MW01094169

Unfaithful Servant

Unfaithful Servant

Timothy Harris

Five Star • Waterville, Maine

This novel is a work of fiction. Names, characters, places and incidents are either the product of the author's imagination, or, if real, used fictitiously.

First Edition
First Printing: March 2004

Published in 2004 in conjunction with Tekno Books and Ed Gorman.

Set in 11 pt. Plantin by Minnie B. Raven.

Printed in the United States on permanent paper.

ISBN 1-59414-184-3 (hc : alk. paper)

Chapter One

It was a foggy evening in late January and cold ocean air was leaking through the old window frames of my Santa Monica office on Fourth Street. I'd just about decided to close up for the day when the phone rang.

"Are you Thomas Kyd?" It sounded like a child's voice on a car phone and I could hear someone arguing in the background.

"Yes," I said. "Who's this?" There was more arguing, as if the phone was being fought over, and then the line went dead. I'd been getting a lot of prank calls from kids recently. My phone number was only a digit different from a pet store and some little wise-ass liked to call up and ask me if I carried any snakes large enough to eat his sister's dog. A moment later the phone rang again.

"What time do you close?" the same voice asked.

"I'm closing now."

"Wait! Can't you wait? I'm right outside."

"Who is this?"

"Just wait. I'll be there in a second. I promise."

I heard footsteps on the uncarpeted floorboards of the outside hallway and then the door to the reception area creaked open. The person coming in to the waiting room couldn't have been much more than fourteen. He was talking into a tiny chrome-faced cell phone while checking the time on his wristwatch. When he saw me, he said, "Later" into the phone and snapped it into a hip holster. He was rail thin with peroxide blonde hair and baggy jeans draped like curtains over his Alan Iverson basketball shoes. He was tilted forward at an angle to counterbalance the considerable weight of a school backpack that looked rugged and hi-tech enough for Mount Everest. A diamond flashed at his ear; metal hoops had been threaded through his eyebrows. He was not a bad looking kid, but all this shit he was wearing—enough to feed a Third World family for a couple of years—hit you before you noticed *him,* which, I assumed, was probably the point. It was like protective armor designed to conceal the immature body and wide frightened eyes.

"Are you, like, the detective?" He lowered the backpack to the floor with a thud.

"Yes. What can I do for you?"

"How do I know you won't take my money and just do nothing?"

It was a question that, with varying degrees of politeness, most clients eventually got around to asking, but he just blurted it out.

"You don't," I said.

"Are you like an ex-cop or something? Do you have skills?"

"Skills?"

"You know, martial arts, self-defense, surveillance. I'm definitely going to need surveillance." He tried to peer past me into my office, perhaps hoping it contained busy technicians monitoring computer screens of satellite photos, something more impressive than the worn Turkish rug and out-of-date magazines in the reception room.

"Listen," I said. "Who are you?"

"Hugo Vine. One of my friends knows you."

"I doubt it. I don't know any fourteen-year-olds."

"Okay, knows *of* you." Hugo sighed impatiently. "My

friend's parents got divorced. The Marmelsteins? The mom hired you last year to see if her husband was hiding his assets and stuff?"

I remembered the Marmelstein case rather well, if only because I was still in Small Claims Court fighting to get paid what I was owed on it.

"I'm thinking of maybe hiring you to do something for me."

"No offense, but I think I'm out of your league."

"No offense." He hitched up his pants, which kept sliding off his non-existent hips. "But I think I can afford you." He didn't say it rudely, just matter-of-factly. The truth is, he said it kind of apologetically, which made it even more insulting.

"What the hell do you need a private detective for?"

"I want somebody watched."

"Do you know how much that would cost? That's a minimum of five hundred dollars a day."

"Max Marmelstein said you charged his mom two hundred and fifty. I thought you might make me a deal because, you know, it looks like your business is a little slow right now. It's probably the economy. A lot of my stocks are off, too." He slipped the watch off his wrist and held it out to me. "It's worth at least fifteen thousand. I had it appraised."

I don't know why I'd lied to him about my going rate, but I do know there's something particularly deflating about getting caught in a lie by a child. I took the watch and weighed it in the palm of my hand. It was a vintage stainless steel Rolex with a matte black dial and ivory colored hands. The bezel was flawed in one spot, the steel twisted up into a sharp edge as if it had been struck with a chisel. A minute legend on the dial claimed it could tell time to a depth of six hundred and sixty feet, which I suppose could be pretty useful if you were late for an underwater business meeting.

"It's a James Bond Submariner. It's mine," he said. "It's not stolen or anything."

"How old are you?"

"Fourteen. Why?"

"Do your parents know you're here?"

"No."

"Why not?"

"Because *they're* who I want you to watch."

It was such an outrageous request, I suddenly wondered if the whole thing was some kind of adolescent trick, like the prank calls I'd been getting.

"I can't accept this." I handed it back to him.

"Why not?"

"Because you're a kid."

"That is so weak!" he snarled. "Who gives a fuck how old I am? I don't fucking believe this shit!"

"I told you," I said very slowly and deliberately, "I can't help you."

I wasn't ready for how quickly he lost it. Suddenly this gawky unformed kid's eyes had turned into dark unfocused pools and he was screaming abuse at me about how stupid and unfair I was and how he couldn't believe I wasn't dead yet.

"Calm down!" I grabbed him by the shoulders and held on as he struggled, his face flushing with rage. He fought for about five seconds and then he shuddered like an animal and became utterly slack. After a moment he knocked my hands aside.

"You okay?" I asked.

"Fuck you," he said in a trembling voice. "You're not a real detective. You're just a loser." He turned and stormed out, leaving the door open behind him. I watched him swagger down the hall past the broken elevator towards the stairs, legs wide apart, taking big steps as if he was moving down a cellblock. The crotch of his pants was at his knees, his ass was hanging out, and he had no belt. It was the look for gang bangers that winter, and rich white kids from the West Side.

I went over to the window and looked down on Fourth Street. The dense fog softened the headlights of the passing cars and collected in misty halos around the streetlamps. The pavement was empty except for a pair of homeless women pushing shopping carts piled high with their worldly goods into the public parking structures where they were going to bed down for the night. I saw Hugo come out of my building and look expectantly up and down the street. A moment later, a shiny white Suburban came around the corner and pulled in to the curb. Hugo climbed in and the Suburban did an illegal U-turn and vanished into the stream of homebound traffic. I was still smarting from his venomous outburst when I saw he had left his fancy backpack behind.

I'd seen kids humping these things for years, but it had never occurred to me just how heavy they were. As a hundred-and-eighty-pound grunt in Vietnam I'd rarely carried gear that weighed more than half my body weight. Hugo's backpack felt like it held fifty pounds of barbells. I emptied a load of textbooks, an Apple PC, a Palm Pilot, a pager, a Walkman, and a CD player onto my desk. In the side pockets I found a crumpled packet of Indonesian clove cigarettes, some expensive Laker ticket stubs, and a tin of Evergreen chewing tobacco. A zippered compartment contained a collection of pill bottles prescribed to Hugo Vine: some of these medications I recognized as, at various times, doctors had fed me the same ones. Some were to speed you up, others to flatten out the ups and downs, and others just knocked you sideways, until you weren't anything more than a dazed spectator of your own life. I wondered if Hugo's outburst had been a result of his not taking these pills, or was that what he was like *on* medication. I emptied the bottle of *Zendrax* into the palm of my hand and imagined the buzz I'd get if I swallowed a few of the tiny star-shaped pills. Of course I would then need to take the edge off with a lot of chilled vodka, and if I was going to really throw away my sobriety of the past six months, I might as well smoke some Chinese heroin while I was at it. If hell is your ultimate destination, there is really no reason to deny yourself anything along the way.

"Excuse me?"

A young Hispanic woman peered shyly in at the door. She was small and dark-skinned and spoke in a timid girlish voice with a Spanish accent. Despite her submissive manner, her dark solemn eyes were perceptive and there was something long-suffering and stubborn about her mouth that I found attractive. She reminded me a little of the French actress, Jeanne Moreau, who had had a stern, uncharacteristically ordinary face for a movie star. Watching foreign films when I was a teenager, Moreau's air of austere, repressed passion had hinted at smoldering sexual depths I couldn't imagine in any airbrushed *Playboy* centerfold. All that this woman probably shared with the French actress was an upper lip slightly fuller than the lower one, but it was enough to intrigue me.

"Can I help you?" I said.

"I come for his backpack." She averted her eyes.

"And you are?"

"I am the housekeeper."

I returned the pills to the bottle and loaded everything else back into the backpack. "I was looking for his telephone number or an address so I could return it," I said.

"Yes." She nodded encouragingly, eager to help me with my lie.

"He's quite a kid."

"Yes." She laughed nervously.

"Do you know why he came here?"

Her eyes roamed uncomfortably around the room. "No." She shook her head.

"He wanted to hire me to spy on his parents."

She nodded and smiled as if I'd said something about the weather.

"What do you think about that?"

She remained mute, like someone who's taken a huge bite of something forbidden and is trying to pretend there's nothing in her mouth.

"Don't you think that's a little strange?" I persisted. "He tried to pay me with a fifteen-thousand-dollar watch."

From the half-open door she gazed longingly at the backpack on my desk. All she wanted was to get it back, but she couldn't bring herself to cross the floor and take it.

"He has to do his homework," she finally said.

"Why didn't he come back for it himself? Too embarrassed?"

"Yes, that's it," she said, a little too quickly. "He . . . he ask me to apologize to you. He very sorry for anything he did."

She was a touchingly untalented liar, but it was clear she wasn't going to tell me anything about the kid. I helped her hoist the backpack on her shoulders and watched her brace her feet so as not to stagger under its weight. Her hair was thick and black and so naturally glossy it looked almost lacquered. She smelled nice, like expensive hand soap and oranges.

"You'd think these kids would be smarter with all these books they have to carry around." I tried one last time to draw her into a conversation, but she ignored the bait.

At the door she glanced anxiously back at me. "You not going to tell his parents, are you? He a good boy. He really is."

"It's none of my business," I reassured her. "What's your name?"

"It doesn't matter, mister. I'm just the housekeeper." She turned abruptly and left.

Was she offended that I was flirting with her? I'd always assumed that reaching middle age would make dealing with women easier. By then you should have some idea of who you are, and that knowledge should remove some of the anxiety and melodrama from the process. But the act of being attracted to a woman makes you doubt who you are all over again; her rejection made me feel as gauche and humiliated as a teenager.

I watched her from the window as she came out of the building and thought how lucky the kid was to have such a loyal, pretty young woman looking out for him. Her slight body was bent nearly double under the weight of his backpack as she staggered over to the Suburban. He watched her from the front seat but never made a move to help her. When she got inside, she affectionately ruffled his hair and then reached over and fastened his seat belt for him. I remember feeling surprised and a little envious that someone as hostile and apparently flawed as Hugo merited such affection.

Chapter Two

Several months later I was on a surveillance case tracking Alvin Peck, a prominent Hollywood agent whose wife didn't believe he was spending his nights attending Narcotics Anonymous meetings. I found Alvin where he was supposed to be, in a church on San Vicente in Brentwood, sitting in the back row with a number of other upscale professionals who'd become casualties of the fast lane. They all wore dark glasses and black leather jackets and fiddled nervously with their cell phones like worry beads. There were several actors with well-publicized substance abuse problems in the group that night, and a lot of the audience seemed more interested in observing them than listening to the various speakers. At the intermission, I followed Alvin out onto the pavement with the crowd who were chatting to each other under a growing pall of cigarette smoke. I felt a faint tug on my arm and turned around to see Hugo Vine smirking at me.

"Hey, Hugo. How you doing?"

"Okay." He shrugged elaborately. "Are you, like, some big recovering junkie?"

"Aspirin's about as exciting as it gets for me these days. What about yourself?"

"I don't take drugs," he sneered. "They're for fools."

"So what are you doing here?"

"You wouldn't believe me if I told you."

"Try me." I looked around for Alvin Peck but I'd momentarily lost sight of him.

"My mother and my therapist think I'm like this huge drug user."

"But you're not?"

"My mother wants to send me away to this fucking boot camp in Maine for psycho kids." Keeping his eyes coolly trained on me, he shook a Marlboro out of a pack, planted it in the corner of his mouth, and fired it up with an assured flick of his Zippo. "They make you do character-building stuff like get up at the crack of dawn and take ice cold showers. I don't care. I'll just run away."

His bravado was a work in progress, but it didn't lack a certain style. The whole performance with the cigarette would have been more effective if he hadn't lit the filter end. His hand trembled faintly as he held it between his fingers. I looked away so he wouldn't realize I'd noticed his mistake and caught sight of Alvin Peck edging away from the crowd towards the driveway beside the church.

"I'm sorry, Hugo. I'd love to talk to you, but I'm on a job."

I followed Alvin to the parking lot, where he got into a British racing green Town and Country Range Rover with a baby seat in the back. I trailed him to the corner of Santa Monica and Formosa in Hollywood, where he stopped to pick up an Asian boy huddling for warmth in a doorway. They drove all the way downtown and cruised slowly around McArthur Park, finally stopping in front of a gutted Deco apartment building where a vocal group of ten-year-old street dealers clustered around the car. After making a purchase, they went to a motel and took a second-story room overlooking an empty swimming pool with beer cans and a trashed baby carriage at the bottom. I checked out Alvin's freshly waxed Range Rover in the parking lot with my flashlight. The backseat contained some red-covered

CAA scripts, a pair of children's soccer boots, and a grocery bag full of vitamins and carrot juice from Wild Oats. I tip-toed along the balcony past their window and got a few shots of them through a warped panel in the Venetian blinds. They were sitting in separate armchairs like an old married couple, sucking on crack pipes, and watching "Who Wants to Be a Millionaire?" on the TV. The Asian boy had taken his shirt off; his narrow chest and skinny arms were so covered in tattoos that it looked like he'd been dipped in mud. The adjoining room wasn't occupied and its flimsy lock proved no problem. I lay down on the bed and breathed in the depressing stink of disinfectant and stale cigarette smoke that came with the room. I'd forgotten to bring a book to pass the time, which threw me into a panic because I was at the mercy of my thoughts. The bedside drawer contained some torn condom wrappers, but someone had stolen the Bible. I distrusted the Bible with a passion; it was the most insulting and haunting of books. You had to be a slave to accept it and dead in your soul not to fear its beautiful whispered threats, but still it was the only thing that made a skanky motel room like this one bearable. With nothing to distract me from my surroundings, I could feel all my buried despair waking and starting to feed. At such moments it was awful to contemplate how many years of my life I'd spent secretly observing other people fuck up, without ever learning anything of importance myself. At least nothing that had ever caused me to change who *I* was. In all the years I'd been a detective, I hadn't really *grown,* I'd only gotten older. I could hear Alvin and the boy gently murmuring through the particle board wall. After awhile their TV was turned off and I saw the bar of light under the connecting door go out. Whatever they did in the dark to each other was swift and only one of them made animal panting sounds. The TV went back on and then the water pipes rumbled in the wall as one of them used the shower.

I followed Alvin back to his NA meeting just in time to join the tepid audience applause for a white-haired woman who proudly told everyone she had been over forty years sober. It was considerably longer than most of the people in the room had been alive, and the general feeling was she was piling on a bit. Afterwards I sat in my car in the church parking lot and downloaded the pictures of Alvin and the Asian boy into my PC. It took less than a minute to type up the night's activities and fax it all over to Alvin's wife. She was going to have a photo of her husband sharing a crack pipe with the street hustler before Alvin even got home to Beverly Hills from his NA meeting.

I was about to drive home when I noticed Hugo Vine among the last stragglers coming out of the church. Shoulders hunched against the evening chill, face buried in his hooded sweatshirt, he moved among the adults but was plainly not one with them. Emerson said, "Children are aliens, and we treat them as such." Hugo had pissed me off so much the night he barged into my office that I'd never even asked him *why* he wanted me to watch his parents. I'd just dismissed him as a rich kid with an obscene sense of entitlement. I'd never had children and the truth was the older I got the less I cared for them, especially when they hit adolescence. What were teenagers for? What was the point of them? They were like badly engineered adults whose behavior couldn't be relied on or predicted. Adolescence was a brief moment in anyone's life, but they acted as if it was going to last forever and nobody had ever gone through it before. Not that it mattered what I thought anyway, because you could not argue with the young; they had a secret weapon that trumped anything you threw at them: they had death on their side, they knew they were going to bury you.

On the off-chance the cute housekeeper was picking him up, I walked over to where Hugo was sitting on the curb in front of the church.

"You waiting for your ride?" I asked.

"Uh-huh," he said tonelessly. "Where'd you go?"

"I had to keep an eye on somebody."

"I know. That guy Peck. He's my mother's agent. He always ditches meetings, and then he sneaks back just before the end," Hugo said approvingly.

"You noticed," I said. "You're pretty sharp."

"Not really. The meetings are so boring I just look at the people."

"Why'd you want me to watch your parents, Hugo?"

"It doesn't matter anymore."

"You sure?"

"It's gone." He held up his wrist where the fancy Rolex used to be and smiled with bitter satisfaction. "Guess you missed your chance at the big bucks. Now I can't pay you."

"Who the hell asked you to pay me? I just stopped by to see how you were." It wasn't true: I was there for another chance at talking to the housekeeper, but he didn't need to know that. "We both know you offered me that watch and I wouldn't take it."

"You wanted to take it," he said dismissively. "You were just too scared."

He jumped guiltily to his feet as the white Suburban pulled in to the curb. Instead of the housekeeper, there was a heavy-set guy hunched behind the wheel. He was wearing tinted prescription glasses and he made a point of lowering them to get a good look at me as Hugo climbed inside. I was going to say goodbye, but it was clear from the way Hugo was staring stiffly ahead that he didn't want to draw any attention to the fact we'd been talking.

Chapter Three

The next morning I got a call in my office from someone who identified herself as Tea Lane, Sally Vine's attorney. Tea had a whiney voice with the kind of grating Brooklyn accent that people who admire Barbara Streisand find endearing. She informed me that I was to present myself at the Vine house at one o'clock that afternoon to discuss certain charges that had been brought against me regarding her client's son, and that I was to be prompt as a lot of important people had had to clear space in their schedules to make this happen.

"Who's Sally?" I asked just to annoy her.

"Sally *Vine!*" She made it sound as if I hadn't heard of God. "The *actress!*"

I'd seen a few of her early movies, and then lost interest as the studio worked what was fresh about her into a formula. A Sally Vine role now involved a great deal of graphic and unjustified suffering that culminated in a triumph of self-empowerment. The characters she played were stalked by serial killers, raped by U.S. Presidents, and driven to the brink of madness by psychotic husbands. There was always a decadent sexy moment in a Sally Vine movie when she appeared to welcome the pain coming to her. This exciting *frisson,* the unmentionable hope that when pain got bad enough it led to exquisite forms of pleasure, still put customers in the seats and critics sometimes admiringly described it as European. She had had numerous brushes with addiction and a volatile marriage to Daniel Vine, an elderly film producer who had managed every aspect of her career. It was hard to remember if she had ever actually been any good. She was one of those stars whose misadventures are so heavily reported in the tabloids that they overshadowed the work that made her famous in the first place. I remembered reading her husband had died recently in a freak skiing accident in Lake Tahoe. It had never occurred to me that she was Hugo's mother, though of course it now made perfect sense.

"I don't think I've heard of her," I said. "I know a Hugo Vine."

"Hugo is Sally's son. I'm sure you know that and I'm sure that is the basis for your very inappropriate interest in him."

"I have no interest in him."

"Let's not play games, Mr. Kyd. Mrs. Vine is prepared to bring legal action against you that could result in the loss of your license and jail time. I advise you to cooperate while you still can."

"Legal action?"

"Contributing to the delinquency of a minor. We have Hugo's diary. We know he phoned you and went to your office and gave you a very valuable watch, and we know you're still trying to see him. You're in a very poor position to try and play offense, Mr. Kyd. I strongly advise you to be here at one o'clock." She hung up.

Even though I was completely innocent of what she'd accused me of, I should have had the brains to immediately call a lawyer. I didn't because it seemed pathetic not to be able to protect myself from such idiotic charges. Or maybe I just looked forward to showing this abrasively self-important attorney how deeply she had her head up her ass. I went into the office restroom and found myself whistling while I shaved. Since I'd quit drinking, my daily act of taking stock in the mirror had stopped being a source of dread. My eyes were clear, the drinker's bloat was gone, and the face that stared back at me was one I was slowly learning not to hate so much. I debated about what to wear to the meeting; it was either my one really good suit to impress the snotty lawyer with my professionalism, or go totally casual to show how little she scared me. It's odd how you worry about what people you dislike will think of you. In the end I went with the good suit, not because it would impress Sally Vine's lawyer, but on the off-chance I ran into the shy Mexican housekeeper.

The Vine place was near the top of one of those roads in Bel-Air that begin on Sunset and ascend for so long and around so many identically twisting curves that you start to worry you're not actually going anywhere. The gated mansions, hidden from view behind high walls and towering hedges, have all the life and atmosphere of bank vaults after business hours. When I had passed the same grandiloquent pile for the third time I realized I was lost, and so did someone else. A man stepped out of a driveway ahead of me and blocked the road. He wore yellow aviator sunglasses and had a microphone in his ear with a little speaker attached to the lapel of his freshly pressed dark blue suit.

"Are you lost?" He gave my battered mud-streaked Land Cruiser the pained look you reserve for a piece of bad fish.

"I'm looking for 4167 Mountain Crest View." I tried to peer past him to find out what he was guarding but all I could see was a long ascending drive that eventually disappeared into a delicate pale lavender mist of flowering jacarandas. I don't know what it is about jacarandas. I know they're *the* beautiful L.A. tree. Once a year they flower briefly and exquisitely, but they annoy me. When I look at them I think of Monet's *Water Lilies* and all the pretty Impressionist reproductions you see hanging in every medical building in the city, as if the purpose of beauty was to cheer people up about having root canals and colon cancer. Like beauty's going to save you any more than it stopped Van Gogh razoring off his ear.

"Okay. The Vine place," he said. "A lot of people have trouble finding it. Turn around, hang a left and then a sharp right, and don't stop until you get to the top."

I thanked him, pulled forward, and started to back into his driveway to turn around when he suddenly raised his hand and ordered me to stop. He held his other hand to his earpiece and then barked into the speaker on his lapel. "Hold it up. I'm clearing the gateway."

Behind him I could see an old man in a wheelchair being slowly rolled down the drive by a uniformed female nurse. The man was asleep, his head lolling forward, but as I gazed at him he stirred and lifted his head. To my amazement, I recognized the familiar tanned features and luxurious silver and black mane of the former President of the United States. He seemed to perk up at the sight of me. I caught the flash of a welcoming grin and then his head sank back down on his chest and he returned to his nap. They were taking him out for some fresh air, a little spin around the neighborhood, but it looked like he was going to sleep through the whole thing.

"Is that who I think it is?" I asked.

"Just turn your vehicle around, and exit the property." He wasn't being polite anymore and he'd let his suit jacket fall open to reveal a big shiny automatic strapped under his arm.

I backed out of the driveway and carefully followed his directions to the top where the road dead-ended in a dramatic lookout point: you could see all of Los Angeles spread out from downtown to the ocean under the cloudless winter sky. The city was definitely showing its wholesome, innocent side that day. The descending flanks of the Santa Monica Mountains were green from the winter rains, and the air was freshened by a hard breeze coming off the bay. It lifted the smell of eucalyptus and wild rosemary off the chaparral, along with some stirring sweet scent that always made my hands swell. I'd lived in the city my whole life and I still didn't know what it was.

There were no houses at the summit, just an open iron gate festooned with security cameras. I drove through it and followed a cypress-lined driveway that wound back down the hill to an even bigger gate set in an eight-foot-high river rock wall. It was topped with flowering bougainvillea but you could see a flash of razor wire glinting through the blood red blossoms. A hulking guy in a Hawaiian shirt and tinted prescription glasses waved me through into a graveled compound where luxury sedans were lined up like a foreign car dealership. He was the same man who'd picked Hugo up from the NA meeting last night. He opened my door and laughed when I told him my name.

"You getting ready to have a long day, *homes*. I hope you brought a toothbrush."

"You the guy who picked Hugo up from the meeting last night?" I asked, noticing the initials *SFW* tattooed on his forearm: *So Fucking What.* It was a prison ink job done with a small motor, a hollowed-out ballpoint pen, and a guitar string.

"Don't worry about me. I'm the least of your problems." He rolled his eyes in the direction of the house. "They're all waiting for you."

"Who's *they?*"

"The whole *team,* man. Hugo's therapist, his tutor, his mom, and step-pop. Plus his mom's lawyers. And oh yeah. Almost forgot." He paused to relish the punch line. "A lady prosecutor from the Sex Crimes Unit, with a detective from the L.A.P.D.! That's what I'm talking about!"

He indicated two nameless brown sedans that could only have been driven by county employees; they'd been parked in a separate section reserved for the unstylish late model cars driven by the Vines' hired help. I had no idea what kind of lies Hugo had told about me, but the words, *Sex Crimes Unit,* stopped me dead in my tracks. It still wasn't too late to walk away from whatever trouble was waiting inside the house. I had my car keys in my hand; the gate was still open; the guy looked more than big enough to try and detain me, but I didn't think he cared one way or the other.

"Maybe I should think about this," I said.

His lips curved in a scornful smile. "You think about it, *homes.* Failure to recognize could be hazardous to a chimo's future."

I'd never had someone call me a child molester before. It's not really the kind of thing you can discuss. He was leaning comfortably against the side of my car and when I kicked his ankles out from under him he went sprawling on his back, his glasses flying.

"What did you call me?" I stood over him.

It took him a second to figure out what had happened. He rubbed the back of his head and groped around in the gravel until he located his glasses and then peered up at me. "I have made a grievous error," he said. "You are a stand-up guy and I am entirely out of line." He slowly got to his feet and brushed himself off. "Seriously, man, I got given the wrong impression about you." He was grinning again, though keeping his distance. "My name's Malahide. I kind of keep an eye on young Master Hugo around here."

I knew for a second I'd scared him, but his fright was mainly surprise at my vicious reaction to his insult. I was a predator and you could see it worried him that he'd wrongly identified me as prey. It worried me, too. His frame was packed with prison yard muscle and he looked too cunning to fool with the same trick twice. He led me through a brass-studded door into a vast enclosed courtyard dominated by an ancient sycamore. In its branches was lodged a two-story tree house that was bigger than my apartment and probably had better plumbing. Some workmen were up a ladder running cable into it. There was a painter freshening up the trim on the little black iron fences enclosing the flowerbeds, and there was a gardener who looked like he was adjusting the petals to catch the April sun at just the right angle. In the corner of the lawn a dog trainer was trying to teach a refractory Airedale to heel. It was obviously a very hard-working household.

He ushered me through some open French doors into a library where a wiry looking young woman in a gray Armani pantsuit was conversing with two other women. One of them had a stocky physique and wore a creased off-the-rack outfit, which told me she'd probably arrived in one of the county sedans outside. The other was a more flamboyant blonde with a glamorous, heavily made-up face. She had on a lot of clinking, vaguely folkloric jewelry and was dressed in a Neiman Marcus version of a Peruvian Indian's poncho. Pretending to follow their conversation, but really checking out the photos of movie stars scattered around the room, was a middle-aged detective with a flabby, disgruntled face and the husky physique of a linebacker gone to seed. A certain kind of cop aspires to look like the nattily dressed lawyers who torment him in court. This guy was dressed in what used to be known in the eighties as a power suit: it was shiny, dull olive green, and pointlessly double-breasted. If it had looked good in the discount store the day he bought it, it had never looked good since. I was wearing a dove gray and soft blue window-pane-check two-piece from Battistoni that was worth more than he made working a month of overtime. It was worth more than the rest of my entire wardrobe put together. It was so nice I was amazed the ex-girlfriend who'd bought it for me hadn't asked for it back when we split up. As I entered the library, he went as still as a cat spotting a bird landing on the lawn.

"Detective Stone, Robbery-Homicide. You're late." He unbuttoned his jacket and put his hands on his hips, staring at me with naked displeasure. I just smiled at him. After Tea Lane, the encounter with the Secret Service guy, and Malahide, I was in a dangerously pleasant mood I remembered from when I used to drink.

"Hilary Flowers, Deputy City Attorney, Special Operations Division," the woman beside him said in a calming voice, looking thoughtfully at me, hands folded together over her stomach as if at any moment she was going to lapse into prayer. She wore no make-up and everything about her, from her short sensible hair to her vaguely orthopedic-looking shoes, was plain and modest. Except for her eyes, which betrayed her completely. They were deep blue and swimming with a little too much emotion and need.

"Hi, I'm Wanda," the woman in the poncho waved. She added with a girlish brightness, "Hugo's therapist?"

"I'm Tea Lane. Miss Vine's attorney," the young woman sighed, running her fingers through her hair in an attitude that suggested she had a great number of more important things to attend to than any of us. She was about to continue when she noticed Malahide still loitering behind my shoulder. "Do you think we could have a little *privacy?*" she snapped at him.

"It's your world, Ms. Lane. I'm just tiptoeing through it." Malahide held up his hands in mock surrender, winking at me as he backed out the French doors.

"Mr. Kyd," Hilary Flowers broke the silence. "Detective Stone and I are here today in response to a complaint we received from Mrs. Vine. We've spoken to Hugo and the housekeeper and Mr. Malahide, and now we'd like to hear from you."

"What exactly am I accused of?"

"There's been a complaint, that's all," she reassured me. "No charges have been filed."

"Yet," Stone said.

"I'm here of my own free will in response to a fairly unpleasant call from Ms. Lane. I don't have to answer any questions until I know what I'm being charged with. Actually, I don't have to answer any questions at all."

"Let me tell you what *unpleasant* is," Stone said. "I can take you into custody right now and stick you in L.A. County Jail. Believe me, you don't want to spend even one night in there with a child molester jacket."

"Slow down, Cedrick." Hillary Flowers put her hand on Stone's elbow.

"I'm serious, pal," he hissed at me. "You'll make bail, but before that I know someone is going to reach out and touch you."

"Cedrick," I said. "Don't you know anything about intimidating innocent people? You don't threaten me with homosexual rape in prison *first.* Now you don't have anything *worse* to threaten me with."

His face reddened. "We'll lift your investigator's license."

"Do that. Because when I make bail there's going to be a whole crowd of reporters and photographers waiting to talk to me. And I'll tell them the story I'm not telling you."

"Why don't you tell us your story, Mr. Kyd?" Hilary Flowers said in her hushed, measured voice.

"I don't know," I said. "I think it would look better in the tabloids. They have a way with words and pictures that an ordinary guy like me lacks."

"He's trying to extort money from us," Tea Lane said to the others, as if she'd suspected this all along. "Sally will not have the media camped outside this house and following Hugo to school again. I want to make that absolutely clear."

"You're not doing a very good job protecting the Vines, Ms. Lane. Obviously, if I wanted to sell my story to the tabloids, I could have done it already."

"Okay." Hillary Flowers beamed at me. "What *do* you want, Mr. Kyd? No, let me amend that. What would you *like?*"

"I'd like to sit down."

"I think that's a very good idea," she said approvingly.

I started to move towards a high-backed sofa facing the fireplace, but Ms. Lane steered us towards the other end of the room where some finely cracked French leather armchairs were arranged in front of a floor-to-ceiling window. A great sweep of green lawn flowed out to the edge of the cliff and beyond that there was nothing but dazzling blue sky, and a pair of hawks circling over the chaparral. Wanda, the therapist, gave me an encouraging smile.

"Go on, Thomas." She rubbed her hands together in anticipation. "I can't wait to hear this."

"Hugo phoned my office and came in one night several months ago. He wanted to hire me. He tried to pay me with a watch. I said I couldn't work for a child. He threw a hissy fit and walked out. His housekeeper came back because he'd left his backpack behind. Last night I was working an unrelated case and I ran into Hugo at a Narcotics Anonymous meeting. He was his normal charming self. Malahide picked him up after the meeting, and today I got a call from Ms. Lane telling me I'd contributed to the delinquency of a minor, which is why I'm here."

"What unrelated case?" Stone asked.

"I had somebody at the NA meeting under surveillance."

"Who?"

"I can't tell you that." It was a coincidence, I suppose, that Sally's fourteen-year-old son and her agent attended the same NA meetings, but not a very remarkable one. The film community of Los Angeles was as incestuously knit together as the inhabitants of a small town. I had no idea what Alvin Peck's wife had done with my photos of her crack-smoking, cock-sucking, CAA agent, soccer dad husband. It was none of my business, just like this was none of my business. "If you don't believe me," I said, "I can print you out the dated billing forms with the name of the client blacked out. They're in the computer in my car."

"I believe you, Mr. Kyd." Hillary Flowers smiled encouragingly but Stone and Tea still didn't want to let me off the hook.

"Why did Hugo write in his private diary, *Kyd probably my last hope*?" Ms. Lane asked.

"I don't know. I try not to read other peoples private diaries."

"You're leaving something out," Stone said triumphantly. "You haven't told us what Hugo wanted you to *do*."

It would have been easy to tell them Hugo had wanted

his *parents* watched. Maybe if Hugo's parents had been there instead of sending a cop, a prosecutor, a lawyer, and a shrink to grill me, I would have told them. But they weren't anywhere in evidence. It was just this gang of strangers discussing the boy's fate, and he wasn't even represented. So far the kid had been nothing but a pain in the ass to me and I certainly owed him no loyalty. But there was something about the number of adults ranged against him that I didn't like. Something about the careless way these people threw their power around rubbed me the wrong way.

"I have no idea what Hugo wanted," I lied. "You read his diary, Ms. Lane. Any ideas?"

"Sally *asked* me to read it," she said, as if that made anything she did totally beyond criticism. "And no, he didn't say anything about that. It's all written in some kind of gibberish code so people can't understand it."

"Did Hugo actually *say* he gave me the watch?"

"Not in so many words." Tea Lane smoothly shifted gears. "You have to understand, Hugo is . . . a difficult child. I mean, he's terrifically bright and amazingly gifted, but sometimes he's a little uncomfortable with the truth."

"Is that a new way of saying he's a liar?"

"His father was killed in a tragic accident. I think Hugo deserves a little sympathy, don't you?" She forced her brows and lips into an expression that I realized was meant to indicate compassion. It looked about as natural on her as a hat on a snake. "When we found out Hugo had gone to see you, and then the diary, and approaching him the other night, well, understandably we had to find out if you were taking advantage of him." She rose to her feet. "Anyway, I'm sure you'll be sending us a bill for your time."

Beyond her I could see a man with a book getting up from behind the high-backed sofa at the far end of the room. He had obviously been listening to our conversation and now he waited for us as we drifted across the room. He was in his early thirties, vaguely Middle-Eastern looking, with the deeply tanned face of a male model. He wore a black silk T-shirt stretched tautly over his gym-sculpted torso, gray cashmere slacks, and a pair of embroidered Turkish slippers without socks. A gold bracelet and gold watch dangled from his wrist and there was a lot more gold around his neck. He was rescued from looking like one more over-accessorized Beverly Hills Persian by a pair of tortoise shell reading glasses perched on the tip of his nose, and the unlikely presence of Isak Dinesen's *Seven Gothic Tales* in his hand.

"Hey. I liked what you said there about lying. I'm Raj, Hugo's stepfather." He squeezed my bicep as he shook my hand and smiled lazily as if the two of us already shared an amusing secret. At the same time, his glossy black eyes performed a swift appraising inspection of me that seemed to meet with his approval. "I want to apologize about the misunderstanding. We get crazy people making threats against Sally and the tabloids going through our garbage; sometimes we get paranoid, you know what I mean? Tea's not really a pit bull except when she's got her lawyer hat on, and the police are here because we over-reacted. I hope there's no hard feelings, Thomas."

"I'm fine." It took an effort to get my hand loose from his grip. He'd mastered the look and talk of a Hollywood player except for his accent, which retained a guttural Middle Eastern cadence.

"Unless anybody needs him, I'd like to borrow Thomas for a minute." He draped a hand over my shoulder.

Sensing a sudden change in the wind, Tea Lane immediately gave my arm a warm squeeze to let me know, contrary to appearances, she had always been a big fan of mine. The other two women seemed happy to let me go, but Stone had a cheated, unsatisfied expression on his face.

Raj picked up on it right away. "Sally asked me to tell you how much she appreciates you coming out, Cedrick."

"Give her my best." Stone almost blushed with pleasure. "My wife and I rented that last movie she did. Tell Sally we really loved her work."

The policeman wasn't just a fan, I realized, he was a critic.

"She'll be pleased to hear that. Those Laker tickets are there at the 'Will-Call' anytime you want to use them." Raj turned effortlessly to Hilary Flowers. "We'd like to write a letter to the City Attorney about what a great job you've done for us."

"That's not really necessary, sir."

"No, it means a lot to Sally." He looked at Tea. "Make sure that goes out today."

Having dispensed the necessary party favors, Raj beckoned me to follow him out the library door. He led me along a passageway lined with books and silver-framed photos documenting the life Sally Vine had led with her elderly deceased husband and Hugo. At a glance, Daniel Vine looked at least thirty years older than her. Their life seemed to consist of ski trips and ocean-going yachts and movie sets and award dinners spent with people I didn't know but whose faces I recognized from magazines and movie screens.

"Check it out." Raj indicated a photo of three-year-old Hugo struggling to hold up one of his father's Oscars. "What a life this kid's had, eh? His father was a giant. One of the classiest producers ever. Most people in the business, they let their decorators do their libraries for them. But Vine was old school. He *read* all these books." Raj held up the copy of *Seven Gothic Tales*. "This is a first edition, signed by the author. It's the same woman who wrote *Out of Africa* with Meryl Streep and Bob Redford."

"Yeah, I like her."

"Meryl? She's great." He looked at me, intrigued. "You do a job for Meryl? Naw, don't tell me. I know you private detectives aren't allowed to tell who you work for. You're supposed to be like a priest, right?"

"I meant the writer, Isak Dinesen," I explained.

"Yeah?" he said. "I was just checking it out. I'm thinking maybe there's a role for Sally; I can option it, develop it, *produce* it, get a photo of *me* up there with an Oscar."

"Is that what you do?" I asked. "Produce?"

He studied me for any glimmer of disrespect. "I married a famous woman." He shrugged. "Daniel Vine's a very hard act to follow for a guy who started out as a ski instructor like me. I know what people say. That's okay. I'm used to people underestimating me. Here." He pushed the book into my hands. "There's nothing for Sally in it. It's yours."

It was the English first edition in perfect condition, the thick cream pages barely touched. "Thanks, but I can't take this." I tried to return it to him, but he stepped back with his hands raised.

"Keep it. You look good with a book." He said it as if books were fashion accessories that didn't work for all people. "But I bet you look better with a gun. You ever carry a gun?"

"Very rarely."

"Ever shoot it?" There was almost a catch in his voice, as if he was trying out an obscene word to see how it made him feel.

"Occasionally."

"Occasionally? I like that. But you're kidding me, right?

Where would you shoot a gun?"

"Los Angeles. Vietnam."

"Man, you look too young for Vietnam. I thought all those Vietnam vets had beards and the matted hair and signs like 'Will Work for Food,' " he giggled.

"You don't look like you could spell Vietnam."

For a second he had the blank, wounded look of a humiliated child. Then the expression was gone and he was laughing again. "No, but I can spell *fucked* and that's what happened to you guys, right? Like in *Apocalypse Now* and *Platoon*. They never gave you your props."

I shrugged to show how stale I found the subject. I think I even yawned, but it didn't stop him from trying to charm me. "You can tell how bad a war was from how many good movies they make out of it. Vietnam? You *know* that war really rocked. Desert Storm? You can't make anything out of that except maybe a comedy."

I realized he was one of those guys who had to flatter anyone he met. The act of seduction was like breathing to him, at once effortless and a necessity. If one compliment didn't work, he'd try another and another until he found the soft underbelly of your ego.

"Was there something in particular you wanted to talk to me about?" I asked.

"Yeah, actually there was," he said. "You're an impressive guy. You're very articulate. You dress nice. *I* saw that suit at Barney's but I knew I wasn't tall enough to wear it. So I look at you and I ask myself a question. At your age, why aren't you running your own agency?"

"I am."

"You know what I mean. You've got some dinky little office in Santa Monica. You could be a chain. You could be nationwide."

"You could be my ex-wife."

People had asked me for years why I didn't expand my business, or nowadays *grow* it. I didn't have an answer really, except that I'd never considered being a private investigator much of a business. At its best it was a vocation, and more often it was like an addiction. It was something I could barely justify doing myself half the time, so how could I ask other people to do it for me? This disinclination to be successful and powerful in a place like Los Angeles was highly suspect. Lovers and doctors had variously diagnosed it as self-loathing, masochism, even a form of insatiable grandiosity. Whatever it was, I suspected it had gone on too long to ever change. Nowadays working alone allowed me the illusion I was special and sometimes let me experience the luxury of telling people far richer and more powerful than me what I really thought. I was aware it was a privilege shared mainly by crazy people who lived on the streets, but it was all I had.

"Why do you care what I do?" I asked.

"I could hook you up with a lot of people. Most of them are assholes, but they're all very rich. And the way I see it, the only thing worse than working for rich assholes is working for poor assholes."

The way the ex-ski instructor delivered the last bit, you could tell he considered it one of the cornerstones of his philosophy. But was it true? To me it sounded like what house slaves had always said to justify not working with their brothers in the fields.

The passageway led into a glass-enclosed sunroom lined with rows of original teak and brass chaise lounges. Wind blew through the open windows and the view was so spectacular it was almost dizzying. It made you feel you were standing on the deserted deck of an ocean liner that had bizarrely beached itself on a mountaintop above Los Angeles. The sunroom opened out onto a wooden balcony dramatically cantilevered out over the hillside.

"You see that?" Raj pointed below to where a three-story steel and smoked-glass office complex had been abandoned in its final stage of construction. The structure not only dwarfed the surrounding chaparral, it looked like aliens had dropped it there by mistake. A single workman toiling with a generator on the roof appeared to be trying to ready it for a return to whatever galaxy it had strayed from. In Southern California, arrangements for cars always come before people. Carved out of the hillside below there was already a ribbon of shimmering black asphalt lined with reserved parking spaces for about twenty future cars.

"Vine International Pictures," Raj said solemnly. "V.I.P. The new company name was my idea. Every movie I produce, I'm going to be aiming for an Oscar. When they hear it's a V.I.P. movie, it's going to be like hearing a car is a Bentley, or a violin is a Stradivarius."

I glanced at him to see if he'd lit a joint when I wasn't looking, or suddenly lost his mind, but there was an expression of deep seriousness on his face. In Hollywood that's when you have to watch out. The joking around ends and they bare their souls. They tell you the *dream*. To a rational observer it sounds like an overblown fantasy, but it's as serious as the fin of a shark.

"That's going to be a very impressive building."

"They stopped construction when Vine died. When I take the company public," he purred, "investors from Israel, Russia, Turkey, and Germany are going to pay to finish it. As soon as I put Sally back to work, I've got ten-million-dollar offers for her lined up like 747s on the runway. Sweet, huh?"

"Very nice," I said, wondering at his compulsion to boast about all this stuff to someone he didn't know and would probably never see again. Was it a sense of inferiority that came from being married to an older, famous wife? He wasn't just going to produce movies, he was going to win Oscars. He wasn't some young stud Sally kept around as a toy; he wanted me to know he was the one putting *her* ten-million-dollar ass on the street. Or was that also wish fulfillment? Sally Vine had not starred in her late husband's two Oscar-winning films, and her last two big studio movies had faltered at the box office. She was approaching the last stage in the life cycle of a female star. It wouldn't be long before the offers to play the romantic lead dried up. Then Raj would have the unenviable job of coaxing her to swallow her pride and consider playing the mother of the lead. Daniel Vine had bequeathed to Raj control of the last and most demeaning stage in his wife's career. It was like inheriting a showy, beautiful luxury car, a Bentley or Ferrari, just as it was falling to pieces.

"When we get V.I.P. up and running we're going to want our own private security." He gave me his inviting bad boy smile, the one that must have charmed Sally Vine into his bed. "What about it, Thomas? A nice corner office down there with a view, your own parking spot, and one for your hot young secretary. Stock options. A nice car. *Serious* money. Tell me none of this interests you?"

"It would only worry me."

"Don't you know there's nothing to worry about?"

"Who said that? Alfred E. Newman?"

"The worst is over. You know who said *that?* Sartre. It means all the really bad childhood shit that can happen to you has already happened." He studied me with a professional eye. "You should wear your hair shorter. But you're very good-looking for your age. You'd make a great character actor. A villain, but a villain with, you know, integrity. I should introduce you to some casting agents."

"I don't think so."

"How could you not want to be in the movies?"

"When I was little I didn't dream of *playing* a guy with a gun. I wanted to be one."

"That's why you'd be good. That could work for you."

In the course of our little chat he'd offered to introduce me to rich clients, make me head of security for Vine International Pictures, and now he was dangling a movie career.

"Don't worry. I'm not gay." He smiled, reading my mind. "I just like to discover people, change them around." He folded his arms and calmly examined me. I might have been an interesting painting he was trying to decide where to hang on a wall.

I didn't like the feeling, but at the same time I could appreciate how creepily seductive this kind of attention might be for an insecure actor. He was giving me a taste of the warm, enervating bath of approval stars received from their handlers. It was all so palpably phony it was hard to believe how often it worked. He could see I wasn't impressed and it bothered him that he still hadn't managed to find anything I wanted.

That's the only reason he made the mistake. It was just an idle, vulgar whim on his part, a need to show off how much more he had of everything than me. He smiled languidly and then he bestowed what he obviously considered the ultimate prize. "Come on. I'll introduce you to Sally."

Chapter Four

She didn't notice us coming into Hugo's bedroom. She was on her knees, with her back turned, running her hand along the underside of a dresser where a sock drawer usually fit. The shy housekeeper stood beside her, head bowed, shoulders rigidly hunched as if anticipating a blow for whatever Sally Vine hadn't yet found in her son's bedroom. Wanda, the therapist who made house calls, sat on the edge of the bed, a faraway, abstracted smile on her face.

"Searching my son's room for *drugs!* I'm so ashamed I want to be sick," Sally Vine said furiously.

"You've got to try and separate yourself from whatever Hugo's doing," the therapist counseled her. "Otherwise it's going to tear you apart."

Raj laid a possessive hand on his wife's haunch, assessing its muscle tone. "Somebody hasn't been working out, babe. I can feel it."

She went still and then slowly turned around. For a second there was a look of cold dislike on her face, but it vanished the second she saw there was another person in the room. She made some imperceptible adjustment to herself, as involuntary as a man sucking in his gut at the sight of an attractive woman. Her face became radiant as she smiled up at him.

"Raj! I didn't know you were home!" She glanced in my direction and gave me a lesser, fading version of the same smile. She had black hair cut boyishly short, a dreamy oval of a face with the kind of Irish skin that flushes with every mood swing. In person, her dark blue eyes retained a strong suggestion of the vulnerable, haunted cast familiar from so many movies. Quality plastic surgery had erased the fine lines that would have normally accrued to a woman drifting past forty, but it had also tightened her face into one characteristic expression. Even when she cried, I thought, she would still look very much the same. She was wearing a tight, intensely stylish halter-top and a pair of pale green satin shorts. Every inch of her exposed body was lean and ripped to the point of looking over-trained. Although she obviously wanted to display her hard-won victory over body fat, there was something not quite sensual about its effect. The will power that had gone into chiseling her arms with muscle only seemed to emphasize her losing battle against time.

"You're the detective Hugo went to see." She stayed on her knees, with her arm twined around Raj's leg. "I am so sorry, Mr. Kyd."

"Please, call me Thomas," I said. "And really, it was no big deal."

"Well, you're very kind." She gazed at the floor for a moment and when she looked back up her eyes were filmed with tears. "I don't know what to do with him. *Why* would he try to hire you? What did he want you to *do?*"

From the police to his therapist and his mother, it was what everybody wanted to know. A *team* had been organized around this kid like a court around a prince but no one seemed to have a clue about his inner life. As Hugo's mother waited for my answer, I was conscious of the housekeeper in the background. She hadn't so much as acknowledged my presence since I'd entered, just quietly gone about her business of tidying up Hugo's bedroom. But now she paused in the act of sliding the sock drawer back into Hugo's dresser, listening.

"Hugo never told me what he wanted me to do." I watched the housekeeper expel a slow breath and resume sliding the drawer into the dresser. When she turned around she took a quick peek at me and I smiled directly into her eyes. She looked like she'd been scalded.

"Hugo's going to be fine, sweetie," Raj humored Sally. "He's just being a teenager."

"Last month I found a dozen bags of grass under his mattress." She turned to me. "We drug test him all the time, but he's figured out a way to cheat the test. Look at this room. Look at this house. I've given him *everything.* I'm not just talking about buying him things. From the day he was born, I've made sure he's had the best tutors and doctors so he could grow up into a happy, functioning person. I've devoted myself to him. I didn't have any of that when I was a child. Why does he *need* drugs?"

"Maybe he doesn't need them," I said. "If he's got that many bags, it sounds more like he's selling them."

"What?" she wailed.

"That would explain why he never fails the drug tests." Wanda clapped her hands. "If Thomas is right, it's actually good news."

"I'm supposed to feel relieved because my son's a drug dealer?" She yanked out a drawer and pawed through Hugo's trove of baseball cards, batteries, skateboard wheels, and outgrown action figures until she came up with a child's ski mitten. She shook it and a stream of colored pills quickly filled up her cupped palm and spilled over on to the floor.

"This is what he does with the medication you give him. He doesn't even take it. He saves it up and hides it somewhere I'll find it." Tears tumbled down her flushed cheeks.

"Why does he do this to me? I bought him these mittens in Lake Tahoe. He wanted them because they had little heaters inside them. It was the weekend his father died . . ." She hugged herself against the sobs that threatened to overwhelm her.

"You've got to give the kid some time." Raj appealed to the therapist for help.

"He's right, hon," Wanda said.

"When I try to hug him, he shrinks away from me. When I smile at him, he looks at me like I'm dirt. I can't stand it."

"It's a phase," the therapist soothed.

"He needs to go away somewhere where there's some structure. Where they make him take his medication and teach him some values."

"If you send him to boarding school, he's just going to run away," Raj said.

"There are schools where you can't run away," Sally said.

"They're pretty extreme places," Wanda said. "You've got to remember, when a child loses a parent the way Hugo did, a part of him thinks it's his fault. He blames himself."

"I'm sick of all this therapy bullshit." Sally wheeled on the therapist. "He didn't kill his father. He had nothing to do with it. He wasn't even on the mountain, for Christ's sake!"

The housekeeper had picked up an armful of dirty laundry and was edging quietly towards the door but Sally Vine noticed her. "He tells you everything, doesn't he, Serafina?" she asked in a charged whisper. "I see you two laughing together. You think I'm going to let you keep your kid in my house while my child is destroyed?"

"I'm sorry, missus," she said. "I tell Hugo he got to act better all the time."

"This is not anyone's *fault,* Sal," Wanda said. "It's something we've all got to work through."

"It *is* someone's fault. Someone's turned him against me. He's poisoned my child and he's trying to destroy me."

I couldn't tell whether she'd passed over into naked paranoia, or touched on a subject no one wanted to discuss in my presence, but suddenly the room went completely silent. It lasted so long that I finally made a move to leave.

"Wait." Sally trained her eyes on Raj. "I want you to get rid of Malahide. You said he'd watch Hugo and make sure nothing happened again. But something is happening. I know it."

"Nothing's happening. Hugo's a little wild."

"He stole a fifteen-thousand-dollar watch!"

"He says he lost it," Raj shrugged.

"He'd never lose that watch. It was his father's." Sally paused dramatically before turning her gaze on me. "How do I know I can trust you?"

"Trust me with what?"

"My husband was killed in a terrible ski accident with a snowboarder, who left him to die. We offered a reward to find the man responsible. A lot of witnesses came forward, but when the police questioned them it turned out they were just after the money. But there was one person. He sent us E-mails. He left messages in our mailbox. He said he knew who killed my husband, but he refused to talk to the police about it."

"He was just a creep," Raj scoffed. "The police said it always happens when a celebrity dies in those kind of circumstances. All the lames and wannabes come out of the woodwork."

"But the police never caught him," she said. "When this ghoul realized I wouldn't have anything to do with him, he started making anonymous calls to the tabloids. We had reporters camped outside our house for weeks. You must have read about it."

"I'm sorry. I don't read the tabloids."

My ignorance of her private life annoyed her. "They've said terrible things about Raj and me. Just incredible stuff. Really evil things. How could you not know about it? They were hounding Hugo on the way to school. This ghoul doesn't care that he's destroying my innocent child. He just wants to hurt me."

"Why?" I asked. "Any special reason?"

"Because he's a sick fuck!" Raj pulled me by the arm. "I brought Thomas up because he wanted to meet you, babe. He's got to go now. He's doing a job for Meryl Streep."

"I always heard she was very difficult," Sally said. "What's she like?"

"I don't know what your husband's talking about. I'm not doing a job for Meryl Streep."

"Okay, for that writer," Raj said, trying to laugh off his mistake. "Isak what's-her-name. She won an Oscar, for Christ's sake."

"I didn't say I was working for her, either. She's been dead for about twenty years."

"Whatever." He frowned, indicating I'd overstayed my welcome.

"Wait!" Sally looked to Wanda for support. "Tell him! I want to know what he thinks."

"This is just a theory," Wanda said in her little girl voice, "but it is consistent with a lot of Hugo's behavior. We think Hugo may blame himself for his father's death and as a result he's trying to solve the crime in his own way. The drugs, the alienation from his family, it's all his way of acting out."

"I will not let this happen to my son," Sally said. "Do you think I *want* to send Hugo to some place where I'm not even allowed to see him?"

"Of course you don't," Wanda comforted her.

"But I will if that's what it takes to save him. I'm a recovering substance abuser, Thomas. I know how easy it is to make that one wrong turn in life and never be able to get back again. Will you do this for me?"

"Do what?"

"I want you to watch him. Make sure he doesn't do drugs. Take him to school. Protect him when he leaves the house. Make sure this person can't harm him."

"Your son doesn't like me very much, Mrs. Vine."

"That's because you wouldn't do what he wanted."

"I really don't know much about children. I think this is probably a job for someone who has more experience."

"But I *want* you." She looked confused, as if not getting her way was some kind of a mysterious injustice that made no sense. "Why won't you help me?"

"I didn't say I wouldn't help you. But what if this whole thing isn't just Hugo acting out? What if this person has real evidence about your husband's death?"

"I see where this is going," Raj jeered. "Thomas doesn't want to play the bodyguard. He wants a bigger part, honey. He wants to solve the whole case."

"He can solve anything he wants," she lashed back. "I want my child protected, which is something nobody in this room seems capable of doing." She walked up to me and took my hand and held it in both of hers. She looked solemnly into my eyes. It felt staged, like bad acting always does, and I was embarrassed that she was making this spectacle of herself in front of all these people.

"Will you help me?"

"Look, I didn't come here for a job," I said. "I don't even like kids."

"I knew you'd do it." She stood on tiptoe and pressed her lips against my cheek. "Thank you, Thomas." As she turned away, I had the dispiriting certainty that this little act of seduction was as practiced as signing her autograph. She walked towards the door, gathering the therapist up from the bed on her way out and telling her, "You've got to give me something else to calm me down. You can see this thing has me totally out of control. I mean, look at me . . ."

Looking at her, of course, was all anybody in the room had been doing. She was the one who'd wept and pleaded and raged, while we were the ones who'd had no control over her behavior. Was she really unable to handle her feelings as a mother? Or had she had an actress's sure hold on herself through the whole thing? It was impossible to tell and perhaps she didn't even know herself. Maybe I was too ready to notice the space inside everyone that didn't ring true. She was one of those narcissistically demanding women whose need for drama seemed to have a demoralizing effect on everybody around her. My father had been a Hollywood screenwriter whose career was shattered by the blacklist. I was shocked as a kid when he told me that most of the movie stars I admired were actively loathed by the people who worked with them. Being in Sally's presence had somehow diminished everybody in the room, as it had kindled a resentment, which, for various reasons, nobody had dared to act upon.

My gaze drifted to Serafina. She'd sunk to her knees to pick up the pills Sally had scattered on the floor. She was dressed in a starched beige and brown maid's uniform that was almost criminally ugly, not so much a dress as a punishment for being a servant.

Raj motioned me out of the bedroom and closed the door. His wife's hiring of me had soured his mood. "I didn't know you liked that illegal stuff." He snorted.

"I don't know what you're talking about."

"Serafina. I saw you checking her out. Too bad she doesn't like guys."

"I'm not interested in dating your housekeeper."

"It's your lie, tell it how you want." He laughed.

"So what exactly does your wife expect me to do here? I've never done a job like this before."

"I thought you were a detective," he needled me. "She's turned you into another fucking babysitter."

I was going to let him have it, and maybe I would have, but Serafina came out of the kid's bedroom then with an armful of his dirty laundry. I stepped back against the wall to let her pass, but Raj deliberately stayed where he was so she had to turn sideways and squeeze herself past us. The yielding weight of her hip brushed against me as I breathed in the familiar soap and orange peel scent of her body. Raj made a show of staring at her butt as she moved away down the corridor, and tried to draw my attention to it with a conspiratorial grin. When I ignored him, it only made him grin more.

"You didn't answer my question," I said.

"I don't know what you're supposed to do with the kid. Keep an eye on him. Help him with his fucking homework for all I care."

"What about the watch?"

"Sure. That would be nice. Find the watch, too. Knock us out."

"My daily rate is . . ."

"Whatever," he said airily.

"I'm going to need . . ."

"See Tea. She does details." He reached out and softly punched me in the chest. "*Great* fucking suit." He glided away down the hall, leaving me feeling like a dog had come on my leg.

Tea Lane cut me a payroll check from a V.I.P. account and made a production of glumly searching for Hugo's phone bills. She worked out of a damp, older wing of the house that backed onto the hillside in a warren of small rooms that had once been used by Daniel Vine as production offices: the shelves still sagged with old scripts, the posters of his movies were gathering dust, and the air retained a strong reek of cigars. "I hate it back here," she groused, "but those idiot workmen are taking forever to finish the new building."

"Is that where you're going to be?"

"Corner office with a view." She tried to say it as if she believed it. "No more working out of this glorified ashtray. I'm going to run the company for Raj and Sally, and make movies!"

Everything about their business was said with conviction, and yet everything was conditional. It was all going to happen *when* the building was finished, *as soon as* Sally agreed to go back to work, *if* the financing came through: they seemed to exist in a perpetual future tense.

"Where'd you go to law school?"

"Harvard," she said with dismissive pride. "But I'm not really a lawyer. I mean I am. I used to work in legal affairs for Vine, but you know, I'm really a producer. I'm just doing this housekeeping shit as a favor to Raj and Sal." She couldn't quite conceal the pleasure she took in invoking their names, as if she was a lowly freshman who'd been befriended by a pair of cool God-like seniors.

"They're great," I agreed. "Too bad about her kid."

"Yeah, he's a nightmare. But you'll fix that."

"What makes you so sure?"

"Sally's this close to sending the kid away. All we need is some evidence that he's screwing up and she'll ship him out."

"It must get frustrating," I said sympathetically. "In terms of your business."

"You don't know what frustrating is. We've had three start dates on *Poison Me, My Love* since Vine died, and Sally's made us miss all of them."

"Good title. Sounds like that Raymond Chandler one, with Robert Mitchum, *Farewell, My Lovely.*"

"No, it doesn't! That is so yesterday." She treated my casual comparison almost as a personal attack. "Our movie is much edgier. It's based on a true story. It's sort of shot through with this . . . this . . ." She pretended to wistfully search for the right phrase, though you could tell she'd used it a hundred times before. ". . . this supercharged hyper-reality. You know?"

I didn't. It sounded like some kind of gas additive for video spaceships to me.

"The studio wanted *Poison Me* as their big blockbuster tent-pole summer release, but Raj said they were like impossible, creatively. The suits would have ruined it. So now we're going independent, but not low rent, Sundance independent. It's going to be a big budget Miramax kind of movie, locations in London and Venice, really hip and out there but totally classy, which, frankly, is so much cooler than the cookie-cutter version the eunuchs at Dreamworks would have made."

Sally's last two movies, I knew, had been the financial equivalent of sucking chest wounds for the studio. Translated into English and minus the spin, what Tea was really saying was that no one wanted to roll the dice on another big-budget Sally Vine movie, especially one with her inexperienced husband as the producer.

"So what's holding Sally up?" I asked.

"She's not sure about the director, who is great. She thinks maybe her character's too unsympathetic, which it isn't. Raj will talk her around. She and Raj are mad crazy in love, but it's tempestuous. They've got like this intense, creative, erotic relationship that you couldn't begin to understand. Anyway, if she doesn't commit soon, I'm going to kill her. I could be in London and Venice right now, and instead I'm stuck here looking up her kid's phone bills for you. But it won't be for much longer, I guarantee you that."

"It's funny," I said. "But when I met you I didn't think you were a lawyer."

"What's that supposed to mean?" she said suspiciously.

"I just had this feeling that you were really something else. More on the creative side, you know." I watched to see if she was going to bite on the compliment. "I don't have a creative bone in my body," I lamented. "Maybe that's why I'm good at spotting it in other people. I suppose it's something you're born with, like nice teeth and curly hair."

She had nice teeth and curly hair, and when she thought about that, it made her a tiny bit less grumpy. "I suppose." She exhaled heavily.

"So what's the story with the guy on the gate? Malahide?"

"He's like this ex-con Raj knew in Tahoe." She fluttered her eyelids in disdain. "He got V.I.P. to buy this pathetic script he wrote and now he thinks Sally's going to star in it. Like that's going to happen."

"Why would the Vines hire an *ex-con* to keep an eye on Hugo?"

"Malahide is one of those 'recovered' criminals who gives inspirational talks to gang kids. Raj convinced Sally that a hardcore role model like Malahide might straighten Hugo out. I love Raj, but he's got this weakness for colorful losers."

"Thanks." I made a face.

"Not *you!*" She frowned. "I'm talking about people trying to make it in the industry. You're just a regular person with a job." She made it sound almost as interesting as being a grain of sand.

"Excuse me."

There was a small boy watching us from the open doorway. He was about four, very dark skinned and husky, dressed in cut-off shorts and flip-flops. He looked as serious as an owl.

"What do you want, Adolpho?" Tea rolled her eyes at me.

"The TV won't work."

"That's too bad." Tea got up from her chair and escorted him out. "You're not meant to be in here, Adolpho. Go back to your room."

"But the TV is no good."

"When your mother gets back, I'm sure she'll fix it. Go on, go to your room." She shooed him out like a dog and shut the door, shaking her head. "They live in back. He comes in at night and tries to pretend he's working on the computers, and she drives me crazy. Like I don't have enough on my plate without giving her free immigration advice. The other day she comes in and asks if I know anybody she could marry for her green card. She has a kid out of wedlock and now she wants to get married so she can stay in the country. That's the level of these people."

"Where's she from?"

"Guatemala, Salvador, who knows? She says she had to leave for political reasons which, translated, probably means she got knocked up." Tea Lane's casual contempt hung in the air like a bad smell, but she didn't seem to notice. "You have to get Hugo's schedule from her before you leave."

"Good idea." I made for the door.

"Wait," she barked. "Sign this."

It was a confidentiality agreement promising that I would never write about the Vine household or any of its members, or try to make a movie about them, or sell their secrets to the tabloids. I was never to take a photograph of them, or make a sound recording of their voices, or even discuss them with another living being. Any infraction of the agreement would result in civil and criminal charges, fines and jail time, the loss of my firstborn.

"Gee, I feel like I'm working for royalty."

"You are," she said without irony. "Sal and Raj are very private people. They don't like to be disturbed."

"I understand."

"No eye contact. They don't like to be stared at, or talked to by people who work for them in the house."

"I'll try not to make that mistake."

"Any information you find out, regarding Hugo, or anything else, you bring to me first. You do not go to the police, and you do not bother Sally or Raj. Is that clear?"

"That's exactly how I'll do it." I signed the confidentiality agreement, and Tea Lane notarized it, pressing my thumbprint into her ledger book. The grainy unique swirls of my identity were there in black and white, along with the prints of dozens of other people who'd taken the vow of silence you needed to enter the service of the Vines.

"Anything else?" I said eagerly.

"Yes." She bared her perfect white teeth in a smile. "I just want you to know. You don't fool me at all."

I was going to ask Tea what she meant, but the phone on her desk started beeping. She snatched it up, listened briefly, and said, "Sally's agreed to attend the event. She's very committed to the gun control issue but no way are she and Raj sitting at a table unless there are at least three other A-list names at it . . . fine. Then she'll do Steven's Cancer thing at Cedars." She noticed me listening and furiously waved me out of her office.

The Vine kitchen was a vast, echoing space of stainless steel and polished granite surfaces, more like an industrial design center than a place where something as messy as food was prepared. Serafina was scrubbing the mud out of the cleats of Hugo's soccer boots while eating her lunch standing up. Idly now and then, she lifted her head to watch the men in the courtyard through a window as they installed cable in Hugo's tree house.

"Tea said you could give me Hugo's schedule."

She put down the soccer boot, and hurriedly washed and dried her hands. "Please, follow me."

At the back kitchen door she stepped aside to let me go first, but I refused, gesturing her forward with my hand.

"No, please," she insisted.

"Go ahead," I said.

When she saw I wasn't going to budge, she finally relented and darted past me, as if she was afraid I was going to put my hands on her. Walking around the outside of the house, I made a point of keeping a good distance between us, but it didn't seem to lessen her nervousness.

"You're very fond of Hugo, aren't you?"

"Yes," she said warily.

"Are you worried about him?"

"A little." And then, as if she might have given away too much, she added, "Maybe."

"We have something in common, Serafina."

"Yes?"

"We both know why Hugo came to my office that night." I looked at her for a response, but she kept her eyes firmly on the ground. "I'm not going to lie to you. I barely know Hugo and what I've seen I'm not too crazy about. But there's something wrong in this house, isn't there? Something not right?"

"I don't know."

"I understand why you might not trust me, but I'm trying to help this kid if I can."

"Why you trying so hard if you don't like him?"

The question annoyed me. Wasn't it enough that I was putting myself out for this obnoxious kid?

"His parents are paying you," she persisted. "But you say you are really fighting for Hugo?"

"It's a conflict of interest." I gave her a big smile. "My life is full of conflicts of interest."

"Yes?" Her eyes swept briefly over my face and then looked away, but in that instant there was so much veiled disdain in her gaze I felt myself flush. I thought of what Raj had said about her not liking guys, but I knew this wasn't about her and men. The scorn she hadn't been able to hide was for me.

I waited outside the open doorway to her room while she searched for Hugo's schedule. This damp portion of the original house looked like it hadn't been touched since the fifties. The white wall-to-wall carpeting had turned gray and shiny from years of dirt, and the stained acoustic tiles in the ceiling sagged with water damage. She'd filled the place with flowers in water glasses and covered the walls with Discovery Channel posters of pandas and herds of wildebeest. Adolpho was curled up asleep on the double bed, which took up most of the space in the room. I noticed a catalogue of U.C.L.A. extension courses on her bedside table, along with a framed photo of a teenage girl in a blue and white school uniform posing with some nuns. As she rummaged in the dresser drawer, the boy stirred on the bed.

"Mama," he murmured. "Hugo's TV won't work."

"Go back to sleep!"

Her harsh tone startled him, and then he turned and noticed me lurking in the doorway. "Why is that man here?"

"Calle-te!" she hushed him.

"I've come to fix the television, Adolpho." I said. "Do you mind if I have a look?" I entered before she could refuse my offer of help and approached the brand new TV. I checked the remote for batteries and hit the power button. All I got was hissing static on all channels.

"The TV is fine," I said. "All you need is cable."

"Hugo gave it to me." Adolpho beamed proudly. "He says now it is mine."

"It was a present to Hugo from his mother," Serafina scolded him. "He shouldn't have given it to you."

"*He's* going to fix it." He pointed at me. "He promised."

"That's not his job!" she snapped.

Adolpho took in a huge, warning gulp of air and went rigid; his face darkened alarmingly. The sound he finally produced sounded like a car alarm going off in the tiny room. As he struggled in his mother's arms, his eyes never left the TV; it was like a shiny new bike that someone had given him with a flat tire: it was perfection with a heart-breaking flaw; it was tragic, and he was never ever going to get over it.

I found one of the cable techs packing up his tools at the foot of Hugo's tree mansion. He had a shaved head and a waxed, braided red goatee that hung from his chin like a lariat. Steel arrows and rings pierced his eyebrows, nose, and lips. A gold tongue stud flashed in the cave of his mouth. Somewhere behind all the metal I located his refreshingly innocent nineteen-year-old eyes. I asked him how much it would be to run an extra line in to the housekeeper's room.

"There's twenty-seven rooms in this place and every one of them is wired for cable, dude. Even the shitters."

"Her room isn't," I said. "I'll make it worth your while."

Half an hour later, Adolpho held the remote in his fist and was triumphantly calling out the numbers of the channels as they flashed by on the screen.

"Look Mama!" He pointed at the screen where a man was breathlessly hawking Zirconium engagement rings. "I'm going to buy you one." He looked at me with wide, adoring eyes. "And one for you, too!" he shouted.

"Be quiet!" she told him.

"I don't mind the noise," I said. "Let him enjoy himself."

"*They* mind." She refused to meet my gaze. "If they find out about the TV and the cable, it is bad for us."

"How long have you worked for the Vines?"

"Almost two years."

"Does anyone ever come back here?"

"Just Hugo."

"Then nobody's going to notice," I said. "I'm your friend. I'm not here to hurt you."

"You're *my* friend," Adolpho shouted.

"That's right," I said. "Maybe I could take you and the boy out someday? No pressure. We could just go to the beach, or the pier, or something."

"Please, don't be offended. You are very nice to help us and make Adolpho so happy. We are both very grateful, *Senor* . . ."

She knew what I was after and she was telling me as politely as she could I was wasting my time. I'd used the opportunity of questioning her about Hugo to ask her on a date. I'd tried to worm my way into her affections by winning over her son. Her beautifully mannered response made me feel shabby.

"It's not a crime to ask," I said. "Or maybe it is."

"You have to pick up Hugo at seven-thirty in the morning." She pushed his schedule at me. "He has to be at school by eight, or his teacher gets mad . . ."

"Is there anything I've done to offend you? A lot of people find me offensive. You'd be in good company feeling that way. I'm just curious."

"*I* like you, mister," Adolpho said.

"Why are you saying these things to me?" she whispered fiercely.

"Fine. We'll talk about something else. Tell me about Hugo. What's he like?"

"He thinks it's *fonny* to break the rules." She backed me out of the room. "Like you!"

After she shut the door in my face, I heard her lock it from inside. It wasn't a very promising start to a relationship, but I thought I'd found one person in the house I could trust.

Chapter Five

When I got home, I pulled up the Tahoe newspaper accounts of Daniel Vine's death on my computer and cross-checked them against the reports in the *L.A. Times* and a few of the tabloids.

None of the major facts were in dispute and all the accounts told the same essential story. The sixty-four-year-old producer, along with family and friends, had taken the last fast-speed chair up the Nevada side of Heavenly Mountain minutes before a white-out closed the runs down for the day. The main party had become separated from him on the way down. When Vine failed to rendezvous with them in the lodge below, he was reported missing to the ski patrol by Sally's agent, Alvin Peck. A nighttime search was mounted and then abandoned due to worsening blizzard conditions. By the time it was over, the storm had dropped over two feet of powder. It wasn't until the end of the next day that a girl wandering away from her ski school spotted a patch of reddish snow with a glove protruding from it. She said she was drawn to it because it looked like a giant snow cone. Buried inside it was Daniel Vine's frozen corpse. There was some initial confusion as to what killed him; the corpse showed some bruising and a cracked kneecap, injuries consistent with a collision, but not enough to have caused death. Instead a razor sharp object had sliced his hamstring to the bone, severed his femoral artery, and caused him to bleed to death.

The Lake Tahoe coroner's opinion was that Vine had

suffered a high speed collision with a snowboarder; the razor sharp edge of the snowboard had cut through his leg like a scalpel and left him crippled. With night falling and the temperature dropping, it was estimated he'd probably lasted no more than five minutes before the shock and blood loss finished him. It was the ski resort version of a hit and run accident and there were thousands of snowboarders on the mountain who could have caused it. The blizzard had obliterated the original crime scene. Sally Vine was a local girl who'd become famous; her husband's death was a big story, but it came under the heading of an accident. After heated assurances that all possible steps were being taken to find a suspect, the police said less and less until they quietly stopped working the case for lack of any leads or witnesses.

There was a tabloid photo of Hugo taken the day after his father's body had been found, which I enlarged and printed out. He was standing beside the toppled remains of a snowman outside the family compound. His face staring into the paparazzi's telephoto lens looked devastated, swollen from crying. Behind him, in the illuminated doorway of the chalet, I could see Serafina beckoning him to come inside out of the cold. Hugo was dressed in a T-shirt and ice-caked jeans; his feet were bare on the snow. On his hands, I noticed, he was wearing the same ski mittens his mother had found in his drawer that afternoon.

I tried to recall how life had felt to me when I was his age. My first year in high school, my father broke his back in a motorcycle accident; it was more the act of a wayward teenager than a screenwriter looking at the twilight of his career. It was something that should have happened to me. He spent almost a year immobilized on the couch, washing down the pain pills with supermarket vodka. By then my mother was hardly ever home. She still described herself as an actress, but she paid the bills working full-time as a paralegal. At night she performed in obscure one-act Beckett plays in theatres so small they could barely contain the audience of loyal relatives who grimly sat through them. By the time I was sixteen it was apparent my father was going to have to spend the rest of his life as an invalid. He wore a flesh-colored plastic cast molded to his body like a gladiator's breastplate. His friends had scrawled "get well" messages on it after the accident and they were still visible when the cast was found one morning propped up in the sand at Surf Rider beach in Malibu. It was where he'd taught me how to surf. He'd left it there like a discarded shield before clawing himself across the sand into the cold Pacific. After he killed himself, I'd run away from home and lied about my age to enlist in the Army. At the time it seemed like a perfect way for me not to think about what my father had done. Sort of like the man who jumps in front of moving train in attempt to overcome depression. By the time I got over there, the war was already lost. In numb terror, in the first month I killed a Vietnamese boy who was younger than I was. He weighed a little more than a hundred pounds, an emaciated doll with tiny child-like hands that looked obscenely small holding a rifle. I slept with my first Vietnamese bargirl and numbed myself nightly with liquor and weed until I discovered that smoking smack was the one thing that could put me where I wanted to be. I remembered the huge distance I felt from my mother when I came home on leave and realized she couldn't understand what had happened to me. I'd taken a fatal fork in the road and I would never be able to retrace my steps. Looking at the photo of Hugo, I wondered if his father's death hadn't done something similar to him, something his cable-ready tree house and retinue of shrinks and minders could never put right.

From his phone bill, it was obvious Hugo was engaged in an investigation of some kind. He'd made calls to several watch dealers to get an idea of the watch's value. Before coming to my office, he had tried some large private detective agencies, which had presumably turned him down. When my father crawled into the ocean, there had been no question of any conspiracy. The body cast left on the beach was his suicide note to me. He was telling me he'd ended his life where he and I had been most happy. Whatever my feelings were at the time, I knew his death was final, and there was nothing I could do about it. With Hugo I couldn't tell what was going on. Was he right to suspect his father's death wasn't an accident? Or was it just some kind of neurotic acting out, a retreat into fantasy because he didn't like the brutal card life had dealt him?

I hadn't thought about my father in a long time and now I wondered if the chilly bleakness of his death might be a foretelling of what I would do one day. I switched off the computer and stared at the screen as the picture of Hugo shrank to a tiny quivering dot of light before fading out. In front of me there was a bottle of twenty-year-old malt whisky I kept on the desk beside the computer, with a shot glass and a pack of red Dunhill cigarettes to remind me of the enemy. I liked having them there right in front of me, knowing the only thing that kept me from starting again was my decision not to reach out my hand.

Chapter Six

Hugo was waiting with Serafina just inside the main gate when I pulled up the next morning. She responded with a polite coolness to my greeting and fussed over Hugo, making sure he had his thermos and lunch. He didn't say anything for the first mile, but I could see him checking out the interior of the Land Cruiser. The car looked like crap from the outside but it let me blend into the great part of the city that bore no resemblance to Bel-Air. Pepper spray, a stun gun, and plastic handcuffs were velcroed to the ceiling; an ocean of CDs and books spread over the seats. Hidden under oily rags in back were video cameras, tape recorders, and a fax machine and laptop connected to the ones in my office and home.

"You didn't have to put cable in her room," Hugo finally broke the silence. "I was going to do that."

"You didn't miss out on anything. It just pissed her off."

"Just leave her alone! She doesn't have anything to do with *this!*"

"You got it," I said in a neutral voice.

In my rearview mirror I could see a tan Dodge van close on our bumper. A young guy was driving and there was a young woman in the passenger seat, with a video camera aimed at us. They looked like college kids. I slowed down to let them pass, but they stayed right behind us.

"They work for the 'turd factory,' " he said. "The *tabloids!*"

"Your parents warned me."

"Raj is not my parent. And my father always said he'd give me that watch one day."

"I understand."

"If you catch me taking drugs, you're going to tell my mother and they'll send me away. I know all that. So could we just not talk?"

"Fine with me."

He leaned forward and popped open the glove compartment. There was a quick release holster with a snub-nosed .38 glued to the inside of the door. "Uh-oh, the man is armed and dangerous." He started to reach for the gun and I slammed the glove compartment shut. He fished a cigarette out of his pocket and put it in his mouth. I took it and threw it out the window. He switched on the radio and turned the volume up. I turned it off. He kicked at the tapes lying at his feet.

"Omigod! Bob Dylan . . . Ray Charles . . . Van Morrison. This really is like a hippie van, isn't it? Do you have like incense holders and shit? I'll bet you sing along to the music. Admit it. You do, don't you?"

"Sometimes. When I'm lonely. You want me to now?"

"Get a life!" He pulled on his headphones and stared straight ahead, quivering with outrage.

I tried to appear calm, but being the recipient of that much anger had made my pulse soar. I was so distracted I didn't see the traffic light on Sunset and Bundy changing from yellow to red. By the time I noticed, it was too late to stop and I had to run through it, nearly getting us killed by a furiously honking tow-truck. Hugo never shifted a muscle as it happened. But when I glared at him he cracked a thin smile of appreciation, as if he thought death was cool. I decided to ignore him and the next time I looked he'd fallen asleep, mouth open, chest rising and falling, hands peacefully abandoned in his lap. He wasn't bad company when he wasn't conscious, and we'd temporarily lost the tabloid van.

The Hart Hayworth Academy was located on Wilshire and Seventh in an old red brick building across the street from Lincoln Park. It had a reputation as a place where wealthy families sent problem kids who couldn't get into the other private schools and wouldn't survive in the public ones. The front door was painted a glossy Wimbledon green and there was a showy brass plaque whose finely etched print informed the public that the school's founding dated all the way back to the early 1990s.

"We're here." I had to nudge Hugo to wake him up. As he gazed drowsily at me, for a brief second unsure who I was, it was possible to imagine him as an innocent and sympathetic child. The illusion only lasted a second before his face resumed its habitual expression of sullen hauteur. He gathered his things and got out of the car without saying a word, leaving the door wide open behind him. He looked indistinguishable from the throng of listless teenagers being dropped off in front; they all slouched under the weight of their backpacks and they all looked like they could have slept another good six hours.

After a few minutes the tabloid van rolled up and parked about forty yards down the street from me. Neither of us moved for about an hour. I was bored, but not as bored as they must have been watching me watch Hugo's school. When they finally drove off, I put on a pair of those impenetrable black sunglasses worn by glaucoma sufferers and a conical Japanese gardener's hat that hid most of my face. I added a gray metal three-pronged walking cane, the kind they give you before you graduate to the full walker. In my experience the best way to draw no attention is to appear old. When you add a disability, you become just about invisible. I wandered around the back of the school and moved from window to window until I spotted Hugo in a classroom. Twenty or so students were watching a TV monitor showing Clint Eastwood's *Unforgiven.* A Santa Monica police officer stood at the blackboard writing in block capitals the words: *drugs, alcohol, firearms, murder. Unforgiven* was one of the few American movies that conveyed the dry-mouthed nausea of real violence. In it, the retired killer played by Clint Eastwood can only take human life when he's numbed and deranged himself with alcohol. It was one of my favorite movies and I assumed this was some kind of drug education program for the students. Hugo was seated near the rear, elbows propped on the desk, face cradled in his hands, very much asleep.

At ten-thirty the students spilled out of the school for their mid-morning break, a lot of them heading down the street to a 7-Eleven to get their blood sugar levels back up. Hugo drifted behind them, slowing to tie his shoe and then casually stepping out of sight down an alley. By the time I looked down it, he was already at the other end approaching a white food wagon with the name *Roach Coach* emblazoned on its side. I watched him from behind a Dumpster as he stepped up to the window where a skinny Hispanic with heavily tattooed arms waited to take his order. Hugo looked around and slid some bills across the counter. In return the man reached down and handed him a refrigerator bag filled with white powder. Hugo stuffed the bag in his underpants and the man laughed at him. The man beckoned Hugo forward and Hugo shook his head, but the man kept beckoning him and finally Hugo put his elbow on the counter and they arm-wrestled each other. The man pretended to be struggling and then he easily pinned Hugo and they laughed together at the result. Hugo waved goodbye and ran back down the alley to school; it was the first time I'd ever seen him really smile. He looked as excited as some kid hurrying towards his first car wreck.

I returned the hat, sunglasses, and cane to the Land Cruiser and headed back to the *Roach Coach.* The guy in the window smiled at me as I approached him down the alley and then frowned as I pulled open the wagon door and stepped into the kitchen.

"What you doing, man?"

"County Health Board." I showed him a shiny laminated I.D. with a California State seal, and gazed critically around. "Open containers." I dabbed my finger in a cardboard tub of cooking lard and bent down to check under the grill. "Rodent feces. Grease build-up. I'm closing you down, amigo."

"What you talking about? You ain't supposed to inspect me again until the end of the year."

Watching his face for a reaction, I ran my hand under the counter and then above the window where there was a shelf lined with candy and cigarettes. I felt something cold and hard and carefully brought down a loaded Saturday Night Special, its plastic handle held together with Scotch tape. I removed the bullets and put them in my pocket.

"That ain't mine," he said. "I never seen it before."

I jammed the gun in my waistband and brought down a carton of Camel filters from the shelf. There was no cellophane wrapping on some of the packs and the silver paper inside had been opened and carefully closed again. When I opened one, I saw several cigarettes had been removed and in their place was a twist of crumpled newspaper. I withdrew it, unfolded it, and smiled at the sight of the colored pills.

"Feel something slip in your ass, *pendejo?*"

"You can't arrest me for drugs," he said confidently. "You're just the rat-shit inspector dude."

"Who says I'm here to arrest you?" I kicked the door closed and banged down the hatch on the window.

"Who are you?"

"You know that kid who was just here?"

"What kid? I sell food to hundreds of kids." He backed away from me.

"You want to know who I am?" I got him in the corner and leaned my forearm up against his windpipe. "You just sold something to my son," I hissed in his ear. "What was it?"

"It was nothing! I swear!"

I rapped him in the solar plexus and he bent double in agony.

"It's asteroids," he grunted. "I sold him asteroids."

"You mean *steroids?*"

"Not the real kind. I mix this weight gain shit from the supermarket with corn flour. He sells it to all his skinny friends that wants to have muscles."

"You're selling him drugs, *cabron!*" I pushed his chin up with the heel of my hand.

"No, man! I'm *buying* from him. Your son selling me Ritalin, Dexedrine, Prozac! *He's* the motherfucking dealer."

"You're lying to me!" I yelled, but I knew in the pit of my stomach he was telling the truth.

"I got kids of my own," he protested indignantly. "I don't sell to no kids. I sell to construction guys."

"I could turn you over to the cops. There's one in the school right now."

"You do that," he said. "They be arresting your little

Hugo right with me, man. See how his skinny white ass likes it in L.A. County."

I couldn't figure out how to extricate myself from the situation with any dignity. I grabbed a steel mallet and broke the firing pin off the Saturday Night Special and dropped the gun in a vat of menudo bubbling on the stove. It was a gesture, but it didn't mean anything and he knew it.

"Taking your shit out on me when *you* the bad motherfucking parent!" He rubbed his windpipe. "That's you, *homes!* That's you not taking care of business! My kids don't do none of that drug dealing shit!" He looked at me with triumphant scorn as I ducked my head to back out the door. "Rich motherfucker be having things, don't even know how to raise a child. How do you like me now? Bee-yutch?"

As his taunts followed me down the alley, I wondered why the hell I'd chosen to say I was Hugo's father. I really couldn't think of a more thankless position.

I licked my wounds across the street in Lincoln Park and waited for Hugo to come out for lunch. Homeless people lay asleep on the grass under mounds of blankets; others were rearranging the loads on their customized baby carriages and shopping carts; a pair of bearded, dirt-ingrained vets in jungle camo were pretending to play tennis with imaginary balls and rackets next to a court where some schoolgirls were playing real tennis with their coach. The early spring sun filtering through the eucalyptus trees warmed us all equally and, if you didn't look too closely at the human details, everything appeared picturesque in that beguiling California way. There was a plaque on the white Spanish colonial building beside the tennis courts, identifying it as the "Miles Memorial Playhouse." It had been *"dedicated in 1929 to the young men and women of Santa*

Monica." Well, here were their descendants seventy-one years later, sleeping their hangovers off on the grass, coughing last night's smoke up from their lungs, gratefully pouring today's first drink of cooking sherry down their parched throats. I thought of Stick Adams, a black Marine I met in the V.A. hospital who later died of an overdose. "You only go around once in this life," he told me towards the end. "And I'm going around fucked-up."

And then I realized it wasn't just the homeless in the park that unsettled me. I'd been to this very exact theatre when I was fourteen. My father had forced me to accompany him to see my mother perform a small role in an Ibsen play. I remember being bored and resentful and then furious when I realized her contribution to this gloomy amateur performance was playing the insignificant role of the maid. How dare they treat my mother like that? Why did she *allow* it? And though I didn't want to voice it even to myself, how could she be such a *loser?* At that age, even I knew doing small theatre work in Los Angeles was not much more than high-minded masochism. No Hollywood talent scout was going to discover her down here. My father and I clapped and cheered when she took her bow, but the noise we generated only emphasized how empty the place was.

"Hey, mister, give you a dollar to buy me some cigarettes at the 7-Eleven?" A squeaky-voiced boy from Hart Hayworth brought me out of my reverie. He was about twelve, staring open-mouthed at me. Across the grass I could see other kids asking the homeless to buy smokes for them at the convenience store across the street. It was lunchtime. School was out.

At first I couldn't see Hugo, but then I spotted him walking around the edge of the park towards Saint

Monica's, the Catholic Church on the corner. A smiling bride and groom were having their photos taken on the front steps. Hugo slipped past the wedding party and vanished inside. I couldn't believe he spent his lunch hour going to church, and soon enough I noticed a succession of other boys entering by the front and coming out by the side exit. I entered and mixed with the guests in the portico. Beyond the bobbing heads, I could see several of the Hart Hayworth boys waiting anxiously in the pews. Hugo had established a position behind one of the church's two sleek, polished wooden confessionals. They reminded me of expensive coffins standing on their ends in the showroom of a funeral home. Each one had the name of the priest who would hear your sins on its locked door. One by one, the boys stood up from the pew and approached Hugo behind the confessional. A real confession would have taken longer, but they weren't trying to save their souls; they just wanted to bulk up. The exchange of cash for his bogus steroid powder took only a moment.

On his way back to school Hugo walked with easy familiarity through the homeless camped out on the grass. He bent down to high-five some of them, handed money to others, waved good-naturedly as they begged him for more. He was like a prince dispensing largesse to the dispossessed. It was a side of him I didn't know existed, and even though he was showing off, it lessened my dislike of him. The truth was, if he hadn't been my responsibility, the criminal ingenuity of selling his Ritalin and Prozac to construction workers and scamming his classmates with fake steroids would have probably amused me. I could think of lots of worse things I'd done at his age.

He came out of school laughing with a group of boys,

and he carried some of his good mood into the car.

"I hope you're not a whiner," I said.

"Huh?"

"The Roach Coach guy says he buys pills from you."

"I don't know what you're talking about."

"And then there's that fake steroid powder he sells you. The stuff you sell to your dim-witted friends in church during your lunch hour. Did you really think I wouldn't catch you?"

"You didn't say . . . I didn't think you were going to *spy* on me!" He looked at me with horror, as he finally realized what I'd been doing all day.

"That's what people pay me to do."

"No way!" He twisted in his seat like a hooked fish. "I'll tell them you hit me. I'll tell them you tried to molest me."

"They won't believe it."

"This is not happening." He kept shaking his head in a kind of willed disbelief. "I haven't done anything to you!" he cried. "Why are you being such a dick?"

I reached over and fished one of his cigarettes out of his shirt pocket. I jammed it between my teeth. "It's not easy losing a parent . . ." I started to try to tell him about my father, but he banged his head against the passenger side window until I shut up.

We drove in silence along the wide-banked turns of Sunset, through the Bel-Air gates, and got stuck going up the hill behind a slow-moving Mercedes station wagon. A pair of twin girls strapped into its rear-facing back seat stared at us all the way up the hill. They had big heads covered with flaxen hair and large stolid jaws and an air of assurance you find in well-adjusted guard dogs. They glared at us without moving their faces, or visibly blinking their eyes, all the way to the top. What was going on? Since I'd been one myself I'd barely registered children and now suddenly they were everywhere.

"I didn't *lose* a parent," he finally said in a strained trembling voice. "Someone murdered my father."

"How do you know that?"

"I can't tell you." He dug his knuckles into his eye sockets to stem his tears.

"Then I can't help you, Hugo."

The Mercedes station wagon ahead of us slowed to make a right turn over a drawbridge into the driveway of a huge mock-French chateau. As they reached the safety of their home, the twins did what they'd been waiting to do all the way up the hill: they stuck out their tongues and gave us the finger.

"Do you have to tell my mom?" he asked in a small voice. "What if I paid you?"

"You already tried that, kid."

As we passed through the first gate at the top I could see Sally and Raj, both in matching sweats, jogging up the drive towards us. They were outfitted with heart monitors, baseball caps, Oakley sunglasses, and hand and ankle weights.

"It's not fair!" Hugo wailed. "Why didn't you tell them yesterday? Serafina said you were on my side and now you're just a snitch."

"I didn't trust them." I pulled the car over and rolled down the window to greet his approaching parents. "Too bad I can't trust you, either."

"Raj killed my father." He gulped as if he was about to throw up.

"Got any proof?"

"I'm working on it." He'd gone white with tension.

"I need more than that."

"I know somebody who saw him," he gasped.

"Hi, honey." Hugo's mother's face filled the window. "How's school?"

"Great." He put a world of rage and sarcasm into the single word.

"How'd it go?" she addressed me.

"So far so good," I replied.

She removed her sunglasses and smiled brightly. Her eyes wandered inquisitively from my face to his, and then surveyed the interior of the car. "Is this what you'll be driving him in?"

"It's fine," Hugo sighed.

"It's got a new engine, new brakes, new tires," I said.

"But no air bags," she said. "You know, if you don't mind, I'd rather you drove one of our cars, Thomas."

"I'm sorry, Mrs. Vine. But I've got my computer and fax and all the equipment I need to do my work in here."

"I'd still rather you drove one of our cars." She continued to smile at me.

"I'm really sorry, but I can't function without this car." I could have used one of her cars, I suppose, but it made me think of the uniforms she forced the help to wear in the house.

"Come on!" Raj called to her. "We have to do five miles."

I flinched as her hand came at my face and then I realized she was snatching Hugo's unlit cigarette from my lips. She held it in front of me and broke it between her fingers. "I don't like people smoking around my son, or on my property." Her smile remained in place, but her eyes were like knife points, sharp with dislike. She put her sunglasses back on, checked her watch, and resumed jogging up the driveway.

Hugo looked anxiously at me. "Don't take it personally,"

he said. "She's on this diet and it's driving her crazy. And it's not about you not having airbags."

"What is it about?"

"It's just your car doesn't look so nice. She probably doesn't want the other parents seeing me going to school in it. It's dumb, but she cares about that stuff."

He was such an impulsive, narcissistic kid, I was surprised he had this other layer to him: an embryonic conscience just strong enough to make him uncomfortable with the way his mother had spoken to me. He was trying to make excuses for her, asking me not to think badly of her.

"I'm waiting to hear about this guy who saw Raj kill your father."

"I can't tell you everything yet."

I turned the car around and headed back up the drive towards his jogging parents.

"What are you doing?"

"I want to let your parents know I'm quitting."

"Why?" He was stunned.

"Because you're putting me into an impossible position."

He reached over and turned off the ignition and the car lurched to a halt. "I'm sorry," he said. "I'm sorry. I'll tell you everything if you swear not to let my parents know about it. But you've got to really swear."

"I can't do that. Tell me what happened first."

"No, first you've got to swear." He folded his arms to let me know this was his final offer.

If he'd been an adult, I would have told him to forget it, but then an adult would never have had his childish faith that I would keep my promise. "I will do everything in my power to protect you from harm," I said. "That is the only promise I can make."

He considered my words carefully, testing them for vagueness, loopholes, and treachery. "That's not even a guarantee." He frowned. "I mean, you could still tell."

"Would you trust an adult who promised you more than that?"

"My father always said if a deal was for real you shouldn't have to trust the other guy."

"We don't have a *deal*," I said. "This isn't a negotiation. You're not paying me. I don't owe you anything. In fact, what I'm doing is completely wrong and I'll probably get in a lot of trouble for it. I'm trying to *help* you."

It was a foreign concept to him. I didn't know if it was his personality or his upbringing, but he seemed to view emotions like affection or trust as dangerous traps.

"Why?" he asked.

I got out of the car, walked around, pulled open the passenger door, and tried to yank him out, but he had his seat belt on. I got it undone and dragged him out and marched him into the brush beyond the driveway. He made an attempt to struggle, but it was mainly to preserve his dignity. He could have called out at any time and someone would have heard him, but he kept his mouth shut. I had him by his jacket collar and his feet had to take little hopping steps to keep up with my big strides. We reached an oak tree and I placed him against it and leaned my hands on either side of his head so he had to look me right in the face.

"It's a good question," I said. "It's not the money. If I wanted money, I could have taken your fancy watch that night. It's not because I'm on your parents' side, or I would have busted you today. So what is it? Is it your winning personality? I don't think so. You're rude and you're a liar and so far you've been about as reliable as a length of frayed rope."

He widened his eyes to give them a look of innocence, pretending to eagerly agree with my stern appraisal of his flaws. I knew I wasn't getting anywhere and it was because I still hadn't honestly answered his question. I thought of the nerve required for him to have come to my office that night, and how Serafina had affectionately tousled his hair and made sure his seat belt was on. I thought of him arm-wrestling with the Roach Coach driver and handing out spare change to the dispossessed in the park. These moments stood out because they were such exceptions to his normal mood of rebellious, nihilistic fury. He wasn't anything like me and I disapproved of just about every graceless, entitled thing about him. So why was I going to all this trouble for him? It wasn't as if children were an endangered species. They were as common as weeds. People produced them as easily as they ate and breathed. It wasn't merit. There was nothing special about him. In a world where so many children were enslaved, abused, and starved he was typical in his blindness to his remarkable good fortune. He perfectly fit Dostoyevsky's definition of man as "the ungrateful biped." But didn't we all? We were eye to eye, and under my disapproving gaze he'd dropped the innocent act and reverted to his habitual expression of cynical distrust. His lips were ready to form into a sneer as soon as he heard what I had to say.

"I like you," I said.

His expression became thoughtful and inward-looking, and then he ducked under my arms and hurried back to the Toyota. "Come on." He waved impatiently. "I have to show you something."

"What?"

"We can't talk about it here."

I parked in front of the house and followed him up to his

bedroom, where he withdrew into his closet for about ten minutes. He came out in a pair of Abercrombie and Fitch cargo shorts and some streamlined new hiking boots complete with valves to adjust the pressure in the soles. He filled a backpack with a hunting knife, snakebite kit, nylon rope, flashlight, energy bars, and bottles of Evian water. The wilderness we were heading for turned out to be no more than thirty yards behind the old section of the house. An overgrown path of weathered railroad ties descended the hillside towards a gorge exploding with flowering vines, prickly pear, and nasturtiums. To my amazement, I saw someone had thrown a mountain bike, surfboards, snowboards, a go-cart, roller blades, and dozens of other perfectly good items down into the tangled vegetation. A little further down, a vast collection of baseball and basketball cards had been scattered over a canopy of ivy and morning glory. The once glossy picture cards had lost all their shine in the rains; there were hundreds of them stuck to the leaves like tiny bits of gray, waterlogged laundry. I paused to retrieve one of them: a Kobe Bryant card from his rookie season with the Lakers that was actually signed: *Hugo, be cool—Kobe Bryant.*

"Come on!" Hugo tried to pull me away from the scene.

"Why'd you throw all this good stuff away?"

"I didn't." He colored in embarrassment. "It's no big deal. When I act wrong, my mom always gets rid of my stuff. It doesn't matter."

"Why doesn't she give it to someone who wants it?"

"She just gets all upset and drags it down here and cries as she's throwing it off the cliff. It's like some kind of therapy." He shrugged defensively. "I don't even care."

It sounded so bizarre I wanted to ask him more about this dumping ground for items from the Sharper Image catalogue, but I could see he hated the subject. I'd found it so difficult to tell him I liked him, I didn't want to risk him shutting down again. I followed him away from the gorge along a narrow, snaking tunnel marked with fresh coyote scat. We walked bent-over for about thirty seconds before coming out into a secluded grove of old eucalyptus. It was late afternoon and the heavily shaded spot was so littered with years of dead leaves it took me a moment to notice the abandoned mine shaft: it was a twelve-foot-square opening in the earth sealed off by a rusted iron grill. Hugo brushed off the leaves and loosened the edge of the grill, sliding it aside.

"The guy who dug this mine was a total loner," Hugo said approvingly. "It's the only one around here."

"Maybe there wasn't much worth mining in these mountains." I looked around for any signs of the man who'd come here to try and strike it rich so many years ago. Whoever he was, chances were he was from somewhere else and this spot must have struck him as a strange and alien place. It was full of emptiness and a kind of beauty that failed to console. He wouldn't have felt he belonged. Generation after generation of ambitious, hopeful people had been drawn to Los Angeles and complained of the same unsettled feeling: the lack of roots, the absence of tradition. There was a tradition, of course, but it was a tradition of feeling unconnected and lost, and everyone experienced it. You didn't have to be some European émigré to sense it. I'd hiked in these mountains since I was a child and driven the streets of Los Angeles my whole life, yet all my attempts to treat it as home felt strangely forced and unreal.

Hugo took the coil of rope from his backpack, tied it around a tree trunk, and let the slack fall down into the mine. He shone a flashlight into the depths and I saw it was only about fifteen feet deep.

"I hope you're not thinking of going down there," I said.

"Don't worry. I know what I'm doing."

"These old mines can be dangerous."

"I'll be fine."

It was the eternal dialogue between youth and age: without thinking, we'd fallen into it like an old married couple. Hugo let himself down into the shaft, and when he reached the bottom he turned off the flashlight and I couldn't see him anymore. I waited, wondering what he was doing. Idly, I played with the idea of somehow getting my hands on the extremely expensive mountain bike his mother had toppled down into the gorge, or the surfboards for that matter. It was infuriating to think of all that fine stuff left out to rot.

"Hugo? What are you doing?" There was no response. I got down on my knees and peered into the darkness, but all I could see were some faint glints in the water that had accumulated at the bottom of the shaft. There was no sign of Hugo.

"Damn it, Hugo!" The echo of my voice sounded panicky to me. The shade in the clearing had deepened and there was a chill in the air. When I yanked on the rope, it came up empty.

"I'm getting sick of this, kid." When there was still no answer, I dropped the rope back down the shaft, checked to see it was securely tied to the tree trunk, and started to lower myself into the hole. The walls were buttressed with rotted timbers that crumbled when I braced my feet against them; water seeped out of the slick clay; it smelled of damp and long dead animals. My feet sank up to the ankles in the muddy bottom. There was not enough light filtering down through the steel mesh above to see anything.

"Hugo!" I shouted and the rope was torn out of my grasp. It snaked back up to the top where I could see Hugo peering down at me.

It was impossible to discern his expression, but his voice, when he spoke, was disconcertingly calm and business-like. "I had to see if it worked. Are you all right?"

"What the hell are you doing?"

"This is where I'm going to catch Raj," he said. "Scream as loud as you can. I want to see if you can hear someone calling for help."

"How did you get out of here?"

"You can't see how to do it without a flashlight." He sounded very pleased.

"Drop the rope," I said grimly.

"No, scream. I have to hear you scream first. Do it!"

I'd been dozily wondering how to get hold of the kid's beautiful mountain bike and suddenly he had me trapped in the dark at the bottom of a foul-smelling mine shaft. It had all happened with the deceptive speed of a household accident: the fall down the stairs that ends in a broken neck, the slip in the bath that results in a cracked skull. One minute you're singing in the shower, the next your lifeblood is washing down the drain. I tried to beat back all the horrible thoughts sweeping through me: *he is not insane . . . he is not trying to kill me . . . he found a way out of here and so can I.* I started blindly groping my way along the slimy walls in search of an opening to freedom.

"Scream!" he ordered.

I tried to do what he said. I screamed, but it came out like an airless bleat. I was starting to hyperventilate now and my vision was turning scratchy; my hands going tingly and numb. I knew where this was going, where it *wanted* to go because all my panic attacks had only one destination in mind. A terrible force was trying to pull me backwards into a tunnel in Vietnam that smelled so badly of shit and rotting fish paste it burned your eyes. There was something hideous at the end of it, and the prospect of having to face it was paralyzing. I was smacking my hands against the muddy walls and muttering disjointedly when Hugo dropped down at my side.

"Are you okay?" He shone the flashlight in my face. "Jesus, I'm sorry. I just thought this would be a cool place to trap Raj. The way out's right over here." He directed the light to a section of plywood leaning against the earth wall. When he pulled it aside I felt a cold breeze on my skin; the sound of running water filled the shaft. I kept my hand on his back as he led me down a short section of framed tunnel that ended where it was bisected by the rusted remains of an ancient drainage pipe. We climbed into it through a jagged opening in its corroded paper-thin wall. Inside the pipe it was almost high enough to stand up; the freezing water filled my shoes as it ran ankle deep towards the pipe's opening a few yards away. I only took my hand off his back when we stepped out into what was left of the daylight.

"I used to be claustrophobic," he said. "But I cured myself."

"I'm not claustrophobic." I fumbled violently in his pocket for the pack of cigarettes, got one in my mouth, and realized I had no matches.

He produced his Zippo and cupped the flame from the wind for me. His hands were warm and steady; mine were shaking uncontrollably. I went over and lay down against the base of a tree, hating him for having witnessed my weakness.

"Everybody has something they can't stand. It's nothing to be ashamed of." He refrained from looking at me. "My dad couldn't stand Disney. My mom hates dog hair on the furniture. I don't hate cats, but I'm allergic to them." He added rather lamely, "I guess with you it's tunnels."

"I don't know why I ever gave these up." I greedily inhaled the cigarette. "What made me think I could live without them?"

"Should I, like, tell you what I know about Raj now?"

"You're feeling kind of cocky because I didn't like it down that hole so now you're going to tell me, is that it?"

"I didn't *know* you were going to get so upset. It's not like I planned it or anything."

"Upset is what your mom gets when she finds a dog hair on the couch. I wasn't upset down there. I was out of my fucking mind."

"I said I was sorry."

"No, you're right—I do have a thing about tunnels." I lit a fresh cigarette from the butt of the first one.

"Is it, like, something you want to share?" He spoke hesitantly, but you could see the therapy-speak was second nature to him; his generation had learned it in school instead of a second language.

"The last time I went down a tunnel was in Vietnam and I killed a boy."

"You *killed* him?" All the secret elation at getting to play my therapist faded from his face. "How old was he?"

"It's hard to tell a person's age when he's starving. He was smaller than you."

"Was he trying to kill you?" It was the question everybody asked.

"I thought he was. He was trying to get away from me," I said. "I didn't even realize it was a kid until afterwards."

"How did you . . . ?"

"I strangled him until he passed out, and then I broke

his neck." I already regretted my confession. Once I started to get close to someone I always told them about this incident from my past, but there was never any relief. With each telling, I seemed to get further away from the grisly truth of what had happened that day. Had I been justified in killing the boy? Or had I done something obscene, which I'd covered over and for which I could never be forgiven?

"Did they find out? Did you get in trouble?"

"No." I pulled myself to my feet. "They gave me a medal."

On the way back we had to walk around the floodlit tennis court where a boisterous game of doubles was in progress: two men playing against two women, all of them beginners, the women hitting cautious lobs, the men going for big shots that went into the net, or hit the fence, everybody doing a lot of fist-pumping and high-fiving whenever a point was actually scored. There were some heavily-built men drinking wine and beer in the small grandstand loudly yelling encouragement. They sported gold chains and wore skintight V-necked ribbed sweaters and pressed chinos over tasseled loafers with no socks. They had the air of young middle managers letting off steam after a boring day at a business convention. When they spotted us passing by, the cheering and yelling slowly died out and everyone looked to one of the male players. He took a step towards us, shielding his eyes against the glare of the lights as he peered into the darkness.

"That you, Raj?" His voice sounded cowed, deferential. "Some of the guys wanted to check out your court. I cleared it with Tea. Hope that's okay?"

It was Cedrick Stone, the beefy L.A.P.D. detective, barely recognizable in a visor and brand new tennis outfit. He wasn't used to feeling in the wrong and I enjoyed his moment of unease as he peered into the darkness. The other off-duty cops looked down into their glasses of Chardonnay, wondering if Stone had landed them in it by bringing them to the movie star's house.

"It's not Raj's court." Hugo's childish voice pierced the silence.

Stone came closer until he could make us both out. "Hey, it's Hugo, right? How's it going?"

Hugo stared at him without answering.

"Your dad said it was okay to use the court."

"He's not my dad."

Stone smiled indulgently. His eyes rested coldly on me for a moment and then he turned on his heel and swaggered back to the service line. "It's fine. It's just the kid," he reassured them. We watched them as they started to play again, Stone clowning and talking trash, trying to get the party mood back up. But his pals had been intimidated by Hugo's remark. They were young, hardened big-city cops, bulked up from the weight room, veterans of shootings, but no matter how tough you are, no one is immune to the discomfort of committing a social faux-pas. Standing under the spotlights, they lowered their voices and self-consciously sipped their drinks, like gatecrashers at a party where they knew they didn't belong.

"None of my dad's friends come and play any more," Hugo said as we moved away. "Raj fired everybody who used to work here except for that bitch, Tea. Boy, would I like to hang her from her 'corner office with a view.' I'd like to get an automatic weapon and just blow those stupid cops away, too. That would be so cool. *Tennis Court massacre . . . L.A.P.D.'s finest gunned down by unknown assailant. Bodies cut to pieces by AK47-wielding killer. More breaking news at ten.*"

I let him riff on his lurid, blood-soaked fantasies. They weren't healthy or mature, but they didn't sound strange either. It was like listening to my own *id* talking. As he enthusiastically described how much fun it would be to run Raj through a wood-pulper, and flatten his therapist with an RTD bus, I felt him slip something solid into my hand. "This is what he gave me . . . the guy I told you about. It's my dad's money clip. You can see the initials, D.O.V. . . . Daniel Oliver Vine. The Tahoe police didn't tell the media anything about the killer robbing my dad. If some psycho tried to confess just for the attention, they said, he wouldn't know that detail. I know my dad had his money clip with him when he went skiing that day." He spoke calmly and deliberately, as if he'd given it all a lot of thought.

"How do you know that?"

"I just know." He hesitated and then expelled a deep breath. "I took some money out of my dad's parka that day, while he was in the bathroom with my mom. I never stole anything before, but they were having this big argument about Raj and I was just pissed off. It was only five dollars. I flushed it down the toilet . . . afterwards."

Afterwards, I realized, referred to after he'd learned of his father's death. It couldn't have been lost on Hugo that, after going through his father's pockets, a few hours later whoever killed him had done the same thing to his corpse. There was no connection between Hugo's theft and the murder; it was just bad timing, but in a child's sensitive mind one might seem to have caused the other. Guilt would bond them together like glue.

"How much money did your dad have on him?"

"At least a couple of grand. Pops always carried a big wad of cash." He shook his head in amazement. "Even when he went swimming. He'd put it in a Ziploc bag in his bathing suit. He used to say, it's kind of lame, but when I was a kid he'd say, 'You never know, you might meet a cute mermaid and want to buy her a drink.' Like mermaids need a drink. It was a joke. But that's how I'm sure the guy who gave me the money clip is for real. His name is Eric. He's a pretty nice guy."

"How did you meet Eric?"

"I was at a concert at The House of Blues and he just kind of came up and started talking. He goes, do you wanna go backstage and meet the musicians? I'm, like, sure, but I'm here with someone. I know, he says, you're here with Malahide, but you don't want Malahide to see *this*. And he shows me my dad's money clip, and I'm, like, I don't believe this. So we go backstage and he says all this stuff about it not being right how my father died, and how he knows what really happened, but nobody wants to hear the truth, and it's, like, totally dangerous for him even to be talking to me. I said, if he knew something, why didn't he go to the police, but he said the police were in Raj's pocket. Everybody was getting paid to be quiet except him. He said he knew everything and he felt bad. He kept talking about how he was, like, an artist, too, and he knew what a hard life it was. He kept saying he felt sorry for my mother, being such a big star, because everybody was taking advantage of her, and it wasn't her fault. It was, like, he knew her."

"And you believed him?"

"He knew what her nickname was from high school. *Mustang Sally*. He knew what Malahide was going to be drinking at the bar that night. It was like he was tight with Raj and all of them."

"What's this Eric look like?"

"He's, like, old, but still pretty hip. Kind of John Travolta. He's kind of intense. He was kind of cool actually."

"What did he want from you?"

"Nothing. He just said he wanted me to have my dad's money clip. He'd never met Pops, but you know, he'd seen a lot of the movies he produced." There was something about the solemn pleasure Hugo took in describing this touching moment that made me wonder if it had really been like that. The money clip was real, but the stranger offering sympathy out of the kindness of his heart had the fairy tale glow of something that didn't occur in nature.

"Did the guy say he *saw* Raj kill your dad?"

"He said he, like, knew what happened." Hugo frowned. "I believe him."

"Did you ask him how come *he* had your dad's money clip?"

Hugo shook his head, irritated by my questions. We had reached the rear section of the house where the garbage cans were kept in a fenced-in area behind Serafina's room. I could hear the TV, and as we came around the corner, Adolpho was momentarily visible through the window, bouncing up and down on the bed as he stared open-mouthed at a breakfast cereal commercial.

"Who else knows about this?"

"I tried to tell Serafina, but she hates all this stuff. Even if I'm right about Raj, she thinks it's too dangerous."

"How long before you accidentally ran into Eric again and he asked you for money?"

"It wasn't like that," Hugo protested. "I was going to Third Street Promenade one night to the movies. It was an 'R' and I was looking around for an adult to help me sneak in and I saw Eric. He was playing guitar and singing . . ."

"Singing what?"

"I don't know. James Taylor songs, *Fire and Rain.* I asked him what he was doing and he said he was sleeping in his car and this was the only way he could make any money. The police had been hassling him because he didn't have a performer's license. *I* was the one who suggested paying him."

"To do *what* exactly?" I was having a hard time keeping the skepticism out of my voice.

"It doesn't matter!" he flared. "You think I'm stupid. I wish I'd never told you!"

The explosive mood swing took me by surprise. He was such a caustic, critical individual, I'd forgotten how abnormally sensitive he was. "I'm sure you're on to something with this guy, Eric," I said. "I just want to know more about him."

"You're such a bad liar. No wonder you have no clients."

"You gave Eric your father's watch, didn't you?"

"It's none of your business," he snapped.

"Here we go," I said. "Meltdown time."

"You're a joke. You think I'm impressed because you don't care about money? I just think you're lame. Oh, *I like you, Hugo.* Like I give a fuck! Why don't you just go away? Why don't you . . . go and strangle a Vietnamese baby or something?"

He was so angry and it was such an absurdly low blow I burst out laughing.

"You think that's funny?" he said.

"I don't know. Should I cry?"

"You're sick." He was still pretending to be outraged, but he'd lost his edge of raw hysteria. "You should, like, get help. Therapy. Something."

"I've tried. Nothing works."

"Try harder."

"You think it would help?" I rolled my eyes back to look like an insane person.

He laughed against his will, and the worst of the storm seemed to be over. At least for now. There was a vulnerable seam somewhere in his personality, a painful opening that I was always touching upon, and I didn't know how to close it. I couldn't even figure out how to avoid it. Had he ever just been an innocent little kid? Had he enjoyed a taste of Eden before turning into this insecure, deeply temperamental, maddeningly opaque teenager? It was like dealing with some grouchy, high-strung diva.

"Did you give Eric the watch?" I asked gently.

"Yes!" he barked. "But it's been a week and I haven't heard from him."

"Okay. What was he supposed to give you in exchange for the watch?"

"I don't know. Information!" He groaned. "He said he *knew* the real players. I thought he could lead me to them."

"You did good," I said.

"*No.* I got tooled. He's going to sell the watch and we'll never see him again. Everything I do turns into shit. Always has, always will." He was plunged in adolescent despair and I have to admit I found it momentarily soothing, a breathing spell, like the silence when a jackhammer stops. I also felt strangely flattered that he'd said *we* instead of *I*.

"This is the main thing." I held up the silver money clip. "This proves you're not crazy and I'm not out of my mind to believe you."

"Yeah, well, no offense, but having *you* believe me doesn't exactly mean a lot. The guy is gone and he's never coming back."

"Yeah, well, no offense," I said, trying to keep my temper in check, "but I guarantee Eric will be getting in touch as soon as he burns through whatever money he got for that watch he scammed off you."

"Bullshit," he said. "You don't know anything. If you did, you'd have a better job than driving me to school."

I turned on my heel and walked over to where my car was parked and got inside. A second before I slammed the door I heard him yell dispiritedly, "You taking me to school on Monday?" A part of me wanted to punish him for his abusive attitude and just drive away, but as I looked back at Hugo, the front door of the house opened behind him. Raj stepped out into the light and took in an appreciative breath of the night air. He was stripped to the waist, his chiseled torso shiny with sweat, his dark golden face glowing from his run. He was chug-a-lugging some protein drink straight out of the blender and looked like an advertisement for some product that made you beautiful and healthy and incredibly rich all at the same time. He smiled faintly at the sound of distant cheering from the off-duty cops on the tennis court and noticed us. He didn't say anything, just ran his eyes over us with a kind of bored majestic insolence. He had the confident bearing of a lion after it has feasted on its prey, jaws stained with gore, looking around at a world that is too weak to threaten him. But then I remembered it was against the rules to make direct eye contact with him.

"I'll be there," I said to Hugo.

Chapter Seven

That night I strolled up and down the Third Street Promenade on the off chance I'd run across Eric. The casually dressed crowd surged past the shops and sidewalk restaurants and bulged out around the multi-plex cinemas. A ten-year-old Asian boy was playing Hendrix's *Voodoo Child* on his electric guitar; his mother sat on a milk crate beside him collecting donations. There was a black guy painted head to toe in silver standing frozen on one foot, while people marveled at his ability to resemble a statue. Some Hare Krishnas in Birkenstocks and pale orange robes danced without rhythm or grace to a monotonously beating tambourine. Their heads were shaved and their pasty faces wore expressions of dreamy, exaggerated rapture, as if they were sure God liked their kind of music best. But there was nobody who looked like John Travolta singing old James Taylor songs.

I passed a bar and a cloud of liquor-scented air wafted out the open door. Inside I could see people packed close together, enjoying themselves, animatedly drinking. I'd washed out of AA after attending a few meetings, allergic to anything that required like-minded people getting together to improve themselves. I'd thought I could rely on my own internal power to quell my thirst, but it was getting more difficult with each passing day. I didn't go into the bar, but I had a bad feeling I'd be going into one soon.

"Hi. Thomas Kyd, right?"

A young woman looked up at me, with her hand confidently extended. She was short with a blunt, full-bodied figure. She wore a beret and was dressed in a white sweat-shirt and plaid skirt that brought to mind a Catholic girl's school uniform. She had inserted her pink scrubbed face and eager sparkling blue eyes an inch or two closer to me than felt comfortable.

"Do I know you?" I took her hand.

"I know I'm not unforgettable." Her accent was from one of those states where hockey and ice fishing are popular. "But, *hey,* I thought you might have noticed!"

I stared at her, mystified.

She pretended to take my picture. *"Hello?"*

And then I got it. She was the tabloid photographer who'd followed Hugo and me to school.

"Now don't look like that. I'll bet I took more pictures of you than your mother ever did."

I instinctively looked around to see if her male counterpart was photographing us together. "Where's the guy who drives your van?"

"He knocked off hours ago," she said. "Jeez, I got so many shots of your mug I feel like I know you, Thomas."

"I've got nothing to say to you people. Sorry. I just don't."

"It's okay." She laughed. "Can't blame a girl for trying, can you? It's not like we're not a teensy little bit in the same business now."

"I can't talk to you."

"Okie-dokie. I'm just hanging out. I saw you and thought I'd introduce myself."

"Yeah, right." I stepped back from her. "I gotta go."

"Go where? Back to your little bungalow, curl up with a good book? I've been watching you. You're walking around trying to decide if you want to blow some brain cells on one of these crummy movies."

I brushed past her and headed down Arizona towards the beach. In a second she was walking beside me again, acting as if the previous conversation hadn't taken place. It was the way people who wanted to get you to join a religion or buy a used car treated you.

"That Hugo's a real cute kid." She had to take quick steps to keep up with me. "He sure has grown since his dad's funeral."

"Why don't you leave him alone?"

"My editor wants to do something on kids of dead celebrities. How are they coping with the tragedy? That kind of thing. I notice Hugo goes to those NA meetings. Guess there's a little drug problem there like his mom."

"Is this something you dreamed of doing when you were growing up?"

"God, yes!" she said. "I *love* sleaze. It's amazing what celebrities do out here. And everybody's in on it. I mean, we get calls from people reporting they saw Meg Ryan go to the ladies' room at some club. Is she in there doing drugs? Is she in there with a guy? No. Dear little Meg's probably just taking a dump. But they think it's interesting. We've got people everywhere telling us what is going on with everybody. Like Hugo, for instance. You know how he gets his urine tested every week?"

"I said, *leave me alone.*"

"I guess Sally hasn't got you doing the real shit work yet. Malahide used to take the kid's little pee-pee container to the lab on Santa Monica a couple of times a week."

"If you weren't a woman I'd slug you."

"I like you." She elbowed me playfully. "So I'm going to give you a little heads-up. Just to show you how nice I can be. Little Hugo not only failed his drug test last week, his urine was awfully weird."

"Weird how?"

"You know, like he not only tested positive for coke, but the poor boy's pregnant." She studied me for a reaction. "Oh come on! His mother substituted her urine for his so he'd fail his drug test. Admit that is the most fabulously bizarre thing you ever heard."

We had reached the end of the block and I couldn't decide whether to keep listening to her or turn around and walk away as fast as possible.

"Now listen up, Thomas," she said. "I respect you. I really do. I'm from Wisconsin and we admire grit and loyalty more than most, but you've got to wake up. Your predecessor, Malahide, used to sell us stuff about the family all the time. The pharmacy tells us about every prescription the Vines get. That stuck-up attorney of theirs tells us when and where Sally and Raj are going jogging. Hugo's teachers have talked to us. Hell, when Raj was the Vines' ski instructor he used to sell us photos and all kinds of information about Sally and her husband. We'll pay cash. No one is ever going to know because we always protect our sources."

"No, you don't. You just disclosed them all."

"Who cares? If anyone asked, we'd deny it. Stop being so damn proud. You can't live on pride," she said. "It's not nutritious."

"I know, but it tastes better than dirt and it doesn't fill you up so much." I expected her to give up after my nasty allusion to her weight, but she just laughed.

"I had a feeling it wouldn't fly, but I had to give it a shot." She cocked her head sideways and looked speculatively at me. "I bet there's something you don't know about me."

"I don't even know your name."

"Prudence Nash. What's more important is," she took off her beret and let her thick dark hair fall around her shoulders, "I'm a girl with a thing for older guys. Why don't I turn off the meter and we can go and have a drink?"

"I don't drink." I didn't say it with any pride; it felt more like an admission of inner dullness.

"And I don't bite." Her audacious smile hardened. "I'm not a bad person, you know. Just trying to earn a buck so I can go to film school. And you know, I'm already making movies now with real stars in them, except the stars aren't doing what the studios want anybody to see."

"Hugo's *fourteen*. I promised the kid's mother I'd protect him."

"So? I promised my editor I'd take pictures of him. It's a job, isn't it?"

"Not really, but you're still young. You'll figure it out." I turned and walked back towards the promenade. She didn't say anything, but after I'd made it halfway down the block she blew a loud, derisive raspberry at me.

I drifted around for another hour looking for Eric among the street performers and waving off people trying to get me to join the Black Muslims. I checked in at the small substation the Santa Monica cops run on the promenade. I identified myself as a private investigator to an impressively bulked up black female officer from the bicycle unit called Corelle Lamb and asked her if she remembered anyone performing on the guitar about a week ago without a permit.

"He was singing James Taylor songs," I said. *Fire and Rain.*

"They all do." She rolled her eyes. "What's he look like?"

"The description I've got says he's 'cool' . . . like John Travolta."

"He didn't look too cool in *Battlefield Earth*," she said.

"Didn't catch that one."

"It was so bad it wasn't even good, you know what I mean?"

I nodded. "You or someone from this station probably rousted him about a week ago."

She tore the wrapper off an energy bar and nibbled daintily at it. "I usually only remember 'em when they're good, and most of the good ones have permits. There *was* a dude in a white suit the other night doing some songs from *Saturday Night Fever*. I told him, I said, 'Eric, you too talented for this place. You got to take your act to somewhere where you can get discovered.' I always mess with 'em a little. Softens the blow of rejection." She laughed uproariously. "They just trying to get themselves noticed. Nothing wrong with that."

I tried to keep the excitement out of my voice. "How do you know his name's Eric?"

"I know him. I chased him off before when he was doing his . . ." She stopped and let out a groan. "Damn! You got me all confused with your first question. See, Eric don't look like no John Travolta when he's doing his James Taylor act. He got a whole other thing working for him then—sandals, headband, one of them Indian shirts that hang out with no collar. But when he's into the disco he slicks his hair back, you know, more like he was in *Pulp Fiction*."

"He sounds versatile."

"Oh yeah. He just can't get it together to get himself a permit like he's supposed to. What you want him for anyway?"

"Contributing to the delinquency of a minor. Do you think he's dangerous?"

"Just when he sings," she said. "But we ain't allowed to arrest people for what they sound like."

I left her my card and asked her to call me if Eric showed up again.

On my way home I stopped at Pavillions, a twenty-four-hour market on Montana, and cashed the Vines' V.I.P. check with the Sri Lankan night manager. He was a thinly built, very dark skinned man in his thirties with a mouthful of crooked white teeth and a refined English accent. I couldn't remember his long unpronounceable Sinhalese name, but I noticed the I.D. tag pinned to his shirt now simply said "Brad Smith."

"My daughters refused to go to school unless I changed it." He chuckled. "The 'Brad' part was their idea. You know, for Brad Pitt."

I had to make a purchase to cash the check, so I bought some gum at the checkout counter. The brightly-colored tabloids in the racks beckoned the eye like fruit in the produce section. The lead story in the *Enquirer* that week concerned an obese elderly couple in Bakersfield who had been abducted from their mobile home by aliens. Instead of sexually molesting them, as was customary, the aliens had given them liposuction and facelifts. Neighbors at their trailer park confirmed the astonishing improvement in the couple's appearance. It hardened my suspicion that aliens were only drawn to people of limited means and education. The world's truly successful people, who normally attracted all the attention, apparently couldn't get arrested by extraterrestrials. In the upper right-hand corner of the same *Enquirer* was a photo of Raj under a headline that read: *GOING DOWNHILL FAST?* I added the tabloid to the chewing gum I was buying. In the past the night manager had tried not to show his concern when my purchases consisted only of liquor and cigarettes. He now giggled: "That is not a very nutritious selection of items, Mr. Kyd. That *National Enquirer* is habit-forming. I am totally hooked on it."

"It's for a friend."

"Of course." He handed me my money with a smile and took a last look at my check. "Vine International Pictures." He raised his eyebrows suggestively. "I've heard of them. You are coming up in the world, Mr. Kyd."

I was living that year in a tiny cottage set behind a weathered craftsman's bungalow on Fourth Street near Montana. I say "cottage," but for most of its life the structure had been bolted to the aft deck of a ferry that used to carry passengers between Santa Monica and Catalina. Twenty years ago the owners of the main house, Jack and Wendy Doyle, had bought it at auction and propped it up on railroad ties. Their children had used it as a playhouse before growing up and moving out. The Doyles had grown older, and over time the untended garden had risen up around it until it was barely noticeable. The wiring and plumbing weren't up to code and the Doyles' property wasn't zoned for a rental unit. If it wasn't for the roots and vines covering the structure, it would probably have collapsed years ago. It was oppressively hot in summer and permanently damp in winter, but I was four blocks from the beach and the Doyles were happy with a modest rent in exchange for me never asking them to fix anything.

I went into the galley and poured myself a glass of *Crodino* over ice and added a splash of soda. The Italian aperitif looked like a real drink and had a semi-bitter medicinal taste that I'd conned myself into believing was more like liquor than cough medicine. The piece on Raj in the *Enquirer* turned out to be an exposé of the lies he'd told about his past since launching V.I.P. He had never been a member of the French Olympic ski team, as he'd claimed; his father was not a highly decorated French naval officer; his Lebanese mother was not a legendary nightclub chanteuse known as "the Barbra Streisand of Beirut." Raj had not studied at the Sorbonne, or served in the French paratroopers either. Lying was no more of a crime in Hollywood than breathing oxygen, but not being able to close was another matter. Despite all of Raj's announcements of big new deals with foreign partners, V.I.P. had yet to make a movie starring Sally Vine. The headline might as well have read—*Is This Man Full of Shit?*

I washed out my glass in the sink and tossed the *Enquirer* into the trash. I was about to take a shower when I heard the sound of someone rapping on the window. I switched on the outside light and threw open the front door. Prudence Nash came around the side of the cottage, her arms folded over her chest, looking at me with an expression that managed to be both aggrieved and sheepish at the same time.

"I couldn't find the front door." There was a hint of liquor on her breath. "I've been out here for ages."

"What can I do for you?"

"I have a bone to pick with you." She peered past me into the house. "Afraid to let me in?"

"Looks like you went and had that drink by yourself, Prudence."

"Just *one!*" she said. "That's all it takes with me." She ducked her head and bulled her way past me into the house. "I bet I'm the kind of girl you look at late at night when the bar's emptying out and decide I'm not worth it. Too fat, huh?"

I couldn't believe she was here because I'd turned down

her offer of a drink. "If I was drinking," I said, with a stab at chivalry, "I wouldn't be able to remember much about it in the morning anyway."

"Worried I'm here to get some dirt on the Vines?" she taunted me.

"If you are, you're wasting your time."

"Only reason I'm here, stupid, is because you *wouldn't* give me any." She became aware of her cramped surroundings. "What is this, a doll house?"

"It's where I live. What do you want?"

"I want you to take back what you said. I am *not* sleazy. I do not eat *dirt* for a living, and you're not my father." She sounded genuinely indignant.

"No problem, Prudence. I take it all back."

"Oh stop patronizing me!" She flopped down uninvited in the single armchair and extended her powerful stocky legs into the center of the room. "You're right!" She glared up at me. "I shouldn't be taking pictures of poor little Hugo who is, after all, only a child. Nothing, not even the directing class at AFI, is worth the loss of my immortal soul. Taking pleasure in the squalor of the lives of the rich and famous is a sin. There, I've confessed. Are you satisfied?"

"I really got under your skin," I marveled.

"I *hate* being in the wrong." She gazed truculently around and shuddered. "There are homeless people who live in bigger cardboard boxes than this place. I feel like I'm in an elevator. This place is *small.*"

The phone rang but before I could get to it the machine picked up: Hugo's childish voice filled the room. "It's me, Hugo. Are you there? I heard from Eric . . ."

I picked up. "Hey, Hugo, what's going on?"

"I heard from Eric," he said.

"You're kidding. What did he say?"

"He wants to meet me. He's going to call back and tell me when and where." His voice was breathless with excitement. "You sound weird. Is something wrong?"

"I don't know if we should be saying all this on the phone. Where are you?"

"I'm right outside, dude," he laughed. "My mom's having a big party. Serafina drove me over to your office, but you weren't there so we came by. Can we come in?"

"Serafina?" I said.

"And Adolpho. We told my mom we were going to the movies."

I couldn't believe everything could turn to shit on so many different levels at the same time. "You know, Hugo, I was actually asleep . . ."

"Come on, dude. Your lights are on. I can see them."

"I'll come out. Stay where you are."

Prudence watched me from the armchair, enjoying my predicament. "I could hide?" She looked around the tiny room. "But I don't know where."

I didn't like the idea of leaving a tabloid reporter alone in my place, but there was nothing I could do about it. The headlights of the white Suburban blinded me as I stepped out into the driveway. As I came closer, I could see Serafina behind the wheel and Adolpho jumping up and down in the passenger seat. I walked around to the driver's side and asked her where Hugo was.

"He's looking at something. I am sorry. I tell Hugo it is better not to disturb you at night at your home." She tried to act very casual, but I could see she was wondering why I didn't want them to come inside. With a woman's sixth sense had she already guessed that another woman was inside my house? But then I realized I had much bigger problems: Hugo was down at the end of the driveway, peering into the windows of Prudence's parked Dodge van.

"Check this out!" He waved me over. "I think it's from the turd factory!"

"I doubt it. Dodge makes a lot of these vans."

"No, you can see all her cameras inside. That fat bitch must've followed you home."

"Maybe she lives around here?" I suggested.

"Of course she doesn't! You're my bodyguard and she just happens to park in your driveway? I bet she's watching us right now." He looked around and shouted. "Come on you big turd! I know you're there!"

It was a game for him, a chance to blow off steam, but the idea of the overweight girl hearing him made my skin crawl with embarrassment. "Keep it down!"

"What's the matter?" He was puzzled. "Why are you acting so uptight? I thought you'd be interested that Eric called."

"I *am* interested."

He knew I was lying, but it still didn't make any sense to him. He looked at me suspiciously, waiting for me to say more, but my mind had gone blank. All I could think was how annoying it was that someone so young could be so infuriatingly perceptive. He was leaning against the Dodge van, looking from me to the lights of my cottage shining through the undergrowth. It was like watching a car accident unfold, seeing his face change as he suddenly realized. "She's in there, isn't she?" He pushed away from her van as if it had bitten him.

"It's not what you think."

"I don't fucking believe you!" he cried as he shoved past me.

"I haven't told her anything." I caught him by the arm. "I'm trying to get her to tell *me* stuff."

"Yeah, right! You're just like all the rest! It's all about the money!"

"It's nothing to do with money."

Now an apparently even worse thought gripped him. "Are you," he made a face like he'd swallowed something disgusting, "having *sex* with her?"

"No!" I could see Serafina reflected in the Suburban's rearview mirror, listening to every word we said. "For Christ's sake," I whispered. "I'm . . . pumping her for information. She knows a lot about what's been going on."

"Like what?"

"When was the last time you got high?" I demanded. "The truth."

"Uh . . . like, maybe a couple of months ago. I didn't even want to. It was just . . . part of selling weed to these jerks at school. It would've looked funny if I didn't smoke some, too. Why?"

"Did you ever screw around with your urine sample?"

"Yeah," he said, as if it was an insult to think he hadn't taken precautions. "I always carried a little thing of bleach in my pocket, or some soap powder to add to my piss, and I'd drink gallons of tea. They *never* caught me. Not even close, man."

"You're coming up dirty at the lab. That's the kind of thing the little lady inside is helping me with."

"She's not *little,*" he cried. "She's a fat creep. Anyway, I thought you liked Serafina."

"My personal life is none of your goddamn business, Hugo," I said. "She doesn't even like me."

"How do you know? Fucking Raj is always hitting on her. My psycho mother's always threatening to fire her. She's just scared."

"I'm not getting into all this right now. I want you to go

home and if Eric phones again, call me. Otherwise we'll talk tomorrow."

"This sucks!" He gave me a withering look and kicked the side of the Dodge van on his way back to the Suburban. A part of him wanted to believe I wasn't lying, but he had a whole history of getting shafted by people who should have been looking out for him. It wasn't my fault, but I had a terrible feeling I'd lost what little trust he had in me.

I didn't know how much Prudence had heard, but when I got back inside she was going through my dusty vinyl collection, pulling out albums, and frowning in amazement at the hoard of ancient popular music.

"Sorry about my van," she said. "I didn't know you and Hugo were an item outside business hours."

"I should have known this was a bad idea."

"If it wasn't for bad ideas, nobody would have discovered penicillin." She kept going through the records, making funny faces at my taste in music. "This is a very bad omen, you know. Only listening to music from when you were young. The only hopeful sign is that you haven't put them in alphabetical order yet."

"I think we're about through here, don't you?"

"Not really. I'd say we're just getting started." She moved from the shelves to my desk and picked up the enlarged photo of Hugo standing in the snow in Tahoe after his father's funeral. "Great picture," she said. "Worth a thousand words. It's the composition, the way it's framed. There's the kid who's been crying next to the snowman who's lost most of his head. It's the funny thing next to the sad thing that makes it work. But the best thing, in my humble opinion, are his little boy's bare feet standing in that icy sludge. The kid is freezing, but he's so miserable he doesn't even know it. And then in the background there's that open door with the warm light shining out, and the maid calling him inside. *Hope!* Every picture needs a little hope."

"Do you always feel that good about your own stuff?"

She laughed at being caught out. "I wish, but that was a great fucking shot, and I'm proud you've decided to collect my early work."

"I'm glad, too. And now I think you should leave."

"You know, I could just call my editor, tell him about what happened tonight. He'd cook up some story about Hugo catching you and me together and the Vines would fire your ass."

"Now you're threatening me? What happened to no more sleaze?"

"I'm Catholic. I'm allowed to sin again so long as I confess. God actually expects me to backslide. For some reason it makes Him love me even more than when I'm good all the time."

"You're cute, but a little perkiness goes a long way. Do what you have to do. I'm going to bed."

"I know more about this case than anyone. I've been tracking it since it broke. What is wrong with us helping each other? It may be for different reasons, but we both want the same thing. You're on the inside. I'm on the outside. Hey, let's solve this fucker together."

"You're wasting your time."

"Give me one good reason!"

"You don't listen. You talk too much. And I don't trust you."

"Is that all?" she asked. "No problem. I'll give you all the information the *Enquirer* has, and in return you don't have to give me anything. What about that deal could you not like?"

I tried to herd her towards the door, but she danced away from me.

"Just can't stand the idea of having a partner, can you?"

"Out!"

"Too old and set in your ways. Too stubborn to admit you're just Hugo's babysitter. That's all you are, you know. And that's all they want you to be. You're never going to crack this case alone."

I went and opened the door and caught her by the wrist and started pulling her out. She grabbed on to a bookcase with her other hand and kept jabbering. "No one is better at what I do than me. I'm on it twenty-four/seven. I'm the best. Frankly, I'm insulted. I don't normally offer to collaborate with people . . ."

After a lot more tugging and pulling, I managed to actually get her physically outside the house. She was breathing hard, her face flushed from the exertion, but from the triumphant smirk on her face you would have thought she'd won the victory.

"Think about what I have to offer, Thomas. And remember, slamming a door in someone's face does not mean you've won the argument. It's a sign you're . . ."

I missed the last part.

Chapter Eight

I tried calling Hugo first thing the next morning, but all I got was his voicemail. I tried the main house, and left messages with the answering service, asking him to call me. After I still hadn't heard back by noon, I decided to drop by the house on the excuse of returning an algebra textbook he'd left in my car. As I pulled in to the Vine parking compound and turned off my engine, I saw a woman in bare feet running out through the brass-studded gate and hopping painfully over the gravel towards the parked cars. It took me a moment to realize it was Sally Vine. She was bundled up in a man's raincoat, head wrapped in a scarf, face hidden behind sunglasses. She beeped her car keys at the half a dozen gleaming vehicles parked in the drive, but none of them flashed their lights back at her. "God help me!" She hurled the car keys away and started rummaging wildly in her bag for another set. She finally found the ones she wanted and was halfway into a silver Lexus SC300 when Raj came tearing through the gate. "Get back in here!" he yelled. I could have said something to let them know I was there, but I wanted to see what was going to happen next. Raj got to her before she could lock herself inside the car, grabbed her by the collar of her raincoat, and started dragging her out of the seat. They were scratching and shrieking obscenities at each other and finally she started screaming for help; the sound seemed to bring out a zest for viciousness in Raj. He drew his fist back, looking for an opening to smack her. I pulled open my car door and loudly slammed it shut.

"Hey," I said brightly. "Looks like it's going to be another beautiful day."

They were so stunned to see me there it took them a second to figure out who I was. A dazed look of hope started to form on Sally's face, but before she could speak Raj stepped in front of her.

"Get out of here!" he barked at me. "I'll drive Hugo to school!"

"It's Saturday," I chuckled idiotically as I walked towards them. "It's his day off."

"I told you to get out of here!" he roared.

"I don't mind. No problem at all." I kept coming closer, with the serene smile on my face, holding up the book. "Hugo forgot his algebra. I promised I'd help with his homework. How are you, Ms. Vine?"

She put her hand to her cheek and watched me as if she was hypnotized. Her raincoat had fallen open and underneath it I could see she was wearing nothing but a zebra-striped thong. She was breathing hard, mouth agape, like someone having a nightmare with her eyes wide open.

"Get off my property!" Raj shrieked. "I'm going to fuck you up!"

"You okay, Ms. Vine? Anything I can help you with?" I said calmly.

"That's it, fucker!" He rushed at me with his fist cocked, but when I didn't react he started walking around me in a circle, trying to work up the nerve to hit me from behind. Out of the corner of my eye I saw Hugo watching us through the half-open gate, his face pinched with fear.

"You're toast!" Raj bellowed. "You hear me? Get your ass off my property!" He was like a dog that had had a chance to bite an intruder, but decided it was safer to just keep barking. I pretended he wasn't there at all. He kept making these little charges at me, the beginnings of kicks and punches, calling me *cocksucker* and *motherfucker,* asking me if I wanted a piece of him, but it didn't sound right. There's something about a guy with a guttural Arab accent trying to cuss like he's a black man that's ridiculous. He'd learned it all from the movies.

"Why don't you put your little dick back in your pants, Raj?" she whispered fiercely. "He's not scared of you."

He stood there, his bronzed face turning ashy as the insult rippled through him, and then he moved stiffly to the open Lexus and climbed inside. "This isn't over. This is just beginning, baby." He tortured the transmission on his way out of the compound, spitting gravel back against our legs.

We stood there listening to the roar of his car going down the hill until it faded out of range. In the ensuing silence a blue jay flew down to peck fruitlessly at the disturbed gravel. The Airedale wandered out of the bushes with a guilty air and stood there looking relieved to have missed the disturbance. I picked up Sally's sunglasses, which had been knocked off in the fight, and saw she had the beginning of a shiner. She noticed me averting my gaze from her nakedness and pulled her raincoat closed with a nervous giggle.

"Sorry about that." She turned and walked towards the gate, lightly tousling Hugo's hair as she swept past him into the compound. For all her concern she might have stepped out into the driveway to retrieve the morning newspaper.

"Hey, Hugo." I walked over to him, but he turned his back on me and fled. I followed him as he stormed across the lawn, past his tree house in the giant sycamore and down the broad marble steps to the villa's green-tiled pool. There had been some kind of party around it the night before that had gone wrong. The bottom was covered in broken terra cotta pots, their rose bushes slowly drowning in the chlorinated water. There was a large portable barbecue unit lying on its side, with charcoal briquettes and burnt chicken and scorched lobster shells spilled out around it. There was a half-full bottle of vodka floating in the water, clanking against the tiled rim of the pool where it was held by the suction of the outlet drain. A light breeze moved over the surface of the water, bending the shafts of sunlight that converged in the green cathedral-like depths. Even with the junk at the bottom of the pool, the scene was unbelievably beautiful: the palatial marble setting, the classically placed olive trees and flower beds, the hot blue sky and breathtaking views, not to mention the comforting certainty that Hispanic servants would clean up any mess on Monday morning. The Vines' Hollywood lifestyle was a variation on a feudal European fantasy that wealthy Southern Californians had been pursuing since they chased the Spanish colonists away. It's a copy of a copy but on a good day and with the right decorator it can look pretty damn close to perfection.

I flopped down on one of the chaises that hadn't been tossed into the water and tilted my face up to the sun. I could hear a tinkling sound and when I looked I saw Hugo was urinating into the pool. I closed my eyes and heard him grunting, followed by the splash of heavy objects and a moment later the muted thud of them coming to rest on the tiled bottom. I didn't say a word. He was a small soul and his rage was so great that morning that relieving it was going to be like defusing a mine.

"I'm sorry, Hugo."

He paused in the act of pushing a ping-pong table into the pool. "What the hell are *you* doing here anyway?"

"Has that ever happened before?" I asked. "Raj hitting your mom?"

"Duh!"

"I guess it's lucky I was here."

"I'm sure she'll thank you," he scoffed. "Now you'll be her big hero."

"What's that supposed to mean?"

"I see the way you look at her. You're just like all the others. My mom snaps her fingers and guys like you drop like flies."

I wanted to protest that I was different, that I was looking out for him, but I didn't think he'd believe it. With a famous mother, his whole experience would have been of her effortlessly stealing away the loyalty of any man who showed an interest in him.

"Why does your mother let Raj treat her like that?"

"You're the big expert. You tell me."

"Well, what were they fighting about?"

"He's pissed because she pulled out of his dorky movie." He smiled grimly. "None of the studios want to work with him. He invited all these foreign investors for dinner last night and she got loaded and made him look like a jerk. He keeps setting up all these deals and at the last minute she says she's not going to do them."

"Why does she do that?"

"Because he's so ghetto. I don't know. She's a star. She can do whatever she wants." He flopped down on the chaise next to mine and put his hands behind his head like a producer working on his tan.

"If she's a star, how come she lets him hit her?"

"That was about something else." He yawned. "Raj found out she had an abortion last week."

"Was it his?"

"I guess. That's why he got so mad about it."

"She doesn't want to make movies with him. She doesn't want to have his children. Why did she marry him?"

"How would I know?" He turned over and flopped down on his stomach, his face turned away. "That's what you were supposed to find out instead of driving me to school and helping me with my algebra." He didn't say it with his usual barbed scorn; it was just a sad fact he was resigned to. "It's not your fault. My mom didn't hire you to find out who killed my dad. I don't even think she wants to know."

"Why not?"

"Ask her," he said in disgust. "I don't know."

"You sound like you're giving up," I said.

"No, I'm growing up. I thought it was going to be like in the movies, you know, with the private detective shooting the bad guys and making it all right in the end. In real life things just suck and keep on sucking and nobody can do anything about it."

When kids say things like that, even if you secretly share their pessimism, you're supposed to reassure them. You tell them evil may exist, but it can be exposed and defeated. But what if it can't? I'd been able to save his mother from a beating at Raj's hands, but that didn't solve the problem of why she let him beat her like that in the first place. I don't know how much time elapsed, but after awhile I noticed his shoulders jerking up and down, and I realized he was silently sobbing. I reached over and placed my hand on his back. His bony spine arched up like a bow. He made a hideous woeful sound like an animal makes when it's been caught in a trap. "I just want to die," he said.

Chapter Nine

I walked back through the grounds to the house and entered the library through the open French doors. It was a weekend and the place felt deserted. Despite the heat of the day and the emptiness of the library, a mesquite fire had been lit in the river-rock fireplace. I walked into the larger formal sitting room, where an identical fire was burning, though here it fought a losing battle against the air-conditioning. Seated on one of the matching gray silk couches, the Airedale was chewing a Flemish milkmaid's rosy-cheeked face off an antique needlepoint cushion. The dog growled in warning but lost interest as I headed up the stairs. I moved down the hall past Hugo's bedroom through a door into a health club-sized gym filled with chrome workout stations set on a zebra-striped carpet. The voice of some aging country western singer, ravaged by amphetamines and bourbon, drifted out of a half-open door where I could see Sally Vine sitting on the end of a massage table. She was tilting her face up as Tea Lane reluctantly took photographs of her bruised eye with a silver digital camera. As I approached them across the carpeted floor, I thought of Sally's zebra-striped thong and wondered if she always wore underwear to match the rugs.

"I know Raj didn't mean to hurt you," Tea was saying. "He started calling as soon as he left. He's suicidal about it."

"Suicidal? Is that what he told you?" Sally snickered and took a slug from a long neck bottle of beer. She'd changed into a frayed tank top and skimpy cut-off jeans and it was easy to imagine her as the teenage hell-raiser, the white trash beauty queen of Lake Tahoe before she mesmerized Daniel Vine and got herself to Hollywood.

"You and Raj are so made for each other," Tea persisted. "I know you can make it work, Sal."

"Don't call me 'Sal,' " she said.

"God, I'm sorry. I didn't mean to . . ."

"Just take the pictures. I don't need a shoulder to cry on." She noticed me in the doorway and stopped talking.

Tea Lane wheeled around and gaped. "You can't come up here!"

I took the camera out of her hands and hit the button to open the lens. "And you can't take photographs with the lens shut. Didn't they teach you about suppressing evidence in law school, Ms. Lane?"

The lawyer froze as if she'd been struck across the face, not moving a muscle as Sally frowned at her.

"Sal, I had no idea," Tea finally broke into a tearful whine. "I . . . I . . . asked Serafina for a camera and she gave me this stupid thing. Honestly, you can't believe I'd . . ." She made a grab for the camera, but I held it out of reach. "Give me that back! I'll find you another one!"

"Get out of here," Sally hissed at her.

Tea stared desperately at the camera and burst into repressed sobs on her way out of the room.

"The bitch is worried she's not going to get her little coproducing credit if I press charges," Sally said.

Without thinking, I raised the camera and started taking shots of her bruised face. She wanted to object but some stronger impulse took over, her head automatically tilting to offer me her best side.

"I need to talk to you about Hugo."

She took two beers out of the fridge and offered me one.

"No thanks."

"You sure?" She kept holding out the beer, watching me with a kind of friendly malice. "Had a little too much fun back in the day? Can't even have a cold beer without worrying you'll turn into a monster?"

I ignored the question. "Your son's talking about killing himself. Did you know that?"

"I know." She held the iced bottle to her black eye. "But he won't."

"You sure?"

"Don't let all that sensitive crap of his fool you. He's as hard as gravel. Just like me." She let her gaze wander around the room, as if inviting me to notice the curious surroundings. The windowless cubicle had been designed to contain nothing more than the massage table, but it was crowded with an old armchair and a rust-stained fridge. There was even a sagging single bed covered in a surplus Army blanket scorched with cigarette burns. A collection of dented, naked Barbie dolls were propped up against the pillow.

"This is my stuff from when I grew up," she said dreamily. "You can take the girl out of the trailer park, but you can't take the trailer park out of the girl. This is where I come to remember the shit-hole I came from. Why I left Nevada and why I'm never going back."

"I've lived in smaller places than this without feeling sorry for myself. I live in one now."

"That's not what Hugo told me. He said you didn't like small, enclosed spaces, or was it *tunnels?*" She let the word hang in the air, observing my reaction. "You look surprised. Do you think Hugo doesn't tell me about the inappropriate stuff you fill his head with?"

It had never occurred to me that Hugo told his mother what went on between the two of us.

"And now of course he's got you believing Raj killed his father." She looked at me pityingly. "It's a fantasy. He thinks he's in a movie. I tried to tell you he came with a warning label, but I guess he'd already set off those tortured father feelings of yours. I appreciate you looking out for him. I appreciate you coming to my aid with Raj today. I really do. I admire courage." She unscrewed the cap on the second bottle of beer and licked the foam off like a cat. She was obviously one of those people who liked to talk when she drank. The sound of her own voice seemed to envelop her in a comforting shell; she was displaying other sides of herself now: the judicious Sally, the compassionate Sally, the wistful but brave Sally. She wasn't boring yet, but it was coming; it was just another beer away. "You won't believe me, but I love Hugo more than anyone in the world and one day everybody's going to realize it. There's just too much you don't understand about me and that boy and life's too short to explain it."

"One thing I don't understand is why you'd substitute your urine for Hugo's on his drug test?"

The blunt question didn't make her flinch in the slightest. In fact, a dreamy smile relaxed her face. "I *knew* that nurse at the drug clinic was a tabloid snitch. I knew it. Don't you hate it when you don't listen to your first intuition about someone?"

"I guess I'm wasting your time here." As I backed up towards the door, I slipped the camera in my pocket.

"No, don't go. I'll answer your question. I'm trying to get Hugo into this special therapeutic boarding school. One of the things they require is a student's drug history. I know he's been cheating his drug tests; I thought I'd make it look as bad as it really is so they'll put him in the right place."

The cold illogic of this coming from a woman getting bombed by herself in the middle of the afternoon apparently escaped her. She stretched out her arms and yawned with a sound that was half sleepy gratification and half longing for something more. With the door closed the room was starting to smell like the inside of a bar. There was her perfume put on a long time ago, but it was being displaced by an odor of sweat that came off her in sharp attractive waves. Her neck was slick with sweat and it shone on her chest and darkened the planes of her breasts where they filled out her tank top. She perched girlishly on the end of the massage table, slowly swinging her legs back and forth, her bottom squeaking faintly against the leather. It was a sound as regular as the beating of a clock and she listened to it as if it was coming not from her but from some outside source beyond her control.

"We've got a lot in common, you and me." Her voice was sleepy and tender.

"Like what?"

"We've got Hugo."

I could see her watching me with a kind of pleased expectancy, like a doctor who's administered a drug and is waiting to see the results. The long muscles in her thighs flexed smoothly as she rocked back and forth; her little white toes clenched and unclenched; her breathing grew slow and deep. There was a speculative wantonness in the way she gazed at me now: her mouth open, the tip of her tongue perched on the edge of her lower lip. She kept swinging her legs, cheeks flushed, her eyes never leaving mine. What did she want? I wasn't deluded enough to think she wanted me; it was more like a game, a test to see if she could activate my desire just by looking at me in this way. It was about control. I stared back at her, thinking of her son's spine arching in agony as he wept on the chaise by the pool outside. He'd welcomed my comforting hand on his back, trusted me enough to let me see the shameful wreckage of his pride. It must have showed on my face.

"Why are you looking at me like that?" Her voice rasped, as if she'd been woken from a deep sleep and didn't know where she was.

I didn't bother to answer.

She swung her legs over the side of the table and stood up. "Ugh, it's baking in here."

I threw open the door and lurched out into the gym. It was flooded with unreal sunlight blazing through the skylights and it felt like I'd gone from the darkness of a movie theatre into bright daylight. I had a ringing headache and an impression I'd been in the presence of a disordered mind.

"I know you think I'm bad to my son, but I meant what I said in there. All I want you to do is protect him for a little while longer."

"Protect him from *what* exactly?" I said.

"Protect him from me and the things I've had to do in my life."

"That's a soap opera line. You can do better than that."

"If I could tell you more, I would." Her eyes turned liquid with sorrow as she contemplated the sacrifice being asked of her. Apparently it was a burden she could not share, even if it included accepting my mockery like a martyr. That's how noble she was. She was acting, of course, but she believed it. It was like watching a sleepwalker driving a car.

"I won't work like that. Fire me. Pick any reason you want." I laughed unpleasantly. "Tell people I made eye contact with you."

"I'm not going to fire you and you're not going to quit."

"Why the hell not?"

"You couldn't stand the idea of leaving Hugo alone with a monster like me."

A moment ago she'd wanted to be desired by me, and now she was trying to get me to feel sorry for her. She was so wrapped up in the drama of being Sally Vine she didn't even understand why anyone might object to the way she treated her son. He was like an extension of her, his behavior only important in how it reflected back on her. It was as if she couldn't distinguish between where she ended and Hugo began. With such a twisted viewpoint, it would not matter much to Sally if her son were suffering because in her mind she was already suffering for the two of them. She loved him unconditionally, but it was the way she loved the toes on her own feet. Except as an audience he was not very real to her. Nobody probably was.

"Just in case you're interested, there's a guy called Eric, who's met your son twice. He gave Hugo your late husband's money clip. Eric's the one who told him Raj was involved in his father's death."

I expected this to produce a reaction at least, but she only tightened her jaw and looked away, as if I was unfairly persecuting her. "How do you know this?"

"It's not really very hard to find out, *if* you want to find out, Ms. Vine. I think I can help you if you tell me what's going on."

"Men have been telling me how much they can help me all my life," she said. "In the end they all just want to use me." She turned and walked across the zebra-striped carpet towards her wing of the house. "You're a nice guy, Kyd. I'm glad Hugo's got someone to look out for him."

"I think you're in a lot of trouble, Ms. Vine. I'm going to

find Eric. I'm not going to stop until I find out everything."

The threat made her turn and look back over her shoulder. "Everything?" she said in a grave, dramatically-charged voice. "You have no idea what a relief that would be to *me*."

Sally walked through into her bedroom and shut the door. It was hard to tell if she was going to die from the injustice of it all, or just take a nap. I'd told her I thought she was guilty of something and she hadn't denied it. I'd threatened to expose her, but she hadn't fired me. Her coldly passive reaction, refusing to take responsibility for anything that had happened, or might happen in the future, reminded me of an iceberg floating across shipping lanes.

Chapter Ten

I looked through the house and returned to the pool, but there was no sign of Hugo. I knocked on Serafina's door and after a muttered consultation she unlocked it and let me inside. She was ironing a stack of the unflattering brown and beige maids' uniforms, with Hugo huddled in a corner on the floor, his head lolling between his upraised knees.

"Give it back!" Serafina ordered Hugo. It was the first time I'd ever heard her raise her voice to him.

Hugo crawled under the ironing board and reached deep beneath the bed, sliding out a snub-nosed .38 Smith & Wesson. He left it on the rug and returned to his spot behind the ironing board without saying a word.

"Is that mine?" I said.

Serafina slammed the iron down on the board. "He take it from your car."

I picked up the weapon, checked that none of the bullets had been fired, and dropped it in my pocket where it clinked against the camera I'd appropriated. "Were you planning on using this on yourself?" I asked him. "Or did you have something else in mind?"

"Someone's got to do something," he muttered.

"He's talking about killing Raj!" Serafina said. "And Malahide!"

"Christ, Hugo!"

"Hey! How would you feel if your mother married the guy who killed your dad? Think about it! Before you came along, they hired the other guy who killed my dad *to drive me to school!* How sick is that?"

"You've got to prove these things first. You can't just go waste people. You'll end up in prison for the rest of your life."

"You think I give a rat's ass? It wouldn't be that different from this place anyway. It's crawling with phonies who belong in prison."

"I know you're upset," I said.

"Tight observation, Sherlock! That really helps a lot. What's next? Family counseling? Maybe Wanda the therapy moron can set up some therapy sessions for Raj and me to work out our emotional issues. Oh wait! I've got a better idea! Maybe I can take some medication that will make me not give a shit like you."

"You should not talk to him like that," Serafina protested. "He's trying to help you."

"Yeah, well trying doesn't cut it!"

She picked up the framed photo of the uniformed schoolgirl and the nun from her bedside table. "Look at it," she commanded him.

"You already showed me." He sighed. "Your little sister . . . she's very pretty."

"She's dead, Hugo. One day the soldiers come to our school and they take Lucretia away. The soldiers are *drunken*. They say she is a, how you say, *guerillerera,* like freedom fighter. Lucretia's not fighting nothing, but they do very bad things to her and afterwards they throw her in the street. That's how we find her. Because of the dogs fighting over her dead body. You understand?"

"I'm sorry." He gulped. "Why didn't you tell me this before?"

"Because you a very *fonny* boy and I don't want to make you sad. Maybe you tell your mother about it and she think

I'm depressing you, and she tell me and Adolpho to leave this house. I tell you now because you have to listen to this man because he is trying to fight for you, I think. My sister don't have nobody to fight for her except some nuns. That's why she's dead."

It was more than I'd ever heard her say before in one stretch and when she was finished I knew I'd been right to trust her. She took Hugo's face between her hands and pretended to shake it like a broken machine. She ruffled his hair and murmured gently, "*Valiente muchacho.* You have to be strong."

I nodded at her, one adult to another, to show my gratitude for her support, but she didn't respond, just held me with her eyes for a moment, not exactly reproachful, but not impressed either. I fished the camera out of my pocket and showed it to her. "Ms. Lane says you gave her this a little while ago."

"No." Serafina shook her head. "I have not even see Ms. Lane today."

Hugo pulled himself to his feet. "It's my dad's." He took the camera and turned on the colored LCD monitor. "He let me use it when we were in Tahoe." He frowned as the recent shots of his mother's bruised face filled the display screen. Holding his thumb on the jog dial, he sequenced back through dozens of images until he reached the first photo. "I took the first picture when he bought the camera. See for yourself."

It was a close-up of his elegant father wearing a black Russian fur hat against a snowbank. Daniel Vine had tanned finely-wrinkled skin, dark slanted eyes, a broken column of a nose, and a sly, genial mouth. It was a shrewd, lived-in face, its cunning held in reserve, its charm on display. He looked more like Hugo's grandfather than father;

his eyes were deeply pouched, and his neck had that loose, fibrous look that surgery can't fix. But life still poured out of him. It was in those glowing Semitic eyes and the wised-up, wicked-looking mouth. It was not the face of a man defeated by life, or depressed by knowledge of his waning powers. It was a face that wanted you to know he still had appetites and knew how to satisfy them. The succeeding photos Hugo had taken were of Serafina helping him build the snowman with Adolpho.

Towards the end there was a badly framed shot taken with the photographer's finger covering half the lens: you could see snow swirling on the ground and filling the air and two dim figures receding into the whiteout. It had been taken at three thirty-three p.m. on December twenty-third, the day he died. Then there was a photo Daniel Vine had taken of himself lying on his back in the snow, holding the camera maybe twelve inches in front of him. It had been taken on the same day, at three thirty-six p.m. Something immeasurably disruptive was at work in his face. The lips were pulled back over the gums in a desperate shout. The distorted features were smeared out of shape like a Francis Bacon painting, as if the corrupt flesh was being flayed off the bone by centrifugal force. It held me with its sick pornographic power long enough for me to know I was staring at a man desperately trying to photograph his own death. I turned off the camera before Hugo could see and casually returned it to my pocket.

"What is it?" he demanded.

"I'm not sure. I'll have to print them and blow them up."

"It's my camera. I want to see."

"I know you do, Hugo. But some of this could be important evidence. You may have to testify in court about it one day. It's better to wait until we've got a lawyer and witnesses."

"I don't care. I want to see it now." He had the trapped animal look he got when things didn't go his way.

"Right now, the less you know the safer you're going to be."

I could see him fighting with himself, wanting to yell at me and sweep my objections aside, another part of him thinking maybe I was right. Maybe he could trust me. *Thinking.* That was something new for him; it took painful effort and the initial reward was feeling unprotected and vulnerable.

"Fine," he groaned.

It wasn't a big moment. He was still barely able to control himself, but he was trying. I decided that I liked this kid all the way down to his core. "When was the very last time you saw this camera?"

"It was . . . oh, man, it was so gross." His disgust was for himself. "I saw it when I took the money from my dad's pockets. It was in his parka . . . and then I saw it when the Reno cops brought all my dad's clothes back from the morgue. They'd just stuffed everything in a *paper bag*. The camera was at the bottom. I was going to take it, but my mom was freaking out. I couldn't think. I just took his watch and forgot all about it."

"What happened to your dad's things?"

"My mom was screaming at this dumb cop because he'd brought them back in a supermarket bag and they still had dried blood on them. What were the cops supposed to do, have them dry cleaned? I didn't care. It wasn't going to bring my dad back. She was hysterical because she got blood on her hands from his clothes. Wanda, like, gave her a shot of Valium or something. I don't know who took the clothes."

"Ms. Lane told me Mr. Raj want me to throw away the clothes," Serafina said. "But the paparazzi are outside in the street going through the garbage. She say to burn them, but I don't think it's my place to destroy the clothes of Mr. Vine. I keep them and bring them back for the family. Ms. Lane, she take the camera of Mr. Vine and his valuables. I don't know what she do with them."

It seemed the camera had passed through the hands of the Reno police without ever being examined. Had Tea Lane stored it away somewhere along with Vine's other personal items, never realizing what it contained? When I'd caught her pretending to take photos of Sally, she'd blurted out an excuse that made no sense, blaming the Guatemalan housekeeper for giving her a *stupid* camera. She'd wanted to distance herself from it, as if it was radioactive. But then she'd looked desperate when I'd refused to return it to her.

Hugo followed me out to my car and watched as I wiped his prints off the .38 and replaced it in the glove compartment. I checked the battery pack and downloaded the last two photos into my PC and printed them out. You could imagine them smeared across the front page of *The Enquirer* and *The Globe* and *Star.* You could see them filling the screen on some late night Fox TV exposé as the experts fanned the flames. How much were they worth to the media? A hundred thousand dollars? Half a million? What would a photo of Nicole Simpson taken just before she bled to death have been worth? All I knew was that I'd never held anything in my hands that was worth that much money. Daniel Vine had tried to shout in his moment of dying, to send a message from the grave, and that attempt could open up the case again. The media would pay a fortune for the photos. But would someone else kill for them? I kept my back to Hugo. I found an old tennis racket with broken strings and pried off the plastic cap at the end of the handle. I rolled the photos into a tube and slid them inside the hollow core and replaced the cap.

"Raj is pretty bulked up. He knows how to kick-box. I don't blame you for just, you know, standing there. I thought he was going to kill you or something."

"Relax. I won that fight."

"Yeah, right." He laughed dejectedly.

"Do you know what I *would* have done if Raj had tried to hit me?"

"No," Hugo said.

"Neither does he. And that's because he didn't want to find out."

My mobile phone was vibrating in my pocket. I walked a few steps away from him and answered it. "Yeah?"

"That Mr. Thomas Kyd?" It was Corelle Lamb, the Santa Monica policewoman from the promenade. In the background I could hear a woman trying to make herself heard over the feedback from a microphone. "I think we got your boy, Eric," Corelle chuckled.

"Where are you?"

"*Abbot's Habit* Coffee House, deep in the heart of Venice. It's one of them open-mike poetry readings. Eric's getting ready to contribute to the delinquency of a whole roomful of people."

"Can you hold him till I get there?"

"I ain't going nowhere near him. Man's got no clothes on. This is some nude poetry-reading shit. The man's not wearing nothing but a watch."

"Can't you hide his clothes?"

"No thanks. Last guy at the mike was an A.C.L.U. lawyer. We're just monitoring the situation according to section 311.8 of the penal code. Make sure the audience isn't getting any sexual gratification from the performance. Eric's getting ready to come on soon as this nasty nude woman finishes reading us her daddy's suicide note. Ain't nobody getting off on *that,* I can assure you." The policewoman hung up.

"Who was that?" Hugo demanded sharply.

"I've been working with the Santa Monica Police. They've found Eric. He's at a nudist event in Venice. He's going to be performing in a few minutes."

"He's going to be *naked?*" Hugo's face scrunched up in adolescent horror.

"Yeah, it's a lot of naked grown-ups all reading their poetry. Wanna check it out?"

"No thanks." He looked sheepishly at the ground. "I . . . I don't like poetry much."

Chapter Eleven

As I came out of the Vines' compound I saw two unmarked cop cars and a restored yellow Sting Ray Corvette blocking the road at the top of the drive. Detective Stone leaned against the Corvette's hood, dressed in tight jeans, cowboy boots, and a Hawaiian shirt. I recognized the four other cops from the tennis court last night getting out of the unmarked cars. They were all wearing off-duty clothes. I slowly dropped my right hand to the mobile phone on my belt and dialed my home number. I heard the machine answer and then the beep telling me it was recording. There were five of them and from their body language it was clear they didn't think dealing with me was going to be any harder than stepping on a bug. I turned on the radio and got a traffic report from KCRW. That would be evidence of the time and date of whatever conversation my answering machine could record in the next three minutes

"This is Thomas Kyd," I said aloud. "I'm being obstructed from leaving the Vine residence by Detective Stone and four other off-duty police officers."

I pulled to a stop and got out of the car. They approached me down the drive in a line, two of them fanning out to either side of me, Stone in the middle. I walked right in amongst them and they closed around me.

"How are you, Detective Stone?" I said, nodding at the others. "You're the four guys who were playing tennis here the other night. You're off-duty cops, right?"

Stone nodded to the cop behind my left shoulder, a

nervy looking redhead, smaller than the others, with a flat, bitter face.

"Hands above your head, asshole," the redhead barked.

"Whatever you say, officer." I placed my hands on my head. While he roughly searched me, emptying the contents of my pockets into the dirt, I kept talking. "What's the problem, Stone? Why are you searching me? What are you looking for?"

The redhead pulled the camera out of my pocket and tossed it to Stone.

"Is that what you're looking for, Stone?" I asked. "Daniel Vine's camera?"

The stilted way I was talking didn't sound quite right to them. I wasn't reacting normally and it was making them nervous. The redhead jabbed me in the right kidney. To him it was a disciplinary tap, but it flooded me with pain and nausea, dropping me to my knees in the dirt.

"Jesus!" I groaned. "What'd you hit me for, officer? Sally Vine asked me to take pictures of her face because her husband punched her. Tell him to stop hitting me."

Stone still refused to answer me. He turned on the camera. He stared into the viewfinder at the last photo of Sally's bruised face, which would come up first. I had to get him to say something so I'd have his voice on the answering machine tape. He sequenced back and then he frowned as he peered at Vine's grisly self-portrait. He hadn't been expecting it. It took him a moment to realize what he was looking at, and then his face smoothed out and became self-consciously bland.

"You looked funny playing tennis, Stone. Your ass is too fat for those tight tennis shorts and your gut hangs out."

The others waited for Stone to react to the insult. But he was still thinking too hard about the photo and what it might mean. He was like a man who's been handed a winning lottery ticket and at the same moment asked to fix the water heater. He couldn't take it all in.

"*Hel-lo?* Is that the camera?" the redhead finally asked Stone.

Stone put it in his shirt pocket, and nodded. He'd seen the photo of Daniel Vine, but he wasn't sharing the knowledge with the others. He was trying to calculate something of huge importance, while appearing to the others to be thinking of nothing at all. It gave him an inert, constipated look.

"It must make it hard to fuck your wife, with a gut like yours," I said. "She must have to sit on top and look down at your face. Hard duty."

He stepped forward and swung his pointed cowboy boot at my face. I blocked most of it with my crossed forearms, but the sharp toe ripped into the side of my skull above my ear, and knocked me backwards.

"You kick a man in the face, Stone? When he's on his knees?"

"Keep talking, I'll shit in your mouth." He was breathing hard.

"Who asked you to get the camera back, Stone? Was it Raj? Tea Lane? Who are you *protecting* and *serving* on your day off with your four fellow officers?"

"The fuck's wrong with him?" The redhead looked at Stone. "Why's he talking like that?"

"We received a complaint that he stole a camera belonging to the Vine family. We investigated him earlier for stealing a watch." Stone looked around at the others, trying to drum up their support, remind them of why they were justified in doing what they were doing. "An eyeball inspection of his van shows him in possession of a computer and other items also believed stolen from the Vines." He pulled open the back doors of the Toyota and hauled out my PC and printer and handed them to the others. "Put it in my car," he ordered.

"That's all my own equipment," I said.

"Makes no difference," he assured them. "He's been downloading confidential information into his computer."

The others turned and walked back to their cars. Stone leaned down on one knee and whispered in my ear. "I'm going to tell you what time it really is. You may have scared that sand nigger in front of his wife today, but you're dealing with me now. You are going to drive away from this house and never come back."

"And if I don't?" I asked.

He dabbed his finger in the blood streaming down my brow and drew a little bull's eye on my forehead. "I'll put the boots to you, bitch. Then I'll drop you on to a freeway and watch cars run over your dead body until you're as sad as a dog lying flattened in the middle of the road. No one will ever know about it. And no one will give a fuck."

His face was so close I could see flecks of food jammed between his teeth. It was a red, shiny, sensual face, packed with fat like a baby, confident and used to being obeyed. I could smell the tuna fish sandwich he'd been eating while he waited for me to come out. But something had changed in his eyes since he'd seen the photo of Daniel Vine. The other cops had come to get the camera and warn me off, a favor to Raj for letting them chill around a celebrity's tennis court. But Stone was taking it to a dangerous new level and the strain of crossing that line into unfamiliar territory showed in his eyes. He'd gone dirty. When I'd seen the photo of Daniel Vine I'd imagined him shouting something, a plea from beyond the grave. Not for help because he was already dying and nothing was going to change that, and not for justice because justice could only be enjoyed, if at all, by the living. He was fighting for *truth*. Why else spend the last moments before he froze to death taking his own picture? Hugo's father didn't want his killers to get away with it. His horror of death was not as strong as the horror of its true meaning being airbrushed out and forgotten.

Stone had looked at the same photo and pretended not to see or hear a thing. Outwardly, he was still a high ranking cop, armed with all the violent moral power of a badge, but inside his guts and brain and nerve endings, everything had changed forever. He put his hand on my shoulder and shoved himself back to his feet. He towered over me, off balance on the high-heeled cowboy boots; they were expensive and brand new like his tennis clothes, props for some fantasy life he'd decided to chase in his off-duty hours.

"No one's going to ever believe we had this conversation," he said and walked after the others, grinding my sunglasses lying in the dirt under his boot heel, never noticing Daniel Vine's money clip beside it, not hearing the electronic *beep* as my answering machine finished its three-minute loop and turned off.

Chapter Twelve

A Santa Monica police cruiser was pulled up in front of *Abbot's Habit,* the landmark Venice espresso joint on the corner of California and Abbot Kinney Boulevard. A sign on the closed front door proudly announced the nude poetry reading was Sold Out. I parked in the lot behind Hal's restaurant and used its restroom to wash the blood out of my hair and scalp. Then I walked over to join the overflow crowd gathered outside the coffee shop windows. I edged forward like someone in a peepshow line until it was my turn to peer through the cloudy glass. In keeping with the religious jest of its name, *Abbot's Habit* was furnished with old wooden pews from some demolished church. The space was filled with a nonplussed audience of resentfully fidgeting spectators. They stared at the ceiling fan, they studied the oil paintings of tattooed lesbian mermaids on the walls, anything to avoid looking at the obese, gray-bearded naked man shaking his sad Jell-O hips as he crooned into the microphone at the front of the room.

"I do not take a lover," he said, *"because I want to be friends with the whole world. I do not love one man because I see the man in all men. I am the flesh of the poem and I sing the poem of my flesh to your flesh."*

The man was so fat you could not even see if he *had* a penis; it was buried out of sight under the folds of his belly: another unkept promise, like his claim of being a poet. Only in Venice, I thought, could absolute freedom of expression end up being so utterly fucking lame. It had always been a drain trap for a certain kind of bohemian mediocrity: all the people parading on the boardwalk, with snakes wrapped around their necks, parrots on their shoulders, their faces stained with tattoos, all the exhibitionists screaming: *look at me.* Sometimes it made you pray for a real anarchist to come along and show them what it was really about. Why hadn't Ted Kaczynski blown *this guy* up, for instance, instead of some harmless square of a physics professor at Stanford? At the side of the room I could make out Corelle Lamb standing with her bicycle beside some fellow officers. They looked defeated by the sheer tedium of the event. Dotted among the audience were a few of the other naked people who'd performed, but none of them resembled Hugo's description of Eric. I rapped hard on the window. Every face in the room turned around, grateful for the interruption, including Corelle Lamb, as I gestured to her to meet me around the back.

"Eric got cold feet right after I called you," she told me in the parking lot. "He put on his clothes and slipped out the back. I think maybe he recognized me from the promenade."

"Can you describe him to me?"

"He's tall. Kinda cute in a girly kind of way. Got that long Jesus Christ hair parted in the middle and hanging down to his shoulders. Looks like he works out. Looks like a waiter in one of those restaurants that only hires people who don't think they should be waiters."

"What do you think he was doing here? Is he trying to get discovered? Is he gay?"

"This is freak central. Everybody's trying to get discovered. Eric just hasn't figured out what for. Is he gay? He don't make my heart go pitter-patter. But even Denzel walking around naked with a guitar in front of his Johnson would turn me off."

"Did you see which way he went?"

"Remind me again why I'm supposed to answer all these questions." The warmth in her eyes had cooled. "Maybe tell me a little about that big old skid mark on your forehead."

"Eric's got a fifteen-thousand-dollar watch he scammed off my client's son. He also was in possession of a piece of evidence connected to a homicide investigation in Tahoe."

"*Homicide.* Now that's what I'm talking about. You in the big leagues, baby. So you working with the po-lice on this homicide, right?"

"Just you, Corelle."

"Oh, now it's Corelle. We on a first name basis all of a sudden. So tell me, mister sweet-talking silver-tongued man, exactly what homicide is Eric connected to?"

"It's somebody famous. I can't say."

"Movies or TV?"

"Movies."

"Movie celebrity . . . got a son . . . a homicide in Tahoe. I'd say Sonny and Cher, but old Sonny got baked on Vicodin and skied into a tree. That's not homicide, that's just careless. Tell me when I get warm."

"You're not going to guess who it was. The coroner called it an accident."

"Give me a second here. I waste a lot of my time on this stuff." A broad smile slowly creased her face. "That guy married to what's-her-name! Vine! Sally Vine's husband. Skiing accident, I remember. But you're calling it a homicide and you think Eric's connected to it."

"He told my client's son he knows who did it."

"So how come old Sally don't pick up the phone and call the po-lice? I'd be happy to arrest Eric for her."

"There's a problem," I said. "Sally and her new husband

aren't exactly jumping through hoops to re-open the investigation."

"Oh, so you doing all this on your own? I gotcha. Kind of sneaking around behind your clients' backs."

"They've got a fourteen-year-old son. He wants to know what happened to his father."

"Oh, so you really working for the son? I gotcha." She nodded. But she couldn't hide her growing disappointment in my story.

"It sounds fucked-up, I know."

"Sounds illegal. How'd you hurt your head? Don't tell me it was trying to stick your head up your own ass because I *will* believe that."

"Can I trust you?"

"Hell no! I'm a cop."

"That's interesting because a cop did this to me. An L.A.P.D. Homicide cop."

"I'm sure you deserved it." She took a step back from me as if I was contagious.

"I thought you dug homicide, Corelle. Maybe you like pedaling around on your bike more."

"Don't play me." She waved me off in disgust. "It was a mistake talking to you. I see that now."

"This cop who kicked me in the head. He said he would kill me if I didn't drop the case."

"Uh-huh." She folded her arms to defend herself against my nonsense. "Threatened your life, did he?"

"You ever heard a cop threaten to murder an innocent person before?"

"Only on TV," she snorted.

"I got it on my answering machine. Wanna hear what it sounds like?"

She sighed. She looked at me with the disgust you reserve for people with holiday snaps of the Loch Ness monster. I explained how I'd managed to record the voices of the policemen. She glanced back into the coffee shop where, to my amazement, the bearded poet's performance was actually receiving some faltering applause. I dialed my machine, punched in the code, and handed her the phone. She looked like she wanted to kill me, but she put it to her ear.

She never moved, or said a word for the three minutes it took to listen to the tape except to hold her hand to her other ear when a car roared by.

"That's illegal what you did." She handed me the phone back after listening to it. "Wouldn't be admissible in court. You couldn't even say you just happened to have left your phone on by accident because right at the start you're saying—'This is Thomas Kyd. I'm being obstructed from . . . blah blah'—like you're setting them up. And you were disrespectful to the officer, saying that about his wife. Shit, maybe you did steal the camera. *I* don't know. This is all a long, long, long way from being any part of *my* business."

"That's what I thought you'd say." I nodded understandingly. "And what you *should* say as a police officer presented with this kind of evidence. Being a police officer yourself. Anything else would be disloyal."

"Ain't got nothing to do with loyalty. Got everything to do with survival. Something you don't seem to know much about, I might add."

"So you think that cop was serious, about turning me into freeway road-kill?"

"No saying what someone might do to a sneaky motherfucker like you if you irritate him bad enough."

"Thanks for the heads-up, Corelle."

"I see you working. Trying to make me feel guilty. I ain't gonna help you. You already told me a shitload more than I ever asked to know, and all I did was try and do you a favor." I started to speak, but she held up her hand. "Don't be telling me something else I don't want to hear."

"Just thought you'd be interested in seeing what was in that camera."

"I thought the cop took it away from you." Even as she spoke, she regretted getting pulled back into it.

"Not before I downloaded it."

"I thought he took your PC." She was desperate to catch me in a lie, any lie, so she could discount my whole story.

"I printed the important stuff out before that," I said. "Vine took two pictures just before he died. One of them is of two people walking away from him. The other one's of him, yelling, like, you know, *Hey, I'm being murdered. Does anybody out there give a shit?*"

She was glaring at me now like someone who'd put her hands in wet paint and then got it on her clothes and didn't know how to wipe it off without getting something else dirty. "Two things can happen now, Mr. Big Mouth," she said. "I can take you down to the station and you can file a complaint against these officers, and present your piece of illegally obtained evidence . . ."

"I'm not ready for that yet."

"Didn't think that would appeal," she said. "Or you can just drift away like a gum wrapper in the wind, and I'll pretend none of this ever happened."

"Another one of those conversations no one's ever going to believe took place." I nodded. "No thanks. I've had those before. They're starting to make me feel like a ghost."

"What the hell do you want me to *do?*" Her voice rose in indignation, her open hands pushing outwards, as if to fend me off, though I hadn't moved.

"You already did it. You listened to my story. Now if there's a paragraph in the *Metro* section about an unidentified dead body found on the freeway, you can tell them who I was. And if they say I jumped, or fell, you'll know it's not true."

"And that'll make it all better?" She grimaced at my sentimentality. "Having one person know the truth about your sad demise?"

"Depends on who that person is, Corelle. If it's someone who's willing to speak up, it could mean a lot. If it's your average person, you're right, it won't mean shit."

We barely knew each other, but she understood exactly what I was asking. I was trying to spread my trouble around, create a record in case something bad happened to me. I was putting her in my will and leaving her something, but it wasn't money, it was an onerous, thorny obligation. Why should she bother with such an unrealistic, outrageous appeal from a stranger? To survive as a cop you had to learn to hide any inner tenderness you felt beneath a contempt as impervious as a Kevlar vest. Otherwise all the scamming assholes would just eat you alive. And I was appealing to her *what?* Her religious sense? A fantasy longing she may have had as a kid to do something incredibly heroic, even saintly, no matter what the cost to herself. Something that would make her not ordinary little Corelle Lamb, but someone ready to take one for the human race. It was pathetic, of course. Most cops may start out with that idealistic gene in their make-up, but life on the street sandblasts it right out of them.

She fished her wallet out and removed the business card I'd given her. "This a real state investigator's license number, or something you made up at Kinko's?"

"It's real."

She asked for my driver's license and a credit card and wrote the numbers down in her fat notebook. "I can't say if I'm going to *remember* you, but I *will* be checking you out, sir."

I started to thank her, but she curtly told me to wait where I was and went back inside the coffee house. Several moments later she came out and brusquely handed me a Polaroid of Eric taken by the woman organizing the reading and a contact number Eric had given her when he signed up to appear.

"Thanks, Corelle. I really mean that."

"Don't want your thanks." She shooed me away. "Don't ever want to see you again."

Chapter Thirteen

The number Corelle had given me had a local Venice prefix. When I dialed it, I got an answering machine, a man's husky theatrical voice telling me I'd reached Dieter at something called *Zeus and His Play Things.* Against background music that sounded like Bobby Short playing piano at the Carlyle, he went on to tell me they were closed on weekends because *"All work and no play makes Zeus a dull boy."* The message meandered on in a cheerful, spiteful vein, full of quips and campy asides, Dieter hoping I was having as good a day as he was, though he doubted it, and apologizing for the fact he was doing all the talking, but as he concluded before hanging up, *"that's the way Zeus likes it."* Did Dieter compose a fresh message every day, I wondered? Did he crack himself up? Was he always this *on?* My head ached and the muscles around my kidney were starting to spasm. It wasn't Dieter's fault, but I blamed him anyway. Apart from being irritatingly flamboyant, Dieter had omitted to say what *Zeus* was, and where it was located so I called directory enquiries for the address.

Zeus and His Play Things turned out to be not only close by, it was on the other side of Abbot Kinney a few doors down from where I was standing. It was an antique junk shop housed in a one-story wooden bungalow that probably dated back to when Venice had real canals. The garden in front was decorated with cacti and restored 1940s metal lawn furniture all arranged with the staged precision of a department store window. The porch contained a pair of chrome yellow old-time recliners, and an array of hanging orchids and red lacquered birdcages. A neon sign framed with lightning bolts above the front door flashed weakly in the afternoon light. Through the half-shaded windows I could see racks of vintage clothing, old movie magazines stacked in piles, some glass display cases filled with silver flasks, Deco costume jewelry, pocket knives, and watches. An old pit bull bitch lay collapsed on the hardwood floor, warming herself in a patch of sunlight streaming through the window. She watched me through one cloudy eye, not moving her grizzled muzzle, waiting to see if I was going to make her get to her feet and bark.

I walked around the side of the house. The small back garden was piled with more stuff, old ceramic tubs and sinks, Victorian mantle pieces, sections of spiral staircases waiting to be restored. At the rear of the property, a ramshackle wooden garage with a rusted tin roof backed on to the alleyway. I could hear the plangent strains of Jimmy Cliff's *Many Rivers to Cross* coming from inside:

Many rivers to cross
And it's only my will that keeps me alive
I've been hurt, washed up for years
But I merely survive because of my pride.

It was music freighted with an acceptance of loss. The biblical words, the longing in the Jamaican's voice, the way he'd taken the pain in his life and fashioned something beautiful out of it, always gave me the chills. The song stopped abruptly and after a moment resumed again, but now a live voice was straining to sing along with him.

And this loneliness won't leave me alone,

It's such a drag to be on your own
My baby left, and she wouldn't say why,
Now all I do is cry . . .

The live voice was in tune, but it couldn't come close to matching the dirge-like melancholy of the original. Even Bruce Springsteen hadn't been able to do that. I moved carefully around the side of the garage and peered in through a screened window. The space was dimly lit by a bare bulb hanging from the exposed rafters. An old VW van plastered in decals was parked against the far wall and the remaining space was taken up by a sleeping bag on a box spring, and a card table where Eric sat hunched over a boom box. In the heat of the tin roofed garage, he had stripped down to boxer shorts. When he hit the rewind button I saw he was wearing the Rolex. I moved from the window to a door in the side of the garage and quietly tried the handle; it was locked. I knocked hard three times and stepped back to the window to see his reaction. He stood frozen in a half crouch, staring at the door. I waited a moment, just long enough for him to believe the person knocking at the door had gone away, and rapped hard on the window behind him. He wheeled around and saw my face framed in the glass a few feet away. I didn't say a word, just stared in at him, letting the fear build up.

"I'm a friend of Hugo." I finally waved. "I need to talk to you."

It took him about half a minute before he cracked open the door and warily examined me, leaning his head out to make sure I was alone. "Who are you?"

"My name's Thomas Kyd. I'm a private investigator working for the Vine family."

"How did you find me?" It was what most concerned

him. He'd pulled on a pair of white drawstring pants and a white collarless Indian shirt, but the watch on his wrist, I noticed, was gone.

"Can we talk inside?" I took a step forward and he grudgingly moved aside. The garage smelled of creosote and old newspapers and the mice that fed on them. There were several outfits in dry cleaning bags suspended from hooks on the wall. An entire shelf was covered in vitamin bottles, whole-wheat muffins, bags of grains and cereals. They gave off that raw, sweetish smell of organic decay that lurks in health food stores. Up close I could see that, for all his boyish looks, Eric was already in his early forties. He was meticulous about his clothes, he was an aspiring musician, he ate like a hamster, and he shared a tin-roofed sweatbox of a garage with an army of mice. Who was this guy?

"Before we go any further," I said. "I'd like to see some I.D. Just to make sure you're who I think you are."

It was what he should have said to me, and it confused him. "I don't even think I have to talk to you," he said. "*I* haven't done anything wrong."

I leaned forward and placed Daniel Vine's money clip on the card table and stepped away from it. I didn't say anything. I let the silence do the work for me.

"Look . . ." he finally said.

"Your I.D., Eric."

He hissed in exasperation and pulled a worn, bulging wallet from his pocket and handed me an expired Nevada driver's license. His name was Eric Weaver, age forty-three, with a Tahoe City P.O. Box for an address. I copied the details down in my notebook.

"Your license expired six months ago."

"I *know*," he said. "But that's not a crime. Well, not a big one, anyway."

"Got insurance on your van? Any outstanding citations, warrants, that kind of thing?"

"I know you're not a policeman so I don't think I have to . . ." He got a petulant look on his face and clammed up.

"You're not going to talk to me?" I smiled.

He shook his head, lips pursed shut, a furtive defiance in his eyes. I started going through his wallet, emptying it out on the card table. It was stuffed with movie ticket stubs, scraps of paper with phone numbers scribbled on them, about twenty dollars in small bills. No credit cards, nothing laminated, nothing official. I made a little pile of it on the table. It was his life and you could have made it disappear by striking a match. I walked over to his van and opened the door.

"I don't know what you're looking for," he said, putting a little threat in his voice, and crossing his arms to show me he'd had about enough.

"I don't know either." I rummaged through the van. "But that's usually when you find the most interesting stuff." What he had in his van was mainly a lot of clothes. He was a quasi-homeless guy with a huge wardrobe. He'd installed a wooden sleeping platform with a futon and drawers beneath it. The first drawer was full of the average vegetarian's dirty little secret: cheap candy bars, the real sugary synthetic kind. The second contained about six months' worth of *National Enquirer*s dating back to Daniel Vine's death. When Eric wanted to give himself a party, I guess, he binged on Baby Ruths and the tabs.

I took the *Enquirer*s out of the van and laid them on the card table. He was watching me with a fixed, slightly martyred look on his face, still refusing to speak. "I know you've got the watch, Eric," I said. "Hugo told me he gave it to you. I've even got a photo of you with it." I took out the Polaroid Corelle had given me. "There you are, butt-ass naked with your guitar and there's the watch on your wrist. It's a pretty good shot. Make a nice album cover." I laid the photo on top of the *Enquirers*. He had to struggle not to look at it.

"A Santa Monica cop got that picture for me." I took out my phone. "She'd be happy to come over here and search for the watch. Shall I give her a call?"

He finally broke his silence. "Why are you doing this to *me?*"

"I need the watch, Eric."

"Fine!" He crossed to the shelf, dug it out of a bag of raisins and nuts, and indignantly slammed it down on the card table. "I didn't even want it! Okay?"

"Why not? It's worth a lot of money."

"You wouldn't understand," he said. "Just take it and go."

"You're very indignant, Eric." I put the James Bond Submariner on my wrist and compared it to the twenty-dollar imitation Cartier I'd bought off a Nigerian on the Venice boardwalk. I liked my knock-off better. "You sound like the victim of an injustice. Are you?"

"Complaining about karma is a waste of time," he said with a dejected air of superiority.

"Thanks for sharing. Instead of calling the police, would you like it better if I called Malahide and told him where he can find you?"

"*What?*" He staggered back.

"Take it easy, Eric."

"Sweet Jesus." He put his hand over his mouth and made a dash out the door. I sat down at the card table and listened to him retching in the weeds outside. There was a Latin inscription on the back of the Rolex, but I didn't know what it meant. It probably meant *stirred not shaken.* When he came back inside, Eric slumped down at the card table and buried his head on his arms and dry-sobbed for a while. I let him be. His own imagination seemed to be frightening him more than anything I could say. Up close you could see his beautiful, wavy dark hair was threaded with gray. The gray hairs were actually white, brittle and frizzy, the kind of hair I imagined the body keeps growing after death. He stopped sobbing and we sat in silence, breathing in the captive dead air of the garage, and listening to the old wooden structure make tiny creaking noises in the heat of the day. Something heavy, an avocado maybe, thumped down on the tin roof and rolled off. A car slowly cruised by outside and stopped, filling the alley with the menacing percussive thud of a rap song: the words, *big pimping . . . niggaz . . . bitches . . .* hanging in the air. Someone bragging about his dick, his Porsche, the fear he inspired in his enemies. A bottle shattered against the pavement, and the car accelerated away.

"Eric? Either tell me what you know, or I'm calling Malahide."

"No," he said.

"I *will* call him."

"I don't believe you. If you were going to call him, you would have done it already." He lifted his head and warily examined me. "But you can't do it." There was a look of cautious triumph on his face now as he tried to convince himself it was true. "You're just trying to freak me out. This is all bullshit. I don't have to take this. You can just get out of here, buddy. You can just get out of here before *I* call the police."

I'd seen him vomiting at the mention of a name, and cowering on the floor, but he'd recovered. Something close to spite brightened his face as he got to his feet. He was one of those people who looked ugly when they became confident.

"Go on!" he yelled. "Get the fuck out of here!"

I was going to have to make him sick with fear again, and the idea repelled me. I walked over to the tool bench and found some wire and pliers and an oily rag to stuff in his mouth. I could feel a pressure mounting in my skull, nausea rippling through my stomach at the prospect of having to hurt him. There was a trick to getting over it, which I'd learned in the war. You took all that dread building up inside you, all your horror at the violation you were about to commit, and you blamed it on the enemy. Why? *Because he was making you feel that way.* Maybe I wasn't angry enough for it to work anymore, or maybe I was just too old and scared of how I'd feel afterwards. Whatever the reason, I couldn't do it, and I was almost relieved when I heard steps coming around the side of the garage. A face passed fleetingly in the window and then the door burst open and a man stepped into the garage with a sawed-off pump shotgun pointed at me.

"What's going on?" He was in his early fifties, bulked up, a monumental head with a waxed Marine crew cut, a powerful jaw, and deep-set blue eyes. He was wearing a see-through black mesh tank top with an AA sobriety pin, and tan and gray Desert Storm camouflage pants tucked into combat boots. A few strands of ladies' pearls were loosely knotted around his bull neck below a flying eagle tattoo of the 101st Airborne. Another faded tattoo—Vietnam Vets Cooling Their Jets—snaked along his forearm, which had been shaved as clean as his face.

"Nothing," Eric mumbled. "It's fine."

"Don't shit me. You were just yelling for the police."

The man stepped into the garage, the shotgun dropping to his side. He noticed the photo of Eric at the nude poetry reading on the card table and snatched it up. "For Christ's sake!" He turned on Eric. "You went to that fucked-up thing?"

"Dieter! It's my life. I can do what I want."

So this was Dieter, the flamboyant owner of *Zeus and His Play Things.* He tossed the photo back and spotted Daniel Vine's money clip. I watched his hand readjust the grip on the lowered shotgun, finding the trigger with his index finger, as he turned to face me.

"So who are you, cupcake?"

"I'm a private investigator, Dieter."

"Well, isn't that peachy keen?" He glared at Eric. "I thought you told me you gave that money clip back. What have you done now? You answer me, goddamn it, or I'm sending your ass back to mom."

"I haven't done anything."

"What'd you do?" Dieter towered over Eric. "The truth!"

"There was this kid . . ."

"A *kid?*" Dieter's shoulders slumped, all the wind knocked out of him. "You swore to me, man. You swore you weren't going to ever . . ."

"It's not like that." Eric glanced uneasily at me, and dropped his voice. "It was Sally's *son.* I ran into him at this concert. I gave him the money clip and I said a few things about Sally and Raj, that's all."

"That's all?" Dieter said bitterly. He went and sat down at the card table and ran his huge hand through his hair. His eyes wandered over the tabloid cover photos of Sally Vine and then he swept them to the floor. The shotgun dangled loose in his hand, the barrel scraping on the concrete floor. The same car cruised down the alley again, blasting shock waves of rap against the metal garage door. It sounded like the amplified thump of a human heart as it went by. A heart racing on amphetamines. Dieter raised the shotgun and pantomimed tracking the car. *"Boom,"* he snarled softly. *"Boom."* The aged pit bull poked her head around the door and barked in protest as the music faded away. She walked on arthritic legs over to Dieter and slumped down at his feet, out of breath, her sightless eyes shining like dark, melted glass.

"What's the deal with Eric and kids?" I said softly.

"Don't talk to him, Dieter!"

Dieter turned and looked at his brother with withering dismay. "Our old man worked as a handyman at a brothel outside Reno when we were growing up. Mom was the maid. Half the kids in town, their fathers went to that brothel, but we still got shit about it everyday at school."

"I'm not listening to this," Eric said.

"When Eric was a little kid mom used to make him sing at . . ."

"Shut up, Dieter!"

"I want him to understand. Maybe he'll cut you some slack if he knows how you got involved in all this." Dieter sought Eric's eyes, but Eric stared sullenly at the wall. "Our mom's always had a drinking problem. She used to make Eric sing for the girls at the brothel. He was kind of the mascot of the place. He could sing anything. He could sound like anybody you wanted. Everybody said he was going to be famous one day. I don't know if you've ever lived in a small town. You watch TV and you go to the movies and it's like seeing there's a whole other world, only you're not allowed to be a part of it. The only kid Eric was close to in school was Sally Vine. Her name was Sally

Tourette then and she wasn't any movie star. She was just this skinny, tough little girl who was always getting in trouble for fighting and taking drugs. Her old man was in and out of jail and her mother worked the truck stops along the interstate. Eric and Sally Tourette were like brother and sister. But back then everybody had Eric pegged to be the star. Sally was a ragged little glue sniffer who was probably going to end up giving blow jobs to truckers like her mom."

"I'm not listening to this." Eric got to his feet.

"It's your life, little bro'. It's time to own it."

"You're just a big faggot who's been to too many AA meetings," Eric hissed. "You're worse than an old woman. You don't know anything about my life."

"Just what the cops tell me," Dieter said evenly. "Just what your probation officer says."

"This has nothing to do with that! I just talked to Hugo because he's Sally's kid." Eric sat down in a huff. "And I never did anything with those other kids. We were just good friends. It was all blown out of proportion."

"Eric had a gig teaching music at a place called The Tahoe Academy the last few years. It's a residential school for rich kids with drug problems. Kids who are so fucked up their parents can't control them. When he was younger, Eric had some misdemeanor molestation charges brought against him in Reno. It's not what you think. There was never any physical contact. He just likes being around kids. He gets attached to them and he pesters them, but he doesn't touch them."

"You sure you never touch them?" I asked.

Eric kept his head down, refusing to answer. I looked at Dieter, who seemed torn between a desire to tell the truth and his need to protect his brother. "His probation officer says it's because of what happened to Eric when he was growing up. He's trying to relive his childhood, but this time he's successful and popular. That's mainly why he likes hanging around teenage boys."

"Did this probation officer ever mention the term 'grooming'?"

"I don't remember," Dieter looked uncomfortable. "He could have."

"It's when an adult gets close to a child, buys him stuff, takes him to fun places. It's a long-term strategy. It's like petting a dog until it trusts you."

"Maybe he did mention that," Dieter conceded.

Eric had an asexual quality, an immaturity that fit the passive-aggressive profile of a groomer. They weren't impulsive risk takers like other pedophiles; they had the built-in patience of a parasite that could wait for months before making a move to take over its host. But the eventual goal was always sexual contact with a teenage boy. I didn't press the matter. I just wanted Dieter to know he hadn't succeeded in glossing over it.

"Eric didn't mention his record on his employee application for the Academy. When the school found out about it, there was a stink and now Eric's on probation. He's supposed to be seeing a therapist in Reno once a month, but the guy's about a hundred years old and lets Eric do his sessions over the phone. One of the conditions of the probation is he's not allowed to be alone with a minor."

"I wasn't alone with Hugo. I saw him at a concert, for Christ's sake. There were hundreds of kids there."

"You don't belong at a concert for kids," Dieter growled. "Any more than a drunk belongs at a wine tasting."

"How do you know Malahide?" I asked Eric.

"I used to take care of the Vines' ski lodge for Sally when

they weren't there." He shrugged. "Malahide was working at the school as a ski instructor and he asked me if he could stay with me."

"Did the people running this school know Malahide was an ex-con?"

"I guess."

"I need you to do more than guess."

"Okay!" Eric squirmed. "Mr. and Mrs. Dalgleish are like this Scottish couple that run the school. The tuition's, like, seventy grand a year for these kids, and the Dalgleishes don't like to pay the staff that much. I don't even think some of the staff are accredited teachers."

"So you're caretaking the Vines' ski lodge and teaching up at the school. Why'd you invite Malahide to live with you?"

"I didn't invite him. He invited himself."

"Couldn't you have said 'no'?"

"He knew I was on probation for that stupid other thing."

"So he was sort of blackmailing you?"

"You think I'd let a lowlife like that into Sally and Daniel's house otherwise?" Eric shuddered. "He was a total pig. He broke into the wine cellar. He spilled stuff on the rugs. He slept in their bed. It was a nightmare."

"And how does Raj fit into all this?"

"During the off-season Sally and Daniel used to lease the lodge out. The realtor would call me and I'd have to show the place. That's how I met Raj. The realtor brought him over to look at it. Raj said he was a French film producer scouting locations for some big movie. He said the lodge wasn't big enough for what he needed. When I showed the house, I always put on music to make a nice atmosphere. That day I just happened to play a tape I'd made of a song I'd written. I don't know how it came up," he continued, "but Raj asked me about the song. You know, he really liked it."

I doubted Eric just happened to play one of his songs that day. I was sure he always played his songs when anyone visited the house. He'd wanted Raj to notice his talent that day, too naïve to realize that for Raj a person's talent was just another name for their weakness.

"Raj said he was looking for a theme song for his movie and he asked me if I had anything else. He invited me to dinner in his suite at Caesar's. He was interested in me. A lot of people, they just want to know me because they think I'll talk about Sally. I don't do that. But I thought Raj was different. After that, we hung out a lot together. There was a problem at Caesar's with Raj's hotel bill. He was supposed to be getting money sent from Europe, but . . . I don't know, there were problems with the financing of the movie. He said his best friend, Johnny Depp, had kind of stabbed him in the back in the negotiations. He was thinking of going with an unknown in the role."

"Someone like you?"

"Well, it was discussed." Eric flushed. "You know when you're singing a song it's a kind of acting. A lot of musicians have crossed over, like Mark Wahlberg. By then Raj was hanging out at the lodge most of the time and then he was sleeping over and pretty soon he was living there and I was loaning *him* money. I even got him a job at the resort as a ski instructor. I thought he was something special, but he was just a lying piece of shit. I lent him clothes and money and a lot of other stuff. I gave him everything and he just . . ." Eric's face creased in anguish at the memory. "He lied about everything."

"You know, Eric," Dieter said gently, "when you get the

short end of the stick in a relationship, it feels like you were betrayed. But sometimes it's just you got rejected."

"I *was* betrayed!" Eric yelled. "And it wasn't some romantic *relationship,* you stupid faggot! I was just trying to help the guy."

"Sorry. I forgot you save your relationships for teenage boys."

Eric had called him a faggot several times and Dieter had finally retaliated. It was a window into how the Weaver brothers chose to hurt each other when things got down and dirty.

I tried to get Eric focused back on what had happened. "Do you think Raj consciously planned the whole, thing, Eric?"

"It was all about Sally. Her favorite songs, her favorite food. What she liked. Stuff from when we were kids. He was picking my brains from day one. Sally did some pretty wild stuff before she married Daniel. She wasn't going to be a waitress, or take some tacky job like the other girls. She was working outcall massage at the hotels on the state line when she was still in high school."

"Is that the kind of thing you told Raj about Sally?" I asked.

"If you think Raj is holding her sordid past over her, think again. Sally flipped for him the second she met him." Eric seemed to take some consolation that he wasn't the only one who'd fallen under Raj's spell. "I tried to warn her, but she never listens to anybody when she wants something." He sounded almost jealous of Sally's freedom to indulge her impulses. Eric had impulses of his own but his were secret and had to be kept on a tight leash. "It was usually just sexual with Sally and guys. I still don't understand why she married him. The day after Sally met Raj he was giving Hugo snowboard lessons and hanging out at the lodge. I always stayed out of the way when Sally and Daniel were there. Sally never let me come near her family. She liked to keep her past in a separate box. But it was okay for Raj and Malahide. They got asked to ski with them and invited for meals. They were welcome."

"Tell me about the money clip."

"It was the day after Daniel died. The school had found out about that stupid thing in Reno and asked me to leave. Malahide must've told them. Raj came over and let me know Sally wouldn't be requiring my services as a caretaker any more. She didn't have the guts to tell me in person. I was cleaning my stuff out of the guesthouse, looking under the beds, and I found the money clip under a chair where Malahide's clothes were hanging. It had fallen out of his pocket."

"There was more to it than that, Eric."

"I don't know what . . ."

"Yeah, you do. You were righteously pissed off that day. Malahide had turned you in to the school, you'd lost your job, and a woman you'd loved and been loyal to since you were kids had just sent the person who'd fucked you over to evict you. They treated you like shit, Eric. You don't strike me as a person who takes that kind of thing lying down."

"I went through Malahide's pockets, okay? That's how I found the money clip."

"You're telling me there was no money in the clip?"

"There was a little."

"Like a couple of thousand dollars?"

"If you know, why are you asking?" he snarled.

"Daniel Vine had that money clip on him when he went up the mountain. Any idea how it found its way into Malahide's pocket?"

"No idea at all." He said it with triumph, as if he'd known all along where my questions were leading and was pleased he could disappoint me. "I wasn't there. *If* I'd been invited to ski with them, I might have seen something, but I wasn't. I don't know a fucking thing about what happened on that mountain. For all I know it was an accident. I hope it wasn't, because I'd like to see them all burn in hell."

"I thought you told Hugo you knew who killed his father."

"I was just trying to . . ."

"Trying to what?"

"Just strike up a friendship with him." He swallowed. "I was blowing hot air. It's not a crime."

I had a feeling he was telling the truth, but it still made me want to hit him. Under all his talk of friendship, I could sense a callousness towards others that was pitiless. "And when you accepted the watch from him was that also just blowing hot air?"

"What watch?" Dieter seemed to come awake.

"Hugo gave Eric a fifteen-thousand-dollar watch to help him get information about who killed his father."

Dieter exploded out of the chair and slammed the heel of his hand into Eric's forehead, snapping him out of his chair and across the floor into the side of his van. The dog struggled to its feet and then abruptly collapsed back down again. "You motherfucker!" Dieter pulled Eric to his feet and shook him. "Crying the blues about how you get fucked over by people and the whole time you're putting the moves on her kid." He held Eric by his shoulders and pounded him against the van, sobbing as he did it. "You are so fucking *low!* You are such a disappointment to everyone! I'm ashamed to be your fucking brother!" Eric's head lolled on his shoulders, as Dieter jerked him back and forth. The blow to Eric's forehead had been delivered with conviction, but you could see Dieter was incapable of inflicting serious damage on his baby brother. He was just going through the motions now like an exhausted contestant in a dance marathon and finally he dropped his hands in disgust.

I wondered how many times over the years this scene had played itself out. Dieter wanting to physically beat the sickness out of his brother, but when it came to it, being incapable of really hurting him. If someone you loved was an alcoholic, or drug addict, there was always hope for a turnaround, but what cure was there for a pedophile's hunger?

"When I told you Raj and Malahide might be interested in your whereabouts, you got so scared you puked. I want to know why."

"Don't you understand?" Eric rubbed his head where Dieter had hit him. "They'll kill me if I tell you."

"What are you talking about?" Dieter demanded.

"I can't talk about it," he said with a catch in his voice.

"I want to know. Tell me, Eric."

"I saw what they did to Louis Pike, man. You don't want to mess with this."

"What happened to Louis Pike, bro'?" After nearly knocking Eric unconscious, Dieter was suddenly flooded with a guilty tenderness for his brother.

Eric gave him a frightened, pitiful look. "A few days before Vine died, Louis came over to see Malahide. Hugo and his father were outside making a snowman and Malahide pointed out Vine through the window. 'You'll know him from the hat.' That's what he said to Louis. Vine had this *Dr. Zhivago* kind of fur hat he always wore."

"Who's Louis Pike?" I interrupted.

"Just some drunken bum we went to school with. He's a chair lift operator on the Nevada side of Heavenly." Dieter turned back to Eric. "What did Malahide want Louis to do?"

"I'm not sure." Eric did a quick check of Dieter's face to see if he still had his sympathy. "But right after Vine died, Louis bought this brand new snowmobile. He was showing it off to everybody at the *Bierhaus,* buying drinks, and Malahide comes in and suddenly Louis looks like he swallowed a shot glass. The next day they found the snowmobile about a hundred yards from Louis's trailer. He was lying in a snowdrift next to it. The police said he'd passed out from drinking and froze to death."

"Do you think they hired this Louis Pike to kill Vine?" I asked.

"No." Eric broke into sobs. "He had a wife and kids. Louis wasn't a murderer. And neither am I."

"Would you be willing to testify to all this, Eric?"

There was a pause while he wiped the tears from his eyes and delicately touched his bruised forehead. He looked beseechingly at Dieter, who nodded in understanding and retrieved his shotgun.

Dieter refused to meet my eyes. "I'm sorry, but my brother's got nothing more to say to you . . ."

"Do you really think this is just going to go away because Eric bursts into tears?"

Dieter racked a round into the chamber. "If you tell anyone Eric is hiding here, I'll find you, pal. I'll stick *my little friend* in your ear and blow your brains out."

"If he wants to hide, tell him to stop taking his clothes off in public."

"I'm holding you personally responsible if something happens to him." The more Dieter threatened me, the less conviction he seemed to have. Eric watched me from behind his brother's massive shoulder, a smirk on his face.

"Tell your brother if he talks to Hugo again I'll castrate him."

The dog made a lunging attempt to get to her feet and snap at my leg, but she missed and splayed forward.

"And get a new dog," I said uncharitably. "This one isn't going to protect you from anything."

Chapter Fourteen

A wall of fog was blowing in from the bay, drifting block by block through Venice as I drove back to my office. The crowds deserting the beaches had added to the normal snarl of Saturday afternoon traffic in Santa Monica. I finally found a space on the top level of a public parking structure near my office. There was a homeless woman lying near the stairwell. She was sipping a Starbucks *latte* and watching the Discovery Channel on a portable color TV that she'd propped up in her shopping cart and plugged into a utility outlet. It was a program about the Aztecs and how they'd perfected the art of turning the corpses of their human sacrifices into different kinds of musical instruments. I had a similar model TV in my office, but I noticed she was getting much better reception than I did.

I held my breath going down the urine-scented stairwell and exited out on Fourth Street. I hurried past the dance studio on the corner, full of couples practicing their Salsa moves for that upcoming Caribbean cruise; the travel agency, with its displays of exotic holiday destinations; the jewelry store with its gold and platinum watches nestled in gray velvet boxes. I passed the bar and blues club where I'd spent the nineties drinking myself into a stupor, and the tobacconist where I bought the English and Turkish cigarettes I used to smoke. A vision of forbidden pleasures was trying to take shape in my mind, an inner voice urging me to sell Daniel Vine's watch, buy a plane ticket, and start drinking again. I knew that voice well and it bothered me that it had returned. I walked into the lobby of my building past the broken elevator and took the stairs up to the third floor.

A sharp acrid scent of black tobacco hit me as I came out onto the landing. The door to my office was splintered open. The reception room appeared untouched, but the office itself had been turned upside down, contents of drawers emptied out, files strewn around the floor. They'd left the CD player, the Xerox machine, the printer, the fax, but the TV and my computer were gone. Whoever had tossed the place had urinated in the wastepaper basket and left a filtered *Gaulloise* floating on the surface. Was it Stone? He hadn't smelled of cigarettes when he whispered in my ear, and I doubted he smoked French ones. Still, whoever it was, had suspected the film in my car's computer had automatically been stored in my office computer as well. I figured they would be going after my home computer next, if they hadn't taken it already.

The homeless woman in the parking structure must have decided Aztec human sacrifice was too tame because she'd switched over to Ricki Lake. She was buried in blankets and layers of clothes, just a patch of soiled face peeking out beneath her nest of wildly matted hair.

"Nice TV," I remarked.

"It's mine," she croaked.

"Bullshit. Someone just stole it from my office. Tell me what happened and I might let you keep it."

Her eyes flicked warily at me and she sank deep into her blankets like a tortoise withdrawing into its shell.

I pulled out my phone. "You can tell me, lady, or I'm calling the cops." It was starting to occur to me it would have been simpler if I'd just *become* a cop.

She withdrew a red swollen hand from her blankets and

pointed at the line of parked cars beyond the stairwell. "I didn't steal nothing. They left the TV over there."

"Who are *they?*"

"I don't know. I couldn't understand what they were saying."

"Were they speaking French?"

"No!" She sounded outraged. "I understand that *comment parlez-vous.* I know French. This was . . . they were . . ." She glanced around to make sure we were alone and whispered, "They were *dune coons.*" She displayed her toothless gums in a conspiratorial smile.

"Dune coons?"

She laughed in delight when I said the forbidden words and put a finger to her lips. "Shhhhh! They don't like being called that."

"They were Arabs?"

"Sounded like it. The big one got mad at the little one and made him leave my TV behind."

"What kind of car were they driving?"

"Big black Mercedes. You couldn't see them inside."

"Was one of them carrying a computer?"

"He had something. It had a screen, but it wasn't a TV," she said with an airy disdain. "I wouldn't have wanted it."

I wanted to question her more, but I had to get back to my house. I jumped into my car and reversed hard out of the space and accelerated towards the exit ramp. The woman started yelling and waving her arms at me.

I lowered my window. "What?"

"Where's the remote to the TV?" she shrieked. "You didn't give me the friggin' remote!"

I watched her receding in my rearview mirror as I rolled down the ramp, shaking her fist, her mouth torn by words of abuse I couldn't hear. She was old and wretched, but she insisted on her ingratitude as if it was a right, proof of her humanity. For all I knew, maybe it was.

I forced my way across a honking stream of slow-moving traffic and headed north along Fourth Street. Up ahead cars were being funneled into a single lane by a road construction project. I cut the wrong way down an alley, and hit even worse conditions on Fifth. There was nothing I could do and, as I sat there watching the fog obscure my windshield, I realized I was making a mistake. It didn't matter if the two men took my home computer because I had copies of what they were looking for in the handle of my tennis racket. It was better if they thought they'd solved the problem. What I needed to do was secure the evidence I already had.

I stopped at a Kinko's on Wilshire and made copies. I went to several photo developing places and finally found an Indian Sikh who said he could make color enlargements right away. While I waited I checked the messages on my home answering machine: Hugo had called three times, his voice sounding increasingly worried. I called him back on his cell and he answered on the first ring.

"Where've you been?" he demanded. "Did you find Eric?"

"Are you alone? Can anybody hear you?"

"I'm in my tree house. You were supposed to tell me what happened. You promised!"

"I don't remember us having that conversation. I recall me telling you there were certain things it was safer for you not to know."

There was a pause on the line.

"There's some shit going on here," he said, "that it might be safer for *you* not to know."

"What kind of shit exactly?"

"Tell me about Eric first."

"I don't negotiate with terrorists, Hugo. It always ends in tears. Just tell me what's going on there."

"There's these two dorky Lebanese bodyguards that just showed up in front of the house. They came to the party with Raj's uncle last night and now they're back."

"Raj's uncle?"

"Uncle Firooz from Beirut," Hugo said in his most deadpan voice. "He's a short guy. I think he's almost shorter than me, but he weighs about two hundred pounds more."

"Where did *he* come from all of a sudden?"

"He's one of the film investors I told you about. It's so cool. Raj is scared to death of him."

"What do Uncle Firooz's bodyguards look like?"

"They wear like a lot of *Bijan* aftershave."

"That's not a description."

"They're like guys on the Persian cable channel. They have big moustaches and unibrows. They're wearing these shiny suits with vests."

"Are they driving a black Mercedes with tinted windows?"

"Yeah. How'd you know that?" he demanded.

"Is one guy a lot bigger than the other?"

The frustration in his voice was mounting. "I'm the one who found you, not Raj and my mother. I don't care if they're paying you. I *discovered* you. Tell me how you know all this stuff!"

"You didn't need to *discover* me, kid. You could have looked in the Yellow Pages."

"I can't believe you're doing this," he said. "If it wasn't for my input you never would have found out a thing. I'm the one who gave you all the good ideas and stuff."

"We'll talk about this later." I failed to keep the irritation out of my voice. "Right now it's important for me to know what you know. All that other stuff can wait."

"Uh, I don't think so," Hugo said coldly and hung up.

The Sikh, pretending not to have heard my end of this bizarre conversation, slid the enlargements across the counter and offered me a magnifier. Daniel Vine's self-portrait looked more blurred when it was blown up but I could see new details I'd missed before. His eyebrows and nostrils were rimmed with snow. There was blood smeared in his silver hair and around his yellow neck protector. The photo of the two figures receding into the whiteout had been fuzzy to begin with, and now it was so enlarged the fine grain of the print was almost breaking apart. The figures didn't even look human; they were apparitions trying to materialize out of a background of shimmering dots. It was possible to establish that both figures wore dark clothes, but there hadn't been enough light for their color to register. They were definitely walking *away* from Daniel Vine. The bulky shape of their outlines suggested they were dressed in something with the looser fit favored by snowboarders. Something black and forked like a pair of horns extended from the head of the nearest figure. A hat, maybe. What gripped my attention most, however, was a dark smudge that seemed to be coming out of the blizzard towards the two figures. It was impossible to tell if it was a third person, or just a tree stump. I studied it so long the Sikh finally cleared his throat and told me how much I owed him. After I paid him I showed him the smudge and asked him what he thought it was.

"It is all black from top to bottom, you see." He tapped the spot with the elongated nail of his little finger. "But just below the top there is a little speck. It could be many things. It could be a patch of snow. It could be a person's face."

The time code on the photo showed Daniel Vine had waited for three full minutes after his killers vanished into the white-out before taking the last picture of himself. His kneecap was shattered and he was rapidly bleeding to death. It would have been nothing but windswept whiteness wherever he looked. What had passed through his mind as the blizzard closed around him? I wondered if he thought about Hugo and the unfolding of the boy's life, which he was never going to see. Maybe he was just hoping somebody would come back for him.

"If you bring in the camera I can achieve greater resolution of the image," the Sikh said.

"That's my problem. I don't have the camera anymore."

I couldn't see the black Mercedes parked on my street, but just to be on the safe side I cruised around the block twice, and then pulled into a neighbor's driveway. I climbed over their fence into the Doyles' back garden, went around the side, and studied my cottage from the rear. From that unfamiliar angle it was almost impossible to detect it beneath its blanket of bougainvillea and morning glory vines.

The splintered front door hung open, and inside the same acrid smell of French cigarettes lingered in the air. A dust-free circle showed on the desk where the round base of my computer had rested. To my relief, the answering machine with Stone's voice on it was still there. This time there had been a similarly half-hearted attempt to make it look like a conventional burglary. Uncle Firooz's bodyguards had pulled over one of the shelves that held my album collection and then trampled over the spilled LPs, cracking the records. I picked up an old Ray Charles album and shook the shards of vinyl out into my hand. He was probably my all-time favorite singer. When someone asked him why he sang, the blind heroin-addicted Ray Charles answered simply, “I want people to feel my soul.” Not his wallet, not his rage, not his bitches, but that eternal gnawing human desire for something *more.* My car, my office, and now my house; it was starting to scare me how easily these people could enter my world and *take* things from me. There was another odor masked by the cigarette smoke and I followed it to the alcove, which contained my bed: someone had drenched my pillow and blankets with urine.

I called Hugo. He answered on the first ring, but I could tell from his listless, jaded manner that he was still sulking about our last conversation.

“I’m coming over, Hugo, but I need to get into your house without being seen. How would you do that?” I knew perfectly well how to get into the property, but I thought asking his advice might get him over his funk.

“What do you want to come over for?” he asked sluggishly.

“Quite a few things.”

“Like what?”

“I found your dad’s watch. Thought you might like to have that back.”

“No way! How did you find it?” The surprise in his voice gave me a little glow.

“It’s a long story.”

“Wow, man, that is really good, you know. I didn’t think you’d . . .”

“You didn’t think I was up to it, I know.”

“Well . . . I mean you haven’t exactly been making much progress, but now I think you’re like . . . doing much better.

Uh, good work, Tom." It was the first time he'd ever called me by my name, and it sounded experimental and awkward.

"Call me Thomas. That's what my friends call me."

"Got it," he said. "It's not just Firooz and the bodyguards. That cop who was playing tennis is here talking to Raj, and Malahide is back. I don't know what's going on."

"Where's your mom?"

"She's upstairs with Alvin Peck, her agent. She hasn't come out of her room since this afternoon. It's like there's a war going on around here. Not with guns of course, which would be cool, just cell phones."

"Give me about an hour. I'll hike in by that place where your mom throws your stuff and meet you in Serafina's room."

I hung up and phoned someone I hadn't spoken to in five years. Ken O'Doul was a student who'd befriended me years ago at U.C.L.A. when I'd been taking Criminology classes and he was trying to pass the Bar. We'd both started out as one-man operations, but Ken had quickly moved from defending indigent felons to the far headier world of celebrity clients. He'd given me a lot of work in those early days and wanted to invest in my agency and turn it into a much bigger business. Ken knew how to run a large operation and he had an insatiable appetite for making money. But I was too contrary and too much of a loner for such a collaboration to ever work. What we'd really had in common was a shared hedonism that took the form of getting as high as possible and chasing women, but when I declined Ken's offer he took it as some kind of personal rejection. Defending celebrity clients was one of those awesomely tacky and obscenely lucrative fields where the profits were so great everything else was beside the point.

To my mind, it was about as real as publicity and professional wrestling. Ken had accused me in a cognac and cocaine haze one night of looking down on him for what he did for a living. Why should he be ashamed for wanting to be incredibly rich? I told him I didn't look down on him, I just didn't see why I had to look *up* to him. Ken was diabetic and drank too much and the last time we'd run into each other all he talked about was his new plane and how easy it made getting to his three vacation homes.

A woman answered the phone.

"Hi, it's Thomas Kyd," I said. "Is that Veronica? I think we met a long time ago."

"No. This is Suki. Veronica was wife number two."

"Sorry about that. I'm looking for Ken."

"Aren't we all? Hold on. I'll transfer you to the sauna."

Ken, I recalled, didn't believe in controlling his weight through any form of dieting; he had a stubborn conviction that sweating in a box produced the same results as vigorous exercise.

He came on the line sounding like he'd already had a few drinks. "Thomas Kyd. Where the hell have you been?"

"It's been too long, Ken, and I'm embarrassed because I'm calling to ask you a favor."

"The last time I tried to do you a favor you nearly bit my head off."

He was referring of course to his offer to invest in my agency. It was as if our long-ago quarrel were starting right up again. "I didn't realize it was a favor, Ken."

"It wasn't," he groaned. "Jesus, let's not get into all that again. How are you?"

"Good. You?"

"Terrible." He laughed. "How did Suki sound when she answered the phone?"

"I don't know. How does she normally sound?"

"She's leaving me. Can you believe that shit? Well, I know the next one won't be marrying me for my money because there isn't going to be any left after what the first three took."

"Yeah, I'm broke, too," I laughed.

"No, you're *poor.* You have to have had something to feel broke."

"You're right."

"But that's what you wanted." He couldn't stay away from the subject. I could hear the slosh of ice in a glass and picture the tumbler of Jack Daniels he liked to suck on when he was in the sauna. "I mean you're smart, you're white, you got a college degree. A guy with your advantages has got to work awful hard to stay broke. So I figure it's a conscious decision on your part, like wearing a hair shirt."

"Believe me, most of my decisions are pretty damn unconscious. My life has been a blur. Half the time I think a stranger lived it for me."

"Me, too. I guess I'm sore because it could have been a lot more fun if we'd done more stuff together."

"Maybe it's not too late," I said. "You know Sally Vine?"

"Little long in the tooth now, but she was really something in those early movies. All tightly wrapped and neurotic and underneath you know there's a whole other sexual thing going on. Didn't her husband die? Fell off a ski lift, or ran into a tree or something?"

"He may have been murdered, Ken. She's hired me to look into it."

"Hey." He sounded genuinely pleased. "That's a . . . that's a pretty big client for you, Sally Vine. Congratulations."

"You got a minute? I could use your counsel."

"Sure, man. Just hold on a second. I need to . . . hold on." I could hear him opening a fridge, the rattle of ice cubes as he built himself a new drink. When he came back on the line, he sounded out of breath. I wondered how much weight he'd gained in the years since I'd seen him.

"I'm listening," he said.

I gave him the whole story in a compressed version and, to his credit he never interrupted and, after the first few minutes, I stopped hearing the periodic clink of ice cubes in his drink. When I was finished, there was an awkward silence, and then he sighed.

"Let me get this straight. They hired you to drive their kid to school and now you're investigating them for murder?"

"I know Raj is involved. I'm still not a hundred percent sure about her."

"It doesn't even sound like you have a client, Thomas."

"She hasn't fired me yet."

"If she's letting her husband slap her around, she could be dirty, too. This L.A.P.D. hard-on, Stone, makes it very hard to go to the police. On top of that, none of this evidence sounds close to being admissible."

"I know that," I said. I could hear him taking a long pull on his drink.

"That's the bad news," he chuckled. "The good news is, you got 'em right where you want 'em."

"Glad you think so."

"Give me the name of this chick from the *Enquirer*. I know all the players at Fox and the other tabloid TV shows. We'll get them in a bidding war and this thing will turn into a feeding frenzy. Let me handle this and you'll make a killing. It's just a big open wound that's going to hemorrhage money and ratings for months and months." The prospect of such a deal had infused his voice with excitement and genuine affection for me. People knock money, but in Los Angeles the expectation of it can produce an emotion close to love.

"If I sell this evidence to the tabs," I said, "it can never be used in court against the killers. There goes my case."

"You have no case. What you have is a shot at making some serious change for once in your life."

"I'm a private investigator. I can't go public with a case."

"Oh boy . . ." he groaned. "Listen to me. You owe nothing to these people. No one will ever object to you blowing the whistle and cashing in. In fact, they'll be lining up to hire you. It'll give you some real exposure."

"I want to retain you as my attorney. I'm going to FedEx a package over to you with all the evidence for safekeeping in case something happens to me."

"I'm really jazzed, Thomas. I always wanted to work a big deal with you. We're going to make out like bandits on this thing."

"Not that way. I don't want you to approach the tabs or do anything else with it. Do you understand?"

"Why not?"

"I'm not fucking the kid over like that."

"Can't you ever just do something without turning it into a Humanitarian Aid mission?"

"If this is a drag, man, I'll find someone else. It's no big deal."

"No," he sighed. "Tell me what you want."

"I have a question. Can a minor legally hire a private investigator?"

"Who the fuck knows? Can he afford you? How much allowance does the kid get?"

I ignored his jibe. "Could a minor also hire an attorney?"

"You want me to take some fourteen-year-old as a *pro bono* client?"

"Think about it. This kid is heir to a fortune and he's from showbiz royalty. It's been a couple of years since I saw you on the evening news defending some celebrity for dislocating his wife's jaw. Might be a boost for your profile."

It took him a brief moment to picture this new scenario, and he was off and running. "No one's bothered to write law on what private investigators can and can't do in these kind of situations. The kid can probably hire you the way he'd hire a clown to perform at his birthday party. But as a minor, he doesn't have the capacity to contract with an attorney. Of course I could petition the court to appoint a guardian and the guardian could hire me on the kid's behalf, which is what I'm going to do. A wealthy guy like Daniel Vine would have had a living trust so there was probably no probate, no public reading of his will. First thing we do is contest the will, find out what the kid has coming to him. I bet it was a lot. For all we know, the kid is sitting on a gold mine and doesn't even know it. I want to meet this kid."

"Slow down, Ken. You haven't got the job yet." It wasn't true, but I enjoyed saying it. "The best thing I could do is put in a good word for you. Hugo's going to be looking at a lot of other attorneys."

"Come on! I'm perfect for this job. Criminal and entertainment law, we offer the whole package. We protect him and sell the story at the same time. It's one-stop shopping, and we have the best investigators." In between sips of his drink, he'd gone from reluctant buyer to motivated seller.

It didn't even surprise me that he was already talking

about replacing me with his own investigators. A good idea in Hollywood is like a baby that passes through the hands of ever more powerful foster parents. Whoever manages to most profitably exploit the baby gets credited with having given birth to it. The tantalizing possibilities of representing Hugo had taken such a grip on Ken's imagination he'd already forgotten I'd given him the idea. He liked it so much it was as if he'd had it himself. From there to convincing himself he'd truly generated the idea was the shortest step in Hollywood. It was time to yank the prize out of his grasp.

"Anyway, Ken, we'll keep you in mind. I've gotta run."

"What's the rush?" Ken protested. "Where you going?"

"To see my client." I hung up on him.

Chapter Fifteen

The marine layer still hung suspended over Santa Monica and Brentwood and it only melted away once I got up into Bel-Air. I parked about a hundred yards down from where the road dead-ended at the top, armed myself with my .38 and a twenty-four-inch Mag-lite, and started walking up towards the Vine place. It was very quiet on the moonlit street. High overhead I could make out the winking lights of airliners moving silently through the patterned stars on their heading towards LAX. It was a Saturday night, but the illuminated mansions on either side appeared lifeless behind their gated walls. I kept to the middle of the road, out of range of the security cameras guarding the entrances to the houses. I kept listening for voices, a snatch of music, the sound of a TV coming from one of the houses, but all I could hear was the scraping of my feet on the road. Disturbed by the noise up ahead, a coyote stepped out from behind some trash cans and pinned me with its phosphorescent eyes. I shone my flashlight on the animal. There was nothing bedraggled or furtive about it. It looked sleek and healthy, its coat shiny from a diet rich in upscale garbage and plump household pets. It held its ground as I approached, as if I were the one who didn't belong there. I could hear a car coming down the hill fast and I hurried to the trash cans to get out of sight. The spooked coyote darted across the road as a black Range Rover came around the corner. I heard a mingled squeal and thump followed by the sound of the car screeching to a stop down the road.

I stayed crouched behind the trash cans. After a moment a car door opened and slammed shut and someone started walking back up the road towards the dead coyote. It was Malahide. He was wearing a black Adidas warm-up suit, black gloves, with a black wool skullcap covering his hair. The sound of screeching brakes hadn't produced any reaction from the houses on either side of the street. It was the kind of neighborhood where if you were getting your throat cut and screaming for help the people inside would first check to make sure their doors were securely locked before reporting a *disturbance* to the Bel-Air Patrol. Malahide prodded the coyote with his running shoe to make sure it was dead. He glanced up and down the street and then grabbed the animal by its hind legs and started dragging it towards the trash cans. I could not believe I could be this humiliatingly unlucky. He was going to be a good citizen, dispose of the unsightly road-kill, and find me. Absurd weak scenarios ran through my head, all designed to explain why I happened to be hiding there on my hands and knees behind the garbage. But there was no reasonable explanation. Just before he got to me, Malahide suddenly stopped and tittered sarcastically to himself.

As I watched, he bent his knees and swung the limp carcass around once, twice, like an athlete in the hammer throw, and sailed it right over someone's garden wall. There was the sound of a distant splash as it landed in a swimming pool. The effort of swinging the dead coyote around had pulled his warm-up jacket above his waist. The casual malice of his gesture and the physical strength he'd displayed were chilling, but not as much as the chromed shine of the revolver that I could see tucked in his waistband. For trendy Los Angeles all-black clothing was *de rigeur,* but Malahide's gloves, wool cap, and gun weren't a fashion statement. It's what you wore to commit a crime when you didn't want to leave prints, or be identifiable by a witness. I waited until I heard the Range Rover start down the hill before stepping back into the street.

When I reached the lookout point at the top, all I could see was a dense blanket of fog where the city should have been. For a moment I felt confused by the absence of lights and landmarks. A great silence had engulfed the coastal plain. And then I detected a faint distant roaring, irregular and never-ending, like surf, and realized it was the San Diego Freeway coursing invisibly below the fog. I wondered why Malahide was packing a gun. He was somewhere down there in the murk now, another pair of headlights moving anonymously through the pea soup. It made me think of the blizzard in which Daniel Vine died and the storm that had half-buried Louis Pike beside his snowmobile. A low visibility marine layer didn't afford the same protection as a snowstorm, but it still provided excellent cover. I had a guilty feeling that instead of hiding I should have cracked Malahide across the skull with my flashlight and taken his weapon away. One of the reasons I hadn't was because he scared me in a way that Raj didn't. The cops referred to victims of crimes as "vics," but in jail a *vic* was not a victim but a seasoned, hardened convict. Malahide was pure *vic.* He'd been belly-chained, foot-locked, and handcuffed. It was written all over him. He wasn't someone you could hurt and hope you'd taught him a lesson. You had to be willing to kill him and I didn't know if I could still do that anymore.

The gates of the private road down to the Vine compound were locked. Peering through the bars, I could see the entire house was lit up, as well as the gardens leading down to the pool and guesthouse. Two men in dark suits, one tall and broad-shouldered, the other short and sturdy, were smoking and kicking a soccer ball back and forth on the spot-lit gravel. Uncle Firooz's bodyguards were in their twenties and had the lazy contained grace of skilled athletes. They trapped the ball on their thighs, let it drop to their shoes, flicked it with practiced insouciance back and forth. I was sure these were the guys who'd kicked their way into my office and house, stomped on my record collection, and pissed on my bed. It was impossible from that distance to tell if they were armed. Nestled in among all the luxury foreign cars were Stone's bright yellow Corvette and Alvin Peck's green Range Rover with the baby seat in back. Something was bringing all these people who served the Vines together, but I still couldn't fathom what it was. All I sensed was that if Daniel Vine hadn't died, none of them would have been there, and the only person in the house who still mourned his father was Hugo.

I followed the wall around the property line until I was out of sight and scaled it, dropping down into overgrown brush. I located a coyote trail and made a wide detour through the chaparral before working my way back to the house. The deserted tennis court loomed ahead in the darkness. Coming from the vicinity of the guesthouse I could hear what sounded like Middle Eastern pop music and the occasional voice bellowing in a language I didn't understand. Up ahead, the lighted windows of Daniel Vine's old production offices came into view. Through the angled Venetian blinds I could see the drawers of all the filing cabinets and desks were pulled out and the floor was piled with stacked documents. Tea Lane was on her knees going through the contents of a manila envelope, a phone cradled to her ear. Her nose looked raw and pinched from crying. It was nine o'clock on a Saturday night and the brash adrenaline-fueled confidence that she was making movies seemed to have deserted her.

Hugo answered the door and hustled me inside Serafina's empty room. He had put the metal hoops back in his ears, lips, and eyebrows. He'd covered his bare arms with wild swirls of magic marker ink to make it look like he was tattooed, and buzzed a highway down the middle of his peroxide blonde hair. There was something tight-jawed and manic about his behavior that made me suspect he was on something. I handed him his father's Rolex, but he barely glanced at it before shoving it in his pocket.

"I have just done the coolest thing!" he said. "You know, all day, I've been going around acting like I'm insane, just talking all kinds of crazy stuff. I told Raj I could hear my Dad's voice coming from the attic and I told his fat uncle the guesthouse was haunted. When they try to talk to me, I act like a zombie. I talk to them in *Latin!*"

"Latin?"

"We just started taking it in school. You should see Raj's face. He doesn't know what to do with me. It's freaking him out."

"I don't get it," I said. "What are you trying to do?"

My failure to understand offended him. "They're worried I'm having a nervous breakdown. I can do and say anything I want. I just barge in all over the house and find out stuff."

"Like what?"

"What's wrong? Why are you looking at me like that?"

"I'm just worried if you act nuts they'll call your therapist and stick you in some psych ward. Are you high?"

"Stop being so uptight, or I'm not even going to tell you what I did."

The truth was, I couldn't stand all the metal stuck in his

face and the mess he'd made of his hair. He reminded me of the druggie homeless kids who hung around the fountains in the Third Street Promenade. It was as if he'd turned back into the tormented, painfully distraught boy who'd barged into my office so many months ago. It was a trap to take his appearance and mental condition so personally, I knew, but I couldn't seem to stop myself.

"Go ahead. Tell me what you did."

"When that creep cop arrived, Raj took him in the library to talk in private, right? So our dog Genghis is, like, really badly behaved, you know, he jumps on everybody and takes dumps all over the place. The trainers are always trying to discipline his ass, but Genghis is just this extreme animal. He won't, like, obey at all. So he's supposed to be locked up in the kitchen at all times, but I let him out and chased him into the library where Raj and the cop were and he jumped all over the cop and started slobbering on him. And they got really pissed. It was so fucking cool. And then I caught Genghis and took him out."

"That's it?" I said.

Hugo studied me for a moment, registering my confusion and disappointment, almost savoring them. "I left my tape recorder behind in the room. It's got a ninety-minute tape in it and this awesome microphone that can probably pick up a fart at fifty yards."

"Jesus Christ, kid. I'm impressed."

He scoffed, "It probably won't even work. I bought it online from this company in New Jersey. They *claim* it's the same equipment the CIA uses, but it's probably just Radio Shack junk they sell to suckers like me."

"Don't be so down on yourself. You did good."

"I had a couple of *doppio espressos* because I figured I might have to stay up all night. That's why I'm kind of nervous. So." He shrugged, dropping his good humor. "What have *you* got?"

"Remember that night you came into my office I said I couldn't take you as a client?"

"Yeah, I was a little rude. I'm sorry."

"You were very rude actually, but I was wrong. I talked to a lawyer, and there's nothing illegal about it. So if you want to officially retain me, we can do that, and I can retain this lawyer and he'll be part of our team."

"Who is he?"

"His name's Ken O'Doul."

"O'Doul?" He sounded dubious. "An Irish lawyer? I don't know. Is he, like, with a powerful firm, or is he like some small time guy you just happen to know? Like a guy who wants to help kids and stuff because it's the right thing to do?"

Hugo had a mordant contempt for everybody, including himself, but he seemed to reserve his keenest distrust for anyone who professed to operate from selfless motives. He assumed the world was full of phonies and that most forms of idealism were a sham. The annoying thing was I pretty much agreed with him, but for his sake I had to pretend I didn't. This constant need to project a positive image of the world to Hugo was starting to wear me out.

"No, I didn't find Ken in the Yellow Pages under 'Lawyers who feel sorry for people,' " I said. "The guy owns his own plane."

"Is it a jet?" Hugo asked. "Anybody can own a plane."

I let my breath out very slowly and tried to remember he was only fourteen. "Yes, it's a jet. Ken's about as wealthy as you can get practicing law in this town without going to jail for it. There's nothing altruistic about him. The only reason Ken wants to take your case is because he loves money and publicity."

"I didn't mean anything." Hugo squirmed. "It's just that Pops always said in business you should never hire your friends. This guy, Ken, sounds great. What else have you been doing, or is that it?"

"Let's see. Stone and some other cops grabbed me right after I left you and took the camera and the computer out of my car. Stone also tried to kick a hole in my skull with the toe of his cowboy boot." I lowered my head and pointed out the scabbed-over laceration.

"Wow," he said, abashed. "I wondered what that was."

"Let's not get sidetracked feeling sorry for me," I said. "I found Eric, who's living in his gay ex-paratrooper brother's garage in Venice. Eric did go to high school with your mom and he used to be the caretaker of your place in Tahoe."

"I didn't know that."

The sound of Hugo admitting there was something he didn't know was so gratifying I had to stop myself from asking him to repeat it. "Eric's also on probation on a child molestation charge. He claims that Malahide pointed out your dad to a local drunk called Louis Pike and paid him to do something, but Eric doesn't know what. Whatever it was, it's going to be hard to discover because Louis Pike is dead. Eric believes Malahide killed him to shut him up. Eric's brother threatened me with a shotgun and basically told me Eric was never going to testify because it was too dangerous."

"What a pussy," Hugo scoffed.

I gave him a disapproving look. "Eric's scared to death. I don't know why you're not scared, Hugo. I'm scared."

"Okay . . . I didn't mean it. It's just, you know, frustrating that no one wants to help."

"When I got back to my office, Uncle Firooz's goons had

broken in and taken my computer. When I got home I found they'd taken my other one." I left out the fact they'd smashed my records and urinated all over my bed. The humiliating light it put me in still rankled too much.

"I'm sorry," Hugo said. "I'll . . . I'll reimburse you for everything. I want you to tell me about the photographs."

"It's actually good for us they took them. Now they think we don't have them any more."

"Tell me about the photographs!" he persisted.

"Well, if I wanted to, I could sell them to the tabs for a fortune. Get some fancy offices in Beverly Hills, a bunch of new clients. Hell, maybe *I* could buy a plane."

"I know, I know. You're being really good to me and . . . and I'm truly deeply grateful." He laughed at how artificial he sounded. "I am *extremely* grateful! But tell me about the photographs."

"I don't want you to know anything about those photos. When I came up the hill, Malahide was driving down and he ran over a coyote."

"Did he see you?"

"No, but he was wearing gloves and he was carrying a gun. One of the logical places he might be going is to my house. Not because he thinks I have the photos anymore. But because I know what's in them."

I held his gaze and for the first time the seriousness of the situation seemed to penetrate his fourteen-year-old brain.

"Do you think Malahide would actually . . . ?" He swallowed. "I mean, I know he was in prison, but I think it was for drugs and stuff. All he ever did was talk to me about living right and having more self-esteem. He even wanted to talk to my class at school about how drugs screwed up his life and everything, but they wouldn't pay him. I know I said I was suspicious of him, but I didn't think he really, you know . . . I thought it was just Raj."

"We don't know who it was yet really, do we?" I said softly.

"I guess not." Hugo looked away.

"Does it worry you that your mom maybe isn't being that helpful in all this?" It was a painful thing to ask, but I didn't know how else to put it.

"Who cares?" Tears suddenly spurted out of his eyes and he furiously wiped them away. "It doesn't mean I'm going to quit, though!"

"Just tell me if it gets too tough, okay, Hugo?"

"Don't worry," he said. "I'm way past all that."

The least I could do, I thought, was pretend to believe him. We could hear Tea Lane yelling at someone in the production offices outside, her voice sounding more and more hysterical. "This is all your fault! You're lying! How do I know you did? If I find out . . ."

A moment later, a shaken Serafina and Adolpho burst into the room.

"Why is she yelling at you?" Hugo was incensed.

"Just a minute." Serafina got on her knees and gave Adolpho a hug. "It's okay, *mi amor,* she make a mistake." She got the boy comfortable on the bed, turned on the television, and handed him the remote. Adolpho surfed through the channels and became absorbed in helicopter footage of a high-speed police chase. He watched hypnotized as the suspect's truck raced the wrong way down a freeway, opening a path in the oncoming traffic, like a smart bomb homing in on its target.

"Tea can't talk to you like that," Hugo scowled. "I'll kick her ass."

"Is okay. Just calm down." Serafina turned to me. "She

keeps saying she give me this camera with the clothes in Tahoe and that I give it back to her yesterday. I think Mr. Raj is very upset with her. She is just telling terrible lies."

"What else was she asking you about?"

"If I burn Mr. Vine's clothes. I have to swear on my parents' grave that I burn them on the barbecue in Tahoe. But I don't burn nothing for that *malita puta asquerosa.*" Her chiseled coppery face glowed with color and her eyes sparkled with a defiance I'd never seen before.

"What does that mean?" Hugo asked.

"I use bad words," Serafina said huffily. "Use your imagination."

"What did you do with Mr. Vine's clothes?" I asked.

"I put them in the attic with Hugo's things from when he was little. His little shoes and picture books and toy animals." She looked at Hugo. "One day when you are older I think maybe you go up there to look at your things from when you were a child. And you see your father's clothes and you remember him. He was a good man. Your father told me once his own father is an illegal immigrant like me. A Jew from Russia. He sneak into this country like a criminal. He say, 'If you go back far enough, nobody has any papers, everybody is illegal.' I like this man very much, and also his son."

Serafina put her arm around Hugo's waist and squeezed him. She was already an inch or two shorter and soon he would tower over her. They made an incongruous pair. Her hair was pinned back and she wore the self-effacing maid's uniform I hated so much. Standing beside her, with his punky peroxide buzz-cut and faux tattoos, Hugo looked like someone from a violent dystopian cartoon. Yet they had never seemed so emotionally linked to each other. I searched Serafina's face for some sign that she now considered me a part of this intimacy they shared, but it wasn't there. She wasn't cold towards me any more, but in her eyes there was still a deep, watchful reserve. She was like a foreign country that I didn't have the right papers to enter.

"I need you to bring me Mr. Vine's clothes down from the attic." I looked at Hugo. "What kind of hat does Raj wear when he snowboards?"

"It's one of those hot dog showoff things with the bells at the tips, you could always hear him coming, like a medieval . . ." He searched for the right word. "Like a clown."

"With forked horns like a court jester's hat?"

"Yeah!" Hugo said. "Why?"

"I know this hat," Serafina said. "It is stored with Mr. Raj's winter clothes in the attic."

"Check if it's there, but leave it where it is," I instructed her.

After she left the room, I explained to Hugo the significance of the hat and how it had to remain where it was to preserve its integrity as future evidence. I needed him to know that we had caught a break with the camera, thanks to his father, but from now on nothing was going to be that easy. Without his mother's cooperation it would be almost impossible to approach the authorities in Tahoe about his father's death. Had an autopsy been performed on his father? Had any trace evidence been found at the murder scene? Or had the blizzard rendered it as blank of clues as a patch of ocean where a man has been drowned? Had a skilled forensic pathologist looked at the body, or was the matter handled by a local coroner? Half the coroners in America weren't even medical doctors but were undertakers. Hugo listened in silence to my gloomy recitation of all the problems we were up against and then headed for the door.

"Where are you going?" I asked.

"Jeez!" Hugo sighed. "Outside, *okay?*" He slammed the door, leaving me alone with Adolpho.

"What's that about?" I protested.

"Shhhh!" Without tearing his eyes away from the TV, Adolpho made a disapproving tsk-tsk sound. "You are Mr. Grumpy! You are Mr. Buzz-Kill!"

"Yeah, well . . ." I started to defend myself, but realized you cannot really defend yourself against the low opinion of a four-year-old.

I stepped out the door and watched Hugo. Keeping to the shadows where the flowerbeds met the walls, he moved cautiously around the lit-up courtyard, paused for a moment, and then strolled quickly across the grass and vanished up into his tree house. I gave him a few minutes to settle down before I followed the same route, climbed the ladder, and knocked on his door.

"It's open."

I let myself inside and at first I couldn't see anything in the darkness but the glow of Hugo's cigarette. He was standing by the window, peering out through an inch of open curtain at the bodyguards out front. They'd taken their suit jackets off, and stood with their arms draped around each other's shoulders, urinating against the side of the house.

"Are they, like, gay?" Hugo asked.

"I don't know. It's a cultural thing. They probably hold hands, too, but it doesn't necessarily mean what it does here."

"Why are they pissing on my house? I'd like to . . ." He stopped as they turned around, seeing for the first time the holsters with nickel-plated automatics stuck in their belts. The cigarette burned on, forgotten between his fingers.

"Do you really think Malahide went to your place tonight to kill you?" Hugo asked in a small voice.

"I doubt it," I lied.

"I don't know. All of these guns all of a sudden. Maybe this is, like, too much for us to fight against. Maybe we should just call the police and tell them what's going on. Oops, I forgot. The police are already here, in my house. Maybe, seriously, we should just forget about the whole stupid fucking thing and pretend like everything's normal. Isn't that what most people do? Just ignore stuff? Pretend everything's great when it really sucks ass?"

I tried to sound calm. "The first day I came out here Stone was with a Deputy D.A. called Hillary Flowers from the Sex Crimes Unit." I moved to another window that gave me a view of the library, but I couldn't spot Raj or Stone. On the floor above it, however, I could see Alvin Peck leaning dejectedly against a Stairmaster in the gym. He was turning his head to watch Sally as she paced back and forth in front of the window. "Flowers realized pretty quick that the child molestation complaint against me was bullshit," I said. "I could give her a call."

"What's *she* going to do?"

"You'd have to make a complaint. Say there're people with guns all over your house. Raj is beating up your mom. That'll get you out of here. If you want to speed it up, tell them Raj is trying to molest you."

Hugo considered my suggestion. "Could I stay at a hotel? I'd want to take Serafina and Adolpho with me."

"Like the Beverly Hills Hotel?"

"Shutters on the beach would be better." He frowned in concentration. "It's right next to the ocean. I could walk to school."

"They don't put your ass in a luxury hotel with your

housekeeper, Slim. You get placed in a foster home. Location unknown. Foster parents unknown. And then county employees start investigating the complaint at about the same speed they repair the roads."

"No thanks." He looked thoughtful. "Why couldn't I stay with you?"

"It has to be a relative," I said. "Don't you have any family?"

"Just my dad's brother, Uncle Miles. But he's like about a hundred years old and it's really hard to talk to him." Hugo smiled faintly. "His real name is Moishe, but he called himself Miles after Miles Davis."

"Where does he live?"

"He used to live here when I was a little kid. But he didn't get on with my mom. Now he's in some old folks home in Beverly Hills. My dad used to take me to see him when I was younger, but they always had these stupid fights."

"About what?"

"Just stuff. Miles was the older brother and it pissed him off that Pops had to take care of him."

"Would Miles help you?"

"I don't know!" Hugo was trying to spit on the end of his cigarette to put it out, but he kept missing in the dark. The smoldering filter was starting to stink.

"Once at the old folks home, when my dad left the room, Miles told me something. He said my mom had accused him of trying to, you know, get with her."

"Do you think it was true?"

"I doubt it. Miles couldn't stand her. He was always complaining and kind of making fun of how much money we had. He was nice to me. He took me to learn how to box at the Police Athletic League. I was the only white kid. It was kind of cool, but my mom freaked. She thought it was tacky. She wanted me to have a bodyguard like Prince William and Prince Andrew." Hugo put a finger down his throat to show what he thought of his mother's fantasy.

"When was the last time you saw Uncle Miles?"

"He came to the funeral in L.A. . . . they had to bring him in an ambulance from the old folks home. I never really got to talk to him because he got into a fight with my mom and Tea."

"About what?"

"Uncle Miles kept screaming, 'I'm in the will! Daniel called me! I'm supposed to be a guardian!' It was like so embarrassing. Finally these ambulance guys just picked him up in his wheelchair and took him away."

"Any idea what was in your dad's will?"

"No," Hugo said. "I don't even want to know."

"Why not?"

"I don't want anything from them." He was grimly vehement. "When I'm old enough I'm going to change my name. I'll make my own money, my own movies."

His response surprised me. Not his horror at the idea of profiting from his father's death, which was understandable, but his suddenly announced resolve to follow in his father's footsteps. It's always a shock when, under the apparent chaos of their lives, you realize kids have a plan, which they carry around like a concealed weapon.

"Where can I get in touch with Uncle Miles?"

"I don't remember the name of the old folks home, but I know where it is. Near Barney's. We used to stop at the restaurant on top to get lox and white fish to bring him. Once we visited him at the Veterans Hospital. He was having some operation on his leg."

"Uncle Miles was a vet?"

"Yeah, he was always talking about the crazy stuff he did fighting the Nazis. I asked him if he ever killed anyone. 'No,' he said, 'but I screwed so many German girls there's probably a Vinovksy bastard running the show in every town in Germany.' "

"Vinovsky?" I said.

"Yeah, Moishe Vinovsky. My dad changed his name to Vine."

The French windows to the library opened and Stone let himself out into the garden. He paused for a moment to listen to the wail of Middle Eastern pop music floating up from the guesthouse and then ambled across the lawn and passed through the gate. As the two bodyguards converged on him, Stone angrily raised his voice. The short one held out a warning hand and gripped his gun, while the other one punched numbers into a cell phone. After a moment, Raj stepped out of the library with his cell phone and turned around, trying to find decent reception. He barked something into his phone and, when we looked out the other window, we could see the bodyguards taking a step back from Stone. The detective shook his head in disgust and yelled at them as he made his way to his car. He pulled his Corvette up to the closed gate and leaned on his horn until they waved the remote to open it. He accelerated up the drive to the next gate, honking his horn over and over, taunting them. The gate came open and he sailed through it, still honking, rubbing it in, as if he was celebrating something.

"Do you think we should get the tape?" Hugo asked.

"Wait." I cracked the door a few inches and watched Raj in the garden as he punched out another number. He started talking in a lilting guttural language that I didn't understand, waving his arm, bending at the waist, pleading into the phone. "Any idea what's going on?" I asked Hugo.

"That's how he looks when he's talking to Firooz. Like he's going to cry."

"Why would Raj's Lebanese uncle want to invest in *Poison Me, My Lovely*?"

"It's not that bad a script. A lot of people wanted to make it."

"You've read it?"

He nodded, poker-faced. "My dad asked me to. He bought it with his own money from the writer. He paid her a million two in cash. It was a big deal. Practically no one ever does that. Pops hated producers whining about the studios. He said if you weren't willing to gamble your own money like the studios did, you ought to shut up and go suck on federal tit." He smiled. "I never knew what that meant, 'suck on federal tit,' but he said it a lot."

"It means work for the government, be a civil servant, low pay, but lots of security. Your dad sounds like he was a special guy. I wish I'd met him."

Raj ended the call and was punching in another set of numbers as he stepped back into the library. After a moment, I could see Alvin Peck in the gym, stepping away from the Stairmaster and putting his cell phone to his ear. The agent started shaking his head at what he was hearing from Raj. He responded furiously, jabbing the air with his finger, laying down the law, and then all at once he looked as if someone had spit in his face.

Hugo wasn't paying attention to any of this. He'd lit another cigarette and was pacing around, making the floorboards of the tree house shake.

"I know Raj is like good-looking and young and everything, but, man, I don't get it. He tries to act so hip and everything and it always just makes me cringe. In comparison to my father, I mean, how could she be with him?"

"You're asking the wrong guy, Hugo," I said. "If I knew anything about women, I wouldn't be up in a tree house on a Saturday night talking about them. I'd be home with a wife and kids of my own."

"You just didn't want to settle down." He nodded approvingly, wanting my bachelor existence to be voluntary, a hard-partying success story. "Kids are a pain in the butt. I'm never having them. And I'm never getting married. *Ever.*"

"You don't know what's going to happen," I said. "And what's worse, when you're as old as me you still won't know."

"I'm not planning on getting as old as you."

"What's that supposed to mean?"

"I'm not trying to freak you out or anything, but I don't really get it. You know, life. Like what's the point? Everybody's always talking about how important and meaningful everything is, but from where I am, I don't see it. I don't think I'd be missing out on that much."

"I thought you wanted to make movies."

"I just say that because I can't think of anything else."

"I bet there's something that'll make you happy. You just have to find it."

"I don't think so. The only time I was really happy was when I was a kid. My dad used to take me to the beach in Malibu. He didn't have those little plastic shovels and buckets. He wasn't into sand castles. He brought like a heavy-duty shovel and he'd dig this big-ass hole in the sand. I mean really deep, and we'd get inside it together and just sit there. People would walk by and look down at us and they'd always say, like, 'Wow, that's big enough to be a grave.' But we knew it wasn't a grave. It was just this totally cool place to be, hidden away from all the bullshit."

His voice was full of nostalgia. I felt him nudge me in the darkness and when I looked over I saw he was holding out his pack of Marlboros. I took one and stuck it between my lips. He lit his Zippo with a practiced flip of his wrist. In the light from the flames I was aware of his dark blue eyes concentrating on performing this adult act in the most casual manner possible. There was a faint tremor in his hand as he strained to hold the flame steady. This hunger to be an adult made Hugo look heartbreakingly young.

Out of the corner of my eye I noticed Alvin Peck leaving the gym. He appeared in one window after another as he trudged slowly along the second story hallway towards the stairs. He was a young athletic guy, with a dimpled chin and a handsome baby face. He wore a beautifully cut Armani suit, a snowy white shirt, a silk tie held in place by a gold collar pin. But it was as if something had aged the CAA agent by ten years. He kept stopping and staring at the ground, up at the ceiling, out the windows, but he wasn't taking anything in. He had the body language of an old man walking down a hospital corridor after being told whatever he had was inoperable.

"How long has that tape been running?" I asked Hugo.

"About an hour and a quarter. It'll turn itself off in about fifteen minutes."

"Where did you leave it in the room?"

"Behind a photograph of my dad above the fireplace. I figured that was something Raj wouldn't want to look at."

"Does it make a *click* when it turns off?"

"Shit. I forgot about that."

We studied the ground floor, but Alvin Peck didn't come out. He must have descended the stairs into the drawing room and entered the library from inside the house. He was in there now, talking to Raj.

"I could go in and get it," Hugo said. "I'll pretend the dog got loose again."

"That kind of stunt doesn't work twice." I checked on the bodyguards and was alarmed to see the tall one coming through the gate. He ran his eyes over the tree house and walked into the kitchen and turned on the lights. After a moment, he came out and headed around the back towards the production offices and Serafina's quarters. Was he doing a sweep of the perimeter, or did he have something else in mind?

"Give me your lighter and cigarettes," I said.

"Why?"

"Just give them to me. I want you to go back into the house and wait in the drawing room. I'm going to create a diversion. When Raj and Peck come out of the library, go in and grab the tape and meet me back in Serafina's room."

"What are *you* going to do?" He handed the Zippo and smokes over.

"I'm not sure yet. But after what's happened today, I don't know if your mom and Raj are going to want me driving you to school anymore. We need a safe place to meet. Don't stop giving spare change to those winos in the park by your school. If something goes wrong here, on Monday morning I'll be one of them."

"Okay," he said. "I know you think I never trust you and everything, but I just want to say . . ."

"Yeah?" I said encouragingly.

"I think this is a terrible idea. Why don't we just . . ."

"Go!" I turned him around and propelled him out the door.

The heavy-duty extension cord from the main house was stapled to the trunk of the tree and entered through a hole in the floor. It plugged into a power strip lying on the carpet behind a table next to the window. The TV and lights in Hugo's tree house all ran off it. I eased the extension cord plug half an inch out of its socket, exposing the live metal prongs. I searched through my pockets and amidst the small change found a paper clip. I waited until I was sure Hugo had taken up his position outside the library, and then angled the bottom of the curtains over the power strip. I dropped the paper clip on the exposed prongs. Sparks flared up and the white power strip went smoky black. I hadn't expected the short to set the curtains on fire, but later it might look that way to an arson investigator. I opened the door and window to get a draft going and lit the curtains with Hugo's Zippo. By the time I got down the ladder and across the lawn you could see the shadows from the flames dancing inside Hugo's tree house. The fire made a dry cracking noise as the smoke billowed behind the windows. A foul chemical smell of burning carpet and melting plastic drifted across the courtyard, but the direction of the wind was blowing it away from the cars parked in front. A window exploded out of its frame.

"Hakim?" the short bodyguard in front called out. "Hakim!"

I withdrew into the shadows and started edging around the side of the kitchen. The brass-studded door opened and the short bodyguard stepped into the courtyard. He saw the fire and started yelling at the top of his lungs. A second later Raj and Alvin Peck came out of the library and ran towards the tree house. Sally Vine poked her head out of an upstairs window and stared at the flames.

"What happened?" She sounded slurred and unfocussed.

"Call the fire department!" Raj yelled at her.

She vanished from the window and then suddenly reappeared. "Where's Hugo?" she asked in a faltering voice. "Is he in there? For God's sake! Is he in there? Where's Hugo?" She was screaming now.

"Chill, Mom. I'm right here." Hugo stepped out of the library and calmly looked up at her. I felt pride flare up inside me because I suddenly knew he had the tape. I could hear footsteps charging along the cement pathway behind the kitchen. I flattened myself against the wall as the other bodyguard came around the corner and blew past me. There was more shouting now, but it was coming from the other end of the courtyard. A man I took to be Uncle Firooz was coming up the steps from the swimming pool, yanking a flowing yellow silk robe around his body as he bellowed in a harsh despotic voice. His thinning gray hair was matted to his scalp, a pair of ugly black frame glasses on his face. He was puddled in heavy flesh and he waddled as he came forward, but still there was something unmistakably formidable about him. He shouted at the bodyguards, pointing at the garden hoses along the wall, slapping and kicking them like donkeys, as they rushed to turn on the taps and get some water on the fire. It was too little, too late. The flames from the tree house were spreading up into the crown of the tree and shooting up into the sky.

I heard footsteps racing along the cement path and caught Serafina just before she ran out into the courtyard. I clamped my hand over her mouth and dragged her kicking out of sight behind the kitchen. Her teeth bit down on my hand and I let go with a repressed scream.

"You!" she gasped. "What are you . . . *where is Hugo?*" She was in her bare feet and soft flannel pajamas.

"He's not in the tree house! He's fine!" Her teeth had pulped the soft inside of my two middle fingers with the force of pliers.

"What happened?" She struggled to look past me. "What have you done with Hugo?"

"I'm trying to help him for Christ's sake! He's going to meet us in your room."

She kept looking at the black smoke pumping into the sky and then back at me. It was still too much for her to comprehend. "Are you a crazy man? Why you set his tree house on fire?"

"Because I had to! You want to scream for help, go ahead. I'm going back to your room." I turned and ran. A second later I heard her bare feet slapping down the path after me.

Inside her room she locked the door and checked on Adolpho, who had fallen asleep in front of the TV. She got down on her knees and pulled a black garbage bag out from under the bed.

"In the attic I see Mr. Raj has a hat like you say, with horns and bells. And I bring you this." She handed me the bin liner. Inside it was a grocery bag stuffed full of Daniel Vine's ski clothes. They were stiff with blood and in tatters from having been cut off his body.

Someone tried the locked door and started banging on it. Serafina grabbed onto my arm in fright. "Who is it?" she whispered.

"It's Hugo," he said impatiently. "Open up."

She let go of my arm and hurried to let him inside.

"That seriously is an awesome fire, dude," he said, looking uncertainly at us. "They think I was smoking up there."

"I fixed it so the arson investigator is going to think something shorted out the power strip and set the curtains on fire. Deny you were ever in there tonight."

"Whatever you say." I could tell his adrenalin-charged

elation was starting to wear off.

"Well?" I demanded.

He reached into his pocket and handed me a black tape recorder the size of a pack of cigarettes. "I want to listen to it," he said. "You've got to tell me what it says."

"Right now you've got to go back and act like you're heartbroken about your goddamn tree house."

He suddenly noticed the blood dripping off the tips of my fingers. "Hey, did Genghis bite you?"

"*I* bit him." Serafina's face burned with embarrassment.

"Why?"

"It was an accident, okay?" She checked to make sure her pajama top was buttoned and started to roughly shoo him out. "Do what Thomas says. Go back to the house."

Hugo stared at us with a look of growing hurt and suspicion on his face. He started to protest and then thought better of it and slammed the door behind him.

"Can you believe that?" I said. "He's jealous because you bit me."

Serafina pulled me into the bathroom and found some Polysporin and smoothed it over the lacerated flesh of my hand. I tried not to dwell on the fact she was naked under the flannel pajamas, or the memory of what her body had felt like when I'd grabbed her. Her pajamas were patterned in tiny cowboys tossing lariats and I tried to distract myself by seeing if they all looked alike. They did. I wanted to say something conciliatory, maybe even amusing, something to bridge the tense silence that always seemed to separate us. But it was as if I'd forgotten how to talk to women.

"If you were a dog, I'd have to get a rabies shot." It was the best I could come up with.

"I didn't know who you were," she said.

"You know who I am now and you still look like you want to bite me."

"Hold still!" She slapped my wrist.

"That felt pretty good," I said. "Definitely better than the bite."

"Stop talking so much."

"Hit me again," I said. "I like it when you're affectionate."

"You have to go now," she said. "One of those bodyguards came to ask me to make them food. Afterwards, when I'm putting my clothes on, he tried to watch me through the window. He could come back."

I followed her back inside the room. We could hear sirens now as the fire engines from the Benedict Canyon substation labored up the hill. I gathered the bag and my flashlight while she turned off the lights and went to check the coast was clear.

"Go now." She squeezed my good hand with both of hers. "Please be careful, Thomas."

Sparks from the burning sycamore tree were shooting into the sky like tracer rounds. The blaze cast a flickering radiance over her face. She stared up at me and was on the verge of saying something more when one of the burning branches separated from the tree with a pistol-like *crack*. She pressed herself against me in fright and I held her to my chest. I don't know how long we clung to each other like that, but it felt like a long time before she pushed me towards the safety of the chaparral.

By the time I'd hiked through the brush and climbed back over the Vines' wall, the black smoke from the fire had already changed into a steamy yellowish haze. A collection of fire engines and police cruisers were pulled up in front of the house. As I made my way back down to my car, neighbors were streaming up the hill in their dressing gowns to get a look. A fine mist of ash was falling like dirty gray snow on their curious upturned faces and no one paid me the slightest attention.

Chapter Sixteen

Two Secret Service men were talking into walkie-talkies in front of the ex-President's residence as I drove down the hill. A fire with police cruisers and fire engines racing to the scene was probably the highlight of their year. They were so engrossed in determining what level of threat was posed by the smoke overhead they never noticed me go by. I dialed Ken O'Doul's number but it wasn't until I reached Sunset that the reception improved enough for me to get through.

This time he answered the phone himself. In the background I could hear his wife's voice rising to a shriek as she catalogued all the things wrong with Ken. It was not a particularly original list of defects, but then the collapse of a marriage always seems to follow a more predictable script than the strange elusive forces that make people decide they want to spend the rest of their lives together.

"It's Thomas," I said. "This a bad time to call?"

"Nah. Suki and I were just going over our pre-nuptial agreement." He sounded extremely relaxed, which with Ken, I remembered, was always a danger signal. "I must have been on medication when I signed this thing, honey."

I could hear his wife telling him how he had drained and destroyed her and no matter what the size of the divorce settlement, nothing would make her whole again. Those were not her exact words; she sounded more like she was in a knife fight in an alley, but that's how it would come out when her divorce lawyer explained it in court.

"Give me a second." Ken put me on hold and came back

on the line five minutes later. "Okay. I think she's hotel for the night. You know, maybe you should out for me. I've only been married to her for eighteen months and I think she's been fucking her ex-boyfriend the whole time. For all I know *he's* the one who's making her so miserable."

"Get one of your hotshot investigators to do it, Ken." I told him about Uncle Miles and the ski clothes and setting the fire and the tape.

"You did all that since we talked?" I could hear him scooping ice out of the fridge for another drink. "I don't think that kid's paying you enough."

"You interested in listening to the tape, or would you rather call it a night and let that Wild Turkey peck out what's left of your liver?"

"It was a joke," he said. "Bring the tape over. I'll put on some coffee."

I followed Sunset almost to its juncture with the Pacific Coast Highway and then took the road up into the Palisades Highlands. Ken's new house was in one of those gated, planned communities that appear like scars in the mountainous wilderness of live oak, sumac, and coyote bush overlooking the ocean. To provide a patina of instant tradition the streets are coyly named after French Impressionists and Italian Renaissance painters. The relentlessly identical mansionettes have an air of chirpy unreality that suggests Disneyland and the Universal Tour more than a flesh-and-blood neighborhood. There is nothing *unreal* about these communities, of course, for they are the growing reality of Southern California. Unlike theme parks, which are at least full of dazed, obese consumers, these are essentially devoid of human beings. They offer privacy, security, and convenience, and they are as legal as inflatable sex dolls. A security guard noted my license plate number and the time of my arrival, checked with Ken that I was expected, and waved me though.

Ken was standing in the open door, backlit by the domed cathedral-like foyer of his new mansion when I pulled into his circular drive. He'd gained a lot of weight since I'd last seen him and adopted some bizarre new strategies to hide the fact. His puffy face was now largely hidden by a dyed reddish beard; his thinning silver hair was combed forward like Napoleon, and he was wearing a warm-up suit several sizes too large that failed in its purpose of hiding his swollen figure. He had sad, hooded brown eyes that were always covertly assessing you, trying to discern what you were thinking, while hiding their own intent. If you met his gaze directly he quickly looked away. Most people just thought he was shifty, but over the years I'd come to realize he suffered from a debilitating shyness. Hidden inside the fat and reflexively cynical lawyer was a touchy, over-sensitive person whose real worry was that nobody in the world liked him.

"This is one ugly-ass house," I said.

"Always the charmer, Thomas." He mournfully embraced me, turning his head aside to spare me his bourbon breath. "But you're right. I wasn't sure if this marriage with Suki was going to work out so I figured, why sink a lot into a great house if my wife's going to end up with it anyway?"

"That's why you bought this place?"

"Well." He chuckled. "The security gate also makes it hard for people to serve me with subpoenas."

I followed him through the foyer into a tiled living room sparsely decorated with white leather couches and glass and chrome coffee tables. The only personal touches were the giant black-and-white framed photos of Ken's collection of cars and airplanes on the walls. The thirty-foot-high ceiling gave the room the chilling acoustics of an airport hotel lobby. I placed the tape recorder on a table, hit the rewind button, and sank into one of the couches.

"Drink?" He smiled. "I seem to remember you're a single malt guy."

"No thanks."

"Come on. Have a drink."

"I quit a while ago. Couldn't stand the hangovers." I tried to be as casual as possible about it, but I knew Ken would find my sobriety threatening. We had been very close in the old days and any change in me had to be weighed up to see if it somehow diminished him

"Then I won't drink either." He kept smiling, looking for clues of what abstinence might have done to me. "You look good, Thomas. I tried to go to AA once. I couldn't handle that one day at a time thing, and all those reformed drunks. It was so competitive. I like to think of myself as more like Winston Churchill. The guy was drunk the whole of World War Two. But he said he took a lot more strength from alcohol than alcohol ever took out of him. You're not doing yoga, too, are you? Eating bran? Meditating?"

"Just not drinking, Ken."

"I just never thought you'd be the one to pussy out like that. Go all politically correct. What happened to your *inner demons?* All that stuff that made you interesting and dangerous?"

"I'm scaring you more right now, cold sober, than I ever did when I was drinking."

"Yes, you are. I've missed you, Thomas. Sure you won't have a little one?" His eyes shone with affectionate mockery. "I promise not to tell."

The tape reached the end of the reel and clicked off.

"My client's only fourteen, Ken. He had the balls to plant this tape recorder in a room under the nose of an L.A.P.D. cop and a guy who may have killed his father." I hit the play button. At first all we could hear was the dog barking, while Stone and Raj yelled at Hugo to get it out of there.

Stone's ingratiating voice came out of the tinny speaker, so close it was as if he was in the room with us. *"I never realized what a photogenic guy you were, Raj . . ."*

"I'm kind of busy, Cedrick, a lot going on with the movie, you know, so if you could just let me have the camera back . . ."

"Oh sure, no problem. There's just one picture of you and Malahide that I thought I might keep as a memento. Maybe you could sign it for me. You know, 'To my good pal, Detective Stone of the L.A.P.D., Your famous friend, Raj.' I can put it on my office wall at the station house. You know, like those autographed glossies of celebrities you see in the Korean dry cleaners. 'Thanks for doing such a good job cleaning the skid marks out of my underwear. Love and Kisses, Kevin Costner.' "

"Is there something bothering you?" Raj said.

"Oh, and there's a snap of Daniel Vine I kind of like, too. He doesn't look that good, but it's probably hard to say 'cheese' when you're bleeding to death. I guess in that blizzard you and Malahide couldn't hear the old guy calling to you for help."

In the silence you could hear the tape running.

"I have no, absolutely no idea what you are talking about." Raj sounded like he had a dry cracker stuck in his throat.

"You sure? What about this? You know what this is?" On the tape you could hear the policeman unzipping his pants. *"This is what I'm going to be using to fuck you from now on."*

Raj's voice was squeaky with horror. *"What . . . what are you doing? Are you a crazy man? Put it away."*

"What's the matter? You've never seen a dick before, you

dumb Arab cooze?" Stone wheezed with laughter.

"I'm not an Arab. I'm French."

"You're a fucking towel-head camel jockey piece of shit."

"Would you please keep your voice down and put that thing away?"

"Oh sure, Raj, no problem." Stone zipped himself back up, his tone cloying and hateful. *"What are you going to do now? Offer me some Laker tickets? Tell me I can use the tennis court, but you don't want me going in the jacuzzi?"*

"I've never meant to offend you, Cedrick, I swear it. We are friends."

"Not friends, babe. We're much more than that now. We're partners."

"Of course we are."

"Do you know what I mean by 'partners'?"

"Yes. I think . . . I think we have to do something more for you. A lot more. When you're off duty, you should be our permanent head of security. V.I.P. needs one. We could work out profit sharing for you, a pension and health plan, a great car, your own staff, you could travel with us on location, London, Venice, you could bring your wife along. Or leave her at home? Take a little hottie intern with you as your personal assistant. I can tell you're a guy who likes women."

"I don't need a pimp like you to get me laid."

"Fine," Raj almost yelped. *"I'm just telling you all the things I want to do for you."*

"I'm not interested in being your rent-a-cop."

"No problem. We'll find something else for you. What would you like?"

"I want to be involved."

"That's good. I want you to be involved. What do you want to be involved in?"

"The movie." The policeman tried to say it casually, but

his voice sounded husky, almost ashamed.

"The movie? What do you mean?"

"Poison Me, My Lovely! *You know what I'm talking about."*

"Not really, Cedrick. Tell me, tell me what you want." Raj was like a hooker trying to coax a nervous john into revealing a shameful sex fantasy. *"Do you want to be in the movie? I could do that. No problem. We could put you in some scenes. Maybe even get you a close-up."*

"I'm not interested in being some fucking extra!"

"There's just no speaking parts that you'd be right for. But maybe I could get the writer to create one for you. Why not? You're a fantastic looking guy."

"Save that blowjob for someone else. I'm not interested in being some fag actor."

"What about technical advisor? I could probably hide that in the budget."

"Let me ask you a question. Were you born a producer? Is it like being born royalty? Or maybe you've got some kind of degree *in producing? You go to some higher institute and take courses in eating lunch and lying and cheating and stealing?"*

"*I don't understand what you're saying."*

"See this gun? I'm trained and qualified to use it. When I go to the range, there's a little white paper target that tells me exactly how many times I hit the bull's eye and how many times I miss. Same with my gold detective's badge here. You don't get one unless you prove to the satisfaction of the authorities that you know how to make cases against scumbags. You say you're a producer, but I don't buy it. You're just like some street whore who decided one day to announce she's got a Master's Degree in sucking dick. You're no more a producer than I am."

"Wait a minute," Raj gasped. *"You have to know people. It's about relationships."*

"I know you. We *have a relationship."*

"It's a little more complicated than that. You have to be able to get people to . . . do things . . . persuade them . . . things they maybe don't even want to do."

"I get people to do things. You're doing something you don't want to right now. I see film credits all the time. It says 'Produced By' and there's a whole list of fucking names. I want to be one of those names."

"Come on, man, be serious!"

"I showed you my cock and I showed you my gun. How much more serious do you want me to get?"

"The business just doesn't work that way." There was the sound of a scuffle and then Raj shrieked in pain. *"Stop! No! No! Please! Don't do that! I beg of you!"*

"What?" Stone whispered. *"What doesn't work that way?"*

"Please . . . I'll do whatever you say. I swear. Please, let go of me."

Ken caught my eye and shook his head in amazement.

"There's something you have to learn about me, Raj," the policeman grunted. *"I didn't get to where I am by* asking *for shit. I got here by* taking *shit. I'm going to do fine in this business. Here. Have some Pellegrino."*

On the tape you could hear Raj slurping water, and coughing as it went down the wrong way.

"Relax, pal." Stone's manner was warm now, almost collegial. *"It's all over. It's going to be fun now, you'll see."*

"You don't have any idea of what you're getting into. This fucking movie is a nightmare."

"You had a problem with that prick detective. I ran him off. What else are you worried about?"

"I had to sign the director to a play or pay deal, or he was going to take another project. Now I have to pay him three mil-

lion dollars whether we make the movie or not. My uncle loaned me the money and now he wants it back."

"Tell him he's going to have to wait."

"You don't tell Uncle Firooz that," Raj said glumly. *"Do you believe there's an afterlife? Mess with my uncle and you'll find out."*

"What's he going to do, sic those two towel-heads on me?"

"Do you have to be so racist?" Raj flared. *"This is why I'm having so many difficulties. I had Sally Vine as my star! I had a wonderful script! I had an A-list director! And not one studio would do business with me because they're Jews and I'm Lebanese."*

"I don't think that's it."

"Of course it is. Look at the way you talk to me. You're prejudiced just like them."

"Stop your fucking whining. This is Hollywood and the last time I looked, Hollywood is in the good old U S of A. You just got to show people in this town you know how to make money and they won't care if you have hair on your forehead and eat your own young."

"That's easy for you to say. Now I have to beg these piece-of-shit European investors for money, and my wife says she doesn't even know if she's right for the part. Everybody resents me because I married Sally Vine. They think I slept my way to the top. Believe me, Cedrick, my life is not any walk in the park."

"Nobody gives a shit about that either. Your problem is you can't control your wife, my friend."

"My financiers won't release the money to make the movie until she signs her contract," Raj wailed. *"Alvin Peck won't lift a finger to help me. He's upstairs now telling her not to do it."*

"Alvin Peck?" Stone asked.

"He's this reptile from CAA. I told him he could package the whole project with their clients. I offered him things under the

table. I can't get anywhere with him. He's got mineral water in his veins."

"I know who Alvin Peck is," Stone said.

"You knowing who he is does not help," Raj snapped. *"Everybody knows who he is."*

"Don't get snotty with me, Raj."

"I'm sorry. I'm just incredibly stressed. No offense to you, but what I really need here is a really strong producer who could apply some major pressure on CAA."

"You mean a guy like Daniel Vine?" The policeman chuckled derisively.

"Okay, you think that's funny. I think it's in poor taste, you know."

"Fuck taste, Raj. It's not about taste. It's about getting the movie made. And that happens to be something I can help you with."

"What are you going to do, expose yourself?" Raj snarled.

"That private detective? When I scared him off, I not only took the camera off him, I grabbed the computer from his car."

"Yes, and Firooz's guys got the other ones. I know all this."

"Would you shut the fuck up and let me finish? That first day he came over here he said he had someone under surveillance, but he wouldn't tell me who it was. It was Alvin Peck. I found pictures in Kyd's hard drive of Peck smoking crack with an Asian street hustler."

"*Alvin smokes* crack?"

"Yes, he does. And he smokes underage pole, too. Tell him if he doesn't get Sally to do this movie, first thing Monday morning everybody who's anybody in this town is going to open their E-mail and find an attachment with pictures of him on the pipe."

"I love this," Raj gasped. *"Cedrick . . . my man! This is so fucking outstanding!"*

I heard a sharp *smack* on the tape, which I presumed was the sound of Raj and the policeman high-fiving each other. They continued to laugh, their voices fading as Raj showed Stone out of the library. The voice-activated tape continued to run for a moment before shutting off.

"I love that cop," Ken said drolly. "If we don't do something about him, he's going to be running a studio."

I carefully lifted out Vine's ski suit from the grocery bag and spread it out on the glass coffee table. I placed the socks at the bottom and the hat, throat protector, and goggles at the head.

"What the hell is that?" Ken asked.

"The clothes Vine was wearing when he died."

"How the hell did you get them?"

"The Tahoe police returned them to the family. Their housekeeper gave them to me." I started going through the pockets.

"You're wasting your time. Once the cops returned the clothes it broke the chain of evidence. You could find a signed note in there from Raj saying he killed Vine and a D.A. is going to yawn in your face. A cop who wants to be a film producer fighting over credit with Raj is very funny, but it isn't going to play in court either. They could be threatening to poison the Hollywood Reservoir and a judge is still going to say you didn't have the right to record their conversation."

We stopped talking as the tape was activated by a knock at the library door.

"Come in," Raj said.

"I think you're making a terrible mistake." Alvin Peck spoke in a trembling voice. *"You can temporarily hurt my standing in the community, but I'm not the first person in this town to have a problem with drugs and drinking. It only shows*

I'm human. You can out me, but frankly, anybody who matters already knows or suspects I'm gay. You can't even wreck my marriage because my wife has already seen those pictures. I don't really see what you'll accomplish by going public, except to cast yourself in the unflattering light of being a vindictive homophobe. When it comes out that I'm suffering this persecution because of my loyalty to a client, well, it's going to make me look even better. I'm not going to lose clients. I'm going to gain them. I'll come out of this stronger as an agent and a person."

Raj let the agent's plaintive hopeful spin hang in the air for a moment. *"I've always liked you, Alvin."*

"Then why can't you just . . . ?"

"But nobody else does. Everybody is scared of you. Smoking crack for a person in your position is like getting caught having sex with animals. It makes you look dirty and desperate. People are going to laugh and enjoy your humiliation. The boy in the photos is underage. And that is going to destroy you forever."

"I can't believe you would . . . Jesus . . . what do you want from me?"

"Get Sally to sign her contract and have your agency start treating me with the same respect it gave Daniel Vine."

"But what reason do I give Sally for suddenly changing my mind?"

"Do I have to teach you how to do your job? Tell her Julia Roberts loves the script and wants to do it."

Their conversation was interrupted by the shouts of Uncle Firooz's bodyguard outside discovering the fire in the tree house. A moment later you could hear Hugo rushing into the library and grabbing the tape and then it turned off. I waited for Ken to say something, but he just stared at some point slightly to the left of me, and then he grunted peacefully and closed his eyes.

"Am I putting you to sleep?"

"I'm thinking." He rubbed his eyes and got to his feet. He walked over and removed a blown-up photo of an early model Porsche from the wall, revealing a recessed safe. He twisted the dial until it chimed like a microwave and the door came open. He collected the evidence from the coffee table and stuffed it inside the safe and then withdrew a plain brown manila envelope and counted out some packets of crisp banknotes. He shut the safe and handed me the banknotes.

"Ten thousand ought to be enough to get you started."

"I don't need nearly that much."

"This is my moment to be generous, not your moment to show how honest you are."

"I appreciate it," I said. "So? What do you think of the case?"

"The truth? It's going to be almost impossible to prove they killed Daniel Vine."

"Why?"

"Too much time's gone by. All your evidence is illegally obtained. You can't really investigate anything without the mother's permission, and she won't give it to you because she's a prime suspect. But I like it. It's a great story."

"Who gives a fuck what kind of *story* it is? They whacked the kid's father!"

"The kid part is okay. Lotta sympathy there. Could be a little problem with the kid trying to convict his own mother. Putting your own mom in the electric chair is kind of un-American, but maybe she did terrible stuff to him."

"What the hell are you talking about?

"I'm trying to see how this could play down the road. It could be a book, a mini-series, maybe even a movie if we structure it right."

"Stop it, Ken!"

"You were right about not taking it to the tabloids. This should be packaged in a much classier way."

"I want to protect this kid, not exploit him. Do you understand?"

"You're attached to him. That's good. It makes it a better story."

"I'm not *attached* to him!" I stormed to my feet. "The kid is already a mess. The last thing he needs is someone trying to make a mini-series out of his life."

"There is no way a murder case involving celebrities won't generate publicity. People are going to write about it whether you cooperate with them or not. All I'm trying to do is think ahead so we can control it a bit. Would you please sit down and stop looking like you want to strangle me?"

I sat down, but I couldn't do anything about my face.

"Right now in the eyes of the law you're just a disgruntled employee. You've got two illegally obtained tape recordings, some ambiguous photos from a camera you stole, plus some ski clothes you lifted while you were committing arson. This isn't going to get anyone thrown in jail except you."

"I'm just getting started. I'm going to track down the kid's uncle tomorrow."

"I just don't want you to have any illusions about what you're up against."

"I know. I appreciate your help."

"There's something else you should consider." He studied me with his sad hooded eyes. "If by some miracle you end up proving the kid's mother helped whack his dad, chances are he's going to hate your guts."

"He says he wants to know the truth."

"He may not be the same person when he finds out what

the truth is. Just don't expect gratitude at the end of this, Thomas."

"I don't expect anything."

"Really? Your whole face lights up when you talk about this kid." He watched me with amused suspicion. "What's his name again?"

"Hugo."

"Hugo?" He snorted dismissively. "What did they give him a fucked up name like that for, anyway?"

"What's wrong with *Hugo?* It's a great name. *Ken* is a fucked up name. It makes you think of *Ken and Barbie,* or *Ken fucking Starr.* And *O'Doul?* That's the name of some piss-poor, non-alcoholic beer from Canada. You're the one with the lame-ass name."

"Jesus, it's worse than I thought." He chuckled at the reaction he'd provoked.

"What?"

"You're obsessed with this fourteen-year-old kid and you don't even know it."

I felt the blood suddenly leave my face and simultaneously an image of that other boy whimpering in the tunnel filled my mind. For a second my stomach heaved at the pornographic violence of the memory. When I spoke, my voice sounded so thin and dazed I barely recognized it. "I don't like what these people are doing to him, Ken. That's all."

"Are you okay?" He stared at me. "You look terrible."

I muttered something about it having been a long day and got out of there before he could ask me any more questions.

Chapter Seventeen

I headed back to Santa Monica along the Pacific Coast Highway. It was after one in the morning, the traffic thinned out, people driving with that stolid caution that's meant to fool the Highway Patrol into thinking they're sober. The fog had retreated back a few hundred yards out over the water where it lay massed in an immense gray wall like a battleship towering over the coastline. A new BMW convertible full of laughing kids screamed past, weaving wildly in and out of the slow-moving traffic. The driver had one hand on the wheel and the other on a cell phone, his young face alive with an expression of dazed, intense happiness. I watched him as he took the curves up ahead, doing eighty in a forty-mile-per-hour zone, in a rush to get to the next party, or a date with death. His parents had bought him a sixty-thousand-dollar car and he was feeling the immortality that rises like sap on a Saturday night. I had a loaded .38 in my pocket and ten thousand in cash, but I didn't feel immortal. I felt scared. I kept to the speed limit and wondered if Malahide was out looking for me tonight with that hi-tech Glock jammed in his waistband.

When I got home I drove past my house several times looking for the black Range Rover he'd been driving, but there was no sign of it. My broken front door yawned open and when I stepped inside and turned on the lights I knew nobody was there. The place was still a mess, but I couldn't face cleaning it up. I pulled the piss-stained bedding and mattress out of the alcove and tossed them out front. Then

I cleared a space on the floor among the shattered remains of my record collection, wrapped myself in a sleeping bag and fell into a deep sleep.

"Hey, wake up!"

I opened my eyes and blinked at the sunlight pouring into the room. Hugo stood in the doorway peering curiously down at me.

"Why are you sleeping on the floor?" He slid some records out of the way with his foot and stepped inside. He smiled at the mess, somewhat alarmed. "Don't you ever, like, clean your room?"

"I clean it. Sometimes other people kick in the door and trash it."

"Oh right. I forgot." He glanced at the empty sleeping alcove. "Why'd you throw your mattress and stuff out?"

"They pissed on it, okay?" I threw off the sleeping bag and got to my feet. I was sore and stiff and it annoyed me that he'd caught me in such a defeated, squalid position.

"Gross." He made a face. "What did you do with my cigarettes? You never gave them back to me."

"I'm going to take a shower, Hugo." I jerked my thumb at the galley. "There's coffee, there's eggs, there's bread. Why don't you make us some breakfast?"

He looked at me like I'd asked him to fly to Mars. Before he could respond, I went into the bathroom and shut the door. I stripped out of the clothes I'd slept in and stepped into the shower. The water pressure was weak and half the showerhead holes didn't work, but the water was steaming hot and I took time to enjoy it. In the past I was almost always hung-over, or still bombed from the night before, when I took a shower. There had been periods in my life when washing myself in the morning was the only act of my day that I could be even marginally proud of. Now I relished the sensation of the water cleansing my skin and allowed myself to imagine a day when I might feel the same way *inside,* the dread and rage locked in my chest also washed away, but I had a feeling you only got that when you were dead. For now, it was enough that my moods weren't coming out of a bottle. I dressed in clean clothes and joined Hugo in the galley. He'd put fresh-roasted coffee into a cup and added hot water from the tap and swirled it around as if it was *instant.* Some of the undissolved coffee grains still floated on the surface. He'd fried two eggs without butter and scraped them on to some slightly charred-looking toast.

"I don't know how to do breakfast. If you don't want to eat it, it's okay."

"It looks fine." I ate the food as if it was edible and washed it down with the disastrously prepared coffee. "Anybody know you're here?"

"I just got up early and took off," Hugo shrugged.

"You *walked* all the way from Bel-Air? I'm impressed."

"I took a taxi." He stuck his hands in his pockets and looked out the window, scowling. "I wish you'd told me you were going to, like, burn my tree house down. If I'd known, I could have got my stuff out first."

"It would have looked a little funny if you'd just happened to get your wide screen TV and sound system and video game collection out ahead of time."

"Whatever."

"At the time it seemed more important to get hold of that tape so we could find out what Raj was talking about, don't you think?"

"I guess."

It struck me as odd that last night he'd been desperate to

listen to the tape, but this morning he hadn't even mentioned its contents. Instead he was complaining about me taking his cigarettes and grousing about the loss of his fancy tree house. "I'm sorry I had to burn it down, kid. But I had to hear what was on that tape."

"I don't care about my video games! You can burn the whole house down for all I care." He kicked impatiently at the galley wall. "Are we going to visit Uncle Miles like you said or not?"

"Something bothering you?"

"Nothing's bothering me! Can we go?"

"Why are you so upset?"

"Stop bugging me!" His eyes had a wild look. "You want to know what I'm pissed about? You think I'm some spoiled brat whining about my PlayStation and X-box? I don't even want them! Adolpho can have them! I don't want any of it!" He was shrieking now, but there was something not quite right about it. His arms flailed out and his head twisted back as if he was yelling at God. It reminded me of the first time he'd lost his temper, that night he walked into my office, and because I'd seen the real thing I knew this was a performance.

"I had . . ." He was panting now, staring fixedly at me. "I had some photos of my dad in the tree house, okay? Stuff I can never replace. Wouldn't you be upset?"

I hadn't realized what a skilled actor he was when he needed to be. He was really good, I thought, as good as his mother. He knew how to use the real stuff, the emotional pain to sell what was merely invented. It was why Dante had reserved a special place in hell for actors. I didn't believe there had been any photos of his father in the tree house last night, but something else was poisoning him with anxiety. I'd just have to wait until it worked its way to the surface, like a splinter buried under the skin.

We drove in silence along San Vicente, past the red blossomed coral trees that run in an unbroken chain for miles along the grassy median strip to Brentwood. It was the first really hot, bright day we'd had in weeks and because it was a Sunday there were more joggers and cyclists out than cars. When we got to Beverly Hills, Hugo finally broke his silence and directed me to park in the underground garage at Barney's. We took the elevator to the top floor where there's a sort of designer delicatessen that makes a religion out of high-priced smoked fish. The place was packed with prosperous looking married people taking their kids and elderly grandparents out for brunch.

Hugo took a ticket and we waited in line at the counter. There is so much plastic surgery in Beverly Hills that it's almost like visiting another planet. The faces have been tautened, the noses shaved, the eyes permanently stretched open, as if they've seen something from which they can never recover.

"So what did the tape say?" Hugo muttered. Apparently we were going to have the conversation he'd avoided at my house in the take-out line at the deli.

"My lawyer friend says the tape's illegal and we can't use it in court."

"That is so typical," he said, but without his customary indignation. It was almost as if he was relieved.

"But we do think Raj and Malahide conspired to kill your father."

"You *think?*"

"Okay. We're sure of it."

Now that he knew what he'd been trying to find out, he appeared dejected. His eyes wandered around the noisy room, avoiding mine. "Are you going to tell my mom?" he finally asked.

"I don't know what I should do. I'm not saying she was involved, but . . ."

"I know. I know." He hissed in impatience, as if we'd been discussing the subject in detail for days and it made him sick to keep going over it.

"Look," I said. "Do you think it's *possible?*"

"How would I know? *I don't know.*"

But not knowing was a way of saying *yes*. It was possible and he knew it, and at the same time I could sense everything inside him recoiling from the terrible weight of what it would mean. He turned away with relief as the counterman called out his number.

A man in his eighties stood doddering in line behind us. His pencil-thin legs were encased in black leather pants tucked into some Prada version of motorcycle boots. An exquisitely soft black leather jacket with epaulettes like the one Brando wore in *The Wild One* was tossed casually over his sparrow shoulders. His complexion had the faded translucence of a discarded snakeskin. He watched as Hugo ordered a plate of sturgeon, whitefish, and lox, an assortment of bagels, and a six-pack of Dr. Brown's black cherry soda.

"Your son?" He indicated Hugo.

"No," I said.

"A nice looking boy." The effort of speaking had caused his tiny chest to puff in and out like a bellows. "Emphysema." He rapped his knuckles against his chest. "Don't let him smoke."

"Good advice."

"The apple didn't fall far from the tree. He looks just like you." His rheumy eyes shone with tears as he gazed fondly at us. He hadn't heard me deny Hugo was my son, or had heard and just didn't care. He wanted this sentimental father-son picture to be true and in his mind it was.

Hugo grimaced in embarrassment as the man reached out and ran his trembling hand across his spiky waxed blond hair.

"It feels like little needles," he said. "Electric . . ."

"Jesus Christ, Percy!" A man marginally younger but similarly dressed grabbed the old boy by the arm, pulled him towards the exit. "You said you were going to the bathroom!"

"I have a place in line," Percy protested. "I'm getting us food."

"We've already eaten, you putz!"

Hugo gazed after them and rolled his eyes at me. "You think that was bad," he said. "Uncle Miles is worse. Uncle Miles is, like, the most embarrassing person in the world."

After searching for Uncle Miles' retirement facility up and down the streets north of Wilshire, Hugo finally pointed out an anonymous-looking beige building off Burton Way. A sign on the lawn in front identified it as *Mansion Park-Towers*, though its stucco façade and metal-framed windows didn't resemble a mansion and there was no tower or park in evidence. We took a doctor's parking spot in the underground garage and Hugo led me up the emergency stairs to a landing where an elderly female patient in a green hospital gown was propped on a walker smoking her head off. She screeched in delight at the sight of Hugo and made a grab for him, but he ducked past her. We came out into a deserted lobby, its walls incongruously decorated with the artwork of kindergarten children. A receptionist glanced at us without interest as we walked to the elevator. We went up to the third floor and followed a corridor past an empty nurse's station and a row of wizened patients in wheelchairs who had the same involuntary reaction of delight at the sight of Hugo. They chirped and shrieked, pawing at him with claw-like hands as he rushed by. In their world of ruined bodies and stroked-out brains, the sight of a fine looking boy was like the appearance of a god. Every inch of the facility was hygienically spotless and brightly lit. The air smelled like every effort had been made to keep it clean and inoffensive, but it was still awful. It carried the taint of what finally cannot be denied about the human body. Hugo paused outside a closed door and handed me the bag of food.

"You give it to him." He sighed. "He likes to eat."

Hugo knocked and we entered the room. Miles Vinovsky was propped up in bed asleep, his mouth open but caved-in looking without the teeth that rested on his bedside table beside some pill bottles and an unemptied plastic urine container. His fierce bird-like face was decorated with a dour Zapata moustache, and a little soul patch. Despite his great age, he had lank, very fine black hair that hung down over his brow in boyish-looking bangs. The TV bolted into the wall opposite his bed had the sound turned off. On the screen a powerful looking man with a bit in his mouth was dragging an airplane along a runway like a horse just for the hell of it, or because someone had said it wasn't humanly possible. We stood for a moment looking down at Uncle Miles and I noticed the other bedside table was piled high with books: Le Carre, George Higgins, Evelyn Waugh, a biography of Hitler. On the window ledge there were more books, some jazz tapes, and a gag photo of Hugo appearing on the cover of *Time* as Man of the Year. It looked like it had been taken when he was about ten.

I turned on my tape recorder and nodded to Hugo that I was ready.

Hugo laid his hand on Uncle Miles' chest and tentatively shook him. Uncle Miles opened his eyes, smiled at Hugo with such pleasure it was almost agonizing, clamped the boy's hand to his chest so he couldn't escape, and at the same time with his other hand found his teeth on the bedside table and got them smoothly into his mouth. It was as seamless as good card trick.

"Where have you been?" Miles shouted. "They changed the phone numbers at your house. That fucking lawyer whore bitch Tea gave me wrong numbers so I couldn't call! I knew you'd come to see me. I had a feeling all day. I think about you so much I might as well be praying!"

The old man dragged Hugo's head down onto his chest in a headlock, squeezing and kissing him in a paroxysm of joy. In between he measured me with the same wised-up heavy-lidded eyes that I remembered from the picture of Hugo's father. Miles was an older, bitterer version of his brother; the moustache and soul patch giving him a Jewish hipster look from another era.

"I brought you some fish." I held up the bag.

"You're a *fisherman?*" he scoffed.

"He's a private detective." Hugo finally managed to wrench himself free of the old man's grasp. "He's trying to find out what really happened to Dad."

"What happened to your father, and I say this with all respect and affection because I always loved him, not that he ever gave me credit for that, not him, not *Mr. I've Got Two Oscars* and everybody can kiss my ass because I've changed my name and married some psycho *shiksa* movie star, is something you'll never understand, kid."

"Don't start," Hugo pleaded. "I've heard this all before."

"Yeah, well certain things are worth saying more than once. They had a lot of balls throwing me out of my own brother's funeral. That was unforgivable. And I'm never going to get over it. I just want you to know that." He glared at me as if I'd missed an important cue. "Are we going to eat or just look at the bag?"

"Your brother was murdered, Mr. Vinovsky," I said.

"Says who?" He fumbled for his pills.

"At his funeral you claimed to have been unfairly cut out of the will. Something about a phone call you were supposed to have received from your brother before he died about being a guardian." I glanced at the chart attached to the end of his bed. "But you're, what, seventy-nine years old. And they've got you on so much Percodan you probably can't tell when your phone's ringing and when it's just the TV."

"I have to take this from this guy?" He looked reproachfully at Hugo. "I'm an old man. I got liver cancer for Christ's sake."

"You're alive, Mr. Vinovsky, and your baby brother isn't. You haven't even asked me who killed him. Does it even interest you?"

"Who?" he gasped, struggling with the pill container. "Who killed him?"

"Hugo's stepfather."

"Why didn't anyone tell me?" There was a whine in his voice. "You come in here saying all these terrible things. How am I supposed to know?"

I'd made him feel guilty and it confused him. He was used to making others feel guilty. It was how he'd learned to approach the world, imposing his imperious, tactless personality before people could do it to him.

I pressed him before he could summon up his outrage again. "Why didn't you go to the police? Or get a lawyer? Even if you hated your brother, you had an obligation to look out for his son."

He pawed the pills into his mouth and gestured impatiently at Hugo to fill his water glass. "I didn't hate Daniel! We were brothers. We had disagreements like anyone else. You should be ashamed talking to me like this." He got the pills down and gasped for air. "And let me tell *you* something, the last conversation I had with Daniel, it all came out. Everything I'd been telling him for years about her. From day one! Daniel admitted I'd been right from the very start. He apologized to me. He begged *me* for forgiveness." Tears welled up in his eyes at the memory. He roughly wiped his face with the edge of the sheet and looked pleadingly at Hugo. "Your father was such a great guy, you know that? He was such a fucking prince among men. He should have never . . ."

"Married my mom! I'm sick of hearing that! Just tell him what Dad told you on the phone!"

Hugo's raised voice and evident distress didn't deter Miles. If anything, they seemed to harden his determination to have his say. "I'm just saying it doesn't surprise me that a woman like your mother has the gall to marry the scumbag who killed my brother. After everything that's happened to me, this is what I get at the end of my life. It's not right."

Miles looked defiantly at us, daring us to deny that he was the greatest victim in all this. His self-absorption was staggering, world class.

"Let's get out of here," Hugo said to me. "This is a waste of time."

"You can't leave. You just got here." Miles looked to me for support. "We're family. He's got an obligation to suffer this thing with me."

For Miles, the word *family* was the last resort, a switchblade he only pulled out when it looked like the fight was going against him.

"Tell us what my dad *said* to you on the phone!" Hugo bellowed at him.

"You wouldn't want to know what your father said about you."

"What's that supposed to mean?" Hugo looked horrified.

"It wouldn't be fair to tell you."

"What did he say about me?" Hugo cried.

"Hugo," I said. "Why don't you go down to the lobby and wait for us? I want to talk to Uncle Miles alone."

Hugo stumbled out of the room, his shoulder clipping the doorjamb on his way out. I drew a chair up to Miles' bedside and brought my face close to his, but it didn't seem to unnerve Miles in the slightest. He regarded me with obdurate scorn, as if he could weather anything I had in my repertoire, as if I was a punk. And yet a look of agonizing pleasure had suffused his face when Hugo had woken him up. It was pure, unrehearsed emotion and had seemed to erupt from some well of feeling in the old man that was even deeper than the roots of his grievance. Despite his injured pride, his continuing resentment of a brother who wasn't even there anymore, perhaps he truly loved the boy. Maybe I could soothe his ruffled feelings, appeal to his better nature, and get him to tell us what he knew. But I also recalled the desperate way he'd grabbed for his teeth like a man whose vanity won't allow him to appear in public without his wig. Only after he got them in his mouth had he felt free to speak and rev up the engine of his abrasive personality.

I put my fingers into his mouth and pulled out his slick dental bridge. It made a sucking *plop* as it came loose from his gums. For a second the expression on his face was almost comical, the look you see on people who have died so suddenly all they have time to feel is surprise. I dropped his teeth in my pocket with my car keys and spare change and walked towards the door.

He made a piteous whimpering sound.

I stopped and turned to look at him. His lips had caved in, his mouth puckered into a beseeching O. He made the whimpering sound again.

"Are you going to behave?" I asked.

He nodded. There was no hatred in his eyes now, not even fear really. It was as if what I had done to him was so unexpected and atrocious it had created a kind of intimacy between us.

I tossed him his teeth and he slid them back into place.

"I was going to tell you . . ." he said in a small voice. "I just wanted to teach the kid a lesson."

I leaned over and pretended to reach for his teeth again.

"Okay okay! I get the picture." He cringed back against the pillow. "I got a call from Daniel! We hadn't spoken in over a year and the first thing he says is he's changing his will. He can't cut Sally out completely, but he's leaving the production company and everything else of his to Hugo, and he wants to appoint me as co-guardian. Why? That's what I ask him. Because I know it ain't because he suddenly *likes* me. After what we been through over the years, I'm the last person in the world he'd ever want to call. I realize something else is going on here so I stall him a bit, you know. Why me, I ask? I don't know if I want the responsibility. And what's the big rush all of a sudden? Doesn't a big shot like you have lawyers and agents to handle this kind of thing? You got people to walk your dog for you. You got *Feng Shui* people to make sure the furniture and the toilets are lined up facing the right way in your house. Why me? And then it all comes out. See, Daniel don't trust any of them people to stay loyal to him once he's dead. They'll all go over to her. But he trusts me because he knows how much I hate her stinking guts. If something happened to him, he knew I'd give her hell. It was done to piss her off and make her life a misery. Naturally, in the end it never came to anything because he died before he could change his will."

"What did he think was going to happen to him?"

"He wanted to divorce her. He'd had it."

"Why?"

"She was fucking that low life, that Raj. She'd always been a slut, but she used to be careful about it. He could never prove it. But this time she wasn't even hiding it. It was humiliating. People were coming up to him and laughing in his face."

"Who?"

He leaned back against his pillows and let out an exhausted sigh. "He said some guy on the ski lift, they're riding up the mountain together, just the two of them. He can't even see the guy's face because it's covered with one of them ski masks. Just before they get to the top, the guys says, *'Your wife's a hoor, grandpop. Mustang Sally. Everybody's riding her. And guess what? That kid of yours? That ain't even your kid!'* And before Daniel can say anything, the guy jumps off the lift and skis away. That wasn't the only time. He was getting these awful calls about it. Young guys phoning him up and laughing at him for letting them have sex with his young wife. A guy wrote him a letter thanking him for having raised Hugo. When he showed this stuff to Sally, of course she denied everything."

"And you were going to tell Hugo this?"

"No!" He looked embarrassed. "I just said it to keep him in line. The kid has no manners." His painkillers were starting to kick in and Miles was having a hard time keeping his eyes open.

"Did Daniel Vine *think* Hugo was illegitimate?"

"He didn't know what to think. He was seventy years old and he was in torment from all this. But he never blamed Hugo. Even if the kid wasn't his real son, he was still going to leave him everything. That kid was all he had left in the world."

"Do *you* think Hugo is somebody else's child?"

"Not a fucking chance," he scoffed. "The kid's got his mother's looks, but from the day he was born he was a Vinovsky. He's got a real temper, he's got a terrible mouth on him, and he's hung like a horse, which also happens to be a family trait."

"Did your brother say anything about people trying to kill him?"

"They were killing him just saying these terrible things to him. Daniel was a very proud guy. In answer to your other insulting question, the reason I never got a lawyer was because someone pointed out to me that I couldn't prove any of this and if I didn't shut up about it I'd be sorry."

"Who told you this?" I asked.

"A guy just like you. Never told me his name, just like you. Just said how easy it was to walk into this place and put a pillow over my face."

"What did he look like?"

"Younger than you. Big guy with sunglasses. He must've been blind without them. The lenses were so thick they made his eyes look like fish."

"His name's Malahide. He's a very dangerous person," I said.

"You don't need to tell me. They could kill me just for talking to you." There was a swagger in his tone now. The idea of being the object of a murderous conspiracy appealed to Miles. Perhaps it was a relief when real life became as threatening to him as he always made it out to be.

"I think Malahide killed the guy who said those awful things to your brother on the ski lift."

"I don't understand any of it." His eyelids were drooping as he fought the narcotic pull of the medication. "This is too much for me. I don't even know who you are, or who you work for . . ."

"Sally Vine hired me to be Hugo's bodyguard. But I'm not working for her anymore."

"I can't believe Sally killed my brother." He sank back on the pillow, and closed his eyes.

"Maybe she didn't know about it," I suggested.

"How could a flaky bitch like Sally pull off something like that? She needs twenty takes to say half a line of dialogue. Every other word out of her mouth is . . . a lie. If she hadn't had a nice ass and a pretty face she would have been locked in a nuthouse, but instead she's . . . a movie star."

"From now on I'm working for you, Mr. Vinovsky," I said. "You're hiring me to investigate your brother's death. And you're hiring an attorney called Ken O'Doul to petition the court to appoint you as Hugo's guardian."

But Miles had drifted off into Percodan limbo.

I filled out an employment contract and asked a cleaning lady mopping the corridor outside to come in and witness him signing it. She was a heavily made-up middle-aged Russian woman, with marcelled platinum blonde hair and a grim mouth decorated with too much lipstick. She could have been Bette Davis's sister, the harsh one, from Vladivostok.

"Cost one hundred dollar to witness," she said in a guttural voice. She had one blackened stainless steel front tooth and she looked like she had a price for everything, including pushing patients out the window. I gave her the money and we shook Miles awake.

"That's Ludmilla," Miles said, giving the woman a sly mocking glance. "She wants to marry me to get her green card."

"No," Ludmilla stroked his brow. "I want to marry you because you kill so many Germans in the War, my little Moishe."

I placed the paper in front of Miles and handed him a pen.

"What's this?" he protested. "I'm not signing anything."

"It's going to help get the bastards who did this to your brother."

"You sign!" Ludmilla gripped his shoulder. "Or maybe no more Percodan for Moishe."

Miles Vinovsky scratched his name at the bottom of the page and fell back exhausted on his pillow. "I hope you kill them. Let 'em suffer for what they did to Daniel. Give the murderous pricks a kick in the teeth for me. And tell the kid I'm . . ." He paused. "Tell him I didn't mean to say all those things about his mother, but he shouldn't have provoked me. I got feelings, too."

"I'll just tell him you're sorry," I said.

"I didn't say *that.* I said . . ."

I got out the door before he could start it all up again.

Chapter Eighteen

On the drive back, Hugo lay slumped in the corner with his face flattened against the window. I tried to interest him in the paper I'd got Miles to sign, but after a brief glance, he let it fall from his fingers like an expired lottery ticket.

"They'll just say it doesn't count, like the photos and tapes."

"Miles said he was sorry about the way he behaved."

"Like I believe that."

"He did. Honest." I smiled over at him. "When he saw you'd come to see him it nearly broke his heart. He's old and he's dying alone in that place. He adores you. He just doesn't know how to tell you."

Hugo grimaced as if in response to some barely audible but painful noise, which only fourteen-year-olds could hear. It was how he treated all my little attempts to mentor him. He didn't contradict me, he just politely endured it the way you do when an old lady passes wind.

"How did you get Miles to sign this piece of junk anyway?"

"When he wasn't looking, I grabbed his false teeth out of his mouth and told him I wouldn't give them back unless he behaved."

Hugo sat up in his seat and stared at me. "What did he do? Did he scream?"

"Why would he scream? It made him feel like a total victim. He was in heaven."

"That's what I don't get about you, Thomas." He lapsed

back into his wan mood.

"And what is that, Hugo?"

"I don't know if you're, like, really smart about people and good at your job and everything, or just, like, you don't even know what the hell you're doing."

"Considering what I was given, I don't think I'm doing that badly."

"No way. That cop beat you up. Those Arab dorks totally trashed your house and pissed in your bed. And then you burn down my tree house to get the tape back, but the tape doesn't mean anything, and now we've got this authorization from my psycho uncle that you got him to sign by stealing his teeth. I mean, do you have a *plan* or is this what it's going to be like forever?"

We were on Wilshire just past the San Diego Freeway overpass, the Veterans' Cemetery coming into view on our right. Whenever I passed it, if only for a second, I used to think about guys I knew from Vietnam who were buried there. I barely remembered them as individuals anymore; they'd fused over time into a kind of fog. There were faces in the fog that tried to come into focus, but I'd trained my mind not to dwell on them. The whole experience of feeling that malaise and forgetting it was normally over in the time it took to glance at the cemetery and return my attention to the traffic ahead. But something about Hugo's criticism of my performance seemed to react badly with the memories I was trying to repress that day. It made no logical sense, but there was something about Daniel Vine's murder that reopened my buried resentments about the war. It felt as if once again I was being asked to solve a crime by the same people who were actively committing it. It didn't help that Hugo, the person I was trying to protect, didn't want to know the truth and had no confidence in me.

"I tried to talk to your mother and I got nowhere. If you think she's innocent, we can go see her right now and play her the tapes and show her the photos. She's Sally Vine. All she has to do is make one phone call. She'll have an army of cops and prosecutors lining up to help her."

"Yeah, but what if we show her all this stuff, and she *is* guilty?"

"Then I imagine she'll stonewall you, tell you you're imagining things, but she and Raj'll know you know what they did."

"What if we *prove* they're guilty?"

"They'll go to jail."

"Who am I supposed to live with then?"

He was trying to imagine what his future would be like with one parent dead and the other in prison. I hadn't thought that far ahead, but from a child's practical perspective, I suppose, it was the ultimate question.

"I guess the court will appoint people to take care of you. They'll do whatever they do in these situations."

"Would I be allowed to see you?"

The doleful note in his voice touched me so much I couldn't answer at first. "Hey, even if you're *not* allowed to see me, I'll find a way for us to hang out."

He sat back with a sigh and folded his arms and crossed his legs. It was a defensive pose he assumed when he had to think hard about something. After several minutes had passed, he rolled down the window, and put his face into the breeze. "I don't want to go home," he said. "I'd rather find out what really happened."

There's a point in every relationship when it either warms into real affection, or stops at a fixed level where it stays for good. With most of the people you meet in life you reach that limit pretty quickly, like the wheels of a car settling into a rut in the road. It's not that you know them, so much as you've decided you're not interested in knowing them any better. That moment in the car with Hugo was when our relationship turned into a real friendship. We drove back along San Vicente in a companionable silence past the Tour de France wannabes in their garish Lycra outfits, and the heart-monitored joggers, and weirdly gaited power walkers. Hugo indicated them with a little ironical smile and I nodded that they were, indeed, hopelessly square. We were involved in a surreal nightmare that these people knew nothing about. It was a secret that for that one sunny moment seemed to empower us because we were in it together.

The good mood lasted until I pulled into a spot in front of my house and saw Pru Nash jumping out of her van across the street with a video camera aimed at us.

"Wait!" she yelled. "Wait!"

"Come on!" I pulled Hugo through the gate into the front garden.

"Thomas . . ."

Out of the corner of my eye I could see old man Doyle signaling to me from the front porch of the main house. He'd probably noticed the kicked-in front door.

"I can't talk now." I hurried past him.

I pushed open my front door and stepped inside and turned back to make sure Hugo was following me when a hand grabbed my shoulder. I spun around and cracked my elbow into someone's head and then I was tackled and wrestled to the ground. My face was jammed into the carpet and there was a knee on my neck and what felt like at least three bodies squirming on top of me. I kept trying to kick and scratch but my arms and legs were pinned and there wasn't any flesh close enough to bite.

"Get the kid!" a voice yelled.

Through a gap in the pile of tangled limbs I could see a floor-level view of Hugo's cargo pants pooling over his scuffed skateboard shoes. I screamed at him to get out, but before he could move a pair of bare brown legs encased in black trainers blocked the doorway behind him.

"Fucker broke my nose." The knee twisted harder into my neck.

"Get his hands, dude!"

My arms were bent back inch by inch, but as they shifted their weight to get a better grip on me, my left leg came loose. I kicked out and connected with something that produced a serious grunt of pain. My teeth closed on something solid that turned out to be a leather belt, then I bit through fabric into flesh and ground it between my jaws. A shriek of pain split the air and the knee came off my neck. I tried to get up on all fours, pushing against the suddenly reduced weight on my back.

"Don't fucking move!" A gun barrel dug into my cheek so hard it nearly cracked my teeth. I stopped resisting and they twisted my arms back and cuffed my wrists. They got off me and I rolled onto my back to see who they were. One guy was Asian, built wide and low to the ground, with a Marine buzz-cut, dressed in Doc Martens and a black hooded sweatshirt. He was red in the face and completely winded. The other guy was a big soft Hispanic. He was holding a hand to his bloody nose and dancing around on one foot, while he pulled up his pants to check the bite marks on his calf. The third guy had the gun and he was bent over, trying not to puke from getting kicked in the stomach. Standing in the doorway, gripping Hugo by the arm, with a look of haughty dismay on her face that suggested she disapproved of what she'd witnessed but wasn't about to even grace it with a comment, was Corelle Lamb of the Santa Monica Police bicycle unit.

"You said he wouldn't be any trouble." The Asian guy glared at Corelle.

"He wasn't no trouble to *me*. But looks like the three of you finally got him subdued." There was something about Corelle's tart, salty personality that reminded me of somebody, but I couldn't think who it was.

"He better not have AIDS. Fucker bit me, man." The Hispanic buried his foot in my ribs, but as he went to do it again, the guy with the gun shoved him aside.

He kneeled down on my chest and put his hands around my throat and squeezed. "What's wrong with you? Huh? We're cops, motherfucker!"

I was already out of breath from the struggle and the weight of his knees squeezed the last air out of my lungs. The fight had erupted so violently I still didn't understand what had happened and now I was blacking out. As I lost consciousness I had the horrible but familiar impression I'd wiped out on a huge wave. It was holding me down, churning me against the ocean floor, which explained why I couldn't breathe. The world was turning gray and I was going to drown just like my father had in Malibu. There was something sad about this, but it didn't matter because the ocean was infinitely more powerful than my puny emotions. In fact, it dawned on me that from the day I was born, death had always been there waiting for me, had always had the power to win this unequal contest, and now it was taking what had always belonged to it. Very faintly I could hear a voice, the sound eerily close at hand yet far away, the way you hear things underwater.

"Get off him! Leave him alone!"

The weight lifted from my chest, and as I sucked in precious air I became aware of the three cops looming over me. They turned their eyes on Hugo and then looked at each other, trying to decide if he was someone whose opinion they had to give a shit about.

"He didn't know who you were!" Hugo said in a quavering voice. "I saw the whole thing. You never identified yourselves as police officers."

The procedural error meant nothing to them. The only thing that saved me from their retaliation was the fact he was the son of a prominent movie star.

"Yo, Sanchez," the Asian guy said. "Call the kid's mother, tell her to come pick him up."

Sanchez limped out of the room and the Asian guy pulled up a chair next to me and dangled his I.D. in front of my face. "Detective Hama. Santa Monica P.D." He looked intently at me. "Dude, we identified ourselves as police officers to you when you *violently assaulted* Detective Quesada and then proceeded to *inflict grievous bodily harm* on Detective Pope and myself while *resisting arrest.*"

"Okay," I gasped in agreement. "I can see that."

He checked my response for any hint of mockery, but it had all been beaten out of me. Hama waited for me to regain my breath and I used the respite to try and get a read on him. He seemed awfully young to already be leading a crew of detectives. He had smooth, mask-like Japanese features, but his body language and the way he talked suggested he'd grown up surfing in the South Bay. He'd made the mistake of underestimating me once and he now seemed determined not to let it happen again. His eyes catalogued the room, absorbing every detail, and when they settled back on me they were as bland as a blackjack dealer's. This look, more than anything else, should have warned me I was in trouble for something a lot worse than chewing on a cop's leg.

"Officer Lamb tells me you made certain allegations against an L.A.P.D. detective yesterday. Played her a tape recording of him threatening you?"

Why had Corelle chosen to report the matter after insisting she wanted absolutely nothing to do with it? I looked her way, but she gave me no clue.

"Officer Lamb further tells me yesterday afternoon she furnished you with a telephone number for an Eric Weaver? Can you account for your whereabouts between, say, eight and ten p.m. yesterday night?"

Hugo started to speak, but I beat him to it. "You know, I'd really rather consult with my attorney before answering any questions," I said.

"Sure thing," Hama nodded. "Just so you know, dude, this is a double homicide we're investigating and you're a prime suspect, so if you've got an alibi now would be a good time to tell us."

The casual way he said it, he might have been giving me a heads-up on the most effective way of paying my parking tickets. I could feel the muscles in my face firing in all different directions, as I tried to work out the details of an alibi explaining where I'd been and what I'd been doing, while at the same time maintaining an air of amazed indignation. I guess you have to be a psychopath to pull that kind of thing off. My mind stayed guiltily focused on what had actually happened: I'd passed Malahide coming down the hill around eight and set the fire in Hugo's tree house at around ten. I was sure Hama could read this information off my face like a teletype.

"Saturday night?" I said. "I was here, reading."

"What were you reading?"

I couldn't recall the title of a single book I owned. "The

Bible," I said. It was a safe choice. The house was full of ones I'd swiped over the years from motel rooms.

"You were home on a Saturday night reading the Bible?"

"That's my best recollection. It was pretty quiet around here. I think I would have remembered if I'd committed a double homicide."

"We have reliable witnesses who saw you enter the Weaver residence on Abbot Kinney yesterday afternoon. They report a violent argument between you and Eric and Dieter Weaver and sounds of a struggle. A neighborhood kid looked through the garage window and saw Dieter Weaver brandishing a shotgun at you. What were you arguing about?"

"If I wanted to kill Eric Weaver, do you think I'd identify myself to a *police officer* and ask her to help me find him?"

"Murderers do stupider things than that all the time. Answer my question."

"I can't. It's a confidential matter between me and my client."

"Not any more. According to Raj LaSalle, the boy's stepfather, you're no longer employed by the family. You physically threatened Mr. LaSalle yesterday afternoon and he's taken a restraining order out against you. They intend to prefer charges against you for theft, child endangerment, and child molestation. These will be in addition to the charges we will be bringing against you for resisting arrest, assaulting police officers, and interfering in a murder investigation."

"He didn't do any of those things!" Hugo tried to shake free of Corelle's grasp. "I was there! It's all bullshit!"

"It's okay, Hugo."

So far the cops didn't suspect we'd been together or they would have never questioned me in front of him. If Hugo would just keep his mouth shut, I thought I could get him off the hook.

"It's not okay! You kicked their ass and now they're lying!"

I hadn't kicked anybody's ass. I'd reacted like a wharf rat on adrenalin and now I was lying handcuffed on the floor for my pains. But to my alarm I saw Hugo considered it a point of honor to earn his share of the same treatment.

"Get your hands off me!" He swung a wild blow at Corelle, who calmly caught his fist in her free hand. He tried to pull away to kick her, but she moved him easily to the side against her hip. If you couldn't hear the obscenities he was yelling, it would have looked like she was giving him a dancing lesson. While everyone was occupied with Hugo, I braced my back against the wall and slid myself up into a standing position.

Sanchez limped into the room, a cell phone to his ear. "The stepfather's outside. He doesn't want to come in until we get rid of the reporters."

"That's not our job," Hama said. "If he wants his potty-mouth kid back, tell him to come in and get him or we'll take him to the station and hand him over to social services."

"He's got some L.A.P.D. detective in the car with him. The guy says he's undercover and doesn't want his picture on the news. Detective Cedrick Stone. He's asking you as a professional courtesy to clear the media out. He says he's got information on our cannibal friend here."

"Fine!" Hama snapped. "Do whatever the fuck they want."

Sanchez limped back outside.

As it sank in that the police were handing him over to Raj and Stone instead of his mother, Hugo started to fight in earnest. "I want to be arrested with him! They're going to kill me like they killed my father!"

Corelle was having a hard time holding him. "Don't you bite me, boy! Don't make me mace you like a dog!"

"Stop it, Hugo!" I yelled. I was afraid if he kept fighting they'd hurt him, but I don't think he even heard me.

Hama finally had to help Corelle pin him to the ground.

Out the window I could see Sanchez backing Pru Nash up to her Dodge van. He put his hand over her video camera lens and barked something at her. She gave up and tucked it under her arm like a purse, but she kept talking a mile a minute, and there was that maddening smile on her face that nothing was going to wipe off. Sanchez kept backing her up and she kept smiling like *Lucy* trying to convince *Desi* there wasn't really an elephant asleep in their bedroom and if there was she could explain everything. She had Sanchez so distracted he never noticed she was still recording him with the camera tucked under her arm. I took a step back and kicked out the windowpane.

"I'm getting arrested," I yelled. "Call my attorney! Ken O'Doul! He's in the book!"

Pope, the detective who'd choked me earlier, yanked me away from the window and pushed me towards the kitchen. Corelle and Hama had Hugo subdued on the floor now. A little blood trickled from the corner of his mouth, and his right foot vibrated like someone having a grand mal seizure. I tried to make eye contact with him, to reassure him this was not as bad as it looked, but I didn't recognize the boy staring back at me from the floor. The Hugo Vine I knew had gone somewhere else.

Pope got me into the narrow kitchen and re-handcuffed me, not nearly as tightly as before, to the handle of the fridge. He looked curiously around, idly turned on the sink, tested the gas rings.

"No hard feelings, pal," he said. "This whole thing was a goat fuck."

I didn't respond to his overture.

"Hey, man. Sanchez has a wife and kids. He's worried you've got AIDS."

"If I do, I got it from him."

"That's funny," Pope chuckled, his eyes drifting over my face. "I could never live in a place this small." He shuddered. "It's like a coffin, but I suppose it's rent-controlled."

The reason for his friendly overtures suddenly became clear to me. He was a Santa Monica cop, but he couldn't afford to live in the zip code where he worked. He probably had to commute from deep in the Valley, or from somewhere even less desirable. But if I got sent to the slammer, the sonofabitch thought he could move into my place.

In the main room I could hear Stone arriving, followed by Raj, his voice, smooth and ingratiating, as he thanked Hama.

"Detective, Sally and I owe you something that can never be repaid. You've given us back our son. Omigod . . . Hugo, are you all right? What happened to the poor guy? Is he okay?"

"He got a little over-excited," Corelle said. "But he's cool now, aren't you, Hugo?"

"You want to go home, Hugo?" Stone's hearty booming voice seemed to fill every corner of the house. "Sure you do. On your feet, big guy. You're going to be fine."

They said more things to Hugo in that vein, as if he was a little kid who'd got lost in a crowd at the beach, and they were big manly lifeguards who were going to take him back to his mommy. I kept waiting for him to rip into them, protest, at least complain about what had happened to him, but he didn't say a word. Something in that room had made Hugo stop talking. A terrible nausea filled me as I realized I'd led him into a place where I could no longer protect him.

"Got to be rent-controlled." Pope pretended to yawn. "In this neighborhood got to be."

I just looked at him. Maybe Hugo was right. Maybe the time for talk was over.

Chapter Nineteen

After Hugo left, they moved me from the kitchen back into the main room and Hama asked me questions for about an hour. He began pleasantly enough but my silence finally made him lose his temper and he threatened me with punishments ranging from growing old in prison to IRS audits. Pope tried playing nice cop then and Sanchez tried playing even nicer cop, but I acted like I had nothing but the furniture for company. Finally they marched me in handcuffs out of the bungalow past my watching landlord and the neighbors. Corelle locked me in the back of the squad car and joined Hama in the front seat. Sanchez had already departed to have his broken nose attended to, and Pope was staying behind to search my car and house for evidence. As we pulled from the curb he was already on the Doyle's front lawn, shooting the breeze and admiring the old man's hydrangeas. My landlord loved cops. It was one of the reasons he'd rented to me in the first place. His wife was scared of burglars and he'd convinced her having a private investigator as a tenant was almost as good as a policeman on the premises. I wasn't worried about Pope finding anything incriminating about me. The most shameful secret I had was how dull my private life really was.

It was a short drive from my place back along Fourth Street to Santa Monica Police Headquarters. I took the same route every day to work, and it looked the same from the backseat of a police car except that people checked me out now with that quick half-guilty glance drivers give victims of a roadside accident. As we paused at the crosswalk in front of my office building, I saw the old crone from the parking structure digging through a wastebasket on the pavement. She looked up and recognized me and started shouting and shaking her fist, still incensed about the missing TV remote.

"Friend of yours?" Corelle glanced back at me.

"I've got supporters everywhere," I said.

"I told you he could talk," she chuckled at Hama.

I didn't speak the rest of the way. I was trying to figure out the chain of events that had got me into this jam. Confiscating the camera from Tea Lane had been like pulling the plug on a hand grenade. She'd reported it to Raj and within half an hour Stone and his crew had showed up at the house to shake me down. After that I was pretty sure Raj had told Malahide to follow me and I'd led him right to Eric in Venice. He'd waited until nightfall and then returned under cover of the fog and killed both brothers. When Corelle heard about the double homicide she would have immediately alerted her superior about our previous encounter. It was the kind of lucky break that might get her a promotion.

I was fingerprinted and locked into an interrogation room at the station house. There was a beige linoleum floor, a scarred Formica table, and a few beige plastic chairs. I tried to figure out which of the walls was the two-way mirror and who was watching me from the other side. I don't know how long I did that for. It felt like a good hour, but it might have been only two minutes. With my hands cuffed behind my back I couldn't see my wrist watch. I couldn't sit comfortably on the chairs either, so I finally lay on my side on the linoleum floor. Hama's gun barrel had cracked one of my right molars and my ribs were sore from the kick, but that wasn't what was bothering me. All I could think about was Hugo and what was going to happen to him now. I was trapped inside this room and he was miles away, but he might as well have been imprisoned inside me. My sense of dread and guilt only increased as the hours passed.

I couldn't tell, but I had a feeling it was already dark outside by the time Corelle walked into the interrogation room with a clipboard in her hand. She left the door half-open and folded her buffed arms over a bosom that even an industrial strength sports bra could not truly flatten.

"Two things I'm scared of," she said, "and one of them is dogs, so if you got any ideas about biting *me,* tell me now and I'll get you a nice muzzle."

"I've never bitten a woman in anger."

"That's what I like to hear from a man. Puts you right at the top of Corelle's list." She helped me get to my feet and stepped behind to remove the cuffs. "Take off your clothes and place them on the table."

"Isn't there supposed to be a male officer who does this?" I asked.

"Ain't nobody interested in what you got. Just strip to your shorts. I have to search your clothes."

"You're a bicycle cop. Why isn't Hama questioning me anymore?" I handed her my jacket and started unbuttoning my shirt.

"He thinks you're prejudiced 'cause he's Asian and you killed all those poor yellow people over in Vietnam."

So that's why I'd been left to cool my heels for so long: they'd been pulling up my records. I'd done a lot of things wrong in my life and I'd been caught for some of them, but they were mainly in the misdemeanor category, the religious equivalent of venal sins. When I was a boy, a priest had once warned me that you can commit so many venal sins that they start to count as mortal sins, but I hadn't believed him. I operated from the position that sailing close to the wind was permissible and even desirable up until that last inch when you capsized. They could look at my records all they wanted. There was only one thing in there that sickened me and I was confident it was too obscure for them to decipher.

"Bullshit," I said.

"Okay," she agreed. "It's 'cause he thinks I'm the only one you'll talk to." She found the employment contract with Miles in my jacket pocket. "Who's *Moishe Vinovsky?*"

Nobody apart from Hugo knew I'd made contact with Daniel Vine's brother, and from their names they didn't even sound related. Considering what talking to me had done for the Weaver brothers, I thought it best for the moment if Miles remained alone and forgotten in Beverly Hills.

"When you ain't gonna answer one of my questions just touch the tip of your nose." She smiled. "Save us both a lot of time."

I suddenly realized who Corelle reminded me of. I'd had an English teacher when I was about ten, a willowy pale woman with pre-Raphaelite auburn tresses and luminous green eyes set in a delicately boned face. *Miss Agniel.* She used to toy with me in the same caustic, playful tone. I adored Miss Agniel so much I used to forget how to walk in her presence. I felt like the *Invisible Man* model: my brain, my organs, my heart all embarrassingly revealed to her. I'd stumble just walking up to her desk. Corelle Lamb could have bench-pressed Miss Agniel with no trouble, and I certainly didn't adore her, but she seemed to have the same safecracker's touch for unlocking the secrets of my affection.

I touched my nose.

"That's better." She nodded. "Now we got ourselves a *system.*"

"I want to call my lawyer."

"Take off your pants, shoes, and socks."

I stripped down to my underwear and tried to stand as straight as possible. My underwear was clean and I was much leaner than when I'd been drinking, but no one was ever going to put my body on a billboard. She consulted her clipboard and checked it against the tattoo on the back of my right shoulder.

"Amor Fati." She pronounced it like *fatty*. "That *Fati* an old girlfriend of yours? Girl's parents give her a name like that and then she got *you?* Bet she killed herself."

"It's Latin," I said.

"Oh, she a Hispanic girl?" She bent over and examined the soles of my feet.

"It's not a girl. It's a saying."

"Well, don't leave me in my state of ignorance, professor. What's it mean?"

"It means—love your fate," I said a little huffily. "Sort of like no matter how bad things get, your life is all you're given, so treat it as something beautiful."

"I liked it better the other way when you were all sweet on a fat girl. See, after dogs, it's fat I'm scared of. I used to be one of them nasty Jell-O-ass girls. I was carrying so much blubber I'd get out of breath just eating a candy bar."

"You look pretty good now."

She heard the compliment, but didn't choose to acknowledge it. "Loving the next installment of your fate's going to be quite a trick," she said coldly. "You can get dressed now."

"What about my phone call? I get a phone call."

Corelle gathered up the contents of my pockets without answering and headed out of the room, leaving the door a few inches open.

I decided she wasn't at all like Miss Agniel. It must have been the experience of being locked up that was bringing back all these childhood memories. I had to be an idiot to think she had any purpose other than skinning and filleting me for Detective Hama. I finished dressing in a despondent mood.

I could hear Stone now, approaching down the corridor in conversation with Hama. They were discussing Laker point guard Derek Fisher's latest foot surgery. They stopped outside my door.

"You're *giving* me free Laker tickets?" I heard Hama gasp.

"Courtside. Right across from Jack and about three seats down from Pamela Lee. And I told Sally Vine about you. She's going to be giving you a call to thank you personally."

"Sally Vine's going to call me? That'll be a first. Hey, thanks, Captain."

The door opened and Captain of Detectives Cedrick Stone stepped inside. A belted blue suede safari jacket was draped casually over his shoulders. Underneath he had on a canary yellow cashmere turtleneck sweater. His cowboy boots had been replaced by brown suede loafers with little gold chains. He even had sunglasses pushed modishly back in his hair. Maybe he was right, I thought, maybe you didn't need a degree to become a producer in Hollywood. Maybe you just needed to go shopping.

He gazed expressionlessly at me for a moment and then he was gone. Had he stopped by to show me his new wardrobe? No, I thought, it was to remind me that I was in his world now and his influence was as inescapable as the dead air filling every claustrophobic inch of the room.

An hour or two passed and Corelle returned.

"I'm going to give you a heads-up," she said. "The big cheese from L.A.P.D., Captain Stone? It's a Sunday night but he's got a top judge in his pocket. Says the judge is setting your bail at two hundred and fifty thousand dollars. No assurety. *Cash* only. That means they're sending you to L.A. County so you ain't even going to be arraigned until Tuesday morning. I don't know if you've ever been there, but it's full of strong young men who have been sexually interfered with when they was growing up. The paperwork accompanying you into County is confidential, but you know what prisoners are like, always gossiping. Word will get out that you an accused child molester. They some angry people in there. You can love your fate all you want, but your ass ain't going to care for it one damn bit. You forty-six years old. You don't want people trying to fuck you."

"When do I get to call my lawyer?"

She pretended to consult the pages on her clipboard. "Says here in my paperwork you already got your call to your lawyer. You called twice, but nobody was there."

I shook my head. I don't know why, she was a cop, after all, but I was surprised by her betrayal. *"Et tu, Corelle?"*

"What's that supposed to mean?"

"That's Latin. It means, it looks like the fucking's already started."

A blush of shame started at her throat and spread up over her cheeks. "All you got to do is *talk* to us!" she pleaded. "We got two dead white people on Abbot Kinney and one of 'em paid taxes and was in charge of his local Community Watch. We got to be perceived as doing something about it."

"I'm not saying a word to you people."

"Then I guess you going to County."

"I guess I am."

She doodled on her clipboard and surreptitiously tore off a corner of the paper. "Last chance," she said. "You work with us, you can get bail and walk out of here. Sleep in your own bed tonight without worrying about getting jumped."

She was staring intently at me, leaning her weight against the Formica table top with one hand. I'd assumed we were being watched through the two-way mirror the whole time, every piece of her behavior a performance for the benefit of her superiors. But now I caught a wrong note. Her facial expression wasn't matching up with her words.

She cut her eyes to the table where her hand was resting. Then she stood back up and walked out of the room. There was a match-length piece of tightly rolled up paper on the table where her hand had rested and I covered it with mine. I waited for several moments and then curled up on the floor as if I was taking a nap. I carefully unrolled the paper on which she'd printed in tiny block capitals:

I recognize Stone's voice from the tape. When you get to County declare yourself gay. Do not let them put you in the general population. Now eat this paper.

I put it in my mouth and chewed. It had no more taste than a Communion wafer and the hope it held out was equally suspect. Could Corelle possibly be my savior? Or was it just another police mind game designed to scare me into talking? I could hear shouting in the hallway outside now, feet running, cops cursing. Someone slammed the interrogation room door shut. It reminded me of the door I'd slammed shut in Pru Nash's face not so long ago. Would she have contacted Ken O'Doul for me? Had she even heard what I'd yelled at her through the broken window? Where were the tabloids when you really needed them?

Several more hours passed before Corelle stepped back into the room, accompanied by Hama. He wasn't jumping out of his skin at the thought of sitting courtside with Pamela Lee anymore. He looked like he'd been in an earthquake and was waiting for the next aftershock to bring the roof down. Corelle's eyes were red and she was clearly in some kind of major disgrace with her superior.

"Officer Lamb has informed me that she *thinks* Captain of Detectives Cedrick Stone may be the policeman she heard *allegedly* threatening you on some *illegally obtained* tape. She has written an official declaration to that fact and further stated she *feels* your life may be in danger if you're put in County."

I glanced at Corelle, but she was staring furiously at the ground. She'd made a huge professional sacrifice for me and I had the distinct feeling she was never going to forgive me for it.

"I will not communicate with you through *her!*" Hama exploded. "Stop looking at her and tell me what the fuck is going on!"

"When do I get to call my lawyer?"

"You don't need to call your fucking lawyer. He's here. The man is a dung beetle. I don't know how, but he's managed to move a mountain of shit off you."

"So what happens to me now?"

"Let her explain it. I'm going to a basketball game." He checked his watch and screamed. "Shit! It's already friggin' halftime!"

He rushed out of the room and his running footsteps faded down the corridor. If he turned his police siren on, he might just make it to Staples Center in time to catch the last minutes of the second half. Unfortunately the Lakers were playing the last-place Golden State Warriors and all the celebrities left early when it was a blowout. The odds were against Hama. Like everyone drawn by the amphetamine radiance of show business, chances were he was going to get his heart broken.

"Thanks, Corelle."

She angrily waved me off, not trusting herself to speak. "I knew it." She spit the words out. "Second I saw you sniffing around me on the promenade that night."

"I never meant to get you in trouble."

"You act like this nice, polite gentleman. Got yourself a little problem. Need a helping hand. But that's just the tip of the iceberg floating on the surface. Underneath where you can't see it, that's what's really going on. I don't know what game you playing, but you done shipwrecked my career."

"You saved me."

"And I ain't ever going to be happy about it. You can take your gratitude and blow it out your rear-end. I'm through with you. Never want to hear or see you again. Get on out of here. Your lawyer's waiting out front. He got himself an even bigger judge to release you on your own recognizance."

After spending so many anxious hours in that room I should have been dying to get out, but I didn't want to leave. "I'm going to find a way to make this up to you."

"After what I did today, I am finished in this police department. My momma always told me, 'Corelle, baby, it's the weak that bring down the strong,' and you have brought me down."

"Oh fuck all that, Corelle," I said. "I'm innocent and so is that kid. They killed his father, for Christ's sake, and you probably just stopped them from getting me murdered in prison. You're the most amazing woman I've ever met."

She made a rude dismissive sound, but I could tell she liked what I'd said.

"Hell, Eric Weaver was a convicted pedophile who was violating the conditions of his probation, and you found him. Stone is one of the dirtiest cops in the whole city and what you did is the beginning of the end for him."

"It'll get my ass fired is what it'll do. I'm telling you, you *better* be innocent. If I find out I lost my job because you played me for a sucker, I'll come get you myself."

Chapter Twenty

"I had to put up my house to get you out on bail," Ken remarked as we walked down the station steps. "I hope you're grateful."

"That's funny. They told me I was being released on my own recognizance."

Ken chuckled at being caught out in a lie right out of the box. "The point is, I was *ready* to put up my house for you. I'm an officer of the court and you've been released into my custody. You have to do what I tell you."

I showed him my contract with Moishe Vinovsky. Ken didn't bother to read it, just checked I'd listed him as the attorney to be retained, and put it in his pocket.

"What's our next step?" I asked.

"It's going to take time. But a disgruntled relative gives us some legal leverage."

"What are we going to do about the kid?"

"All in good time, Thomas. You just got out of jail. Take a deep breath. Enjoy the beauty."

I could see the upper half of the Santa Monica Pier ferris wheel lighting up the night sky. The ocean-borne wind smelled of rain. I followed him through the all-but-deserted parking lot towards a customized black Hummer flying two American flags. The Spartan army vehicle had become the weapon of choice for rich suburbanites in the highly competitive SUV wars of Southern California. Ken had angled his across two handicap parking spots.

"You disabled?" I asked.

"They put in all these spots and they're always empty. There's actually a shortage of handicapped people these days, but they don't want you to know that. They want you to think things are worse than they really are. It's a kind of intimidation. They *dare* you to park in one of these spots, but nobody does. It's not because they're basically decent, either. They're scared they'll be turned into cripples if they do. I park here on principle. It's my way of saying my heart is pure and I trust God not to turn me into a paraplegic."

This indignant diatribe was delivered with a defensive heat that seemed utterly uncharacteristic of Ken. He clicked his key remote and the interior of the Hummer lit up. Ensconced in one of the backseats, a laptop balanced on her knees, a cell phone pressed to her ear, was Pru Nash.

"What the hell is this?" I took a step back.

"Relax! I haven't told her anything. I haven't made a deal."

"What's she doing here?"

"If it wasn't for Prudence, *I* would not be here. I was in my airplane flying to Santa Barbara and she managed to track me down. She had to bribe an air traffic controller. She's a very capable girl. A team player. I'm so impressed with her I'm thinking of hiring her."

"I can't believe you're doing this. She works for the tabloids."

"Prudence works for whoever looks like they can help her the most. This is a huge story. She's not going to blow it with some premature announcement that lets everybody else in on it."

"Is that your deal with her?"

"Yes, it is," he said reassuringly.

"You said you hadn't *made* a deal with her."

"This girl is smart. She's cool under pressure. And she'd

sell her parents into slavery for a chance at film school. Frankly, she worries me a lot less than you do, and she's a helluva lot more fun. Either get in the car or I'm going back inside and telling them I can't take responsibility for your custody."

"Hey there, Thomas." Pru gave me a wave as I settled into the front seat. "You must be starving. Where do you want to eat?"

"They're holding my table at the Ivy," Ken said a little importantly. "It's noisy as hell, and full of phonies, but no one will be able to hear us talk."

"So, Thomas," Pru said. "Ken's been very vague with details, but it sounds like you got some killer photos."

"I love her enthusiasm." Ken smiled at her in his rear-view mirror as we pulled out of the parking lot. "You're a breath of fresh air, Prudence."

"Just so you know, Thomas," she gushed, "anything the *Enquirer* has is yours for the asking. We've worked up some information on Malahide's criminal record, for instance. But nothing like the great stuff you've been getting. Obviously I haven't heard them, but those tapes sound . . . huge. Mega huge. I can't believe you had the *cojones* to bug an L.A.P.D. Captain of Detectives!"

"That wasn't me. It was Hugo."

"Right," she said. "I think we're being followed, Ken."

"I see them." Ken nodded. "They were waiting in the parking lot when we came out."

I checked my side mirror. A dark brown late model Plymouth with two men inside it was behind us. The driver was the red haired cop who'd taken the camera off me. "They're Stone's people," I said.

"You pissed the man off." Ken shrugged. "He had you all lined up in his sights and you got away. You're going to have to lay low until things cool down."

"Lay low?"

"Your job is pretty much done, Thomas. Take a vacation. Go up to my Santa Barbara place. I'm right on the beach at Rincon. You can get out of bed and walk down to the water in your bedroom slippers. The surf's fantastic."

"Yeah? And what are *you* going to be doing while I'm surfing in my bedroom slippers?"

"I don't know, Thomas." He pulled the Hummer into the mouth of the Ivy's underground garage and took a ticket from the valet. "But right now I'm going to have a drink."

For ten o'clock on a Sunday night the Ivy was still going strong. I ordered grilled shrimp and the swordfish and washed it down with two large bottles of mineral water. Ken and Pru had jalapeno Bloody Marys and a bottle of Gaja Amarone to go with their Cajun prime rib, most of which I ended up finishing off. They were much happier talking about the food than eating it. When they weren't looking into each other's eyes, they were both checking out the crowd in the same dazed way to see who was there. Pru didn't have the physical attributes that Ken normally required in his wives. She didn't resemble a Laker girl, but she clearly had something he liked. Her cheeks burned with color from the wine and in the candlelight, if I'd been drinking as much as Ken, I might have been able to convince myself her eyes had the liquid depth of a Vermeer portrait.

"So tell me about Malahide," I asked her.

"He sold us some holiday snaps of Sally and Raj when they went to Bali to recover after the funeral. Malahide's a character. Loves to talk. Born in Tahoe. High school dropout. Since he was seventeen he's either been in prison for using and selling drugs, or working as a counselor helping kids get off drugs and alcohol. He sort of cycles between serious drug bingeing and the recovery movement. His last stint was two years in Idaho State for transportation of marijuana. The warden loved him. Malahide made Honor Farm, ran the prison AA group, and won a statewide creative writing prize."

"Any arrests for violent offenses?" I asked. "Any suspicion of violence?"

"Nothing we could find."

"Did he ever scare you?"

"Let's just say I always made sure I had someone from the paper with me when I saw him. Physically he's kind of intimidating and he has a sense of humor that goes way past anything I'm comfortable with."

"What's that mean?"

"I don't know. He's seen some pretty extreme behavior in prison, I guess. Really sick, gory stuff. Like he told me about this one pedophile who wore a chain around his neck with a little miniature yellow school bus on it. He was a weightlifter and he'd molested dozens of kids. He was proud of it. 'Everybody needs *something* to feel good about,' Malahide said. It was meant to be a joke, but really it was like he was telling you, 'I'm comfortable with *anything*. I've been to places you're too scared to even think about.' "

"When did he get out of Idaho State?"

"Sometime late in 2000. He went back to Tahoe and got a job as a counselor at The Tahoe Academy. He came up on our radar at Daniel Vine's funeral because he offered to sell some Vine family pictures to one of our photographers. After that his job seemed to be driving the kid to school."

What she said confirmed Tea Lane's description of Malahide as a reformed drug abuser with ambitions to be a writer. It also fit Eric Weaver's account of Malahide blackmailing him into sharing the Vines' luxurious ski lodge while they both held jobs at The Tahoe Academy. Yet there had not been a whiff of violence until Raj, the playboy Lebanese producer, self-invented Olympic skier, and friend of Johnny Depp, had blown into their provincial lives. Soon after, Daniel Vine conveniently died in a skiing accident, a drunk Louis Pike froze to death, and everybody moved from sleepy small town Tahoe to the bright lights of Los Angeles. Raj had married Sally Vine and tried to take control of her career, but he was like someone handling a sophisticated jetfighter whose knowledge of flying came from *Top Gun.* Making movies was a mystifyingly difficult business, and beneath the mystification the actual machinery was itself irrational, ruled by luck and timing as much as anything else. Even the very best, the proven winners, knew that most projects never got off the ground and of those that did a majority were failures. The article in the *Hollywood Reporter* about Raj's floundering performance, *Going Downhill Fast,* was an obituary of a dream that was as old as the city itself. In retrospect, murdering Daniel Vine had been the easy part; getting his neurotic star of a wife to make a movie had proven harder than rocket science.

That day on the terrace at the Vines', when out of vanity or insecurity Raj had decided to show off Sally to me had been his undoing. It betrayed him as an amateur, a wannabe. You didn't introduce outsiders to movie stars, ever. You tried to keep them as isolated from the real world as possible. They were like the Red Queen in *Alice in Wonderland* whose every whim was law. You never knew whose head they were going to chop off, or how they were going to exercise their capricious power. As if to bear it out, Sally had impulsively fired Malahide that day and hired me to look after Hugo. I must have struck her as unthreatening, a faithful drone, who could be trusted to watch over her son, as safe as hiring one of his schoolteachers. Or maybe she'd wanted to pay Raj back for acting as if he owned her, for the proprietary contempt of fondling her butt in front of me and disparaging her muscle tone. Who knew what made them tick? In the end it didn't matter which tiny spurt of egotism had triggered my entry into their world. Killing the Weaver brothers for talking to me was an index of what Raj and Malahide would do now to protect themselves. The only thing of real importance anymore was how much danger Hugo was in. I tried to put myself in Raj and Malahide's position, and imagine what they would do if they thought the boy was a threat, but it was impossible without knowing what his mother's role had been.

"I told you Pru could help us." Ken waved impatiently for the bill. Normally he dragged out a meal with balloon snifters of cognac or hundred-dollar shots of Grappa, but he seemed eager to end the evening, or at least the part of it that included me.

The cops followed a few cars behind us on the way back to my house. Ken kept recommending his place up in Santa Barbara as a place to lay low until my arraignment on Tuesday morning. I said I would think about it.

"You're my responsibility," he said. "Whatever you do stay away from that kid. The parents have taken a restraining order out against you. I mean it."

"He's right," Pru said. "This child molestation charge is bullshit, but it scares me. Once that kind of thing hits the wall, it makes a stain you can't remove. Definitely stay away from that kid."

That kid. It was weird how he didn't seem to exist for them. No one had mentioned Hugo at dinner and when I'd brought him up I'd felt their attention shrinking, as if I'd become one of those bores who drones enthusiastically about his child's achievements. I said my goodnights and watched them drive off. They were going to Santa Monica Airport so Ken could show her his new airplane. The cops didn't follow them, but pulled into a spot near the end of my block and switched off their lights.

As I crossed the lawn, Doyle materialized from his porch where he'd obviously been sitting in wait for me. He was a reserved little man with a shock of silver hair. He was shy and did everything possible to avoid meeting one's gaze. I'd known him for two years and in that time we'd had dozens of conversations, but they had always been about the weather, a subject that interested him, I suspected, as little as it did me.

"Mr. Doyle," I said. "I'm sorry about the disturbance today."

"Yes, well." He tried not to look at me.

"The police made a mistake."

"That detective said they were arresting you on suspicion of *murder,* Mr. Kyd."

"It's not true."

"That detective borrowed my tools and fixed your front door. He even patched the window. He's a handy sort of fellow. Now, when I rented you the place it was on a strict month-to-month basis."

"If you want me to clear out, I understand, Mr. Doyle."

"No. The place is yours for as long as you want it," he said. "I just came over to tell you what the little turd did. I saw what his game was right from the start and I strung him along. After he fixed the door and window, I got him to air out your mattress and reprogram Mrs. Doyle's VCR. I was going to ask him to wash your car, but I didn't want to push it."

"I don't know what to say, Mr. Doyle. Thanks."

There was an awkward silence. He looked up at the night sky where a nearly full moon was coming out from behind some cloud. I could see that he was about to resume our normal pattern and say something about the weather, but he caught himself. He cleared his throat and for the briefest of seconds managed to meet my eyes.

"I've been watching you." He nodded towards the bungalow. "You're all right."

Then he turned and walked stiffly back to his house.

As I lay between fresh sheets in my own bed that night, I thought of Doyle's surprising endorsement and how Corelle had risked her career to save me from going to County. The idea of people showing me kindness and support felt very strange. I didn't know what to make of it and it gave me confusing dreams in which I pursued some elusive prize that danced ahead of me, driving me mad because I knew it was immensely valuable, and yet it was always out of reach. Hugo was jumbled in these dreams, and Corelle made an appearance in an erotic role that was so outrageous in its bounty and detail that I knew it had to be a dream even as I was having it.

Chapter Twenty-One

When I picked up the *L.A. Times* from the driveway the next morning I checked for the unmarked police car, but it was gone from its spot. I went back inside and got dressed in some torn jeans, an oily T-shirt I normally used to clean my guns, and an ancient Army surplus rubber poncho. I got in the Land Cruiser and studied the cars parked up and down the street. None of them moved, but a plume of exhaust smoke suddenly appeared behind a green Buick parked fifty yards down the block as its engine was turned on. I took Fourth to Montana and pulled into the Pavillions supermarket, where I bought a bottle of the cheapest California Port I could find. The Sri Lankan manager gave my filthy clothes a puzzled look and raised his eyebrows at the sight of the rotgut wine on the checkout counter. He had an immigrant's sensitivity to the dangers of slipping through the cracks. The last time he'd seen me I was sober and cashing a Vine International Pictures check and now I was buying booze early in the morning. He put the rotgut in a brown paper bag and handed me my change with a fastidiously averted gaze, saving us both the shame of acknowledging my moral and economic collapse.

I lost the cops in the St. Johns Hospital parking structure, a maze so poorly lit and confusingly designed, sick people drive around it for hours trying to find the exit. Ten minutes later I was settled under a tree in Lincoln Park with a good view of Hugo's school across the street. The grass was still damp and littered with sleeping bags, their homeless occupants just beginning to stir awake. A few of them checked me out. Their eyes went to the brown paper bag with the bottle of wine in it, trying to assess if I was someone who would share. I must not have looked very friendly because no one approached me. At ten-thirty the park filled with students from Hart Hayworth on their morning break, but I couldn't spot Hugo among them. There was a teacher in attendance and none of the kids approached the homeless to buy cigarettes for them. By the time they went back to class the sun had come out and people were putting away their bedding and lining up to use the public restrooms. A pick-up basketball game had started on the park court and was on the verge of degenerating into a brawl, players fouling hard on every shot, jawing at each other. The lone white guy playing was the worst offender, throwing elbows and getting in the face of anyone who protested. I was embarrassed to use my cell phone with all the homeless people around, so I pulled my ratty poncho over my head as if I was going to sleep. In the darkness I jabbed out Ken's number.

"Hugo didn't go to school."

"Where are you?" Ken demanded. "You're supposed to be in Santa Barbara."

"I'm worried something may have happened to him."

"He's probably home sick, or something. What difference does it make?"

"I've got a bad feeling."

"Thomas, you have to let go of this until we've taken the proper legal steps."

"How long is that?"

"It could be weeks. It could be months. Even if the court rules that Moishe Vinovsky has the right to contest the will, the other side can appeal."

"The guy is dying. I doubt if he's going to live that long."

"Hey, we'll just have to take our chances. I told you from the start this was probably going to be one of those unsolved mystery deals. You did not bring me a steak. You brought me a lot of *sizzle*. But that's okay. I actually prefer it to steak. Steak is when a famous person gets murdered or murders someone and they catch who did it. It's got a beginning, a middle, and an end. *Sizzle* is O.J., it's Jon-Benet Ramsey, it's Gary Condit. It's knowing someone famous is guilty as hell and walking around free. You can sell that shit forever. Why do you think after more than half a century they *still* run stuff about Hitler being alive in the jungles of South America? People don't want it to be over. Where are you, anyway?"

I heard footsteps on the grass and heavy breathing and a shadow suddenly blocked off the sunlight shining through the holes in my old poncho. Someone was standing over me. I tried to peek out, but all I could see was a pair of basketball shoes, and two hairy powerful calves disappearing into baggy rayon shorts. I pulled the poncho aside and looked up into Malahide's quizzically grinning face.

"I thought that was you," he gasped. Sweat was pouring off him.

The phone in my hand was still out of sight under the poncho. I pushed the *End* button and then the digit I used to activate the message recording tape.

"What are you, *slumming?*" he asked. My presence in the park seemed to genuinely mystify him. "Checking out the lower depths? Trying to meet a whole other end of the gene pool?"

"What are *you* doing here, Malahide?"

"Playing basketball." He jerked his thumb over at the

court where the winded players were taking a breather. "I got into a regular game here when I drove the kid to school." He squatted down on his knees next to me and did a casual sweep of the park to see if anyone was watching us. "Now I get it. You thought you'd meet the kid here."

We were out in the open in broad daylight and I was sure he didn't pack a gun on the basketball court, but I couldn't shake my fear of him. He had the psychopath's dilemma of wanting my approval while at the same time wanting to hurt me very badly, which made him deeply unsettling company.

"They took a restraining order out against me," I said. "I'm just chilling with the unemployed."

Malahide looked at the sorry figures surrounding me on the grass. "They're not unemployed, my brother. They're homeless. What they really are is *phoneless*." He let out a little yelp of pleasure at his *bon mot.*

"I think they're waiting for you." I indicated the players on the court.

"Fuck those limp-dick bitches. They thought I was another white boy born with a tie on. Shit, I'm blacker than they are. I got the punks' hearts." He said everything with a cheerful manic zest, his pale blue eyes burning with a kind of bipolar zaniness behind his thick-lensed glasses.

"You and me got business to discuss." He brought his face close to mine. "I know where you live. I know where you work. I'm even starting to get a feel for the people you *care* about. You're real big on caring. I got that the first time I saw you. 'This is a man who cares deeply,' I said to myself. Well, I know about that kind of thing. Making up for past transgressions, giving back, that's what I'm all about. And I recognize it in others. It's all over you like a rash, my brother. The mark of the guilty man thirsting for salvation."

"I don't know what you're talking about."

"I saw this joke on a T-shirt once. Shows this busy career woman dressed up in her business suit. And her mouth is open in horror and she's tearing her hair out because she's just realized something. The caption reads: *Oh shit, I forgot to have children!* I've seen you with the kid and Serafina and her little brat. Pretending you're one big happy family. I know what you're thinking. No more lonely nights reading at home for you. Look, ma, no hands! I've got an instant family! Look, my life is a Kodak moment! Yes, sir. Your biological clock is beating so hard . . ." He laid his mocking face close to my chest, like a doctor listening to my heart. "I do believe I can hear it."

It was doubly humiliating because I *had* indulged in such wishful fantasies. I was prone on the ground. Having him stick his face so close to me was a violation, an insult, but I was afraid to move. It was like being sniffed over by a predatory bear. He leaned back on his haunches and inhaled, his nostrils flaring with pleasure at the fear he'd smelled on my body.

"I knew restraining orders weren't going to do it," he said. "I told 'em, but nobody listens to me. Threatening *you* is just a waste of time, isn't it? So now I'm going to tell you what time it really is. Those people you care about? They aren't going to survive this if you keep pushing. You act like some crazy motherfucker with nothing to lose, but I know what scares you. It's just one word."

"What's that?"

"Hugo." He waited for me to respond and when I didn't he jumped to his feet. "Great kid," he said. "Lot of promise. Thinks you're the man, the big war hero. Oh yeah! He even told me they gave you a medal for something you did in a tunnel. What was it? You went in and killed some

dink with your bare hands? But afterwards you realized it was a *child?* That's heavy, man. Take a child's life like that. I don't think we'd want to do that twice, now would we?"

He gave me an avuncular nod of the head and walked back towards the court. After a moment my cell phone *beeped* to signal that my answering machine tape had stopped. I couldn't believe what he'd just done to me. He was like one of those charlatan surgeons from the Philippines who appear to dip their hands into a patient's chest and pull out his beating heart. But he'd really done it. He'd ripped my shameful secret out of my body and held it up for me to look at as a warning. *You've killed one boy and if you don't stop you will cause the death of another.* I unscrewed the cap of the Port bottle and smelled the sweet alcohol fumes. Some of the homeless watched me from the grass as I prepared to drink. Their wind-burned faces were shiny with dirt, their hair was matted, but it was something else about them that bothered me. Their clothes were too big for them and it made their faces and hands seem unnaturally small. And then I realized it was because they had to wear all the clothes they owned. Swaddled and bundled up like that, they looked like children whose parents have dressed them against the cold.

I don't know how long I lay there gripping the open bottle, feeling the wound that Malahide had opened up inside of me. The man had taken my will to live. I thought about getting the gun from my car and walking up to him on the basketball court. Putting it on his chest and seeing the surprise in his eyes as I pulled the trigger. But would that fix the pain I felt when I thought of the boy in the tunnel? Would it take away the memory of his neck snapping? I screwed the cap back on the bottle and laid it in the grass. Drinking wasn't going to give me any release. I'd consumed swimming pools of booze in my life and none of it had dimmed the image of that dead boy in my mind. There was always my father's way out, of course, the long swim from which you didn't return. I'd always pretended to find a Viking austerity in his suicide, a man choosing to die rather than exist as something less than he once was. The fact he'd left his body cast standing upright in the sand facing the ocean like a warrior's shield had given the whole thing an air that I badly wanted to believe was heroic. But the truth was my dad had turned into a drunk before the motorcycle accident paralyzed him. The nature of his suicide was not heroic, but self-regarding, and I had never recovered from its aftershock. My father was only forty when he killed himself, still a young man. His mind was intact and he could still perform sexually. Why did his body have to matter so much to him? Death takes its first bite of youth at its moment of perfection; after that an adult's whole life is a kind of falling away from the physical ideal. Didn't he know that humans were meant to ripen inwardly as they grew older? In physical decay there was a promise of fulfillment and deeper vision. It was the trade-off that humans had to embrace to achieve maturity, the price for life on earth. But my father had balked at the terms, refused to endure the journey. There was a message in the legacy he'd left me, but until now I'd been unwilling to decipher it. I'd always assumed I hadn't been a good or interesting enough son to make my father's life worth living. The truth was he had never been all that strong a person to begin with, and the idea of leaving Hugo with what my father had left me was more than I could stand.

I abandoned the bottle and the poncho on the grass and walked out of the park. The Hart Hayworth students were breaking for lunch and I thought one of the boys looked vaguely familiar. He was gangly and stoop-shouldered with a long neck and the beginning of facial hair. He flapped his arms like a pigeon as he waddled aimlessly through the groups of chattering students, making a burbling clucking sound and pretending to peck at their snacks. Kids yelled at him to go away, but he kept bobbing his head and ruffling his imaginary feathers. He was an oddball, an outcast, and for that reason seemed, of all the kids milling about the safest to approach.

"Do you know Hugo Vine?" I asked.

The boy dropped his noisy impersonation of a pigeon and became a stammering self-conscious boy. "Uh yeah. Hugo's my friend."

"Did he come to school today?"

"Uh no. He's not going to Hart Hayworth anymore."

"Where'd he go?"

"I don't know, Mr. Kyd. We were going to do our science project together, but Mr. Goldfarb, he's like our biology teacher, said Hugo's not coming back. It was going to be like this outrageous ballistics experiment. Hugo said we could borrow some of your guns to do it."

The sudden turn in our conversation alarmed me. Borrow my guns for his science project? How did this kid even know my name?

"You don't remember me, do you?" he asked sheepishly. "I'm Max Marmelstein. My mom hired you to, like, get the goods on my dad in the divorce? I'm actually the person who recommended you to Hugo. From what he tells me, it sounds like you're doing like an incredible job."

It was unnerving to learn that Hugo had such a loose mouth, and at the same time I was flattered. He'd told his mother and Malahide about my war experiences and apparently he gave his pals at school daily updates on my progress. It was a total eye-opener. He'd always made me feel I wasn't doing a good job at all and now I found out he bragged about me behind my back. I'd always thought of our meeting that night as a random accident, but from Hugo's perspective, I suppose, it had been part of a carefully researched plan. The same went for his treatment of me. That first night in my office he'd intuitively grasped that his best hope of getting me on his side was to suggest I wasn't up to the job. When he saw that it worked, he'd kept doing it, withholding his approval and calling my fitness into question at almost every opportunity. Whether it had been done consciously or not, he'd motivated me into action like a coach inspiring a sluggish self-doubting athlete. The discovery that Hugo had approved of me all along was wonderful, but it was sad to think he had never dared tell me himself. Up to the very end he'd been afraid I'd prove to be a false friend like all the other adults he'd known. I hadn't been able to give him any peace of mind, and now I couldn't even protect him.

I suggested to Max Marmelstein it would be best if he didn't mention to anyone that I'd been asking questions about Hugo.

"Oh, no problem," he reassured me. "No one believes anything I say anyway."

I walked away and when I looked back he had become a pigeon again, dipping his beak into some screaming girl's tuna fish sandwich.

Chapter Twenty-Two

I had to find out what they'd done with Hugo. There was only one way up to the Vines' house by car and I couldn't risk driving up there in daylight. On the other hand, any car coming down from the top had to pass through the Bel-Air gate on Sunset where it met Beverly Glen. I parked in the shade of a tree and watched the endless stream of cars, keeping an eye out for Serafina's white Suburban. She didn't know I was waiting for her to come down the hill, of course, but I found myself becoming impatient with her all the same. They say the time you spend waiting for someone is often passed listing their faults in your mind, but I couldn't think of anything wrong with Serafina except that she didn't share any of my romantic feelings.

The cars kept pouring through the Bel-Air gate and turning left or right on Sunset. After awhile I felt like I was observing the activity of an ant colony. The numerous gardeners in trucks and housekeepers in family SUVs were the busy worker ants, the executives in luxury cars were high-ranking soldier ants, and the unseen passengers behind the smoked windows of the stretch limos were obviously the reclusive queens. I watched for so long I began recognizing cars that had left hours ago and were now coming back. Finally, when I was about to risk driving up to the Vines', a familiar white Suburban flashed through the gate and turned south on Sunset. I ran a yellow light and forced my way in a few cars behind Serafina. At the next light I honked and drew up alongside, lowering my window.

"Where's Hugo?" I asked.

"They took him." She looked ten years older than the last time I'd seen her.

"Follow me."

We continued on Sunset towards the Palisades, turning off on the winding road that leads up into Will Rogers State Park. We left our cars and sat on the grassy verge overlooking the vast expanse of the polo field. It was one of my favorite spots in the city, only minutes from Sunset yet already wrapped in the quiet of the mountains. The late afternoon sun slanted through the eucalyptus trees, casting long shadows across the freshly mown turf and creating small rainbows in the mist from the sprinklers. It was an awesome stretch of lawn, the size of four football fields, deserted except for the birds, which looked as small as fleas as they hopped from one spot to another. Serafina spoke in a hushed voice, as if afraid her words would echo.

"He would not say anything when Raj and the policeman brought him home. Everybody tried to get him to talk, even his mother. I made him some food and brought it to his room, but that therapist woman was there with Ms. Lane. They said I was treating him like a baby. That's why he wasn't getting better. I tried phoning him on his cell, but I think they take it away from him. I went to bed that night, but I can't sleep for worrying about him. After midnight I hear the two *maricons* who work for Raj's uncle opening the gate. The therapist is there with two men and they come in the house. I go into the kitchen, but I don't turn on the light. I follow them upstairs and hide in the furnace closet by Hugo's bedroom. I can't see anything, but I can hear them talking to him. They talk very nice, very friendly, say he has to get dressed now. He doesn't have to worry. They already pack a suitcase for him with his clothes and toothbrush. They have a letter for him from his mother explaining why this is happening. They are going to give it to him when he's on the airplane. Hugo asks to see his mother. They say it would make it harder for him. 'Harder for *her,*' he says. But he is not screaming or anything. He is very quiet. He asks if he can go to the bathroom. The man says okay but he has to keep the door open. Hugo goes inside and I hear the toilet flushing and then water running and it keep on running and running. I'm afraid maybe he's trying to swallow some pills. 'Hugo?' the man says. 'What are you doing?' And then they run out of the bedroom because Hugo climb out the window on to the roof."

She heaved a huge sigh and patted her chest to calm herself.

"I come out of the closet and I see his mother at the other end of the hallway. She has been listening, too. She is crying and looks like she is *muy borracha.* 'What happened?' she ask me. 'Why you do this to your son?' I yell at her, but she don't answer me. She starts crying how much she loves him, how this is hurting her so much she's going to die. Then Raj comes and takes her and I think the therapist give her a shot. I don't see her again. Tea Lane catches me in the house and locks me in my room. She says it will be easier for me. I can hear people running on the roof, everybody yelling. They got the two men and the *maricones* all trying to catch Hugo up there. I don't know what to do. Adolpho is hiding under the bed he so scared."

"Tell me what happened!"

"They catch him." Her face twisted in grief. "They put him in handcuffs like a criminal. I think they give him a shot, too. They take him away in the car. One of the Arab guys fall off the roof and break his ankle." An involuntary laugh bubbled up out of her tears. "I think Hugo *push* him."

"Where did they take him?"

"Nobody will tell me!" she wailed. "They just say it's for his own good, a place to make him better. They kill his father, but Hugo is the one they put in chains. They have the police and the doctors and the lawyers on their side. Tea Lane say to me, in front of my child, 'If you don't behave yourself, I'm going to report you to the *migra,* the INS. They will send you back to Guatemala.' I cannot return to my country. Because of my sister they have my name on a list."

"It's going to be okay." I put my arm around her. "Right now you have to sit tight and stay where you are. It's the best thing you can do for Hugo."

"And then what?"

"We have lawyers working for us, too. Hugo's uncle wants to help."

"The crazy old man?" she said with despair. "I understand you like Hugo very much, Thomas, but I think it would be better if you had never tried to help him."

I wasn't surprised that she'd come to that conclusion, but it stung all the same. "That's one way of looking at it."

She looked sadly at me, taking in my filthy, stained clothes, my unshaved face. They seemed to confirm the doubts she had always had about me. "I almost forgot." She dug in her purse and pulled out the Rolex. "Hugo say to give it to you. Not to keep. Not to sell. For safekeeping." She got to her feet. "Now I have to go."

For a second I thought she was going to say more, but she ducked her head and hurried back to her car. Through the tinted window of the Suburban I could see her head falling forward on the steering wheel, her shoulders going up and down, her whole body rocking with grief. I finally understood the curious absence of chemistry between us from the first night she'd come to collect Hugo's backpack from my office. I'd never been in love with *her.* What I'd fallen in love with was her fierce unconditional love for Hugo. He wasn't her son but she'd protect him with her life. I'd only experienced that intense connection with others during the war, when you were willing to risk your life to save a platoon mate. It was love conceived out of pure shared terror. Ever since I'd been looking for an equivalent depth in my romantic relationships, something that probably only ever occurred in books and movies: a woman worth dying for. Even that wasn't enough. I wanted her to be willing to die for me, too. It was, my friends said, probably why I had trouble keeping girlfriends.

"I'm going to find him!" I shouted. "I'm going to bring him back."

She gave me a vexed, hopeless smile and drove away.

I searched through the cluttered back of the Land Cruiser, pulled out a small mountain of Yellow Pages, and returned to my spot on the grass. Years ago, when Ken O'Doul wanted to invest in my agency, he'd suggested I expand into the mundane, but lucrative business of transporting people around the country. Private security firms moved criminals within the United States all the time, but there were also licensed agencies that specialized in providing safe escort for the sick, the elderly, the mentally ill, and minors who were considered flight risks. From Serafina's description of their treatment of Hugo, the firm but friendly tone, the mention of a letter from his mother, I was pretty sure the two men who'd taken him away were licensed, bonded employees of such an agency.

There were a lot of them listed in the various Los Angeles County Yellow Pages. Having your child plucked out of his bed in the middle of the night by strangers was an unpleasant business, and deciding who was going to do it was as distasteful as picking out a coffin. It was a task probably handled by the therapist and coordinated with Tea Lane. I assumed they would have wanted it carried out with the strictest secrecy by an agency with an expensive Beverly Hills, Brentwood, or Santa Monica address.

A few polo players had materialized on the field by the far goal posts. Handsome athletic-looking South Americans who looked like they'd been born on horseback. One of them cracked the tiny white ball and they all galloped after it. It was a version of golf on horseback, two sports I'd never learned nor been able to afford. I started phoning around to the agencies. By the time I was on my eighth call, more players had arrived and a full-fledged scrimmage had broken out on the field, although I was still the only spectator.

"Yeah, you escorted my son yesterday. I need to speak to somebody about something that went down." I tried to reproduce the Middle Eastern cadence of Raj's English, his aggressive mixture of flattery and threat.

"And your name?" the woman asked.

"I'm not even sure I'm calling the right place. My wife handled the arrangements."

"I'm sorry, sir. I can't help you unless I have your name." Her manner was professionally soothing, used to dealing with emotionally distraught parents.

"This better be confidential. This can't get out to the press," I said.

"Yes, sir."

"I'm Raj LaSalle."

There was a pause and I could hear her fingers hitting her computer keys. "I'm sorry, sir, I don't see any such person . . ."

"I'm Sally Vine's *husband!*" I said with force. I was getting a taste of the humiliation that Raj must have suffered every time he used his wife's name to open a door. The Raj LaSalle who had existed before was not famous, but at least he possessed a name of his own. It had to be demeaning that none of that counted for anything anymore. Raj the person had exchanged places with someone who had to wave his wife's celebrity like a driver's license to prove his identity.

"Could you hold, please, sir?" There was a faint edge of panic to her voice now.

On the field the game had stopped so the players could exchange their spent ponies for fresh ones. They had no shortage of horseflesh. The glamorous South Americans seemed to have as many ponies as rich Gulf Arabs have wives. After several moments a man came on the line.

"Hi, this is Mitch Biggs. To whom am I speaking?"

"I already told you. Listen, I don't even know if I'm talking to the right place or not. It's a lot of money and I'm not going to just hand it over to somebody because they tell me it's theirs over the phone."

"I'm sorry, sir. I'm not following you."

"We found a money clip on the roof. It's almost two thousand in cash."

"The Vine job?" he said incredulously.

"Yeah, the Vine job. It must have fallen out of one of your guys' pockets. It sure as hell doesn't belong to anybody here."

"Am I speaking to Sally Vine's husband?"

"Forget it," I said. "If it was your money, you would have said so by now. I don't even think I'm talking to the right agency."

"No, wait. I . . . I think it's my . . . my associate's money."

"You don't sound very sure about it. It's all in cash."

"It's his, sir. I . . . just had to confirm that, you know, the attorney, Ms. Lane asked for maximum confidentiality. I was just trying to be careful."

"Did everything go okay?"

"Well, it was a bit tricky at first, but . . ." Mitch Biggs paused, trying to remember the name. "But Hugo settled down really well. He . . . he's a very nice boy."

"Was he okay on the flight?"

"Oh, he did fine. He was pretty heavily sedated. He slept most of the way."

"I know this isn't, you know, your business. But, just between you and me, what did you think of the place we sent him to? Sally's torn up about this. I mean, did it look okay? I don't want anybody being mean to him."

"We just handed him over to the people from the school, sir."

"You never even *saw* the place?" I said reproachfully.

"The Tahoe Academy people met us at Reno Airport. That's what the attorney requested, sir."

The Tahoe Academy.

It was where Eric and Malahide had worked as counselors while caretaking the Vines' ski lodge. "I'll have my assistant FedEx the money over to your office." I hung up.

I felt sure I'd covered my tracks. Greed had lured him into my trap, and guilt would stop him from ever calling the Vines when the money failed to show up. Lying to people wasn't as difficult as polo and it probably didn't pay as well, but at least it was something I knew how to do.

I called information for the number of the school and got a recorded message delivered by a woman with a refined *Miss Brodie* accent who sounded at once patronizing and desperate for business:

"You've reached The Tahoe Academy. No one is available to take your call. If you wish to speak to Jack or Caroline Dalgleish, please press one. If you're calling for information about admissions . . ."

For once in my life I listened to a recorded message without any frustration, grateful for the lack of a live human voice. By the end I knew where the school was and the quickest way to get there from Reno Airport. I knew which colleges at Oxford Jack and Caroline had gone to, and how they'd met and their shared dream of founding a little Athens in the High Sierras where troubled boys and girls from wealthy families could experience intellectual enrichment of a kind found in the best British boarding schools, while benefiting from a highly trained staff of professional therapists and counselors trained to deal with learning disorders, drug dependency, and behavioral problems, all in a majestically scenic environment guaranteed to put the soul of the most agitated teenager in touch with a higher power.

Ken O'Doul had said it might take months to legally reopen the case and with appeals the whole thing could drag out for years. He didn't even believe we would ever be able to prove Daniel Vine had been murdered by any of the suspects. There was a restraining order in place against me. Even if I got through the arraignment on Tuesday without being sent to jail, Stone could have me picked up an hour later for some invented violation. I'd be in the prison system where he could have me murdered with a phone call. That would leave Hugo incarcerated in Nevada where they could keep him indefinitely. Every time he opened his mouth to protest that they had killed his father someone would force-feed him another pill. The kid already had a dark view of the world and that would put the finishing touches on it. It would break his spirit. I didn't really have a lot of hope left, but I had Ken O'Doul's ten thousand dollars and I knew I had to go to Tahoe. Even if I couldn't find enough evidence to reopen the case, I could break Hugo out of there, make a run for it. They'd catch us eventually, but at least he'd know someone had tried to do something for him.

Chapter Twenty-Three

There had been a late season storm in the Sierras and my flight to Reno was packed with skiers in search of the last powder of the season. Conditions were unusually turbulent and it dampened the festive mood of the passengers. Midway through the bumpy flight I ignored the Fasten Seatbelt sign and locked myself in the restroom at the rear of the plane and put in a call to The Tahoe Academy. This time I got Caroline Dalgleish in person. I identified myself as Rick Fisher, an entertainment attorney from Los Angeles and explained that I was calling from my private jet, which had run into some weather over Montana. I was looking at schools in several states and wondered if I could visit the Academy tomorrow.

"Could you tell me a little about your child?"

"There's two of them," I said. "Twin boys. I know you're probably full up, but I've got to place them somewhere. If there's some kind of extra financial charge for taking them at such short notice that's not a problem."

"Yes, well, Rick, tomorrow's a rather busy day, but I think I could show you around the campus at, say, three o'clock. Could I just get some information?"

"Oh boy," I said. "I got this new English pilot. He's flown us right into an electrical storm. Three o'clock you say?"

"If I could just have a contact number?"

"I'll be landing at my ranch in Missoula tonight. You can get me on my global phone. That's 44-34-61 . . ." I scraped my thumbnail across the phone's mouthpiece. "Hello? Hello? Damn, I've lost her. I swear I get better reception in the Swiss Alps." I ended the call.

A flight attendant was angrily banging on the door, ordering me to return to my seat.

At the Reno airport I rented a four-wheel-drive Jeep and made it up to Tahoe in under two hours. It was colder at the higher elevation, the wind off the lake funneling down the canyon of high-rise hotels and casinos. Neon signs blinked on the nearly deserted main drag, telling you what the city had to offer on a bitterly cold spring night: twenty-four-hour check-cashing, instant loans, prime rib dinner for under five dollars, the Moody Blues reprising *Nights in White Satin*. If that wasn't magical enough, you could finish off the evening by getting married in a place that offered a bonus of matching his and her tattoos. Tahoe didn't have the turbo-charged glamour of the new Vegas, where vice had been wholesomely disguised behind overblown fantasies of Venice and Paris. Vegas was like a call girl who'd married a billionaire and become respectable. She had beautiful children now, vacation homes in Europe, and owned a world class art collection. By comparison Tahoe was a small town whore, still buying her sexy lingerie and lipstick at JCPenney.

I checked into the Embassy Suites Hotel on the California side of the main drag, where they were hosting two weddings and a convention for the Association of California State Sheriffs' Departments. Liquored-up cops in leisure wear and wedding guests wandered between the lobby and the packed sports bar where the NCAA semi-finals were being shown.

It was after ten by the time I got into my room and unpacked. I called information and got a phone number and address for Louis Pike. When I dialed it, a man answered, his voice blurry. In the background I could hear music blasting, a party that sounded like it had been going on for a while. I asked him if he'd ordered a bucket of chicken wings and a case of beer. He bellowed my question at the other people in the room and came back on the line.

"You got the wrong number, chief."

"My dispatcher say it was a lady ordered it? A Mrs. Sykes?"

"No," he said. "Deedee *Pikes* lives here. And she ain't no lady!"

This produced a howl of outrage and guffaws in the background and the man hung up on me.

I hadn't wanted to risk carrying a gun in my luggage, but now I decided I needed one. I went down to the lobby and walked out into the cold night air. The invisible state line separating California from Nevada ran between the hotel and a booming casino next door. I crossed the state line with no perceptible change in consciousness and headed down the main drag, peering in through the double plate glass doors. Gamblers were tensely crowded around the roulette and blackjack tables; indecisive onlookers wandered randomly from game to game trying to decide what to play. They moved in a chaotic swarm, making sudden changes of direction, based on complex whims only they could understand. Each gambler had a deeply individual plan, but there were so many of them they ended up creating the illusion of a herd with a single purpose. The less adventurous souls sat welded to the flashing slot machines, feeding in coin after coin, getting the same low fever buzz over and over again. I watched all this ceaseless activity, the noise muted by the glass. It was like watching the aquarium of tropical fish in my dentist's waiting room. Further down the block I found a copy of the *Reno Gazette Journal* frozen to the bottom of a trash bin. I stepped inside Harrah's and checked out the classifieds.

Once you decide to buy a gun in America, it's as easy as locating someone who speaks English. You don't need a driver's license and there's no paperwork involved. You just need a newspaper and a quarter to call one of the dozens of home phone numbers listed under *GUNS*, a category usually found between *FURNITURE* and *HOBBIES*.

I reached someone called Angus Potsdam who was advertising a .357 caliber six-inch Colt Python with Pachmayer grips and a holster for five hundred dollars. Angus had an abrupt unfriendly manner on the phone and I could hear a crying baby competing with a TV in the background. He gave me directions to his home, which was on the lower slopes of Heavenly near the California tram base.

"Is it hard to find?" I asked.

"Nope," he said. "It's the only house on the street that's properly lit up." Then added cryptically, "There's a dog."

The dark streets became steeper and icier as I drove up the mountain; endless A-frames nestled in cramped snowbound lots and there were fir trees everywhere blocking out the night sky. Their snow-laden boughs obscured the signposts. I drove around until I was lost. I tried calling Angus Potsdam again, but my cell phone didn't work in the shadow of the mountain. At a deserted intersection I got out of the car to check a street sign. The thin air and forest gloom were oppressive and I remembered, like a bad taste from childhood, a family vacation somewhere high in the Sierras, my parents quarreling over some forgotten subject. To change the mood in the car, my mother had drawn my attention to the pine-covered ranges. She'd described them with forced gaiety as "whole mountains of Christmas trees."

But it felt like a cheat. A Christmas tree multiplied until it covered every surface and blotted out the horizon was simply monotonous. As I tried to make out the words on the street sign, I heard a door unbolting followed by a dog violently barking. Suddenly spotlights blazed around a house on the next street up and I could see a man waving impatiently at me while his snarling Rottweiler hurled itself at the chain link fence.

"You're not on the correct street!" he shouted, rather pedantically, I thought.

I'd been looking for a lit-up house, not realizing Angus Potsdam's lights only came on if an intruder tried to enter his property. I drove around to his house and shielded my eyes against the prison-yard glare. He unlocked the gate and held on to the dog's collar while it gave me a good sniffing over. Angus was in his late twenties, with sandy balding hair and a mild mannered face offset by surprisingly carnivorous teeth. He wore glasses and was dressed in a flannel shirt and a pair of shiny-bottomed chinos. He was a geography teacher at the local middle school, a Tahoe native, married, with two children. I asked him questions to forestall him asking me any, but I needn't have bothered. Angus wasn't big on sharing personal information. It was a mystery that he'd managed to share bodily fluids with his wife successfully enough to produce two children.

He let me inside a locked Quonset hut beside the main house. It was carpeted in pale blue Astro-turf that squeaked underfoot. It was spotless and empty except for a locked glass display case elevated on a platform against the far wall like a shrine. Within, a collection of handguns was mounted against pale blue velvet backing. The room was as cold as a meat locker and smelled of nothing, but you could tell it was his favorite place in the world.

"Do you have the money?"

I handed him the five hundred dollars. He counted it and put it away in his pocket.

"Don't touch anything." He walked out and shut the door. I took a step towards the display cabinets, but the dog bared its teeth, and I thought better of it.

In a moment Angus returned with the Colt, which proved to be in mint condition.

"You're getting a real deal," he said sourly. "I could auction it on eBay for a lot more, but I need the money to get something else." He seemed to want me to ask him what that something else he was getting was.

"I need ammo," I said.

He unlocked a drawer and handed me a box of 357 silvertip bullets. "Thirty dollars." He held out his hand.

The dog and Angus watched me with the same apprehensive expression as I peeled off the bills.

"Yup, I'm getting something *very* special," Angus said smugly. He had the personality of a snowball, I decided, but one with a rock inside it.

"A life?"

"Very funny." He waved off my juvenile insult. He was a geography teacher; kids probably insulted him all the time. "A Barret M82A1." He bared his carnivorous teeth.

"Is that some kind of dishwasher?"

"Very funny." He blinked. "It's a 50-caliber sniper rifle. It can slice through body armor like a knife through warm butter."

"Sounds sexy."

"Do you know you can shoot someone with it from *two* miles away? Imagine that. You can take out a plane, a helicopter, an oil refinery from a distance of twenty football fields. It doesn't just hit the target, it *explodes* it. Think what some crazy Al Qaeda terrorist could do with a weapon like that."

"How are you getting one?"

"I'm getting it on the Internet." He dismissed me as if I was a student who'd asked a stupid question.

The trailer where Louis Pike's widow Deedee lived was set back from the road in the trees about a mile past the last strip mall on the way out of town. A pick-up truck was parked in front; there were lights on, and the sound of ZZ Top's *Arrested for Driving While Blind* was coming from inside. A collection of abandoned snowmobiles and jet skis lay half-buried under a blanket of dirty snow at the front of the trailer. Around the back a laundry line was hung with frozen white sheets that looked like they'd been left out all winter. According to Eric Weaver, Louis Pike had been found frozen to death beside his newly purchased snowmobile within walking distance of his front door. Eric was convinced Malahide had killed Louis for bragging about his role in Daniel Vine's murder. I was a stranger knocking on his widow's door in the middle of the night. What chance did I have of getting Deedee Pike to talk to me about the man who'd murdered her husband? Did she even care he'd been murdered? He didn't exactly sound like the sort of man a wife would miss that much. He was a drunk, a man who, for money, had been willing to taunt Daniel Vine on a ski lift about the sexually degrading things his wife liked to do with younger men.

I opened my jacket so the Colt in my waistband was visible and pounded hard on the door. There was a sound of scuffling and whispering, a bottle being knocked over, and the music stopped. The blurry voiced man I'd spoken to earlier on the phone said, "Who is it?"

"I'm from Malahide." I put a dent in the aluminum door with my shoe. "Open the fucking door."

Within seconds a haggard looking guy in his underwear threw open the door and quickly lurched back behind the couch where a naked woman sat clutching a bedspread around herself. After the cold night air, the hot sour stink of their bodies was overwhelming. There were empty beer cans and a bottle of Kahlua on the coffee table in front of them, but their eyes had a zombie glow that no amount of alcohol could dull. From the state of the place they were into the second or third day of an epic crystal meth binge. The kitchenette on the right was piled high with dirty paper plates and open pizza boxes. To the left there was a sleeping alcove filled with a bare, stained mattress and some Army surplus blankets and a few naked, headless children's dolls. Something about the dolls disturbed me until I remembered what Eric Weaver had said about Louis Pike: *"He had a wife and kids."*

"I don't have nothing to do with this," the man pleaded as he started pulling on his clothes. "Just having a little party with Deedee, but I'll clear out of your way."

His hair was falling out in fistfuls and he was missing several front teeth. He crashed to the ground trying to get his feet into his pants. It was hard to tell if he was in his mid-twenties or pushing sixty.

"Sit down." I put my hand on the Colt.

He sat down on the floor behind the couch and covered his head with his hands. I couldn't tell if he was ready to die, or thought the couch would protect him from a bullet, or the crystal meth was making him invisible.

"You Deedee?" I asked the woman.

She nodded, staring at the gun in my waistband. Her mouth was pinched shut and her eyes bulged vacantly.

She'd been pretty once, but it took a lot of imagination to see it.

"Where are your kids?"

"Social Services got them. I been a little low since Louis passed."

My eyes wandered over the room and kept coming back to the naked dolls; they were old, the pink plastic skin polished smooth with dirt. And then it hit me: the private room that Sally Vine kept inside her mansion in Bel-Air was just like this scuzzy trailer.

"Why you so nervous, Deedee?" I plopped down on the couch next to her.

The rims of her nostrils were crusted with dried blood and her lips kept pursing together, but no sound came out. She finally got control of her voice. "I don't know what you want. I haven't said nothing to nobody about anything."

"When was the last time you talked to Malahide?"

"He calls, you know, stays in touch. Checking in. He called the other day . . . I think."

In Deedee's meth-buzzed memory *the other day* might mean anywhere from two hours ago to last week. "What'd he tell you, Deedee?"

"To . . . to keep on . . . just the way I've been doing. I do not talk to anybody about anything, mister."

"She don't say *nothing* to me," the man hiding behind the couch said, and then quickly added, "Not that I ask her. None of my damn business."

"Anybody been asking you any questions, Deedee?" I said.

"No. And if they did I'd call Malahide. I got his number right up there on the fridge."

"You and your late husband, did you know Sally Vine personally?"

"*Know* her?" There was a glint of disdain in her eyes. "I knew her since we were kids. Partied with her all through high school. Hell, Louis did it to her in the sixth grade. At least that's what he always said. I don't think he did. Sally never put out unless it was going to get her something."

"Yeah, that's the only way you can make it in the movies," the man agreed.

"She wasn't all that much," Deedee sniffed. "When I knew her she didn't have boobs like that, or that face. They gave her all that in Hollywood. Only thing they couldn't give her was a heart."

"You ever dream of going to Hollywood, Deedee? Having a whole other kind of life like Sally?"

One of her front teeth was loose and she worked at it with her tongue. "Life, in my experience," she said, "is kind of like waiting for an avalanche. You worry about it happening and then suddenly one day it happens and you're dead." She giggled bitterly. "That's my personal philosophy."

The meth had overridden her fear of me. She was revving up to talk for hours.

"You see, Sally's big mistake, and I've always said this, was coming back here. She left town and made a big success and didn't want nothing to do with any of her old friends. That's okay. Just human nature. Doesn't want anything to do with people who knew her before. But then she comes back and builds that big vacation place. Doesn't build it in Aspen where the other movie stars go. She builds it right here in Tahoe, right in our face, to rub it in. And now they can't even sell the place. It's been on the market since her husband died."

"You think she got what was coming to her?"

"Hell no. She's still got the money and the big name.

Sally's fine." She waved a dismissive hand. "She probably thinks she got away with murder."

"Thinks?" I said. "What's that supposed to mean?"

Deedee looked confused by the question. "I don't know. It was just what Louis told me. I don't know what you want from me, mister. I don't know why Malahide sent you."

"Do you know who really killed Daniel Vine?" I asked.

The question produced a sudden uncomfortable silence. It was so quiet in the rank, overheated room I almost thought I could hear their brain cells frying.

"*I* sure as hell don't know," the man behind the couch finally said. "I don't want to know. I'd like to go home."

Deedee moved away from me on the couch, her face mottling and filling with sudden aggression. "You're a cop!" she bellowed in triumph. "He's a cop, Henry! We don't have to talk to fucking cops!"

"You *wish* I was a cop." I pulled out the Colt and laid it on the couch between us so the barrel pointed at her. "I'm going to ask you one more time. Who killed Daniel Vine?"

"Sally did. They all did. I don't know. It was an accident, right? They didn't tell me anything. It wasn't like a *plan*. It happened and they all got rich. Except for Louis and me, but I'm not complaining. I've never asked for anything."

She was like a desperate student trying to come up with the right answer because the wrong one would get her killed.

I got up and walked into the kitchenette. There were some Polaroids of her young kids taped to the fridge with pink heart-shaped magnets. The pictures had been taken at Christmas inside the trailer. Their faces were smudged with food stains from the hands of people opening and closing the door. Deedee had to look at them every time she opened the fridge to get herself another beer, or maybe she'd stopped seeing them. A scrap of notepaper with Malahide's name and a Los Angeles phone number was taped above the fridge handle. I tore it off and put it in my pocket, hoping she wouldn't be able to remember it.

When I walked back into the room, the man called Henry was on his way out the door with one boot on and the other in his arms with the rest of his clothes.

"Party's nearly over, Henry," I said. "The least you can do is stay to the end."

Henry slid down the wall to the floor. He was not a gallant man, but he was very obedient.

"Who are you?" Deedee asked meekly. "You don't have to tell me."

"I've never wasted a mother before." I pointed the gun at her face and pulled back the hammer. "But I don't figure your kids are going to miss you anymore than you miss Louis."

"Please," she begged, "I don't know who killed Vine. I'll say it's anybody you want it to be . . ."

I believed her. She was trying to cry but the meth had dried out her eyeballs so badly she couldn't produce any tears. "Why'd your husband tell Vine it wasn't his kid on the ski lift that day?"

We'd been talking about me shooting her in the face. This new question seemed so inconsequential to her she couldn't even absorb it at first.

"I . . . I . . . I . . . to fuck with his head! Raj said it would drive the rich Jewish guy crazy if he thought the kid wasn't even his real son."

"So it was just a lie?"

"To drive a wedge!" she said eagerly. "Yeah, to make trouble between Sally and her husband."

I put my gun back in my waistband. "Henry? Deedee? It's been such a pleasure meeting you both, I'd like to give you a piece of advice to show my appreciation."

They both stared at me with expressions of stunned idiotic hope.

"This is a very small tightly-knit community you've got here. Everybody knows everybody else. For instance you must know Eric and Dieter Weaver."

Deedee and Henry looked at each other and nodded with relief. "Eric and Dieter? Sure, we know them."

"I had to ask Eric and Dieter some questions in Los Angeles just like I've been asking you some questions here tonight. But Malahide found out I'd been talking to them. And he killed them. Do you understand what I'm saying?"

"Better not tell Malahide." Henry nodded forcefully. "About tonight."

"Good thinking, Henry."

I walked over to their CD player and hit the On switch. ZZ Top's *Tube Snake Boogie* rumbled out of the speakers. I cranked the volume up until the whole trailer was vibrating like a cheap engine that was going to blow up at any minute and left them to their party.

It was after one by the time I got back to the Embassy Suites, the lobby still busy with guests wandering back from the casinos. I picked a local Tahoe promotional magazine off the reception counter and took it up to my room. The Vines' ski lodge wasn't listed by owner, but there was a two-page spread on it complete with color photographs, one of which I recognized from Pru Nash's picture in the *Enquirer*. It had been reduced from 6.6 million to 4.7, and offered lake and mountain views, an indoor/outdoor pool, a tennis court, and a private slip at the local marina. It boasted seven bedrooms and ten bathrooms, an anomaly about expensive homes that had always puzzled me. Did the rich have some deeply-rooted anxiety about staying clean? Or was it the childhood trauma of really having to go and not being able to find an unoccupied bathroom?

I called Anthea Duke, the local realtor handling the listing, and left a message on her voice mail. I was Rick Fisher again calling from my private plane and I was only going to be in Tahoe for a day. I was really in the market for something a bit bigger but maybe the place wasn't as small as it appeared in the photographs. I didn't bother to specify the time of day I'd want to view the house. With the end of ski season fast approaching, I figured Anthea Duke would be desperate for even the illusion of a buyer. Posing as a multi-millionaire, I found myself using the same cold, off-hand tone of voice that I'd used to convince Deedee Pike and Henry I was willing to shoot them. For some reason I felt less of an asshole pretending to be a murderer than I did telling a stranger ten bathrooms weren't enough for me.

There were five messages on my home answering machine. The first one was the grisly recording I'd made of Malahide in the park. Since I'd forgotten the code to delete a message, I had to listen to the whole thing all over again:

"But afterwards you realized it was a child? That's heavy, man. Take a child's life like that. I don't think we'd want to do that twice, now, would we?"

We? I was miles away from Malahide, safe in a warm hotel room, but I still had the unsettling feeling he could read my mind, predict where my emotions would lead me. Had I scared Deedee and Henry sufficiently that they wouldn't report my visit to him? Malahide was a real murderer. He'd already told me if I kept pushing he'd hurt Hugo. In her own way Serafina had told me the same thing.

My attempts to help the boy were destructive because I was too weak to save him. What if all I was doing now was risking getting him killed?

The last four messages were from Ken O'Doul, going from concern to frustration to outraged bluster: where was I? Did I know I was being arraigned in court Tuesday morning? Going AOL on him like this was a criminal offense and a personal betrayal.

The events of the day and the overheated hotel room suddenly had me reeling with exhaustion. I pried open a window and breathed in the bone-chilling air coming off the Alpine lake. It felt like a thousand tiny ice picks stabbing into my lungs. I stuck my face out the window long enough to give myself a ringing headache. I was too tired to phone Ken back. I was too tired to brush my teeth. I was too tired to do anything but get undressed and crawl into bed and turn off the lights. If they issued a bench warrant for my arrest, so be it. I didn't even understand what Ken was so riled up about. If he looked at it the way he always looked at things, my becoming a fugitive was just another twist in that great *story* he was determined to sell to Fox or Disney . . . the one that was actually happening to Hugo Vine, the one that made me dream violently all night while I shivered in the thin mountain air pouring through the window I'd forgotten to close.

Chapter Twenty-Four

"I just remembered, Mr. Fisher. I'm supposed to check your credit rating before showing you the property." The woman at Anthea Duke Realty gazed nervously at me. A second before she'd been gathering up a set of keys and her purse from the cluttered desk, ready to show me the Vine place.

I'd dressed immaculately for the meeting in my freshly pressed Battistoni suit, a gleaming white shirt, and a silk knit Hermes tie. I didn't say anything, just raised one eyebrow in surprise at this last-minute request.

"God, I wish Anthea was here. She is *so* bummed she can't show you the place herself. She's got stomach flu, poor baby. You know, both ends . . . just sick as a dog. Bad shrimp. I never eat shellfish in the mountains, and I never eat it on an airplane. I was a flight attendant for twenty years. A lot of it international. I've been all over the world and I know everything about food poisoning."

I nodded. Her name was Fran and it was the second time she'd told me she'd been all over the world. She had bleached blonde hair cut short, and a wide generous face with a skier's tan. Her eyes were the same steely Scandinavian blue as the color posters of Lake Tahoe filling the realty office.

I glanced at the late Daniel Vine's vintage Rolex on my wrist. "My bank in Geneva is going to close in ten minutes. If you get on the computer right now I'll ask them to fax a financial statement."

"Computers." She gave a little shudder. "Forget it. Let's just go look at the house."

On the drive to the Vines' ski lodge she told me she'd made a terrible mistake by falling in love with a man from Tahoe who had promised to marry her if she quit her job at the airlines. He turned out to have a wife and four children and now she was stuck here working for Anthea Duke who was a bitch and chiseled all the agents out of their commissions. I told her I was a widower with two impossible children I was trying to place at The Tahoe Academy. I'd dreamed of being a civil rights lawyer, but somehow I'd ended up handling the chaotic personal and legal affairs of people like Mariah Carey and Whitney Houston. After that, conversation was no problem. Fran kept asking me if any of the things she read about their personal lives were true, and I just shook my head.

"The sad thing is," I confided, "it's all much *worse* than anything you read in the tabloids. Sexually, it's so sordid . . . a person like you wouldn't want to know."

She colored faintly, imagining it. "Try me," she said. "I'm pretty hard to shock. I've been to Bangkok. Amsterdam. I've been all over the world."

"I'd be too embarrassed."

"It's *that* bad? Come on, what do they do?"

"If I buy the house, I'll tell you what they do. Fair enough?"

"If you buy the house," she laughed, "you can do it to me."

The Vines' ski lodge was a sleek, futuristic affair of gleaming teak decks, rounded concrete walls, and deeply indented arrow-slit windows. The dramatically pitched roof was made of copper covered in a patina of verdigris. What I mainly noticed, though, was the Tahoe police cruiser parked in the driveway. Wealthy people in Los Angeles buy old prop police cars from the studios and park them in front of their estates to deter criminals, but this one looked uncomfortably real.

Fran pulled in behind it and turned off the ignition. She took a deep breath and handed me the keys to the house. "I promised Anthea I'd stay in the car. She says I talk too much and this house sells itself. So I'm going to zip my mouth and just let you wander around inside. If you have any questions you know where I am."

"What's with the police car?"

"Oh, that's Billy Kaplan's. Sally Vine's new husband hired him to take care of the place."

"Scare the burglars away. I get it."

"I doubt if Billy could scare anyone. He's so young he only has to shave about twice a week. He stays in one of the maid's rooms."

"So he's not going to shoot me?"

"Hardly. Anthea told Billy she'd tear him a new one if he didn't have the place looking spotless by the time you got here."

I unlocked the front door and stepped into a wood-paneled hallway dominated by a blown-up photo of the Vine family posing with their skis at the top of Heavenly. It had been taken recently and had a staged look like the ones families send out as Christmas cards. The hallway led into a vast space dwarfed by a vaulted ceiling. Original Craftsman couches, chairs, and tables covered in faded Indian blankets were arranged in intimate groupings around the room. There were some lovely California plein-air landscapes and some sweeping Western vistas of buffalo herds being pursued by Indians, and a collection of Remington bronzes. On the mantel above the stone fireplace, which looked large enough to stable a small horse, Daniel Vine's two Best Picture Oscars stood in solitary splendor. Were these the originals, I wondered, or did you get duplicates for your vacation homes? It felt like a wrong note, like a war hero wearing his medals to bed, and I hoped it was not Daniel Vine who had placed them there.

I walked into the kitchen, which opened through French doors out into the snowy garden. The pool and Jacuzzi had both been uncovered and were sending up clouds of steam into the cold air. Beyond them was a one-story house of weathered wooden shingles that looked like it had been the original residence on the property. I looked through its windows and saw it was now a storage shed housing snowmobiles and ski equipment. Around the side I came across a blackened oil drum that had been cut in half and converted into an outdoor barbecue. Some broken half-burnt skis were sticking out of it. I remembered Serafina indignantly telling me how Tea Lane had ordered her to burn Daniel Vine's bloodstained ski clothes after the police returned them. Was this where she was supposed to do it, while the paparazzi ringed the house with their lights and cameras? I pulled out the skis and examined them. They were top-of-the-line Fischers, designed to withstand the stresses of Olympic downhill racing. The rich bought them just as they bought Ferarris that were hopelessly beyond their driving skills. Someone had sawed them in half to fit in the barbecue, but the fire hadn't been able to do much damage to their titanium construction. In places it had not even touched their original chrome yellow finish. I fit the broken pieces together and realized I was looking at the same skis Sally Vine was holding in the hallway photo. I scratched my thumbnail along the blackened edge until the bright metal shone through. For equipment that was meant to deliver world-class speed, they had not been properly maintained; the edges were as dull as a tired pair of rentals. Still, even in a low-speed collision, a dull ski edge could force its way through flesh to the bone. Why had Sally tried to destroy her skis? Why hadn't the police checked to see if there was any kind of match between the rip in Daniel Vine's thigh and these dull-edged Fischers?

I turned back to the lodge. There had been a bitter little breeze blowing all morning, but now it had suddenly stopped. Snowflakes started falling and within seconds the air was filled with them. Thick soft ones, the kind that stick, descending silently from the dark gray sky. If this kept up, in an hour the footprints I'd tracked from the house to the oil drum with Sally's charred skis would be gone. The visible world was vanishing as I looked at it.

The fireplaces in the upstairs bedrooms were blazing, scented candles flickered in the en suite bathrooms. The young deputy, Billy Kaplan, had done everything he could to help a potential buyer imagine how pleasant it would be to live in this house. I wanted to talk to him. It is not hard to find the maid's room in new expensive American homes. An architectural rule as rigidly adhered to as the Hindu caste system specifies it has to be smaller than the wife's walk-in closet, and hidden away where people can't see it.

As I penetrated further down the hallway I could detect some wintergreen air freshener not quite masking a recently smoked cigarette. I followed the smell to a closed door and knocked.

". . . just a second."

I heard a muffled curse and an aerosol can spraying, followed by the sound of a metal window being slid open.

A moment later a young man opened the door and stared at me with a startled expression on his face. "Hey,

I'm Billy." He waved. "I don't think you want to come in here, dude. It's kind of a mess."

"I like a mess."

"Not this one. Oh man, I'm not supposed to smoke in the house. They didn't tell me you were coming until an hour ago."

Cold air from the window he'd opened wafted clouds of cigarette smoke out into the hall. Billy Kaplan was a very short guy. All through his school years people had probably teased him about it, while he dreamed of those promised growth spurts that had never come. He'd been short for his age and now that he'd grown up he was short for life. But he'd made up for it by working out. He'd grown sideways, which is all you can do when you're short. He had an honest face with a hint of something quarrelsome around the eyebrows. His manner was boisterously adolescent, his voice still high-pitched enough to get him teased.

"I smelled the smoke," I said. "I'm dying for a cigarette."

"Are you kidding?"

Inside he offered me an unfiltered Camel and we both lit up.

"I like this room," I said.

"Are you kidding?"

The room wasn't so much a mess as a place where too many separate activities were being pursued. Encased in a dry cleaner's bag, his Tahoe deputy's uniform hung from a light fixture in the middle of the ceiling. A folded-up rowing machine and set of free weights covered the floor. A flimsy card table sagged under the weight of a computer, a printer, and stacks of film scripts. He tried to position himself so I couldn't see the screen, but I caught a glimpse of what looked like a screenplay in progress.

"What are you writing?"

"It's nothing." He turned pink. "Just messing around."

He eased past me to shut the window and I unfairly sat down at his desk and studied the screen. It was called *Snowmen Don't Bleed* and he was on page 187 of his third draft. A good guy called Jack had just gripped an icicle and was about to drive it into the throat of a bad guy called Lorenzo.

"Jack's a good name for your hero," I said.

"Yeah, well, it's either Jack, Frank, or Harry." He sighed. "That's what heroes always seem to be called, and I'm trying to follow the models."

"You should let me read it. I represent a lot of people in the film business."

"Are you kidding?"

"Why do you keep saying that? Don't you believe me?"

"It's just when I took the job here, not that it's much of a job, basically I just live here rent-free and about once a month I have to turn on the Jacuzzi and light the fires. Anyway, the guy who's married to Sally Vine . . ."

"Raj."

"Yeah, Raj. You know him?" He looked surprised.

"Sure. I know the whole family."

"Oh. I didn't know that. Well, Raj said to me, on account of being a cop and everything, I probably knew a lot of authentic shit and I should write a screenplay for him. He said he was fed up with all the phony plots he was getting from Hollywood. He said one screenplay could make me a millionaire."

"He's right."

"Are you kidding?"

"If it's the right one. You ever hear of a guy using an icicle to kill someone?"

"No, but, you know, it's like the murder weapon melts. I thought it would be cool."

"You're thinking like a Hollywood screenwriter. Think like a cop."

"Between you and me, police-wise, what I mainly do, I breathalyze guys I went to high school with. Tahoe's just not a great place for crime. I know they say you should write what you know, but it's like the guys who are making the big bucks do a lot better writing about stuff that couldn't possibly happen."

I checked my watch. I'd been due in Santa Monica court for my arraignment at nine and it was already past ten. A bench warrant for my arrest would have been put in the works. Now that I was a fugitive from justice, it seemed okay to start chain-smoking. "Can I have another cigarette?"

"I'm trying to quit." He handed me the pack and his Bic lighter. "Keep them."

"You're sitting on a goldmine and you don't even know it." I lit another cigarette.

"I am?"

"The Vine case. You're living in the guy's house, aren't you?"

"Well, yeah, but . . ."

"Didn't it ever occur to you to look around?"

"Yeah, I mean, I kind of *borrowed* some of these film scripts from Vine's office. They helped me see how you do it, but . . ."

"No wonder they got away with it." I shook my head. "A small town like this, I guess, it was easy."

"I'm sorry. What are you saying?"

"It's okay. Go back to your script. Go back to sleep." I headed out of the room.

"Wait! I don't even know what you're talking about. Did I say something wrong?"

I turned and looked at him. "The guy who owned this house was murdered. You do know that, don't you?"

"Daniel Vine?" Billy laughed nervously. "It was an accident."

"Did they do an autopsy?"

"Well, no, because, the family . . . you don't know what it was like around here. The media were driving them crazy. They just wanted it over with."

"I'll bet." I gave him a superior smile.

"What's that supposed to mean?" He tried not to scowl, but I could tell I was starting to piss him off.

"You ever notice those skis in the barbecue outside?"

"Yeah," he said. "I noticed them. Raj *showed* them to me actually. He said Mrs. Vine burned them and swore she wasn't ever going to ski again. She couldn't stand the memories. That's why she's selling the place."

"The memories," I scoffed. "And right after the funeral she and Raj went to Bali to *mourn*. That's like you going to Disneyland to get over your girlfriend dying."

"I don't have a girlfriend." He had a mulish look on his face now, trying to decide how much more of this he had to take.

"Right after Daniel Vine died, a guy called Louis Pike died. Anybody in town notice *that?*"

"That was an accidental death thing. The guy passed out in the snow."

"And the other day in Los Angeles, the previous caretaker of this house, Eric Weaver, was murdered. Someone shot him a couple of times in the head. What do you think? Another accident?"

"I don't know anything about that."

"I think I *will* buy this house." I chuckled derisively. "A cop with your kind of curiosity might come in useful if I ever decide to murder my wife."

"I don't know what you're talking about, mister." His eyebrows were knotted together in warning now. "I'm sorry."

"You ought to be sorry. We've got sharper people in L.A. guarding shopping malls than you've got on your police force."

"Oh yeah? Well, let me tell you something. I don't have to take this kind of shit from you. I don't care if you flew in on your own plane. You can shove your plane. I don't even know what the hell you're talking about. Who the hell do you think you are, anyway?"

"You finally asked me a question," I smiled. "That's a start right there."

"Yeah?" He scowled.

"But it's the wrong question. You ought to ask me how I know all this stuff."

I told Billy Kaplan I was an attorney hired by Daniel Vine's brother to reopen the investigation of his death. By the time I'd filled him in, Billy Kaplan had forgotten all about murder weapons that melted and snowmen that didn't bleed. It turned out he didn't want to become a Hollywood screenwriter any more than he wanted to spend his days issuing citations to people for driving without snow chains. What he really wanted to do, I found out, was nail bad guys.

There was a woman called Claire Chase who worked in administration at the Coroner's Department and he e-mailed her a request for the forensic photos on Daniel Vine. She e-mailed back:

>R u kidding?<

"She's kind of stuck up," Billy said. "I asked her on a date once and she goes, 'You mean say goodbye to my high heels?' "

>*Please, Claire.*< He e-mailed her back. >*Badly need them for this script am writing.*<

>*U r writing a script? Yeah right.*<

>*Trying to.*<

>*What's it about? A midget?*<

Billy's jaw tightened. He was about to flame her back when his computer announced he had mail. He opened the attachment and a whole page of photos of Daniel Vine's naked corpse came up on the screen.

Most of the views were of Daniel Vine's twisted, shattered knee. Since it had been below freezing when he bled to death, there was hardly any swelling. He had some bruising around the hip and shoulder, but no other apparent injuries. There were three shots of the back of his thigh and Billy enlarged each one to the limit. The wound that had killed him showed as a thin dark line with a faint crescent bend at the end. There was no bruising around the wound.

"That looks like a knife cut to me," I said. "Or a razor blade. If it was a ski edge, or a snowboard it would have ripped through the surrounding flesh more."

"I was there," Billy said despondently. "Shit, I helped bring his body down off the mountain. The coroner got his clothes cut off him and started taking pictures, and then these people from the family barged in, a lawyer and some guy who said he was her agent. And Raj. He was yelling about the crazy, fucking snowboarders and how they'd killed Vine. He was getting kind of hysterical, kept talking about Vine's two Oscars. Saying it was an outrage, the man was a national treasure, which was pretty weird. He wanted us to question every snowboarder on the mountain. Like that's going to happen. And then he said Sally didn't want anybody messing with her husband's body. They were going to fly it right back to L.A. and have a service. It had to be quick because he was Jewish. I wasn't in charge, but I should've caught it."

"You weren't expecting it."

"No, that's not why. All the older guys were trying to act real cool around the body, like it was something they saw every day. Making jokes and stuff. I just tried to act like them. I started calling him *the Snowman* and everybody thought it was funny. The truth is I couldn't even stand to look at him. I was afraid I was going to lose my lunch."

I thought of the Vietnamese boy I'd killed. An eerie similarity existed between Billy Kaplan's first encounter with a corpse and my first week in combat. I'd just turned sixteen. I was in with a bunch of hard-core guys who didn't even talk to me. We'd taken a village with almost no resistance, but the sparse enemy fire had paralyzed me. Instead of firing my weapon I'd tried to bury myself into the earth. I was sure my cowardice had been noted. Afterwards we took a break, everyone flopped out on the ground, smoking cigarettes. No one talked to me. I was the chickenshit new recruit, unlucky, marked for death. Out of the corner of my eye I saw a figure scrambling from the back of a burning hooch and suddenly I was on my feet, firing my weapon, charging into the smoke. I suddenly had all the courage I'd lacked during the firefight. I saw the figure drop down ahead of me, scratching at the ground, and then he vanished. I found the tunnel entrance. I crawled in after him and caught him by the ankle and pulled him towards me. Even as it was happening, I kept thinking, there's something wrong, this guy doesn't weigh anything, he's not even fighting. I remember feeling grateful that I wasn't going to have to die, and amazement because killing him was so easy. It was only when I dragged him out by his feet and laid him on the ground that I saw what I'd done.

After that my platoon mates started talking to me. My action had been unnecessary, but the brutality of the result satisfied them. They stopped calling me *shithead.* I'd killed the boy for the same reason Billy Kaplan had laughed at Daniel Vine's corpse: I'd wanted to belong.

Billy kept staring at the screen like it was a bad report card. I reached over and hit the Print key and the pages of photos started sliding into the tray.

"I'm not trying to be a wise-ass," he said after a while. "But I figure it was a left-handed guy who did it. You can see it from the way he pulled the blade back towards himself when he was cutting the poor bastard."

"You're right. *If* it was a guy."

"Shit, you think Sally Vine could have done it?"

I collected the copies out of the printer tray, thinking about what she'd done to Hugo, hoping for his sake she was at least innocent of the act itself, if not the knowledge of it.

"You never know what people are capable of," I said. "But I'll bet when life without possibility of parole gets dropped on her, she'll start telling on everybody."

Chapter Twenty-Five

The Tahoe Academy was a half-hour drive from my hotel, but because of the weather I set out early for my appointment. The snowplows were out in force, but as I climbed into the higher elevation the two-lane highway might as well have been a deserted ski run. Even with my high beams on, and the windshield wipers going full blast, it was hard to see, though strangely there was still no wind accompanying the storm. The snow came straight down, quietly piling up inch by inch, accomplishing its work in deceptive silence. When I came out above the tree line I spotted the turn-off to the school. I followed a road back down for several miles until the trees suddenly parted to reveal a narrow valley ringed by the surrounding peaks. In the summer it was high pasture, but now the fences barely showed above the snow. I drove past some barns and sheds that appeared abandoned for the winter. A sign for the school directed me on to a single-lane track leading across the valley.

It took another ten minutes to reach The Tahoe Academy. It looked like a large, upscale ski resort, constructed out of blonde varnished wood, with sweeping balconies and a steeply pitched, dark blue tiled roof. Lesser buildings of the same design flanked it. The driveway circled around a fenced-in enclosure where, to my surprise, I saw a herd of llamas sheltering inside an open shed. I parked in front and made a dash from my car up the steps into the main building. I walked quickly through a deserted reception area, my heart suddenly beating at the thought of seeing Hugo.

I cracked a door and peered in at a large echoing room where about a dozen kids were silently working at long tables. Hugo wasn't among them. Beyond, more kids moved around an open plan kitchen area, but he wasn't there either. A balcony overlooked one side of the room and I could see an attractive woman with short-cropped auburn hair coming out of an office carrying some papers. My plan was to let Caroline Dalgleish give me a tour of the school and then come back at night to spring Hugo. But what if I got lucky? What if I just saw him? I could whisk him away without ever having to deal with anybody in authority. I waited until the woman disappeared into an office and entered the large room. A few of the kids noticed me, swiveling around to follow my progress across the floor towards some doors on the far side. The doors turned out to be locked. I turned around and saw the woman with the auburn hair staring alertly at me from the balcony.

"Can I help you?" She had a brisk commanding voice.

"I'm looking for Mrs. Dalgleish."

"Why don't you come up here, Mr. Fisher?" She indicated some stairs leading to the upper level.

As I walked past the students, one of them muttered. "Whatever you do, don't send your kid here."

"Who said that?" Caroline Dalgleish demanded.

There was a silence. She surveyed the students and then fixed her gaze on one of them in particular, an overweight scowling Asian girl. "Who was it, Belinda?"

"It was Danny." The girl resumed reading her book.

"Do you want to be an earth person all your life, Danny? Is that what you want? See me afterwards."

Caroline Dalgleish was in her early forties, a coldly poised beauty with a very good figure. She seemed to be inspecting me for defects as I climbed the steps towards her.

She shook my hand and adjusted the corners of her lips into a perfunctory smile.

"We prefer parents to check in at reception." She said it in a bright musical voice, but her implication was unmistakable. She was not a realtor trying to sell me a house. She did not need to soften her behavior with charm, or even much politeness. Only a man suffering desperate problems with his children would blow in out of a snowstorm like this. It was clear she was used to occupying the moral high ground with parents whose very presence at the school was an admission of their failure.

"Sorry. There wasn't anybody there. What's an *earth person?*"

She opened a door, ushering me into an empty conference room. "We divide our students into four groups, earth, water, fire, and air. Earth is the least evolved, as you saw with Danny. Belinda's taken three years to make it to fire. We're hoping in the next six months she can return to her family. Sit down and we'll get you started filling out the forms." She indicated a pile of questionnaires on the table.

"Maybe it would be a good idea if you showed me the school first. I can always do these later."

She inhaled and held her breath, gazing steadily at me, waiting for me to realize my mistake.

"I mean, I'm *sure* this is the right place for them," I said. "It's got a very good feel."

"I'm afraid it's really more a question of whether we want to accept your boys, Mr. Fisher. We're at maximum capacity and we've just had to take another student on short notice."

"I understand." I walked over and glanced out the window. "It's just this storm is getting worse. I'm happy to take the time to fill all this stuff out. I'm happy to write you a check for the year's tuition for both of them as a deposit. That's about a hundred and twenty thousand dollars. I just don't want to get stranded up here for the night."

"We only take children for a minimum of two years."

"Well, then two years," I said. "Money is not my problem. Time is."

She paused long enough to make me feel I'd said the wrong thing, and then shrugged. "As you wish."

She showed me the gym where a desultory volley ball game was in progress, the dorms where the kids slept according to their levels of development, some classrooms filled with students. Wherever we appeared, at the sight of Caroline Dalgleish the atmosphere became muted and constrained. After fifteen minutes I'd seen the whole school and we were back in the main room. There had been no sign of Hugo.

"I don't know," I said. "Your kids all seem so well behaved, so well adjusted. It's like there's nothing wrong with them. My boys are awfully wild. I don't know if this place is tough enough."

"They're well behaved *now,*" she said. "None of them were when they arrived."

"What's to stop them from just walking out the door?"

"It's thirty miles to the nearest town. Running away isn't really an option."

"Well, my two boys would be coming under escort. They're not going to want to be here, and I don't see how you're going to keep them."

"Oppositional children usually spend a brief time in our quiet area."

"Quiet area?"

She selected a key on her chain and unlocked the doors I'd tried to open earlier. She ushered me into a long, brightly lit corridor where a male counselor sat at a desk reading a snowboarding magazine. At the sight of Caroline Dalgleish he put down the magazine and busied himself with his computer. I glanced through the window of one of the doors lining the corridor; a group therapy session was in progress; a girl was sobbing, but I couldn't hear what she was saying through the thick glass. I looked through the next window and saw a body curled on a bed with its back turned. I recognized Hugo's spiky peroxide hair on the pillow, his bare arm dangling over the side of the bed. I willed him to turn over and look at me. Caroline Dalgleish was in conversation with the guy at the desk. I coughed loudly and at the same time kicked the door. Slowly, as if he were underwater, Hugo rolled over and stared in my direction. He looked shocked and apathetic, his eyes at half-mast, his mouth sagging open. I could see the exact second he realized it was me because there was no wonderful flash of recognition. They'd given him so many drugs his face could barely demonstrate any emotion. Instead of jumping up, he yawned, and got shakily to his feet, and staggered towards the observation window. I'd been so excited at the prospect of seeing him I hadn't taken into account how he might react. I'd expected to encounter him while glancing into a classroom, not peering in at him through a soundproofed window. I turned quickly away and returned to join Caroline Dalgleish, while Hugo slapped his palms against the window and kicked the door in protest.

"I hope you're not alarmed," she said as she led me out of the "quiet area." "Some of these children have never had any firmness in their lives."

"How long will he be in there?"

"Not long. As soon as the medication has a chance to help him, he'll go into the woods for a few days with a counselor. The experience of wilderness has a remarkable effect. After that, he'll go solo in a tent on the school grounds until he feels he's ready to rejoin the community."

"I don't know if I can do this," I said. "I'm suddenly getting cold feet."

"We're not for everybody, Mr. Fisher." She masked her disappointment. "We do the things that parents have failed to do for many years."

"I understand. I'm going to have to think about this."

She was aware she'd overplayed her hand, but made no more attempts to convince me. She walked me out through the still empty reception area to the front door and watched me hurry to my car. It was dark and the snow had stopped.

I pulled off the road several hundred yards from the school and switched off my lights, but kept the engine running to stay warm. After about an hour a car passed by with the counselor from the "quiet area" at the wheel, and then half a dozen other cars left the school. They obviously kept only a skeleton staff on at night, which would make my job easier. I tried calling Ken O'Doul, but my phone didn't work. It was almost a relief because I knew he'd tell me to let Hugo sit where he was. Billy Kaplan was taking the photos to his superiors, but I knew it could take a prosecutor weeks to sift through the evidence and decide the best way to proceed. I wanted Hugo in my care, not in the hands of a school where one of his father's murderers could find him.

Only one car passed down the road heading toward The Tahoe Academy the rest of the evening. At nine most of the lights in the main building went off, and by ten the last of the surrounding dormitories were dark. I drove with the lights off to within about fifty yards of the school and turned off the engine. I smoked several of Billy Kaplan's Camels and then got a tire iron, a blanket, and flashlight from the back. The clouds had parted over the valley and the stars in the night sky seemed incredibly close and bright.

A llama stirred in the enclosure, coming to the fence to watch me as I moved around the side towards the main building. It was the size of a small camel, all black except for the liquid shine of its eyes. You're a long way from Peru, I thought, and it spit at me. It didn't get me in the eyes, but it hit the side of my face and hair. The smell was unbelievably foul. I hurried out of range and tried to wash it off with snow.

I was bent over, scooping up a handful of snow, when something exploded into the back of my skull.

When I came to, my arms were trussed to my torso, my face dragging along the ground, bouncing up and down, my mouth choking on leaves and twigs. Someone was pulling me by my feet through the woods, grunting at the effort. I passed out for a bit and when I regained consciousness I was lying on my back in the snow staring up through the trees at the moon. I rolled over on my side and tried to loosen my arms, but they were tied so tight with twine I had trouble breathing. After falling down three times, I finally managed to get to my feet. The world was spinning and the effort of getting up made my head hurt so much I vomited on to my shoes.

Someone grabbed my neck and yanked up my belt in back, pushing me forward, roughly guiding me through the trees. I twisted my head around and caught a flash of Malahide's glasses.

"Walk," he barked.

We were edging downhill through the trees towards a

clearing. In the moonlight I could see the snow-covered remains of a shack and beyond it an outhouse, with its door hanging half-off. I knew I was going to die, but I couldn't think how to stop it. I could make out details—the sound of Malahide's heavy breathing, the smell of his sweat, the moonlight shining on the outhouse—but everything was going too fast to hold on to. He ran me down the slope and sent me crashing up against a tree stump. Suddenly he was crouching over me, his face in mine, spooky, grinning.

"In ten minutes I'm going to be alive, bitch." He chuckled. "And you are going to be one of my memories."

When I didn't answer he stood up and walked over to the outhouse. He ripped off the door and laid it flat in the snow. He unzipped his parka and took out a plumber's wrench and some other tools and laid them on the door. Then he stepped inside the outhouse and shone a flashlight into the depths of an ancient porcelain toilet bowl bolted into the wood plank over the sewer pit.

"What scene in a movie does this remind you of?" He indicated the hole with a knowing smirk. "I'll give you a clue. There's enough shit in there to drown someone. No? Nothing come to mind?"

He walked back and stared cheerfully down at me.

"*Schindler's List.*" He kicked me in the chest. "*Schindler's List*, you ignorant fuck."

He kicked me again, almost playfully, and walked back to the outhouse. He'd said I had ten minutes. The luminous dial on Hugo's father's Rolex told me it was now two minutes past ten. I looked around for something that could help me get my hands free. All around there was nothing but snow, packed into the tree branches, blown into drifts against the ruins of the shack. I rolled over to look the other way and there was nothing but more snow, more trees. I could still smell the llama spit on me, but it no longer seemed foul; it was part of my past life, almost precious. I dug my hands through the snow until I hit dirt and then rubbed them against the ground to get some feeling back into my fingers. My mind desperately tried to find a solution, but I kept thinking about trivial things like the fact I was going to die in a Battistoni suit. I should have killed Malahide after he threatened me in the park. Done it when he wasn't expecting it, executed him in cold blood, but I'd been afraid of being someone who could do such a thing. Fear had ruled me my whole life and now it was claiming me. I didn't understand people who died without regrets. Just thinking about leaving Hugo behind sent waves of hideous sadness through me.

Malahide was hammering metal on metal, trying to loosen the rusted bolts attaching the toilet to the wooden plank. Every few seconds he lifted his head to make sure I hadn't moved.

"The kids at the school," he called over. "This is where we park them for their solos. They spend a couple of days and nights out in the woods on their own, no mommy, no daddy, no MTV, they start feeling it. What a big world it really is, the beauty and terror of God's creation, their own puny smallness in the face of all that indifference. It's meant to humble them. I hope you're taking advantage of it, Kyd, not just lying there feeling sorry for yourself."

I normally carried a Swiss Army pocketknife, but I'd been afraid it would set off the metal detectors at the airport. I checked the watch again. The little hand moved around the glowing dial, counting off the seconds. I'd wanted to take it when Hugo offered it to me that first night, but I'd been afraid . . . always afraid of doing the wrong thing.

"In a few days they'll put Hugo out here to cool him off." Malahide rested from his work to wipe the steam off his glasses. "They'll give him a little one-man nylon tent. He's going to lay in it, listening to all this silence, all this indifference that surrounds him. But I never liked the kids thinking it's just empty out here. Like that's the problem. I always told them about the bears. How sensitive their noses are. How even if they ate up every crumb of their energy bars and always hung their food supply up a tree, a bear could still smell the food on their breath. And the bear would want it. God was in the stars and every snowflake and blade of grass and all that bullshit, but they still had to watch out for the bears. That always got their attention, especially the oppositional ones."

He put his glasses back on. "That's why you're here, Big Time. You forgot about the bears."

I stared at the watch, hating the smug relentless precision of the second hand as it moved and paused, moved and paused around the dial. My breath steamed in the freezing air, but I was sweating uncontrollably. I don't remember the thought, but suddenly I was fumbling with the flip lock clasp on the Rolex, getting it off my wrist. The rotating bezel was minutely indented, as evenly notched as a saw blade except for the flaw where the metal twisted up into a sharp edge. I forced the steel bracelet of the watch between my chest and the binding string and starting pulling the edge back and forth against the twine. Malahide had wrapped the string around my arms four times. To get free I needed to cut one strand, the one he had tied into a knot behind my back.

"We tell the kids they can't just crap in the woods. They got to collect their shit in a plastic bag. But they never do. They always use the outhouse."

Malahide yanked out the last bolt and lifted the porcelain bowl free.

"Hugo's going to use this privy in a couple of days. He's going to sit here on the throne, shivering in the moonlight, holding the roll of toilet paper in his lap, wondering where you are, and he won't even know he's taking a shit on your head. Tell me that's not perfect."

The string snapped and I loosened the remaining strands around my arms.

As he walked towards me, he dropped the plumber's wrench to the ground and pulled a gun out of his parka. He reached down and grabbed my ankle and started dragging me like a dead animal towards the sewer pit. I picked up the wrench as I slid past and yanked my leg back, pulling him towards me. The first blow caught him on the hand and he let go of me, and I got him in the knee with the second one. He had to use his gun hand to break his fall and I rolled over on him, pinning him. I got my fingers into his face and found the eyeball socket and clawed at the softness. He screamed in pain, knocking me off with a sudden convulsive twist of his shoulders that made me realize I'd completely underestimated his physical strength. Before I could recover he'd scrambled to his feet and jumped out of range of the plumber's wrench.

He held his hand to his eye in horrified disbelief, making a terrible yelping sound like a gun-shot hunting dog. He kept the gun trained on me and tried to cup his dangling eye and somehow pour it back into the socket. "You bitch . . . you fucking bitch," he cried.

He stepped close and held the gun with both hands and aimed it at my face. I felt the red laser dot flash into my eyes and then he pulled the trigger. Nothing happened. It didn't even *click*. He'd jammed the slide with ice. He banged the butt of the gun against his palm and tried to fire again, jumping back as I charged him with the wrench. As I raised it to strike him, he pivoted on one foot and kicked me straight in the chest, knocking me on my back. He landed on top of me, pinning his arm against my throat and trying to smash the gun butt into my face. I let go of the wrench and grabbed hold of his hair and got my thumb in his eye socket again and jammed it in as deep as it would go and then I just held on, while he rained blows down on me. I had him hooked and no matter how much he bucked and kicked I kept digging it deeper inside him until he stopped fighting. His whole body was trembling on top of me, shuddering.

"Please . . ." he begged. "No more."

I let go of him and pushed him off me.

"Please . . ."

He was contorting on the ground, his knees doubled up to his chin in agony. Suddenly he reached for his boot and I saw the flash of a blade coming at my face. He missed and I was on him. I found the wrench and used it like a hammer, shattering his collarbone, driving it into the top of his skull, crushing in his face. When he stopped moving I quit hitting him to see if he was dead. His left eyeball was gouged out, hanging by a twisted red thread. His other eye, staring blindly up at the stars, gave him a demented look. He was as dead as a frozen fish.

I dragged his body into the outhouse and checked his pulse just to be sure and then I slid him into the hole.

Chapter Twenty-Six

I stopped at a gas station outside Sacramento and used the restroom to change into dry clothes and wash the blood out of my hair. I threw the Battistoni suit into a Dumpster around back and washed down a handful of aspirin with coffee from the dispenser. When I got back in the car, Hugo was stirring awake in the passenger seat, yawning and rubbing his eyes.

"Where are we?"

"Just past Sacramento. Go back to sleep."

"I can't." He brought the back of his seat up and studied me as I pulled out of the gas station. "What did you do with the clothes with the blood on them?"

After the nightmare in the woods with Malahide, getting Hugo out of the academy had been comparatively easy. I'd used a tire iron to pry off the outside louvered steel shutters and shone a flashlight into his room. His bed had been empty, but then I spotted him hiding underneath it. When he realized it was me, he opened the window and launched himself into my arms, knocking me flat on my back in the snow. He was in his pajamas, still warm from his bed. He hugged me so hard that, despite the pain in my head and neck, I thought I was going to pass out from happiness. He was barefoot and by the time we got to the car he was shivering uncontrollably. I put the heater on stun and wrapped him in a blanket.

"Why are you covered in blood?" he'd said.

"If they heard me breaking in, they'll call the police. I've got to get us off this mountain." I drove like a madman down the icy road.

"I didn't know it was you." His teeth chattered. "After you left, Malahide looked through the window at me. I thought it was him coming back for me. I thought he'd done something to you."

"It's all going to be okay now."

"Why are you all covered in blood?"

"Don't worry about it. Just let me drive now."

"Are you, like, okay? You look like you should see a doctor."

In the rearview mirror my face was a sickly white, spattered with Malahide's blood; a huge lump bulged out behind my ear where Malahide had struck me. I switched on the radio and got some scratchy country music station.

"What's that smell?" Hugo cautiously asked.

"It's not me. It's . . . llama spit."

"I see." He nodded, as if it was all perfectly consistent with the way the rest of me looked.

I reached into my suit jacket and pulled out the Camels Billy Kaplan had given me. "Light me one of those. It'll help kill the smell."

Hugo got the cigarette going and handed it to me.

"I don't look so hot, Hugo, and I don't smell very good, but it's nice to see you again."

"Yeah, me too. Thanks for getting me out of there, man. Really, thanks a lot."

"You're welcome."

After that he dozed off and fitfully snored for the next few hours. I didn't know if it was the drugs they'd been giving him, but I was relieved he felt safe enough to sleep after all that had happened to him.

As I pulled the rental back on to the freeway, I could

sense him struggling with all the questions he wanted to ask. We passed a California Highway Patrol cruiser and I tried to look unconcerned, as they checked us out: a man and a boy driving along the interstate at two in the morning. My act fooled them, but it didn't fool Hugo.

"So are you going to tell me how much trouble we're in?"

"You're not in any trouble, Hugo."

"How did you find me?"

"It wasn't that hard. I called some escort services and pretended to be Raj."

"That's cool." He nodded. "You still haven't told me . . ."

"I'm not going to. The cops are going to question you. Just tell them I broke you out of the school, okay?"

"Nothing about the blood and stuff?"

"That's right," I said.

"Nothing about throwing away your clothes and the lump on your head?"

"That would be helpful."

"I probably shouldn't mention that I saw Malahide at the school then, either."

I didn't answer. He was trying to lull me into some trap, trick me into telling him what had happened.

"Don't you realize, Thomas?" He smiled with beseeching charm. "Whatever you did, it was to help me. I'd never tell."

"I know that."

"Not really," Hugo said sadly.

"Just let it go."

"You don't trust me. I don't blame you. I'm just saying."

"You're fourteen," I said. "It's hard to keep some things

secret at your age. It's not your fault. It's just the way it is."

"I'm fifteen actually. It was my birthday yesterday."

He didn't say it reproachfully, just put it out there for me to think about. What he was really saying, I realized, was that he'd grown up a bit, and I ought to acknowledge it.

I looked sternly at him. "Something happened back there that could put me in prison for the rest of my life. If I tell you about it, you'll be an accessory."

"I'm already an accessory just talking about it with you like this. I mean, that's what a lawyer would say. Just failing to tell the police makes me as guilty as you."

"You're not guilty of anything, Hugo."

"How do I know Malahide isn't going to come back?"

"*I'm* the one who came back. That's all you need to know."

He was silent for a moment, solemnly digesting it. "You killed him to save me. Wow."

"Jesus, Hugo, could we stop talking about this?"

"Maybe when I'm older you can tell me."

"Hugo . . ."

"Fine. I'll shut up," he said.

I'd killed a man who wanted to harm him. He kept quiet for a long time, with the same solemn expression on his face, savoring the enormity of it.

"No offense," Hugo asked delicately, "and like I'm sure you know what you're doing and everything, but can I ask you one question?"

"What?"

"Where exactly are we going?"

It amazed me to realize that up to that moment he'd felt safe enough with me not to even ask the question. "We're going to see your mom and Raj. I've got photographs from the Reno Police that prove your dad's death wasn't from a ski accident. Someone cut his leg with a knife."

"A knife?"

"A left-handed person. Your mom's not left-handed, is she?"

"No, she's not." He couldn't hold down the excitement in his voice. "She's a righty, like me."

"Good." I remembered Malahide loosening the iron bolts over the sewer pit, the wrench in his right hand, his right hand covering the hole where his eye used to be. He had not been the one who wielded the blade, either.

"But Raj *is* left-handed," Hugo said. "You see, I knew my mom didn't do it. She'd never do a thing like that."

"Right."

"Raj must've lied to her," he said hopefully.

"Something like that."

"She probably doesn't even know about it."

I thought of that speck in the photograph coming towards Raj and Malahide, Sally's half-burned skis, her refusal to answer any of my questions, and I knew the really hard test for Hugo was just starting.

"Just before he died, your dad took a picture," I said gently. "Raj and Malahide are walking away from him and there's a third person coming towards them. When that picture's enlarged and enhanced right, there's a possibility that third person is going to be your mom."

Hugo stared coldly at me. "What are you talking about?"

"I'm sorry, Hugo. I think what happened is, there was some kind of collision between your mom and your dad. Maybe she ran into him by accident. Raj and Malahide went to check him out and when they came back, they told her she'd cut his leg open with her skis. I think she panicked. They probably convinced her it was best to just ski back down and report him missing."

"It wasn't her fault." He doggedly resisted the idea. "You said yourself . . ."

"I'm not saying it was her *fault.* I'm just trying to prepare you. The police are going to think she helped cover it up."

"I don't care about the fucking police." Hugo banged his head against the window. "She didn't do it."

I tried to engage him in further conversation, but he angrily cut me off. All his euphoria at being rescued from The Tahoe Academy was gone. At the mention of his mother he'd regressed into a state of barely contained fury, which I could tell included me.

Both gates to the Vine estate were open, but I could see no sign of Uncle Firooz's bodyguards or the black Mercedes. A stretch limo was parked in the graveled driveway, the driver smoking and trying to read the morning paper by the dawn light. While Hugo got out of the car, I gathered up the coroner's photo of Daniel Vine and took the Colt from under my seat and slipped it into my waistband.

"Who are you waiting for?" Hugo asked the limo driver.

"I'm supposed to take Miss Vine to the airport."

"Where's she going?"

"Maui, the 'Women in Film' awards. They're giving her a prize."

The dog charged across the lawn towards us, putting its paws up on Hugo's shoulders, yelping and licking his face. He danced around with it for a moment and then pushed it down as Serafina walked slowly out of the kitchen. He put a finger to his mouth, warning her not to make a noise, and then hurried over and embraced her.

"Are his parents asleep?" I asked.

"Yes," she said. "What are you doing here?"

"Where are the bodyguards?"

"They left."

"Who else is in the house?"

"Just Ms. Lane in the guest quarters."

I pulled Hugo away from her into the house and steered him up the stairs. I could feel his resistance mounting as we passed his room and headed towards his mother's wing.

"What am I supposed to say?"

"You don't have to say anything. I'm going to show her a photograph and we'll take it from there."

"What about Raj?"

"Leave him to me."

"I don't think I can do this."

We were in the gym with the wall-to-wall zebra-striped carpet, the rising sun illuminating the dust motes suspended between the chromed workout machines.

"You know," I said. "Your mother's trapped in something she can't get free of by herself."

"You don't know her."

"Maybe not. But she's a lot more scared than you are, and this is going to help her."

I handed him the envelope with the photo. Was Sally actually capable of being helped by the truth? I didn't know, but I was sure Hugo had to confront her with it. If he didn't, he would keep turning all the unexpressed suspicion and resentment he felt about his father's death against himself. It would blight and stunt him for life.

I eased open the door and stepped inside. In the dim light shining through the Roman blinds I could make out Raj and Sally asleep on separate sides of a huge circular bed. Raj's bedside table was piled high with scripts, phone messages, coverage, copies of *Variety* and the *Reporter*. Balanced on top of them was an open PC and several cell phones. It was the unglamorous side of the job, the endless workload that Raj now took to bed. The only objects on Sally's bedside table were an array of prescription pill bottles and a nearly empty bottle of Chardonnay. I moved silently to Raj's side and switched on a light. He didn't stir. He'd fallen asleep with his reading glasses pushed back up into his hair, which gave him a care-worn look.

I turned around and saw Hugo hanging back in the open doorway. I waved him forward and he slowly entered the room, moving to his mother's side of the bed. He sat down and gently shook her shoulder. "Mom? Wake up."

She made an irritated sound and turned away from him, pulling the blanket over her head. He shook her again and she sat straight up in bed, staring at him incredulously.

"Hugo," she said. "I forgot your birthday." For a second, ripped out of sleep, still half-drunk, she was herself, her face lined with guilt.

"Yeah, I know."

She blinked and swallowed, gasping when she saw me, but still too startled to assemble a coherent reaction to our presence. "What are you . . . ?" She started to speak and then held out her arms to him and he bowed his head and let her embrace him. "Oh Hugo . . . oh my baby . . . oh God I've missed you."

She was genuinely moved to see him, her eyes filling with tears, but at the same time she was already starting to act a little, raising the temperature of her emotion like someone adding hot water to a bath. "Are you, *okay?*" She loosened her embrace to inspect him for damage.

Raj opened his eyes and stared uncomprehendingly at Hugo. He hadn't seen me yet. "What's he doing here?" he said. "What's going on?"

"He has something to show his mother," I said.

Raj froze at the sound of my voice behind him. I leaned over and gripped his collarbone between my thumb and forefinger, squeezing the nerve against the bone. He screamed briefly and fell backwards against the pillows.

"It's okay, Raj. No one's going to hurt you. Be cool." I sat down beside him, keeping my grip on his collarbone. "Show your mother," I told Hugo.

"Show me what?"

Hugo opened the envelope and slid the photo out onto the pink satin bedspread.

"What is this?" Sally edged backwards.

"You didn't kill your husband with your skis. Raj cut his leg open with a knife. You can see it right there in the photo."

"This is bullshit," Raj said. "You can't . . ."

He groaned as I tightened my grip on him. Sally picked up the photo and turned on her bedside light. As she examined it, the color drained from her cheeks and her eyes turned inward; the lines in her face deepened, her lips turning into a bitter line. She was aging as I watched.

"What happened, Mom?"

"I've been . . . he's destroyed me. I've been destroyed."

"It's not your fault," Hugo comforted her. "You didn't know."

"It won't matter." Her shoulders slumped. "No one will understand. I was lied to. They frightened me so badly. They said I'd killed your father. They said I'd go to prison."

"You will go to prison, if you don't shut up, you stupid bitch."

"Bitch?" I pressed the Colt into Raj's throat. "Bitch is what they're going to be calling you in the Nevada pen."

I forced him over on his stomach and yanked his hands behind his back. I took the silk belt from the dressing gown pooled at Sally's feet and used it to bind his wrists. Sally had yet to speak or even make eye contact with Raj and I doubted if she would. She'd turned her back on him, as if he was some tasteless employee trying to make an embarrassing scene about getting fired. He was an irrelevance. He was over.

"I think," I said to Sally, "it would help you with the police if you called them yourself. Tell them exactly what happened. Since they need you to testify against Raj, they're likely to cut you a break. Coming forward, admitting what you did, that'll earn you some sympathy."

"I'll call Detective Stone," she said. "He's a friend."

"No he's not. He figured out what really happened and he's been blackmailing Raj. By the end of the day, Stone's going to be under arrest himself." I opened my wallet and took out Corelle Lamb's card. "Call her. She's familiar with the case. Tell her to bring Detective Hama along."

Sally took the card and glanced at it. "First I want to call my agent." She tossed the card aside.

"He's not a friend, either. He's a gay pedophile who sold you out."

"Alvin Peck? That's impossible."

"You've been sleeping with a murderer and you have really bad representation, Miss Vine. Call the police before they call you."

"Do what he says, Mom." Hugo shoved the phone into her lap. "Do it now!"

Sally lifted her face to Hugo, wounded to the quick. "I can only do it if you promise not to be mad at me anymore." Her voice had become that of a little girl bravely struggling against a world much stronger than her. "Everyone has turned on me. I don't know why. Why? What did I do?" She started sobbing then. "I didn't even know . . . when I tried to ask Raj . . . he hit me in the face . . . you saw him do it. I had no one to protect me, Hugo. You had *him,* your own private detective to watch out for you. That's why I hired him for you. Don't you understand? I did everything I could to keep you safe."

"*I* hired him," Hugo said. "Make the call, Mother, or I'll have to make it for you."

There was a cold, deliberate tone to his voice, and a kind of world-weary disgust which was new and sad to hear in someone so young. Still, the main thing, I suppose, was he meant it. He would call the police and Sally knew it.

"What are you waiting for?" he suddenly yelled at me, indicating Raj. "Get him out of here! And call my lawyer and tell him to get his ass over here."

He was quivering with repressed fury, unable to meet my eyes. With a sickening feeling, I realized that our relationship wasn't going to survive the revelation of his mother's guilt. Hugo had wanted me to find out the truth for him, but the truth was shameful and dispiriting. As the messenger who'd brought the bad news, I was as stained in his eyes as the murderer who'd been sharing his mother's bed. Ken had warned me not to expect the boy to thank me, but it still came as a shock how quickly he turned on me.

I got Ken on the phone and he and Pru seemed to arrive in no time at all. Pru videoed the first exclusive with Sally before the cops even questioned her. Soon there were so many cops and camera crews filling the house that it looked like they were making a movie. I gave my statement to Corelle and put her in touch with Billy Kaplan in Tahoe. She asked me how I'd got so beat-up looking and I said I'd had too much to drink and slipped on the ice outside a bar. That would have been an improvement on the way I actually felt.

I waited around to say goodbye to Hugo, but Ken said he was resting and didn't want to be disturbed. Ken was anxious about the fishy way I'd brought things to a head, and my appearance alarmed him. He said it was probably best if I stayed out of the picture for a while until the authorities could piece the evidence together.

I almost stopped at a liquor store on the way home, but instead I decided to take my rental to the car wash and have them steam clean the interior just in case I'd got any of Malahide's blood on it. When I got home I took a long shower and scrubbed myself raw, but I could still smell the llama spit in my hair. If anything, the smell had gotten worse because I wound up on my knees, vomiting into the toilet bowl. I don't know what happened after that, but Mr. Doyle found me passed out in the garden in my underwear and called the paramedics. I woke up in Santa Monica Hospital and that's when I found out I had a fractured skull.

They kept me under observation for about three hours, long enough to ascertain I had no health insurance, and then sent me home with two Tylenol and a strong warning to avoid strenuous activity. I turned off the phone and slept for the better part of two days and nights, never going out, never even turning on the TV. I didn't want to see anything about the case. I kept taking longer and longer showers, but I couldn't wash out the smell of the llama, or forget my time in the woods with Malahide. I was traumatized and I had a fractured skull, but that's not what was really bothering me. It was the kid. I missed him. I must have started to call him a hundred times, but I always put the phone down, even in my dreams. I couldn't get the last image of him out of my mind: the chilly offhand way he'd told his mother *he*'d hired me. The way he'd told me to get Raj out of there and while you're at it, call my lawyer whose name I can't remember. I should have shrugged it off, but I couldn't. The way I saw it, I'd given Hugo Vine everything I had to give, and it hadn't interested him enough to call and ask me how I was. In my defense, I was more than a little nuts from the fracture. I had double vision and my head ached so much I could hardly eat. When I wasn't having bad dreams I was in a kind of coma.

After two days I decided to call him and realized I'd disconnected my phone. Maybe he'd been trying to reach me, after all.

"Hello," Serafina answered.

"It's Thomas. Is Hugo around?" I hadn't used my voice for so long I sounded barely human.

"Yes!" she cried indignantly. "He's been very worried. He called. We came and knocked on your door, but there was nobody there. Where have you been?"

"I've been here the whole time," I said.

"Your mail and your newspapers are lying outside your front door. Hugo was so worried he wanted to hire a private detective to find you."

"Seriously?"

"Yes, seriously," she said. "Here he is."

Hugo came on the phone. "Dude, are you like okay?"

"Got a little headache," I said. "But it's getting better. How about you?"

"My mom's in rehab. I got to start going back to school again tomorrow."

"Uh-huh."

"So are you going to like take me? I really want you to take me."

Just the sound of his enthusiastic voice was putting a smile on my face. "Yeah, I'll take you, Hugo."

"Thanks," he said.

There was a pause, and I could hear him breathing on the line.

"I miss you, man," he said.

"Me, too, Hugo."

About the Author

A graduate of Cambridge University, Timothy Harris is the author of *Kronski/McSmash*, and the two previous Thomas Kyd novels, *Kyd For Hire* and *Good Night and Good-Bye.* His screenwriting credits include *Trading Places*, *Brewster's Millions*, *My Stepmother Was an Alien*, *Paint It Black*, *Twins*, *Kindergarten Cop*, and *Space Jam.* He was born in Los Angeles and makes his home there and in London with his wife and two sons. He is currently at work on a film based on the life of the Regency boxing great, Daniel Mendoza.